CIRCLE
of the
MOON

Also by Barbara Hambly

Sisters of the Raven

Available from Warner Books

INTO THE MADNESS

Murdered men and women—children, too—lay sprawled in waist-high drifts of dust and sand. A man in the red tunic of the City Guard threw himself screaming out of an open house-door, hacking with his sword. Shaldis held him back on the end of her spear, and he drove himself halfway up its shaft trying to get to her before he finally died. Sickened, trembling, it took her minutes to work the body off the spear, and as she did she could see his flesh and bones blacken and shrink.

PRAISE FOR
BARBARA HAMBLY'S NOVELS

CIRCLE OF THE MOON

"Perfect . . . a believable, fantastic, and colorful world with appealing characters . . . Shaldis and Summerchild are everything a reader could want in the way of heroines."
—**Trashotron.com**

"Hambly's books are powerful celebrations of women realizing their own power and self-worth . . . Her best fantasies in years."
—**FreshFiction.com**

"An enthralling fantasy series."
—**BookLoons.com**

"The culture that the author has created is so realistic and complicated; it's hard to believe it doesn't exist somewhere."
—**TheRomanceReadersConnection.com**

more . . .

SISTERS OF THE RAVEN

"Demonstrates [Hambly's] graceful storytelling style and flair for world-building . . . Highly recommended."
—*Library Journal*

"The world-building is fulfilling and polished . . . [The Yellow City] is nowhere you have ever lived or visited but is somewhere you can practically taste."
—*SFR Newsletter*

"An excellent fantasy . . . lends itself to some deeper and unsettling thoughts."
—**MostlyFiction.com**

"An exciting fantasy tale that contains a strong morality subplot . . . The story line engages the audience from the beginning."
—*Midwest Book Review*

"Smart, thoughtful . . . keenly imagined . . . vividly convincing."
—SUZY MCKEE CHARNAS,
author of *The Slave and the Free*

"This is Barbara Hambly at the very top of her form . . . Read this one!"
—HARRY TURTLEDOVE,
author of the American Empire series

CIRCLE
of the
MOON

BARBARA
HAMBLY

WARNER BOOKS

NEW YORK   BOSTON

Copyright © 2005 by Barbara Hambly
All rights reserved. No part of this book may be reproduced in any form or by any electronic or mechanical means, including information storage and retrieval systems, without permission in writing from the publisher, except by a reviewer who may quote brief passages in a review.

Warner Books and the Warner Books logo are trademarks of Time Warner Inc. or an affiliated company. Used under license by Hachette Book Group, which is not affiliated with Time Warner Inc.

Cover design by Shasti O'Leary Soudant/Don Puckey
Cover illustration by Jethro Soudant

Warner Books
Hachette Book Group USA
1271 Avenue of the Americas
New York, NY 10020
Visit our Web site at www.HachetteBookGroupUSA.com.

Printed in the United States of America

Originally published in hardcover by Aspect
First Paperback Printing: November 2006

10 9 8 7 6 5 4 3 2 1

For Allan

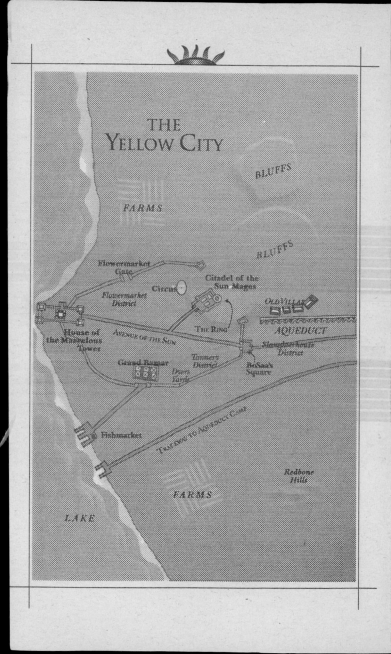

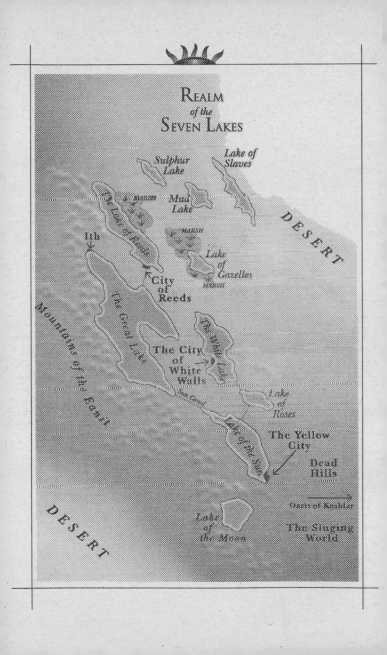

PROLOGUE

Someone was calling for help.

Raeshaldis, Habnit's Daughter, stirred in her sleep.

The call came spiraling up from deep within her dreams, but she knew this was no dream vision, no mental sifting of waking events or past griefs.

Our children are dying. Help us. . . .

A woman; almost certainly a woman of magical power. Even sunk in sleep, Shaldis could sense the shape and color, the taste of the woman's spells. The cry was in no language she had ever heard before—musical and rippling—but the meaning shaped itself in her mind, as words are understood in dreams.

Illness—fever— The wizards cannot help. Healing no longer flows from their hands. We the Craft women—

Here Shaldis's mind groped for the word. In the tongue spoken in the Realm of the Seven Lakes there was no word for women-who-do-magic, as there was for men. Until two years ago there had never been a need for one, for no woman had ever been born with such power in her flesh.

We command the fire and the serpents and the stinging insects, but we cannot wield the power that sends fever away.

And behind that cry, that desperation, Shaldis heard another sound that moved her as if her heart knew what it was or must be. A thick, soft booming, as regular as the beat of the Earth's heart. A rushing like the wind through the groves of date palms, building to a crash like the sound of an avalanche of sand in the dry wadis where the ancients had buried their dead.

But unlike either, and as unknown to her as the language in which the Craft woman called. Yet her dreaming mind felt its power, as it understood the meaning of the words.

Help us. Please help us. Our children are dying.

※

In the village of Three Wells, Bennit the king's overseer also dreamed.

He'd gone to sleep early, not that anyone in Three Wells had any reason to sit up late. The farming village lay far out on the edge of the yellow rangelands, close to the badlands where ancient kings had buried their dead. Sometimes a wandering storyteller passed through or a traveling merchant. Then everyone gathered in Bennit's big adobe house to listen to news from the other villages, or even from the Yellow City on the lake's green shores. For a night they'd marvel over the doings of the king, like a gorgeous peacock in his palace, the House of the Marvelous Tower, or of the great landchiefs of the realm or of the wizards. Poru the salt merchant had brought the astonishing news last year that wizards had indeed been gradually losing their powers all over, as had been rumored for years, and that, of all things, certain women had begun to show skill in magic. Bennit had laughed at this and declared he'd believe it when he saw it and not before.

But such festive evenings were few. Mesquite for convivial fires had to be fetched out of the badlands; sheep fat was more profitably used for cooking than for burning in a lamp. More often, Bennit made his final rounds of the village fields at sunset, checking for evidence of prowling nomads and finding mostly only the marks of jackals and coyotes. He'd count the hairy subhumans—the teyn who did the heavy work of tilling and digging—in their compound, and lock the compound gates. Then he'd return to his wife's corn cakes and beans, a few drinks of corn liquor or strong date wine, and sleep.

If last night, and the three nights before, Bennit had done his final inspections while the sun burned in the sky, well, what of that? And if, contrary to forty-three years of his custom, he found himself looking forward to sleep with the excited eagerness of a child awaiting a treat, it wasn't to be wondered at.

Was it?

He was glad his wife, Acacia Woman, for once made no comment at his change of habits. Such forbearance wasn't like her, but he barely noticed this; in fact, she seemed just as eager to seek her own side of the cornshuck mattress as soon as supper's dishes were scoured and put away. It annoyed him that she slipped so easily into sleep, when he lay awake, watching the dove-colored twilight fade from the sky. When he trembled with eagerness, waiting . . .

Waiting for the music that heralded the coming of those exquisite dreams.

Dreams of things he'd never experienced in waking life. The songs of instruments he'd never heard, of voices in a tongue unfamiliar but teasingly like something he'd once understood. The taste on his tongue of sweets or savories that he knew in no real existence. Kisses—by the names of all the gods, what kisses!—from the mouths of women whose faces were clear and as individual as those of the daughters of his friends, women whose names he could almost have said . . .

And other things still. Deeper exhilarations: of having power, of wearing silk. Of joy so wild that he wanted to weep. He had almost struck old Acacia Woman for waking him this morning, for robbing him of the last smoky whispers of his dream.

He frowned at that memory as he began to slide over into dream. His wife had woken him because when the boys had driven the sheep out to pasture they'd found the body of Klu the teyn minder lying among the cornstalks of the village fields, hacked to death, a look of staring agony on his face. The brother who shared Klu's house was missing—a curious thing, for the brothers had been devoted to each other.

It was his duty to investigate, but curiosity about the matter was pulling Bennit back toward waking. He thrust the matter from his mind, fearful that thoughts of the waking world would somehow interfere with the coming of the dreams. As the sky outside the window darkened and the moon appeared, full and brilliant, fear touched him, as it had last night and the night before—an agony of terror that the dreams wouldn't come.

But they did. First sweet and far-off singing, unfurling like glowing ribbons in the dark. Then beauty that filled him like a bejeweled memory of unutterable sweetness. Stolen lovemaking with the woman he adored—he could see her face like a flower! A single moment encapsulating a hundred meetings, a night of frenzied passion compacted into seconds. Bennit heard himself groan in ecstasy that was half in memory, half in truth. In the next second it seemed to him that he was holding up his baby son, not any of the worthless brats Acacia Woman had given him, but one whom he knew to be the dear child of his soul, and it seemed to him that his heart must break with gladness.

Denser, stronger than ever before, joy followed joy until his heart pounded in his ears, as if someone were pouring the sweetest of liquors down his throat, drowning him.

Then he heard screaming.

Someone screaming in the real world, the waking world, the world that no longer mattered.

The sweet liquor's savor changed to the metallic gush of blood.

Bennit gasped, gagged as pain ripped his belly. A spear impaled him, hurling him to the ground. Men were running toward him, naked swords in hands. Panic darkness swooped upon him, death in agony.

He cried out and tried to jerk himself awake, but only succeeded in sitting upright. Every nerve and joint shrieked in anguish and he looked at his hands, saw them fingerless with leprosy, red-black with running sores. Like a ghost in a dream, he was aware of Acacia Woman leaping to her feet, thrashing her hands at something he couldn't see, as if she, too, were trapped in some fearful dream. She staggered around the room, screaming, fell into the hearth and crawled, her long hair burning, out through the door.

But the dreamworld shifted back into his mind. There were men in the room, soldiers. Though their arms and mail were strange to him, he knew them, knew they were there to kill him, and he leaped to his feet. He was too late. A knife tore into his chest; he felt it cleave his lungs, slice the big muscle of his heart. He was drowning in blood, falling.

Fire was all around him. Shadowy shapes whirled among the soldiers, striking at them—or at something else Bennit could not see—with a burning stick from the banked kitchen fire. The worlds of dream and waking merged, fused, as in the worst of nightmares. Fire roared up the straw mats of the house walls, devoured the woven rush rugs of the floor. Bennit ran out the door, bleeding, dying, consumed with pain and knowing that though he was aware of pieces of reality he was still asleep, unable now to wake.

Dimly he could see the streets of the village as he knew them in daytime, in the waking world that now swam in and out of existence. Men and women he knew with sudden despairing clarity ran among the burning houses, shrieking like the damned, their eyes the wide, unblinking eyes of sleepers who see only their own private shadow shows. Bennit saw his sister run past with her infant in her arms and fling herself into a burning house. Saw one of his cousins crumple, rolling, to the dusty ground, clawing and clutching at his arms, his belly, his throat as if trying to dislodge some horrible thing. Among the houses—Bennit didn't know if it was real or part of the horrors of the dream—he saw something that seemed to be a green mist floating or dimly shining clouds of greenish light.

Only it seemed to him that the clouds had eyes, had mouths—mouths that spoke his name.

The mouths converged on him, singing those beautiful songs. So great was his terror at what they would do—at what they might tell him—that he flung himself back into his own burning house.

ONE

Shaldis woke, the sound of that heavy, crashing boom whispering away from her ears.

She sat up on her narrow cot. The full moon's silver light flooded her cell, glimmered on the drifts of sand that were beginning to accumulate in the corners of the Court of the Novices outside. The dozen or more novice Sun Mages whose daily duty had been to keep the sand at bay were gone. Last spring, when the rains had not come for weeks despite all the efforts of the Sun Mages to bring them, the populace of the Yellow City had rioted and attacked their Citadel. Most of the mages, from master down to novice, had departed after that, facing the fact, at last, that no wizard was able to work magic anymore.

Healing, as the woman in the dream had cried, no longer flowed from their hands. Nor did the power to bring the rains, to ward against rats and mosquitoes, to control the hairy silent army of teyn upon whose labor the great grainfields depended.

Eventually, after everyone gave up trying, the rains had come.

Shaldis didn't know what she and the three remaining

Sun Mages were going to do about the rest of it: mosquitoes, rats, teyn.

She rose from her bed, a tall skinny girl whose fair complexion and thick brown hair proclaimed her descent from one of the half-hundred upper-class clans who had settled in the Valley of the Seven Lakes centuries before. The women of these clans went veiled about their womanly duties. Until two years ago, it was as unheard-of for a girl of one of the great merchant families to go unmarried out of her father's house, as it would have been for her to discover in herself the power to work magic like a man.

Her grandfather had cast her out when she had claimed her own power. At the age of sixteen she had been the first female the Sun Mages had taken in to teach.

Now, almost thirty months later, she was still the only female. She and the three remaining masters—plus the Citadel cook and one male novice—continued to dwell in the nearly empty sandstone fortress on its bluff above the Yellow City, subsisting on donations sent them by the king. Back when the mages had been able to sing the rains out of the skies every spring and cast wards to keep rats from the granaries and grasshoppers from the fields, the great landchiefs of the realm had given them the revenues from land and mines, and thousands of teyn laborers. These had largely disappeared.

Shaldis wrapped the sheet around herself and went to fetch her white novice's robe from its peg on the wall. The predawn air held a taste of the desert's nighttime chill. Even the hundred feet or so that the Citadel was raised over the rest of the city made a difference. Down in the twisting canyons of the city's narrow streets, the air, even at this hour, would be like tepid glue. She pulled on her robe and scooped from a painted pottery bowl on the table a hunk of white crystal as long as two of her knuckles and twice as thick. Yanrid the crystalmaster had let her take it from the Citadel's scrying chamber the day before. It was old and powerful, and worked far more reliably than her own.

A Craft woman, the voice in her dreams had called itself—her mind recalled the shape of the meaning, tried to fit it into words she knew. In the Yellow City they called the women in whom the powers of magic had bloomed Ravens, or Raven sisters, from the fact that, alone among the beasts and birds of the earth, the same word was used for both the male and the female of that species and from the legend that ravens could work magic. The nomads of the deep desert called such women *witches,* a word that originally meant "poisoners of wells." But some in the city were beginning to call the women-who-did-magic Crafty Ones or Crafty Women, the way northern peasants had called wizards Crafty Men sometimes: "those who have a special skill." The term was beginning to be used interchangeably with "Raven." There were still men in the city who claimed to be Crafty Men.

Fewer and fewer believed them.

Carrying the white crystal in her hand, Raeshaldis crossed the Court of the Novices through luminous blue darkness, climbed the rock-cut stairs still higher up the bluff. Well above the rest of the Citadel, she came into the Circle, the open space in which the rites of the Summoning of Rain were worked each spring. It stood empty most of the year, two hundred feet above the dark maze of the city, but the magics that had been raised there every year for six hundred years seemed to rise from its stones and whisper to the overarching stars.

She knelt in the Circle's center, closed her eyes.

I'm here.

She centered her mind on the sun, the source of the power for the system followed by her order. The Sun at His Prayers, this hour was called, the time of stillness. Magics worked through the power of the sun changed from hour to hour, and at this hour sun magic was said to be strongest. Lately Shaldis had begun to wonder if the spells of the Sun Mages applied to the magic of women. Spells she wove exactly as she had been taught by them were wildly inconsistent in their effects: sometimes strong, sometimes weak, sometimes crumbling away like wet adobe—only words like children's games. She drew and released her breath, tried to put from her mind her own frustrations with her failure to control her powers. Tried not to think about her fears of what would become of her—what would become of the Realm of the Seven Lakes—if she and the other small handful of Raven Sisters could not learn to use their powers properly by the time next year's rains were due.

In the ivory light of the full moon the Lake of the Sun shimmered faintly, sunk low in its bed but still a hundred and fifty miles from end to end. If the rains did not come, those who lived along its shores still had time.

The woman calling into the dark of her dreams had none.

Illness . . . fever . . . Our children are dying.

I'm here. Shaldis opened her eyes, angled the crystal to the moonlight so that its central facet was a tiny slab of pale radiance. *Whoever you are, I'm here.*

But she saw no one in that slip of light, and no reply came into her mind. *I'm here. . . .*

For nearly a thousand years, the Sun Mages had spoken

through the mirrors, the crystals, the water bowls in the scrying chamber with mages in other parts of the world, places that for the most part no one had ever journeyed to. It was ninety days by camel train to the barren, foggy villages on the edge of the sea to the northwest; and what might lie beyond that sea—or beyond the deserts that stretched in all other directions—no one knew. Even the constellations described by those alien mages were unknown. It was part of the Sun Mages' training to learn the languages spoken by the outlanders, a laborious process: the language Shaldis had heard the woman speak in her dream had sounded like none she'd studied.

And she had never heard Yanrid or anyone else describe that booming sound she had heard.

And it wasn't a dream, she told herself. *It was real.* A real place, a real woman crying for help.

Our children are dying. . . .

And we are dying, too, thought Shaldis, her mind aching with its efforts to focus on something of the dream that would connect her with that despairing cry.

Unless we learn how to use our powers—among other things, Shaldis had never yet managed to ensorcel either a snake or an insect and neither had any of the women she knew—*we shall die.*

We're on borrowed time as it is, waiting for the time of the rains to come again. Waiting for the next disaster.

We need your help, as you need ours.

The sky in the east stained unearthly blue-green above the Citadel bluff. The fat moon turned the lake waters to shimmering silver among shoals black with reeds and crocodiles. Long lines of bucket hoists stretched out from the grainfields, palmeries, and gardens to the now-distant water's edge. The canal that connected the city's southern gate with the lakeside Fishmarket and docks burned like a sword blade. In a thousand courtyards in the city, a thousand mud-built nests in the rock crags around her, birds began to sing.

Shaldis raised her eyes from the crystal, her head throbbing. The mazes of the Yellow City's streets were still pitch-dark, but the darkness was dotted everywhere now with minute lights as women, or slaves, built up the fires in the outdoor kitchens that nearly everyone used in summertime.

In an hour the three remaining Sun Mages—powerless now but still traditionally the order most closely allied with the king—would descend to the House of the Marvelous Tower, to meet with the king and with the four great landchiefs of the realm. Shaldis could see the Marvelous Tower itself, a gaudy miracle of red and gold in daylight, now a dark spike against the moon-drenched waters, its thousand mirrors twinkling wanly like the fading stars. The thought of the meeting rankled her a little, for although none of the Sun Mages possessed the slightest magic anymore, they would be given a place of honor on the council pavilion's divan, while she would probably be asked to sit behind a screen in deference to the sensibilities of the more conservative landchiefs.

On the other hand, she reflected, that would mean she could sit with Summerchild, the king's favorite and the center of the Raven sisterhood—a far more entertaining proposition than minding her manners under the disapproving gaze of the men.

The rising light showed her the stone arches of the king's aqueduct, stretching away from the city to the south and east. It would, when finished, reach the deep springs of the Oasis of Koshlar and bring water to the Lake of the Sun and to the farms and villages all along its banks: so far it had reached only a few miles beyond the Dead Hills. If it was finished—the desert beyond those parched brown badlands was a deadly place, the haunt of small bands of wild teyn as savage as animals and of nomads barely more civilized who took ill this trespass of their realm.

Once djinni had haunted the desert, too: deadly, brilliant, seldom entirely visible, creatures entirely of magic.

And being of magic, when magic had changed, they had melted away, their powers to sustain themselves gone. One of them at least, Shaldis knew, had taken refuge in a crystal statue in a ruined temple in the slum district beyond the city's eastern gate; after her single interview with it last spring it had not communicated with another human soul. She had theories about what had become of some of the others, but could prove nothing.

She had a feeling that was one of the things the king would ask her at the council—and that one or more of the landchiefs would try to bribe her for help in getting that djinn on their side.

In the mazes of the dark streets more spots of light were appearing. The Dead Hills, with their equally impenetrable mazes of dry wadis and forgotten tombs, lay dark still, save where, for an instant, Shaldis thought she saw a flicker of movement, the passing of a glowing greenish light.

When she blinked and looked again, it was gone.

It was really time to go down. She'd need a little time to scrub herself and fix her hair and get some breakfast before leaving for the council.

Yet she turned her eyes back to the white crystal one last time. The whole sky to the east flooded with light, and the crystal seemed to drink it up and throw it back, burning and pale. Shaldis closed her eyes, dipped her mind back toward trance.

I'm here. I'm Raeshaldis, Habnit's Daughter. I can help you.

And, please, you help us in turn. We need all the knowledge of magic, all the workers of magic—all the Crafty ones—on our side, if we are to survive.

I am here. Please help us.

For a moment she thought she heard, far off like the echoing memory of her dream, that sighing roar, that heavy hammer blow.

Then only stillness and from the city below the crowing of a thousand cocks.

She was definitely late, and nearly ran down the winding stairs from the Circle. Her mind raced ahead of her to what Summerchild would say about her dream, and how they might combine their strengths to scry deeper for its sender. Though she, Shaldis, had the academic training of a Sun Mage, she sensed in the king's graceful concubine a deeper power. The other Raven sisters of the city—a merchant's darkly pretty concubine named Moth, and Pebble, a contractor's big, mousy-haired, good-natured daughter—were newer to their powers and uncertain of them.

Shaldis wished her friend Pomegranate were still in the city. The half-mad beggar woman was another whose powers, she sensed, were as deep as her own. But Pomegranate had gone with the king's former tutor, a onetime Earth Wizard named Soth, to seek among the distant cities on the shores of the other lakes for word of other women who might have power. And the other three Raven sisters she knew were—

She came around the corner into the Court of the Novices, and stopped.

A man stood in the blue shadowy twilight, just outside the door of her room. Not a mage. A tall heavy-shouldered man in a civilian's loose pantaloons and light summer robe, a man whose movement, as he turned uncertainly from her door, was familiar, even before she saw his face.

Then he turned at the sound of her step and said, "Rae-shaldis? Old One?"

Recognition hit her like a dagger in her chest. She stood still, unable to move or speak.

"Daughter?"

"Yes. It's me."

TWO

For over two years, Shaldis had wondered what the first words out of her mouth would be should she ever meet her father again.

Why didn't you protect me? Silly—nobody protected anybody in her grandfather's household when her grandfather went after them.

How could you let him cast me out? Anybody who'd ask that question had never met her grandfather.

I love you? She didn't know if that were true anymore, or whether, if it was, what that meant.

I don't need you? The agony in her heart gave her the lie, but she probably could have come out with the statement, if given enough time to prepare.

Yes, it's me? Too commonplace for words. As if neither love nor agony had ever taken place.

He looked older than he should have, she thought, as he strode across the court toward her, his arms stretched out. Had there always been that much gray in his straggly beard? Had the pouchy flesh around his eyes been that flaccid? The telltale veins on his nose and cheeks that . . . that *telltale*?

Mostly he looked tired. Tired and defeated.

The way everyone came to look who lived in her grandfather's house. She noted automatically how stooped he was for a man over six feet high; how long and thin his ink-stained hands were; how despite her grandfather's wealth, the robe and pantaloons were the same ones he'd habitually worn two years ago. Back in her first year here at the Citadel, when the male novices were brutally hazing her and the masters were demanding why she couldn't seem to make her spells work, Shaldis had dreamed about encountering her father again and telling him coolly, *I have no father.* In her dreams she'd managed to figure out how to make her spells work and was an acclaimed master herself, and her grandfather had sent her father to beg her help for one of his money-making schemes. . . . One of the reasons the wizards were organized into orders was to control the hiring of freelance mages by merchants, landchiefs, and anyone who wanted to use magic to further their own businesses at the expense of their neighbors. Of course, by that time her grandfather, the fearsome old merchant Chirak Shaldeth, would be peeling his own skin off from frustration that he'd let a mage in his own household get away. . . .

I have no father.

As he took her in his arms Habnit whispered, "Old One, I have missed you so."

Shaldis laid her head on his shoulder and began to cry.

"You've grown," he said, after a time of gently patting her back.

She wiped her eyes. "Have the others shrunk, sir?" It delighted her, as it had when she was a child, that she made him laugh.

It was nothing like her dreams.

"It's shocking of me to say so"—Habnit drew back and cupped his daughter's cheek in one hand—"and don't tell your grandfather I said it, but this new fashion one sees for women going about unveiled . . . it suits you. One sees pretty faces in the markets now sometimes. . . . Just because a rose grows in another man's garden doesn't mean passersby can't be cheered by its beauty. Are you happy, child?"

"More than I can say." *More than you ever made me. But you tried.* She sniffled and wiped her eyes again with her sleeve. "Every time I study the books in the library, I thank you in my heart for teaching me the High Script. Even when I got here I read it better than some of the boys." She'd had nightmares for years about the time her grandfather had caught her practicing the formal runes of the script consecrated to poetry, the classics, magic, and the other affairs of men. She had not forgotten that her father denied teaching her, when his father asked who had done so.

She had taken a beating rather than give him away. He'd wept later, in the secrecy of his room. On that occasion her own eyes had remained dry.

The blue shadows in the court were now watery gray, and the upper towers were dyed with the first brazen glare of the sun. Yanrid, old Rachnis the spellmaster, and the even-older Archmage Hathmar would be in the refectory— if they weren't already done with their spare bowls of corn gruel—and here she was, unwashed and starving. . . .

"Have you eaten, Papa?" She ducked into her room, gathered up her sandals, sash, and washing things: the little pan of scrub water in her curtained corner of the kitchen court would be almost cold now. "There'll be bread and honey in the kitchen and coffee, while I—"

"There isn't time, child," said her father, stepping in front of her as she reemerged. "Old One, I know that there was . . . was ill will and anger when you left the house. . . ."

In the midst of her shocked disappointment—*So he only came to seek me because he needs me. Because THEY need me*—Shaldis found herself reflecting wryly how like her father it was to describe as "ill will and anger" the rage and grief when she'd returned from one of her surreptitious excursions to the marketplace to discover that her grandfather had found, and burned, her secret cache of books.

Ill will and anger. Her mother and aunts had had to hold her back from plunging her hands into the kitchen fire to pull the flaming pages out. Had had to keep holding her lest she throw herself at that tall, harsh-faced old autocrat who was cursing her for a disgrace and shouting that he'd had to back down on her dowry in order to get the master harness maker's son to marry her.

Her throat had been raw for days afterward, from the words she'd screamed.

"But we need you. We need your help."

Shaldis drew in a deep breath. Beyond her father's shoulder, the Citadel's other remaining novice appeared in the gateway, a short, stocky dark-browed boy named Kylin. Like Shaldis he still wore the white robe and sandals of the novices—there were bales of them still in the storerooms—though she was now the only person in the Citadel who actually had power, and he was, essentially, a servant these days.

She guessed the three old masters had sent him to tell her they were ready to leave for the palace. But when he backed out again, unwilling to interrupt her, she said, "Excuse me, please, Papa," and called out to the boy. "Tell them to go on without me, Ky. I'll catch up or meet them at the palace."

Kylin glanced at her father, then back at her face, at the red lingering around her swollen eyes. "Are you all right, Shaldis?"

"I'm fine. I won't be long."

Something in the way her father had spoken made her guess that the second part of that statement was as much a lie as the first, and she felt as if her heart had been dipped in pitch and then set aflame. The council, she had already guessed, would be critical, and even more critical her news to Summerchild that, at long last, after years of searching and silence, word—even the tiniest whisper in a dream—

had come to them of the existence of another Raven sister, another Crafty woman, somewhere in the world.

Word, and a frantic plea for help.

But when she looked back at her father, she saw he was scared. Scared and desperate.

And you did not say no to your family.

Ever.

For two years the fact that she'd walked away from them had marked her heart like the scar of a burn.

"What does he want?" she asked, and did not need to say which *he* she meant. "A curse put on a rival's caravan so he can get another two dequins a pound on salt?"

She'd wanted to hurt someone with her words, but when her father looked away in shame she found herself in pain, too. *Even a blow struck in self-defense,* she thought, *still draws my own blood. . . .*

"Last night someone tried to kill your grandfather."

Shaldis opened her mouth to snap something about how wide the field of suspects must be, but closed it. Even two years as a novice in the Citadel—even the unthinkable act of leaving her family's house—hadn't erased the manners beaten into her from earliest childhood, about what a girl-child could and could not say about the patriarch of the house.

Her father, though he might fear and hate Chirak Shaldeth as much as she did, loved his father in equal measure. He was the only one who'd be wounded by such words.

"I came to you because it looks like whoever it was, they used magic to do it."

Oryn II, third lord of the House Jothek to rule as king over the Realm of the Seven Lakes, hated councils. They invariably turned into wrangles about money, a topic that bored him to the screaming point—not that he was so ill-bred as to scream in company no matter how bored he was.

"The point of being king is that one never has to ask what *anything* costs," he argued plaintively as he helped the exquisite Summerchild to the pile of cushions heaped beside the latticed screens that divided the long council room of the Cedar Pavilion into two unequal sections. "People simply bring things to one, and grovel while they do so. Besides, I don't trust a single one of those landchiefs as far as I can have the guards throw him."

He saw the ghost of her smile through the thin celery-green silk of her veil and in the wide topaz-blue eyes. "Perhaps larger guards are in order?" she suggested.

"Mechanization might suit," agreed Oryn, kneeling beside her and offering her one of the several plates of fresh fruit laid out on the low table for her delectation. He was a tall man, and he encouraged his court historians to refer to him as the Peacock King because he suspected the alternative title would be Oryn the Fat. His brown curls, touched up with henna, glittered with gold dust, and the hems of his flame-red robe and tunic sparkled with embroidery two handspans deep—sufficient, he hoped, to impress the lesser landchiefs. "A catapult, perhaps . . ."

"I should be doing this for you," argued Summerchild as the king held out a sugared berry to her lips. "You're never going to get a reputation as a disgrace to the dynasty if you give concubines sugared berries instead of having them beg for the privilege of placing them in your mouth."

"I need the exercise."

And Summerchild laughed.

"Councils used to appall me because they were so dull, you know." Oryn leaned to the latticework, peered through the gauze that backed the exquisite carving, to see into the larger portion of the pavilion, something that anyone could do unobserved from this closed-up and deeply shadowed end. In the main chamber the detachable openwork walls had been removed from between the pillars that held up the ceiling, admitting morning sunlight and the fresh coolness of the gardens. "Lord Sarn always scheming for money and position, Lord Akarian sounding off for hours about whatever fad he thinks will save the world this month . . . Is he still eating insects?"

"I had the cooks prepare some just in case."

"I hope they clearly marked which dishes are which. Lord Jamornid trying to buy everyone's loyalty and respect by having the best and spending the most. . . . Do you think this outfit is more impressive than his? I really should keep spies in his household to let me know what he'll be wearing."

He returned his eye to the lattice. Lord Jamornid, gorgeously turned out in varying shades of violet silk, had just entered the main chamber and was trying to convince the broad-shouldered Lord Sarn that each lord should— and in fact, must—have his individual slaves present with fans, having never apparently encountered the idea that such slaves would not only discuss with their colleagues in the kitchen whatever they heard but also could be bribed to pass the information along to merchants, corn brokers, and landlords.

"Now they frighten me," Oryn said softly. "They

frighten me because each man seems to think that all the old rules still apply. They still think that it's a game about individual power, about raising their House to the kingship. It isn't like that anymore."

He looked down again, in genuine distress, at the woman on the cushions, the woman who had been called the Summer Concubine: the most perfect, and perfectly trained, Pearl Woman of his father's harem. The woman he had loved at sight, fifteen years before.

The woman who had been among the first to develop the powers of magic, when rumors were flying that the Sun Mages—and the Blood Mages and Earth Wizards and the rest—were losing the ability to heal and ward and summon rain.

"We must forget our differences," Oryn went on with an earnestness he would have deplored back in the days when he'd been the fearsome Taras Greatsword's disgraceful dilettante heir. "We must put aside our individual concerns. We must unite, and remain united. Or we will die."

Summerchild lifted one small jeweled hand and wrapped it around Oryn's massive fingers. Though of medium height, she was so slender as to give the impression of childlike smallness, especially against the king's six-foot three-inch bulk. Her fair hair was dressed with elegant simplicity; her linen gown, finer than most silks, was the pale clear hue that exactly matched her enormous eyes. "You wrong them, Oryn," she said gravely. "I think every single one of them would be willing to put aside his own petty concerns and take command of the united realm. They are noble men at heart."

"Yes—just ask them." Oryn turned briefly to the mirror

on the wall, to check his eye paint and unsnag one of his topaz-and-ruby earrings from his hair. "Here come the lesser fry," he added, turning back. "Sarn's cousin Lord Nahul-Sarn, the Great Stone Face . . . the man looks like he was hewed rather than birthed. There's Brother Barún—I'm astonished the Emerald Concubine let him out of her pavilion this early. Here's a gaggle of Sarn and Jothek landchiefs and a couple of the rangeland sheikhs. . . ."

"No sign yet of Lord Mohrvine?"

"No. Drat this custom that the king must arrive last and keep everyone waiting. My uncle will make sure he's the last of *them*, and I have to appear after *him*, and it'll be noon before the council is over and hot as a bake oven. You and Mistress Raeshaldis couldn't manage to conjure a steady, cooling breeze, could you? Or a permanent patch of autumn weather for, say, a hundred feet around the pavilion? It would help things out enormously."

"I shall devote my fullest attention to it, my lord." Both knew that the conjuration of weather lay outside any single woman's power. They both prayed it would respond to combined spells, but had no proof. The Sun Mages had been able to call the rains only at certain times of the year.

"I knew I could count on you, my dearest. Good heavens, that's Benno Sarn with Lord Sarn. His older brother, you recall, who gave up his inheritance to become a Sun Mage. Still robed as a wizard, I see—very tasteful arrangement of astrological signs embroidered on his cloak—he looks like *he's* the one who's going to need to conjure a cooling breeze, in that getup. We should see some excellent glares when the Sun Mages show up. Yes, here they are."

"Oh, let me see!" Summerchild leaned forward and pressed her eye to the lattice just as a tall and grave-faced young guardsman named Jethan escorted Hathmar, Rachnis, and Yanrid up the pavilion's shallow steps. Hathmar, white-haired, bent, and nearly blind, walked past the former rector of the Citadel without a glance; but withered little Rachnis gave Benno Sarn a single cold stare before turning his face aside; and Yanrid, the youngest of the three, traded sneers with his erstwhile colleague that would have done credit to a pair of rival Blossom girls encountering each other in the Flowermarket.

"Where is Shaldis?" asked Summerchild, sitting back onto her cushion. "She should be with them."

"Unless my chamberlain has had an attack of propriety and is leading her here by a separate way. Which sounds like something Geb would do, when you come to think of it. Absurd, when you consider she's the only one of the Sun Mages with any power these days."

"Lord Sarn's certainly treating them with respect." The stocky, powerful landchief had risen from his place on the striped linen cushions of the divan to arrange extra cushions for the Archmage.

"Lord Sarn needs to have people continue to believe in the Sun Mages' power, since his brother seems to be his court mage these days," Oryn murmured. "Maybe Benno's even convinced Sarn he still *has* power—since trying to resume his rightful position as the head of House Sarn would only get him assassinated. Ah," he added, as a slender figure came into sight, strolling along the edge of the marble reflecting pool with a string of deep-desert sheikhs trailing respectfully in his wake. "Here's Uncle Mohrvine at last. Just late enough so that if I make them wait long enough to put him in his place—"

"Great heavens, my nephew is not here yet?" Lord Mohrvine's voice cut through the muted chatter in the pavilion. During the riots of the past spring, when it looked like the nomads of the desert were going to attack the rangeland settlements, Taras Greatsword's younger half brother had begun affecting the bearing and plain dress of a military captain. He'd kept it up, as a pointed contrast to his royal nephew's curled and bejeweled elegance, probably because he'd guessed that eventually the nomads would attack again and people would seek to put their trust in a strongman. He had made a brief alliance with his nephew during the riots, but Oryn did not deceive himself about Mohrvine's intentions.

"It will be noon before we're done here. We might as well hold this meeting in the midst of the desert."

"One of these days I really am going to have to have him murdered, as Sarn keeps telling me I should." Oryn straightened the billowing silk of his over-robe, checked Summerchild's mirror again, and adjusted the set of a necklace. "Only, of course, Sarn knows that as long as Mohrvine is around, he'll never stand a chance of sitting on the throne himself. Wish me luck, my blossoming rose of springtime. I shall need it."

THREE

Naturally, no one on the council wanted to hear that new levies of money, grain, teyn laborers, and beasts of burden were required for work on the aqueduct. From behind the lattice, Summerchild watched the respectful routine of greeting the king as he made his entrance—and Oryn was a genius at making an entrance—erode within minutes into bitter squabbling.

"I admit that more camels are needed now that the workers are farther into the desert, but surely you must see that the division of liability among the High Houses is grossly inequitable!"

"Are you quite certain of your figures, Lord King? Why cannot supplies for the work crews be purchased for far less than four thousand gold pieces? What on earth are you planning to feed them?"

"Five hundred teyn is a tremendous number, now that so many are needed to bring water up from the lakes to the fields."

She observed their faces, men who for the most part would never have dared utter a peep in protest to the demands of Taras Greatsword, Oryn's redoubtable father. Chinless Lord Jamornid was on his feet, forgetting his carefully cultivated dignity and shouting like a fishwife at Oryn's brother, Barún. Heavy-shouldered Lord Sarn was shaking a sheaf of papers at Oryn as if it were a weapon. Only Lord Mohrvine sat silent, his eyes— pale turquoise green, lazy behind heavy lids—moving almost mockingly from lord to lord, not only the great landchiefs but the merchant clan representatives and the lesser sheikhs of the rangelands and near desert, the ones who would have to bear the burden of the new levies. Summerchild had been trained in the finest Blossom House in the city and had retained her connections with the ladies of the Flowermarket District: she knew that Mohrvine systematically entertained these lesser lords nightly, at great expense, in the Blossom Houses. According to her informants he'd purchased concubines for many of them, girls exquisitely trained in the pleasing of men . . .

. . . as he had purchased the Emerald Concubine, who was Barún's dearest treasure, to the fury of Lord Sarn's niece, Barún's wife.

"Yes, my lord, the rains *were* a bit late this year—"

"*A bit late*? Nearly a month?"

"—but they *did* come, and in perfectly normal quantity. Why you persist in believing that we even *need* an aqueduct . . ."

Summerchild knew Barún was absolutely enslaved by that honey-haired, green-eyed girl, but in her fifteen years' residence in the House of the Marvelous Tower she'd seen the king's handsome younger brother absolutely enslaved by numerous other concubines while still retaining sufficient energy to carry on liaisons with circus acrobats, good-looking stevedores, and the handsomer members of the palace guard.

Yet the knowledge that both Mohrvine's mother, Red Silk, and his daughter, the beautiful Foxfire, bore in them the power of the Raven, made her prickle with suspicion every time that handsome, gracious lord made a gift to anyone or asked them to dine. Greatsword, she knew, had mistrusted his younger half brother profoundly, more than once coming close to having him executed.

But even then, it had been too late to do so with impunity.

"For a year now you have been pouring money into this absurd project of yours, my lord, and what have you to show for it? If you had spent the same amount of money and labor deepening the existing wells . . ."

She followed Mohrvine's gaze now to the two sons of Lord Akarian as they raised a protest on the grounds of the failure of magic to protect their crops and investments. "It used to be one could put a spell around the walls of the teyn villages and be sure of them all turning out for work in the mornings," stated Proath Akarian, his whining tenor almost indistinguishable from his father's. "It takes three times the guards to keep an eye on them now, and they slip out of their compounds like weasels, no matter how many of them you string up or how many spikes you put around the walls. When those mages of yours come up with some really reliable means of controlling the teyn again, Your Majesty, then we'll be able to provide you whatever you wish."

And this from a man, thought Summerchild with a resigned shake of her head, who six months ago had been the sworn member of a cult that claimed all workers of magic—both male and female—were in fact demons.

She glanced at Proath's father, wizened, dirty, with his white hair just now growing out of that cult's rather silly obligatory tonsure; he was nodding his agreement. Lord Akarian generally changed answers to the ills of the world every two years or so—his membership in the cult of the magic-hating god Nebekht had lasted nearly three, a record with him.

Whorb, the younger of the two Akarian heirs, added, "And Your Majesty can't pretend to think we have grain to spare! Rats have invaded our granaries as never before, and last fall locusts came out of the desert to devour our farms by the White Lake and the Lake of Gazelles. Locusts! And who knows but that they will return this year in greater numbers!"

"This is not even to speak of the epidemics that have broken out in the villages," added Lord Nahul-Sarn. "I lose workmen daily to marsh fever and pneumonia. Injuries in the mines that once a mage could heal now mortify or turn to fever, lockjaw, and convulsions. Among the cattle and the teyn it's worse."

"Really, my lord," chimed in one of the lesser Jamornid landchiefs, "until Your Majesty is willing to share the benefits of the magic these women of yours make, you can scarcely expect us to keep up with your taxes and demands! It is not only not possible, it is not fair."

"I *beg* your pardon?" Oryn sat up very straight on his cushions—as well he might, thought Summerchild with the cold tension of foreboding tightening behind her sternum. She saw the young landchief flinch guiltily; saw the glance that passed between him and Lord Mohrvine.

In spite of his pomaded curls and eye paint, when Oryn was stirred up he could be terrifyingly impressive. His deep voice, like velvet and bronze, cut effortlessly through the angry clamor of his lords: "Do I understand that there is a belief in some quarters that I am withholding the—the services of the Raven sisterhood from those who need them, simply to increase my own revenues?"

Sarn, Jamornid, and half the lesser landchiefs began a gabble of protest, cut off by the king's lifted hand.

"Is that what is being said about me?"

Glances flashed around the room like birds caught in a windstorm. A lot of them, Summerchild noted, touched Mohrvine.

It was Lord Jamornid who spoke. "Your Majesty has never sent these women who claim power—these women who bow to the commands of one in Your Majesty's household"—it was the closest a well-bred man could come to discussing another man's concubine in public— "out to our compounds, to use their magic to control the teyn."

Silence in the pavilion, broken only by the musical twitter of the green-and-yellow finches in the trees. Summerchild saw the glances flick toward the lattice where they all knew she sat.

Wariness. Resentment.

And in some—whose eligible daughters they fancied had been passed over in matrimony, despite the fact that no king in five hundred years had dared to formally wed a daughter of one of his landchiefs—hate.

"My dear Lord Jamornid . . ." Oryn's beautiful voice was now deadly soft. "If I do not dispatch members of my household to the compounds that house your teyn it is out of regard for the penury you pled moments ago, lest you should be obliged to entertain these ladies to no purpose. The magic of women has proven so far to be unlike the magic of men. Believe me, if the Sisters of the Raven were capable of controlling the teyn with spells of awe, as my lord Hathmar and the Sun Mages for so long did"—he inclined his head toward the three Sun Mages, sitting on their cushions in their robes of white, gold, and blue—"we would have far fewer problems with teyn workers disappearing from the aqueduct than we do. It is one of the problems upon which they are working."

Reluctantly, Summerchild added in her mind—knowing as she did that those "spells of awe" were in truth spells of terror and pain. The labor of the teyn was essential to the aqueduct, to the fields, to bringing water to the city. But every time she passed through the gates of a teyn compound and felt the ancient stink of the accumulated fear spells whispering in the walls, her heart cringed.

"Teyn workers disappearing from the aqueduct," said Lord Sarn drily, "is precisely the reason we are unwilling to send yet more of our teyn out there, under inadequate guard—"

"Not to speak of the curious fact," added Verth, the landchief of the lesser Marsent branch of House Jothek, "that far fewer teyn *do* escape from the royal enclosures than from those of lesser men."

"That is absolutely untrue," said Oryn, startled, and Summerchild saw a dozen pairs of eyes slew again to Lord Mohrvine, who assumed the pained expression of a parent hearing a child claim to have slaughtered dragons and settled a little further back on the divan. "And if that is so—"

"My lords." Lord Akarian rose from his place on the divan and spread his skinny arms wide like the priests of Darutha the Rain God did when blessing the soaked crowds in the temple square in the first downpour of spring. Summerchild guessed that it was the old man's wealth and wide acres, more than awe, that quieted the room.

"Have we not all seen how a man lost in the desert will chase mirages of safety and water, running now one way, now another? Are we not all aware that in doing so he loses even the little life he has left in these foolish quests?" His reedy voice had a gentle, rather dreamy note, like a grandfather speaking to unruly and frightened children. "Do we not all know that if he would but follow a single course, he would come to safety at last, no matter what dreams the sands cast up to lure him to death?"

Barun sighed, and a smile of relief gleamed whitely through his golden beard. "At last a man who speaks the truth!" he cried, obviously thinking he could see where his lordship was headed.

Summerchild—and Oryn, too, to judge by the stiffening of his massive shoulders—had heard far too many of Lord Akarian's half-baked schemes to do more than wait uneasily for what would follow that hopeful preamble. House Akarian had lost far too many teyn and cattle to the aqueduct project for there to be any hope that the "single course" he spoke of was going to lead anywhere useful.

"My lords," continued Lord Akarian, "is it not clear to us all that the gods have deserted our land? In the days of our ancestors, in the days when the kings of House Durshen ruled the Realm of the Seven Lakes, there were none of these troubles. When the lords of House Akarian were kings over the Seven Lakes in the time of our grandfathers, the rains fell and magic lay healthy and strong in the hands of the wise men of the realm. Is there no man in this room—no man in this city—who has the wit to ask himself, *What changed?*"

He was looking straight at Oryn as he spoke. Taras Greatsword, Summerchild knew, would have crossed the pavilion in two strides and smote the old lord to the floor with the back of his hand—if he didn't simply run him through on the spot—before calling his guards to haul the traitor and his sons away.

"A good question, my lord." Mohrvine, after one moment when startled shock widened his turquoise eyes, recovered his composure a split second before Oryn did and spoke into the dumbfounded hush in the room. "Now that you speak of it, a great many things have gone amiss since the death of Taras Greatsword."

All eyes went to Oryn—nobody really wanted the Akarians back on the throne—and it was too late, Summerchild perceived, to unsay the suggestion or to simply silence one half-mad landchief, powerful though he might be. By speaking the name of Taras Greatsword, Mohrvine had deftly shifted the ground of the accusation away from the House Jothek and onto Oryn alone.

"We know the gods are with you, my lord," declared Lord Sarn, leaping to his feet in order to fall to one knee. In his dark-red robe and pantaloons he resembled a brick kiln on whose top a thin crop of grass had grown, yellowed, and died. "How else, when you put yourself into their hands at your consecration? But if indeed a curse is withering our land . . ."

Later, Summerchild reflected that Oryn should have

reacted like a despot and simply yelled, "Guards!" Though at this point that might not have saved him. Not without killing every man in the room.

Instead he said what was clearly the first thought that came to his mind: "That is the most ridiculous thing I've ever heard."

"My lords of the Realm of the Seven Lakes!" Lord Akarian flung up his scrawny arms to heaven. "I call for the Ceremony of the King's Jubilee that he may reconsecrate himself to the gods! For the gods alone can save this land!"

Mohrvine was on his feet as if his cushion had bitten him. "A Ceremony of Jubilee!" He, too, stretched his powerful arms to the heavens; and his voice, the trained boom of a battlefield commander, re-echoed in the carved cedar rafters. "A jubilee!" His landchiefs and the deep-desert sheikhs who had pledged him allegiance sprang up as well and took up the shout. *They were unprepared for this,* thought Summerchild, aghast, noting automatically that it was the Akarian landchiefs who ran from the pavilion to carry the news abroad and that Mohrvine had to gesture to his tall son Sormaddin to get him to follow them out with a half dozen of their own men in the general rush.

He followed this up by striding immediately to Oryn's dais—Oryn was on his feet by this time, speechless—and falling to the floor before him to press his lips to his nephew's embroidered slippers. "We know the gods are with you, my lord," he cried, and Lord Sarn—secure in the knowledge that his niece was married to Oryn's heir, Barún—fell at his other side and grasped Oryn's other foot. Lord Jamornid—who'd been gaping stupidly at the whole business—scrambled to his feet, dashed forward, and joined them, careful to keep a cushion in hand lest some infinitesimal speck of dirt from the marble floor be ground into his purple pantaloons.

"We know the gods are with you, and when the gods show to all the world that you are their own choice, all the evils that beset us will melt as shadows melt with the coming of day!"

The pavilion's polished pillars shivered with the cheering of the lords. Even Lord Akarian seemed swept up in the general delight, though his sons had drawn apart to confer in a corner. Cries and cheers began to be heard from the direction of the Golden Court that lay immediately outside the palace's main gate. With only the slightest extension of her hypertrained senses, Summerchild could hear the news being called out from the Marvelous Tower's red-and-golden heights.

Men shouted thanks for the King's Jubilee, making it impossible for Oryn to accuse Akarian or the respectful Mohrvine of any ill will.

Or, in fact, to do anything but thank his murderers for their loudly expressed loyalty and wonder what the hell he was going to do.

FOUR

"They can't really proclaim a jubilee this early in your reign!" protested Summerchild, the moment the king—having received the final bowed oblations from the last departing landchiefs—stumbled through his private doorway back into the latticed and curtained nook. "Can they?"

"They evidently have." Oryn sank down onto the divan as Barún's massive shadow appeared in the archway that led in from the terrace. "Enter!"

Not only his younger brother took up this invitation but the three Sun Mages crowded in behind. The partitioned end of the Cedar Pavilion began to be extremely full.

Barún's hand was on his sword hilt—its perpetual position when not occupied with one of his concubines or his brother's guardsmen. "Shall I take a squadron and arrest them?"

Summerchild wondered if her lord's brother really thought he could lock up all the great landchiefs of the realm without the whole countryside rising in revolt, and concluded that Barún probably did think it. He was handsome as a god and could crush walnuts in his fists, but he couldn't outthink the kitchen cat.

"Word has gone out by this time," Oryn explained to him. "We'd succeed only in making fools of ourselves, if nothing worse. When one is dealing with doubt that we have the gods' mandate to rule, that's a dangerous thing."

The younger man nodded, brows knit together as he digested this. At last he said, "Then the matter should be simple. The gods led you through the ordeals of consecration once; they will do so again. Perhaps Lord Akarian has the right of it, for once. If you undertake the ordeals again, perhaps they will even relent and bring back true magic. . . ."

He glanced at Summerchild and cleared his throat hastily. "Of course, they will leave the magic of women in place as well, we hope."

"One never knows, with gods." Oryn held out his hand to assist old Hathmar down to the divan; the aged Sun Mage's eyesight had been maintained for years by the finely graded spells of healing worked almost subconsciously on his own eyes. These spells, like all others wrought by male wizards over the centuries, had failed; and even the thick-lensed spectacles he and others of his order had devised over the past few years did not help him now.

"I have always had the teensiest, tiniest suspicion, however," Oryn went on, looking back at the other two mages, whom Summerchild had risen to lead to seats, "that it wasn't *entirely* by the efforts of the gods that I got through the ordeals of consecration when I was crowned twelve years ago. And that leaves me feeling a little . . . concerned. Have I call to be?"

Barún looked completely uncomprehending. Yanrid the crystalmaster glanced at his colleagues from beneath his shaggy brows.

"The King's Jubilee," stated Rachnis shadowmaster in his high, scratchy voice. "Thank you, child, that's very kind of you but I'm perfectly capable of getting up and down myself. In ancient times the Ceremony of the King's Jubilee was proclaimed whenever a king reached the forty-ninth year of his reign, for it was judged that at that age he became a new man, and therefore, a new king. As a new king, he must pass through all the ordeals of his consecration again, to grant the gods their chance to say whether they wished this new king to reign or not. The Jubilee was held in the first new moon of the forty-ninth year. No Akarian king ever achieved forty-nine years of rule, and precious few of the Durshens, and to further complicate the records, kings of old sometimes changed their names after a Jubilee, so we can only guess at how many of the Durshen or Hosh Dynasty kings were in fact continuing to rule under a second name. But the number cannot be large."

The old man tented his skinny fingers, and like a good Pearl Woman Summerchild knelt to him holding the exquisite platter of fresh fruits, candied rose petals, moonjellies, and those exquisite wafer cones of beaten cream called gazelle horns. Aside from its being better manners to serve one's own guests, there were some matters it was better that servants did not hear.

"Upon his deathbed"—Oryn pulled up a low stool usually reserved for the slave who wielded a fan—"my father assured me several times that 'Everything will be all right,' a statement Soth repeated on a number of occasions in the week between my father's death and my own consecration as king—my father having died in the moon's last quarter. By the way, my darling, you had probably better get in touch with Soth and summon him back here. I have the dreadful feeling we're going to need his advice rather badly. And in fact everything *was* all right, though I still have nightmares about the crocodiles, not to mention the pit of cobras and being chased by that damned lion. Did someone drug the lion?"

Barún looked shocked to his soul at even the suggestion that anyone would tamper with the ordeals of consecration, but Hathmar's thin mouth tugged in a smile. "The lion was drugged, my lord."

Oryn heaved a sigh of relief. "I'm glad to hear it. I shouldn't have liked to think of a beast that slow trying to make a living on its own in the wild, poor thing. And I suppose one can simply selectively wet down the kindling on the route one walks through the fire: straw damp with water looks pretty much like straw damp with oil. But the crocodiles . . ."

"That was magic." The pale-blue eyes with their film of white lifted to his face, as if the Archmage could still see.

Oryn drew a deep breath. "Bugger," he said quietly. "I was afraid you were going to say that."

"We know of no drug that will affect crocodiles, my lord," said Rachnis. "Not without killing them. Moreover, they come in and go out from the lake into the lagoon within the temple enclosure. To drug them would involve drugging every beast in the lake."

Oryn raised his brows. "So it's been considered at some point in the past, has it?"

"That I cannot say, Lord King. It is the same with the cobras in the pit of the Serpent King. And the poison that you drank at the heart of the maze in the Temple of Time . . . no one but the single Servant of Time knows whether the cup contains poison or not, but believe me, the spells we cast forth upon you assumed that it was the deadliest venom known."

The old man leaned forward and selected a single grape from the tray before him; his black, sharp lizardlike gaze cocked up at the king. "Myself, I have always suspected that the rites of consecration were originated by the Veiled Priests to screen candidates for the kingship. We know almost nothing of the Zali Dynasty—it was fifteen hundred years ago, and even the land was different then. Myself, I believe the Veiled Priests were in fact mages: mages whose power was not as strong as the Sun Mages who backed the Hosh monarchs who truly united the realm. As far back as our Citadel has stood—long before the rains ceased to fall and had to be summoned by the magic of our order—the Sun Mages have guided the kings through their consecrations."

"Did my father know?"

"Your father guessed." Archmage Hathmar folded his clawlike little hands. "It has always been forbidden to speak of these matters to anyone. The priests of the gods hold great power among the common people, especially in the countryside. But your father came to me the night before *his* father's consecration with some very . . . *specific* . . . promises of support and alliance in return for services which neither of us clearly defined."

"Sounds like Father."

Summerchild, seated now beside Oryn's stool, glanced

up at him worriedly. She'd been only a child when Taras Greatsword had defeated the last of the Akarian kings and had ridden in triumph through the Yellow City to crown his own father, the fat, scheming old moneybags Lord Jothek, King of the Realm of the Seven Lakes. She'd just been sold to the most prestigious Blossom House in the city, whose Mother had seen promise of beauty in her skinny seven-year-old self; from its doorway she remembered watching them ride past.

Taras Greatsword, a golden-haired kingmaker and the greatest war lord of the land. His father—officially generalissimo of the Akarian armies but in actuality merely a superb organizer—slouched in the saddle of a white warhorse and looked as if he were worrying about the cost of every rose petal strewn in their path. The current Lord Akarian, then the head of the formerly royal house's cadet branch. And among them a chubby, curly-haired, overdressed little boy clinging wretchedly to the mane of a mount too big for him, looking around in worried apprehension at the crowds who cheered the end of Akarian incompetence and graft.

That memory had been in her mind when, eleven years later, she'd been informed that Greatsword, now king, had purchased her, the youngest and most choice of the perfect Pearl Women of the realm.

The memory of that curly-haired child.

She asked now, "Is it permitted to teach those protective spells to women, lord shadowmaster? Now that the magic that gave them strength has waned?"

"Sweet of you not to say 'failed,' child." Hathmar extended his hand to touch her wrist with a gentle smile. "We are all of us growing accustomed. The problem is—"

"The problem is," concluded Rachnis grimly, "that for most of the year we have been endeavoring to do exactly that: to teach those spells to the girl Raeshaldis without, of course, telling her how they are used. And she has so far been unable to make a single one of them work."

Oryn closed his eyes for a moment, as if hearing words he had feared all along. Then he opened them again and said, "By the way—where *is* Raeshaldis?"

✳

The house of Chirak Shaldeth lay on Sleeping Worms Street, within a hundred feet of the rose-pink walls of the Grand Bazaar where Chirak was one of the five proctors who governed mercantile law. Like most of the great houses of the city, the lower floor of the main block was given over to warehouse space and its outer courtyard to the stabling of the asses and camels on whom the family business depended. Then came the kitchen and the harem, and last of all the inner garden court, like a jewel of rest from the city's clamor and stink.

A wall circled the whole of the little compound, and around the corner from the big camel gate a small door, heavily barred, opened onto a narrow stair. Shaldis couldn't recall having come in that way more than three times in her life. The teyn porter—Two Shoes, they'd always called him, not that he or any teyn ever wore such things—opened at her father's knock and regarded her for a moment with pale-blue eyes whose slit pupils widened and retracted like a cat's.

For a moment she thought he might speak. But he only made a shuffling bow and stepped back to let them in.

Another teyn—a jenny, profoundly pregnant—was washing the tiled stairs as Shaldis followed her father up: its silvery hair had been clipped all over and shaved off its arms and lower legs, to keep it clean for household tasks. Despite the blue-gray skin that showed through the cheap dust-colored tunic that many household teyn wore, in the dark of the stair it looked surprisingly human. Five Cakes, Shaldis recalled her name was.

"Father—" Habnit slowed his steps as they neared the arched space of the landing, with its wide windows onto the outer court. He hesitated, and Shaldis knew exactly what he was going to say. She'd been sick to her stomach all the way here from the Citadel, wondering how she was going to deal with the situation.

When he couldn't finish the sentence she did so for him. "Is he going to have a seizure if I don't wear a veil?"

They both stopped, a half-dozen steps below the landing, regarding each other in the shadows, united by the past they shared.

"He isn't used to the new ways." He meant—Shaldis could almost hear him think it—*If he goes into one of his rages, you can leave the house and have somewhere to go. He'll take it out on me.*

And on your mother.

The recollection of all her submissions, all the humiliations she'd borne in silence, all the fury swallowed so that her grandfather wouldn't turn his rage on his son's wife rose chokingly to Shaldis's throat, and she trembled as if it were yesterday that she'd been required to wash her grandfather's feet and dry them with her hair. It seemed to her that she'd spent the whole of her life, since she was old enough to stand and think and speak, defending her father or her mother or her younger brothers and sisters from that harsh-voiced furious autocrat.

And it had never been enough.

"If I wanted to please him," said Shaldis quietly, "I'd have married that imbecile Forpen Gamert, wouldn't I?"

"For me," coaxed Habnit, masking his dread with a charming smile.

She sighed. Her stomach hurt. "Let's get this over with, Papa."

FIVE

I thought wizards were supposed to know about things like this," Pomegranate whispered as she strained her senses to pierce the white mists that drifted above the waters of the Lake of Reeds. Her dark eyes were sharp for her sixty-three years, but even with the acute senses of magic she could see little beyond the straw hut where they crouched—she and the former Earth Wizard Soth, and Tosu, the adolescent son of the headman of Shonghu village, about a day's walk up the lakeshore. The fogs that cloaked the Yellow City on winter mornings were a daily phenomenon here in the northern portion of the realm, even in midsummer. Pomegranate could barely discern the shining line where the shrunken waters met the long wastelands of reeds and pools that had once been deep under water, and the waters covered any possibility of using her nose to detect their quarry. Listen as she would, the soft, steady lapping of the wavelets rendered other sounds beneath them indistinct.

When it came, she reflected uneasily, magic or no magic, it would be on top of them before they knew it.

"We are," replied Soth softly. "And we do. But the spells that originally defeated water dragons differed from region to region, and the order of Earth Wizards wasn't centralized until long after the last of them disappeared. The line of teachers of which I'm a part originated in the south. We didn't learn the more obscure rites of the northern school."

"Pardon, Lord Wizard." Tosu bowed to Soth as he spoke—he was a country boy and still clearly had a lot of trouble with the idea that wizards no longer had power and that women might. "But this is not a 'water dragon' that has returned to trouble the lakeshore. This is Hokiros."

And he spoke the name with awe.

Soth's gingery eyebrows pulled together; he had a thin and rather clerkish face, adorned with square-lensed spectacles, and had wound his waist-length graying hair up into a warrior's knot, mostly to keep it out of the way in case Hokiros turned out to be more formidable than the two lake monsters that had emerged over the past year from the deep waters of the Lake of the Moon. "The rites that your father repeated to me last night—they were those that defeated Hokiros before?"

"*Hai*, lord." The boy spoke with the thick dialect of the northern lakes. "In our village the rite was handed down from father to son for a thousand years. Every seven years a man's blood was shed upon the ward stone; every forty-nine years, we brought in a wizard to renew the spells, lest Hokiros wake from his sleep and destroy all the villages of the lakes. In every village along the shore this was done." His voice shook a little. Shonghu village had been destroyed the night before last; villagers, teyn, livestock torn to pieces. Soth and Pomegranate had viewed the ruin yesterday from a respectful distance, for the crocodiles that infested all the lakes had crept out from the water to devour the carrion. Even through his telescope, Soth hadn't been able to tell from the tracks whether Hokiros resembled the long-necked, sinuous dragons that had legendarily inhabited the Lake of the Moon. By the accounts of the survivors, it didn't sound likely.

As close to the village as she'd dared to get, Pomegranate had put herself into a trance, her hands pressed to the earth, trying to call forth images as she'd once done from objects her daughters used to bring her to tell stories about. But the only thing that had come to her had been a sense of darkness and size and moonlight glittering off its spiny back.

"The rites he told me of sound very like those that mages in the south used to ward against the water dragons in the Lake of the Moon," said Soth, who as a trained mage knew thousands of spells, though he was powerless now to work a single one. "Forgive me if I speak from ignorance, Tosu. Back in the days before there were kings, when humankind first dwelled along the shores of the lakes, there were water dragons—"

"This is not a water dragon," insisted the boy. "This is Hokiros."

The form of the name, Pomegranate sensed, was the old form used for the names of gods. . . .

And like a god, right on cue, Hokiros appeared at the speaking of his name.

Just outside the door of the hut—which was rather crowded with the three of them plus Soth's two cross-bows and his satchel of implements—Pomegranate's pet pig, Pontifer, whipped his head around, sprang to his feet with a squeal of terror. At the same instant Pomegranate heard the sloshing rush of the waters and felt the heavy vibration in the ground. From the lakeshore village of Hon, where Soth (and the apprehensive Hon villagers) had calculated that Hokiros would strike next, arose the wild bleating of goats and sheep, left behind in their pens when the villagers had fled inland. Darkness thickened in the light-drenched fog.

Darkness and the monster's hoarse, booming roar.

The earth shivered.

Soth's eyes were huge behind his spectacles. "Bugger all!"

Tosu was right. As the dark bulk condensed into a moving shape, Hokiros looked a great deal more like a god than a water dragon, but a god of what, Pomegranate couldn't imagine. He walked on two legs, like some impossibly huge, naked bird, and carried the immense tail high to counterbalance the serpentine arrowhead of his spiny skull. She guessed already that the old rites, and the dragon wards Soth had unearthed from the millennia-old grimoires in the palace library, probably weren't going to work.

He went straight for the livestock pens. The villagers had, reluctantly, obeyed Soth's order to draw lots and leave enough stock to interest the monster so that he and Pomegranate wouldn't have to hunt him up and down the

shores of the lake. Following Soth's instruction, Pomegranate—who up until last year had been a beggar in the
Yellow City's marketplaces—had circled the pens with
the ward spells that had worked against the water dragons
in the Lake of the Moon. Hokiros jerked back at the line
of them—the line that Pomegranate could see as a smoky
rim of light hanging in the air—and thrashed his long
neck in pain. Then he stepped through the ward signs like
a man thrusting through a thorned hedge and began to
kill, striking at the terrified beasts like a shrike killing
lizards, tossing each into the air, shaking it about with a
murderous whiplash of his long neck, their screams echoing through the unreal world of white vapor and stillness.

Pomegranate whispered, "Got any ideas?"

Hokiros swung his head around, as if he'd heard her
voice. Maybe he had. He'd stepped on the rails of the pen,
the sheep and goats scattering through the village fields
in terror. The black, dripping spines of his haunches
swayed at least twenty-five feet above his clawed hinder
toes—he'd have a stride of nearly forty feet, could catch
the fleeing animals easily.

But Pomegranate saw the red gleam of his eyes trained
on the straw of their observation hut.

She screamed, "Pontifer, run!" but the little white pig
had already vanished. *No fool, he,* she thought.

Soth caught up one of their crossbows and thrust the
other into Pomegranate's hands. "Have you ever shot one
of these things?"

"And at what point in a lifetime of selling fruit in the
streets would I have done that?"

"Load for me, then. Bolt in the notch, string over that
lever. Tosu—"

But as the ground shuddered with the creature's lengthening stride, Tosu ripped aside the thin wall of woven reeds that made up the back of the hut, pushed himself through.

"Tosu, don't be a fool!" yelled Soth, as the boy began to run along the dry ridge land above the waving tassels of the rice fields that surrounded Hon village. At the best of times this wasn't a good idea—even so far from the lakeshore the occasional crocodile crept in among the stalks—and the thought that a human would be able to outrun Hokiros would have been laughable were it not hideously tragic.

The monster came on with horrifying speed, running like the desert lizards. Wizard and Raven sister dashed out of the hut with a single accord, both firing crossbows into Hokiros's black, gleaming flank as he passed.

Then Pomegranate shoved her bow at Soth and tore open her satchel, to reweave the ward spells that Tosu had disrupted by dashing across them rather than passing through the thaumaturgic "gate" in the protective square.

The beast backed from the ward lines before crashing through, thought Pomegranate, struggling for calm. *That means they hurt him.* She concentrated marks of pain in the ward lines copied from those ancient spells used by the mages around the Lake of the Moon. She was barely conscious of Soth loading both bows, waiting. Her friend Raeshaldis had described the Sun Mages' exercises, to teach their novices to form their spells with the proper focus and deliberation even while being walloped by the instructors with thorned switches or screamed at or surrounded by bales of burning straw. Pomegranate had thought those tests excessive and barbaric, but had to admit they made a great deal of sense now. Ancient runes, sourced in the magic of the earth, in the strength of its metals and crystals, bringing fear and pain to Hokiros— here she wove his name into the spell, along with the nearly forgotten glyphs the ancient mages had used for the four-legged, fin-footed water dragons.

Focusing her mind on the earth, on the runes, on the magic that centered somewhere behind her breastbone, just as if that glittering tower of black strength weren't a hundred yards away . . .

She heard Tosu scream, the sound jerking, catching as Hokiros shook him; and for those few moments the earth was still. Her long mare's tails of gray hair hanging in her eyes, she was aware of using the time to strengthen the spell lines, thanking Koan God of Mages that they'd had the wits to ensorcel the crossbow bolts last night with spells of death and malice to water dragons.

Then the earth shook again.

Just go on with your spell-weaving, she thought. *Don't look.*

Pounding, trembling . . .

Glyph of pain, connected at its three points with hands of power formed of salt and ochre. Hook together the lines of the innermost circle with the power curves that continued down into the bones of the earth.

That booming roar that swallowed up the world.

She yelled, "Done!" and looked up as Soth leveled the crossbow and fired, the black, spiny triangular head striking down at him.

Hokiros threw up his head and bellowed as the bolt drove into the flesh just beneath one glaring eye, close— *dear gods, how close!*—above them. Soth leaped back between the two "hands"—scribbled signs marked on the earth in salt and pigeon blood—that bounded the gate of the protective square: Pomegranate trailed the line of salt between them, to close it. If, she thought, she wasn't too terrified to concentrate on the final words of the spell.

The monster reared back, opened his mouth, and spit. From the hillock yesterday Pomegranate had seen scorched and corroded splotches all over Shonghu village's huts, and she and Soth both knew to leap aside. The yellow slime smoked between them on the ground, and Soth fired the other crossbow at Hokiros's gaping mouth, though the head moved too fast and the bolt whizzed past. Pomegranate ducked into the hut, snatched at the pile of bolts that lay beside the wooden trapdoor in the floor. Before her husband's death twenty years ago she'd done all the poor housewife's tasks of grinding cornmeal and doing laundry, and had the arm muscles to prove it, but her hands were shaking so badly she fumbled twice trying to hook the string on the firing lever. Soth, moving faster than Pomegranate would have thought possible for a man of middle age and no conditioning, whipped into the hut; and the next instant the roof was gone, and in its place grinned that terrible black head, those red eyes that seemed to shine with such wicked, watching light.

Soth snatched the bow from her hands and fired, missed, shoved Pomegranate down into the little clay hole, and dropped through himself on top of her. He jerked the trapdoor into place and slammed the latch that held it, gasping for breath. The next second claws like chisels knifed through the wood, raining them with splinters. Pomegranate, balled into a corner of the tiny space, worked frantically at the levers and strings, reloading both bows, heard the trapdoor jerk overhead, then rend apart. The clawed hand, like the forepaw of an enormous lizard, jabbed down, and Soth struck at it with his sword, but the snap of the claw drawing back tore the weapon from his grip and, by the look of it, nearly broke his arm.

Pomegranate pulled her own shorter blade from her belt—though she'd had little more call to use a sword in her life than she'd had to use a crossbow—and when the black gleaming nose slammed down into the square hole above them, struck at it with all the strength of her arm, screaming the words of the ward spell at the top of her lungs. Hokiros withdrew his head and Soth caught up the bow, scrambled up through the trap. Pomegranate saw him kneeling above her as Hokiros struck down again.

The whap of the bow firing echoed in the little hole; she heard Hokiros scream. Soth dropped the bow and Pomegranate thrust the other, freshly loaded, into his hands, then heard it fire with a noise like the breaking of a tree trunk; the ground shook. Soth dropped back into the hole, and in the next second straw, bamboo, and other debris rained down on them as Hokiros smashed the hut with his tail.

Thud. Thud-thud. Not the pounding tremor of his terrible charge but aimless staggering, like that of a drunken man.

Soth fumbled, dropped the next bow Pomegranate handed him, then grabbed it back and scrambled up through the hole. Pomegranate followed in time to see Hokiros reeling away, forehands tearing at his eyes, blood dribbling and splattering. The huge tail struck at the houses of the village, shattering them like toys, crushing fences, splintering sheds. She glanced sidelong at the former Earth Wizard and saw him shaking all over, white as a ghost in the unreal fog light, his hand pressed to his side and his breathing like a leaky bellows.

Together they stood and watched as Hokiros stumbled away into the thinning white mists.

Dislimned into a blot of darkness in the slow-lifting fog.

The water splashed.

A final howl in the mists, hoarse and furious.

Then he was gone.

The fog was clearing. Overhead, the sky was blue and hot. Across the rice fields, the white shape of Pontifer Pig appeared, trotting toward them. He stopped to sniff at something on the path, probably, Pomegranate guessed, Tosu's body.

She estimated the entire attack hadn't lasted a quarter of an hour.

She turned back to Soth as he sat, very suddenly, against what remained of the hut wall. He looked green, like a man about to faint, his face clammy with sweat. For most of his fifty-eight years, she reflected as she unwound one of her many ragged scarves and soaked it from the water bottle, he'd done little but study spells. He'd occupied himself with perfecting his technique in the drawing of wards, in the healing of sick, the occasional spells for good fortune or to conceal tombs from robbers or to keep the teyn of some village or other in awe of their minders. Because of his wizardry, he'd probably never done any manual labor in his life.

Wizardry could be dangerous—seeking out djinni in the desert was never a safe practice—but it was dangerous by its own rules.

And of course for the past ten years, after his powers had vanished, Soth had remained in an alcoholic fog and hadn't done much of anything until the previous spring. Since that time he hadn't touched so much as a glass of wine, but Pomegranate knew that wasn't the kind of damage you got over in six months.

He looked like he would very much like a drink now.

Then he drew a shaky breath, took off his spectacles, and opened his eyes.

She handed him the soaked rag. "Did we win?"

Hon village lay in absolute ruin a hundred yards away: huts smashed, ground scorched with acid, livestock scattered or shredded, the date palms that brought in most of what little money came to the village flattened by Hokiros's monstrous tail. Whatever he was, there was no guarantee that either the poison or the spells of death on the crossbow bolts would work.

Soth dropped his head back against the shattered wall, slapped the wet rag over his face, and said firmly, "Yes. You and I, madam, have ranked ourselves as subjects of the balladeers for years to come." He flexed his right arm gingerly, as if to make sure the shoulder still worked. "And I think we'd better get in touch with the Lady Summerchild and let the king know what's going on here. This is the third unknown creature to—er—surface in a year, and it's by far the worst. I don't think His Majesty is going to be pleased."

SIX

Chirak Shaldeth was sitting behind his desk as Habnit led Shaldis between the tiny beds of jasmine, roses, lime, and avocado trees of the innermost court.

Her grandfather's study, and his chambers off the second-floor gallery nearby, formed a sanctum of silence from the noise of the camel-drivers' court at the front of the house and the smokes and stink of the kitchen yard that lay between. Though both his sons—Habnit and Shaldis's uncle, Tjagan—had chambers off the opposite gallery, Chirak had always forbidden either—or anyone else—to enter the garden when he was in his study. It was the only silence and privacy in the crowded house, and Chirak claimed it as his alone.

The folded lattice wall that would later in the day shut some of the morning cool into the study hadn't yet been put up, and she saw her grandfather as a pale shape looking out from the shadows of his private cave. When Habnit and Shaldis stopped in the entrance, the old man's square red face twisted.

"Veil yourself, girl. Any man would take you for a whore."

There was a time when Shaldis would have retorted that she'd been in such a hurry to come here to save his life that she'd left her veils behind—and would have cheerfully taken the beating for such impertinence—but she'd spent many months now observing her friend Summerchild's impeccable good manners and how the lovely concubine could simply sidestep insults without replying in kind. So now she took a deep breath, salaamed with the exact depth and simplicity that her brother Tulik did when coming into Chirak's presence, and said, "Father told me an attempt had been made on your life, sir."

Rage blazed up in those pale-brown eyes, but so clear were her unspoken words, *I can leave if you don't like the sight of my face,* that he said nothing.

This forbearance left Shaldis speechless with shock. She thought, *He's truly afraid.*

She'd never seen him forgo a burst of rage before, not against a member of his family, only against other businessmen and merchants, whose goodwill he needed.

"What happened?" A bandage wrapped his neck to hold a dressing to the left side of his jaw, and the left sleeve of his robe bunched over more bandages underneath. "You're hurt, sir."

Beard and eyebrows jerked forward. "Of course I'm hurt! It's no thanks to the cowardly imbeciles in this household that I wasn't killed!" All the smoking bile he would have hurled at her for not prostrating herself in the deepest of the twenty salaams proper to women—and a granddaughter of the house to its patriarch at that!—spewed into the glare he directed at his son. "So this is the brat that's grown so crafty, is it, Habnit? Just like any other female, telling me what I already know! She's a fool, and the daughter of one!"

"Have you had anyone look at your wounds, sir?" Shaldis felt sick at the way her father cringed from the words, marveled that her own voice sounded so cool and steady.

The old man rounded on her. "Fat lot of good it would do! There isn't a wizard in the town who could charm a wart off my backside anymore! And if you think I'll let some midwife smear it with rotted leaves and lizard dung you're out, girl! I've good-healing flesh. Ask any man in my company of the militia, when I was a boy."

"Father, you must—" began Habnit, and the old man snarled at him like a dog.

"If I did all you said I must, I'd be a poor man, and a dead one, too! As for this brainless whelp of yours—"

"What happened, sir?"

His hand flinched toward the rod that lay across his desk—the fourfold split bamboo with which he lashed the teyn and which he didn't scruple to use on his sons and grandchildren as well. But he drew it back. Shaldis had thin, straight white scars on her arms and legs from girlhood beatings. It was one of the things that had made her mother plead with Chirak: too many scars could easily sink a prospective marriage, marking a girl as defiant. Parents and matchmakers looked for them.

How did I ever live this way? Day out and day in?

Chirak's lip drew back from his teeth again. "I was attacked in my chamber, is what happened— Didn't you listen to what your father said? I woke hearing a noise— it was pitch-black, even the night-light had gone out, though there's no magic to that: that imbecile Flower never puts enough oil in the lamp."

Maybe that has something to do with your withholding food from all the maidservants—who were all named Flower, the custom in most wealthy houses—*for wasting oil.*

"I felt hands seize me and I pulled aside as a knife slashed into me. I shouted. I've had a couple of the camel drivers sleeping in the gallery outside my room, since those damned protective wards I paid a fortune for have quit working, and the wizard who laid them on the house seems to have skipped town."

He snatched up his bamboo rod and slapped angrily at the wood of his desk. "I pulled away and the slimegot bastard followed me, as if he could see in the dark. When your father and your uncle burst open the door there was no one in the chamber and the door and window shutters were bolted from inside. They ransacked the room and found no one. The drivers were still waking up in the gallery, both of them. Drunken louts and fools, but the door was bolted. It's a pretty pass the world's come to when you can't get a wizard who'll put a spell of ward on an honest man's house, but there's still plenty of them around who'll hire themselves out as assassins! Only a wizard could have got into the room or out of it without being seen."

"Do you keep gold or valuables in your chamber these days, sir? Or anything a robber would have been seeking?"

"Just like a woman, trying to find other explanations for what's staring her in the face! Have you ever known me to keep such a thing in my room, girl? What would I be doing that for, when I have a perfectly good strong room?" He lashed sideways toward the strong room with his rod, then flicked Habnit a stinging slice on the arm. "What god did I offend, to deserve you bringing a stupid female into my house to plague me with inanities? Someone tried to murder me, girl!" He slewed back furiously to Shaldis. His voice shrilled, "Not rob me, not rape me, not kiss me in the dark! How much clearer do I need to make it? Someone put a spell on the guards to send 'em to sleep; someone who could get out of a bolted chamber and rebolt the doors and windows behind him! D'you need it spelled out for you?"

"Yes, I do, sir," replied Shaldis evenly. "I'm sorry if the questions I ask seem trivial to you, but small details help me put together a picture of what happened and who I should be looking for."

"You should be looking for a wizard!" the old man screamed at her, and the rod whistled close to her face. "That's why your imbecile of a father wanted to bring you here! A wizard who hates me! Now can you or can't you find him?"

"Her," said Shaldis.

"WHAT?"

"Her, sir. Every wizard has lost the ability to work magic. If magic was used, then your attacker was a woman."

"That's the most ridiculous thing I've heard in my life! It's the kind of puling bathhouse rumor women pick up and believe rather than look at the facts! Because there's been a raft of charlatans in this city and not a decent teacher in that precious Citadel of yours—and well they deserved to be run out! Let them work for a living for a change!—you and every other fool in the marketplaces just up and decides that all men have lost their power! Stuff! I want to hear no more of it."

He jerked to his feet, not quite as tall as her father but wiry, with a leashed and dangerous power. He slapped the desk with his rod, and Shaldis fought not to jump.

"If that's the best you can do, girl, you can go back to your precious Citadel, and good riddance to you! I told you how it would be, boy," he added, his green-flecked glare raking his son. "Women haven't the brains to see what's under their noses! Now get her out of here before I get truly angry!"

SEVEN

I should probably have a look at his chamber before he comes out of his study," said Shaldis.

Interrupted in the midst of his nervous apologies, Habnit regarded his daughter with surprise. She returned the look with a calm perfected in eighteen months of continuous hazing by the male students of the Citadel. She felt now as she had during those ugly days: knees trembling, stomach hurting, jaw aching from gritting her teeth. In those days each of the masters had been secretly confronting his own loss of power—they had been of no help to a girl who obviously still had it.

In what she hoped was a rational voice she went on, "And I'll need to see every woman in the household."

Her father goggled, then stammered, "Of—of course," and led her through the gloomy passageway that connected the rear garden to the busy kitchen court. "Let's just go up to my room so I can get a—a tablet and stylus for you."

Shaldis had a tablet and stylus in the leather satchel slung around her shoulder, but she followed her father up the stairs anyway. She knew what he really wanted was the wine he always kept in his room.

She supposed, if one had to live in her grandfather's house, it helped to start drinking an hour after sunup. At least it clearly helped her father. She'd seldom in her girlhood seen him staggeringly drunk, but never entirely sober.

The pain of that girlhood awareness returned, but it was an old pain, like the shadow of a cloud she knew would pass.

They took the wooden stairs that ascended from the kitchen court to the upstairs gallery. This arcaded wooden walkway ran around all four sides of that busy heart of the household. From it, they cut back through the maids' dormitory to the gallery that similarly surrounded her grandfather's garden. It would have been more direct to climb the stairs from the garden itself—there were two flights of them, one on the north side leading directly to her grandfather's rooms and one on the south to the smaller chambers of her father and uncle—but in that case her grandfather would have seen them from his study.

Neither Shaldis nor her father felt any need to comment on this roundabout route. But after two years away from the household, Shaldis was interested to see how naturally she fell back into the unspoken set of local rules about not disturbing Grandfather. Fear of the old man seemed to breathe from every mud brick and painted pillar of the house, like tainted water that everyone drinks because there is no other.

At the top of the kitchen court stairs she halted and looked down into the big rectangle below. The pregnant jenny Five Cakes was now sweeping the soft, pitted bricks of its pavement: Shaldis had always found the slow, deliberate movements of the teyn, and their habitual silence, curiously comforting, though she'd heard they could move with terrible speed when roused. Shaldis's mother emerged from the kitchen, unveiled since this area of the house was harem but with her hair bundled under a striped scarf, followed by Fish-Hook, the biggest of their boar teyn, carrying a huge iron cauldron in his arms.

Of course they'd be dyeing cloth the day I come back to investigate in the household, thought Shaldis. The place would stink of boiling urine for weeks.

Her mother, always stout, had put on weight, she saw, under her billowing yellow dress, but her voice as she gave Fish-Hook his simple instructions was as lilting and sweet as ever. The girl who skipped behind her Shaldis took for a very young maid—her grandfather believed in buying children for slaves because they were cheaper—until she heard her mother call the girl Foursie.

Foursie! Fourth Daughter—her younger sister's real name—had been a little girl when she'd left.

And she'd be twelve now. And that fairylike child running out of the kitchen with a gourd of water for the three teyn and two old women slaves grinding corn under the other side of the kitchen gallery: That child had to be Fifth Daughter, Twinkle, whom everyone in the household called Our Little Twinkle Star.

"Daughter?"

Shaldis looked back at her father, waiting in the doorway of the shadowed dormitory of the maids.

"I'm sorry." She followed him through the dim room, long and narrow with the girls' wicker chests crowded against the single wall that didn't have a divan, the bedding stowed out of sight in its few wall cupboards for the day. "Was that Twinkle I saw downstairs? She's going to be beautiful!"

"She is, isn't she?" Habnit smiled with a gentleness that told Shaldis that while she'd been watching her mother in the court her father had nipped on through and gotten his cup of wine from his own room, then come back. A second glance showed her that, yes, he had the half-finished cup in his hand, and there was no more talk of getting a tablet and stylus from his room. "Maybe too beautiful—Strath Gamert tells me his son doesn't want to marry Foursie, and wants Twinkle instead. . . ."

Shaldis was shocked. "Twinkle's only . . ." She counted on her fingers. "Twinkle's only eight! You mean Forpen Gamert? Who was supposed to marry *me*?"

Her father stopped in the doorway that led to the gallery above the garden, his face filled with infinite weariness and infinite shame. "We need Strath Gamert's partnership," he explained—as he'd explained, with that same expression, two years ago when it was Shaldis who had been signed over as bride to the harness maker's foul-tempered son. "Threesie and Twosie were already spoken for—Lily Concubine and Green Parakeet Woman, I should call them." He gave the two sisters their names in the old style, the names their husbands (or more probably their husbands' fathers) had picked for them, with the proper suffixes—*Woman* and *Concubine*—that were now falling into general disuse.

"Forpen Gamert doesn't like Foursie, and because the original contract was breached . . ." There was a trace of accusation in his eyes as he regarded the daughter who'd fled the house and her marriage contract and caused him all this inconvenience. ". . . Strath says he should be able to choose. We're still negotiating."

Which meant Grandfather was still negotiating. *And if you say a single word in reply to any of this*, Shaldis told herself, following her father out onto the next gallery, *you'll be dragged back into the affairs of this family, for another sixteen years of rage and helplessness, to absolutely no purpose.*

But she still felt sick anger at her father and grandfather for little Twinkle's sake.

One more thing, she thought, *to see if I can maneuver.*

As she passed through the arched doorway of the maids' dormitory she reached out and brushed the wood with her hand, and felt it.

The tiniest whisper of magic, as if the fibers of the wood had been slightly warmed.

"But if you say only women can work magic," fretted her father as they turned along the latticed gallery that led to her grandfather's rooms, "surely you can't mean it's a woman in this household?"

"It's either a woman of the household or a woman who's not in the household," said Shaldis. "If it's a woman who's not in the household, it has to be a woman whom Grandfather has hurt, insulted, or endangered; a woman whose family—if she has one—Grandfather has hurt, insulted, or endangered; or a woman who is in the pay of, or being blackmailed by, someone Grandfather has hurt, insulted, or endangered . . . which is a fairly long list of candidates."

"But you're sure it's a woman?" Habnit gestured with his wine cup. By the smell it was *sherab*—distilled wine, nearly as strong as opium. Two years ago, thought Shaldis sadly, he hadn't started in on the *sherab* until after dinner. "Father says—"

"Grandfather doesn't know what he's talking about." Shaldis halted on the gallery outside her grandfather's bed-chamber door. "Men do not have magic. The same way, ten years ago and for all of time before that, women did not have magic. They just *didn't*. And now men just *don't*." *Healing no longer flows from their hands,* a voice had cried in her dream. "The problem is that everything—laws, family, who we're taught to obey and respect—hasn't changed."

"I should hope not!" exclaimed Habnit, truly dis-tressed at the idea. "But a woman in this household."

"I admit that any woman in her right mind who's con-scious enough of her own magic to slip door bolts and elude the camel drivers would use her power to escape the house rather than stick around and try to murder Grandfather." Shaldis passed her hands over the door's wrought-iron handle, over the wood just above it, where the latch inside was.

Magic there, strong and sweet now, like a little song. It didn't feel like the spells of the Raven sisters Shaldis knew best, the ones to whose power and souls she had united her own with the Sigil of Sisterhood: Summer-child, Moth, Pebble, and Pomegranate.

Nor did it feel like the magic of Foxfire, Lord Mohrvine's fourteen-year-old daughter, though Shaldis wasn't as sure of that. When the Sisters of the Raven had united their power with the rite of the sigil, Mohrvine had forbidden his daughter to join them, lest they be aware of it should she work some great spell clandestinely. Mohrvine's mother, the formidable nomad princess Red Silk, had likewise held aloof from the rite of the sigil, as had the seventh Crafty woman of Shaldis's acquaintance, a greedy busybody named Cattail who'd formerly been a laundress.

Magic, Shaldis had long ago learned, did not automatically convey either benevolence or wisdom, any more than blue eyes or a sweet voice did. It simply *was*.

With the magic of these last two, Shaldis had had little acquaintance, but the taste—the vibration—of power she sensed in the wood of the door didn't feel familiar. What Cattail's spells—or Foxfire's or Red Silk's—would feel like if they were sourcing their power differently she wasn't sure. From the earth, for instance, or fire, rather than from the sun. Nor could she tell what difference it might make if they worked magic while drunk or drugged or under any number of other conditions. She simply didn't know.

She followed her father into the room.

Chirak Shaldeth had all four upper chambers along that side of the court, connected by inner doors as well as doors onto the gallery to form a single suite. In the crowded conditions of a city house it was a shocking amount of space, like his claim to the whole of the inner garden. Her brief mental query about why he'd had the camel drivers sleep out in the gallery rather than in one of the rooms of the suite evaporated the moment it formed. Her grandfather despised the men who worked for him as he despised his family, and kept them away with the same mixture of random physical abuse and arbitrary rules.

Of course he'd keep three rooms empty because they adjoined his own. That was how—and who—he was.

He didn't even use them as Shaldis would have, for a library or a laboratory or to fill with pretty or curious things. She raised the latch on the inner door that led from the bedchamber into the next room along, and saw that second chamber was simply empty: cupboard doors shut, floor swept of the city's eternal dust, divan cushions clean and untouched.

The latch was on the bedroom side. The assassin wouldn't have needed magic to dart through and escape the camel drivers, but she would have needed a mage's ability to see in the dark.

Magic had definitely been used in the bedchamber.

It wasn't as localized as the whisper in the wood of the door where the latch had been raised from the other side, but Shaldis felt it everywhere. It clung like perfume to the cedar pillars of the bed, whispered from the folds of the mosquito netting that more and more people were buying now that magic wards against those pests no longer kept them from the windows: every house in the city was beginning to smell of the various smudges people were experimenting with, to drive them away.

None of the Raven sisters had yet been able to place a mosquito ward that worked for more than a few hours.

Yet in her dream the voice had whispered, *We command the fire and the serpents and the stinging insects.*

WE who?

The woman whose power breathed like the faintest of distant sounds in the air of the dim bedchamber?

Like the sound of . . . what? That rhythmic roar.

Shaldis touched the carved doors of the wall cupboards, the chest beside the bed. All of them locked tight, as were the latches on the window shutters: tight as her grandfather's heart. The magic here felt strange, very unlike the spells of opening that lingered on the door. . . . He had spoken of a knife cutting at him out of the dark—had they kept any slashed bedclothes?—but she wondered if the alien power she sensed like the whiff of smoke around the bed was some kind of death spell.

It was very strange, whatever it was. Something she'd never encountered before.

It seemed to her for a moment that instead of the booming crash, she heard the faintest tickle of evil music—

Raeshaldis.

She felt the calling, clear in her mind. The overwhelming urge to look into her crystal or a mirror or a pool of water, anything that would summon an image. "Excuse me, Father," she said, and retreated to the door. Before leaving her cell she'd slipped the white crystal from the Citadel scrying chamber into her satchel, and this was what she angled, so that its central facet caught the light.

And within that facet, like a trick of the light, she saw Summerchild's face.

"Summer, I'm sorry," said Shaldis quickly. "Did

everything go all right at the council? Something came up, something that I need to talk to you about—"

"And we need, very badly, to talk to you."

EIGHT

W hat *was* that?" Pomegranate finished lashing the makeshift sunscreen of palm branches and reed mats into place on the ruins of the hut, and Soth—who'd fetched them from the ruined village while the old woman kept watch on the lake—lowered his telescope from his eye.

"Hokiros," he replied. "Who a month and a half ago was as much a legend as the water dragons in the Lake of the Moon."

While in the village, in spite of an arm that slowly stiffened from its injury, he'd also refilled their water bottles from the well and located a couple of gourd cups and a quantity of almonds and dates. These he proceeded to organize into a makeshift lunch—during her days as a beggar Pomegranate had learned never to pass up food, and the weaving of the ward spells had left her ravenous for sweets. She put several dates on a plane-tree leaf and set it on the hut's clay floor for Pontifer. "He's had a frightening morning," she explained, and patted her rotund pet's head.

Soth replied in a tone of grave politeness. "So have we all."

The fog was entirely gone. Sunlight glared hot on the surface of the lake, burned Pomegranate's face through the light coating of ointment that everyone wore. With luck, the villagers would be back before too much longer.

"At least the wards worked," she added, looking out past the shredded hut walls at the trailing glyphs of pain, of water, of power, scratched in the earth all around them. In addition to putting up a sunshade for themselves, the two unwilling monster fighters had dragged enough straw mats and bricks from the village to cover Tosu's body, which they'd brought back—in several pieces—from the rice field. Pomegranate had drawn wards around it against foxes and dogs, and hoped they'd work on this occasion. "So at some time in the past, somebody didn't think the lake monsters were legends."

"That was our salvation." Soth glanced up from knotting another of Pomegranate's many scarves into a makeshift sling. "Our only salvation, since those spells were so old they'd fallen out of circulation, even out of memory of the lines of any wizard I've ever spoken with."

He moved slowly, as if the battle had taken from him all the energy he had. "I assume that fifteen centuries ago lake monsters were a reality in the Lake of the Moon, and wizards of some kind put heavy wards against them all along the lakeshore. I'd almost say they were too effective, for the water dragons remained deep in the center of the lake, where the water is bottomless, with the result that everyone forgot their existence. They must have done the same with the creature or creatures up here, renewing them by rote and passing the spells along as a religious rite from father to son."

"Until magic changed," said Pomegranate softly.

Pontifer came quietly up beside her and lay down, his chin resting on her sandaled foot. She remembered Hokiros's red glare, the wicked, watching *intentness* of his eyes.

"Until magic changed, and the lake began to dry." Soth folded his long, narrow hands into a double fist, rested them, and his chin, on his drawn-up knees as he gazed out over that glittering blue-and-golden pavement of the open water, beyond the murky pools of the drying lakeshore.

Pomegranate said nothing for a time. She guessed that the former Earth Wizard was reliving all the stages of their journey up from the Yellow City in quest of any information—even the slightest rumors—about other women in whom the powers of magic had begun to bloom.

All along the shores of the Lake of the Sun they had asked, in villages and towns where the mages—if they'd had them—had departed or taken on other work. Most people hadn't even heard that women could do magic now. Many, even in the face of Pomegranate's repeated demonstrations of fire lighting, scrying, and ward spells, had simply refused to believe. Again and again, Soth had been approached under the assumption that he was working through his companion—and that she or her services could be bought from him.

And all along the shores of the Lake of the Sun, the other story had been the same as well: the long flats of drying mud, the acres of shallow reedy pools thick with crocodiles and mosquitoes, that lay between what had once been waterside villages and the current shoreline. Everywhere, makeshift canals stretched across this no-man's-land to bring water to the old fields, the long lines of bucket hoists worked by teyn—the growing effort to keep the teyn enslaved in the face of the failure of the spells that had kept them cowed. Everywhere, maddening infestations of mice, of mosquitoes, of locusts that the mages had once kept at bay.

The Sun Canal, between the Lake of the Sun and the Great Lake that stretched at the foot of the Mountains of the Eanit, had been nearly impassable, even by barges of the shallowest draft. Teyn work crews labored to deepen it, and foremen labored even harder to keep the crews from vanishing in the night and grumbled about the king. The New Canal, which stretched from the Great Lake north to the City of Reeds, was as bad or worse, and that stilt-legged city that had once stood in the midst of the lake's sparkling waters now balanced mostly above dry land or reeking mud. Nars, a former Pyromancer who'd met them there, told them that the canal which had once connected the Lake of Reeds with the Lake of Gazelles further north was now no more than a ditch choked with brush and young acacia trees.

Nowhere, Nars had said, had he heard of any woman coming to power, and he had journeyed far among the more northerly lakes beyond Gazelles.

It was while they were in the City of Reeds that villagers from Shonghu and Hòn had come to them with tales of another peril still.

Pontifer raised his head sharply. Following his wise black gaze, Pomegranate saw the little band of village men making their way along the paths of the rice fields, their simple tunics of stripes and checks like strange colorless flowers among the green. They approached gingerly, poised at each step to spin and race back inland if the waters of the lake so much as rippled.

Having encountered Hokiros, she could not find it in her heart to blame them.

Soth got to his feet, put his spectacles back on—he didn't, Pomegranate noticed, put down his crossbow. The village councilmen seemed to be determined to speak to him rather than to her, possibly because he was a man—though she admitted that with her ragged, brightly colored cast-off garments and the jangling collection of beads, amulets, sashes, and mirrors that hung about her person, they probably came to mistaken conclusions about her. She was used to this. All her life she'd preferred invisibility anyway.

"My lord Silverlord," she heard the headman say, and all the villagers bowed down to the tall, bespectacled mage. "You have gained forever the reverent gratitude of Hon village and all its children, down to the tenth generation. Was Hokiros in fact dying, as he returned to the lake? Will he come again?"

"That I cannot tell," replied Soth. "He was wounded, certainly, and perhaps unto death. But at a guess he wasn't the only one of his kind. You say he has not come forth for nearly fifteen hundred years, and I think it more likely that the thing that destroyed your village today was one of a small group of such things."

The men stared at one another, grasped one another's arms and clothing in terror.

"Until such time as we can deal with the others, if they indeed exist, you'll need to be prepared to sacrifice livestock to Hokiros, to draw him away from the village. Pomegranate will put wards around the village, but you must pen sheep and goats nearby, so that if he comes out he will have something else to eat besides the village."

"But it is so that we would not lose our sheep and goats that we called you!" exclaimed the headman peevishly.

Pomegranate stooped and whispered to Pontifer, "So much for the tenth generation."

"How can you say—"

Pomegranate.

The thought sliced into her mind, clear as crystal.

Look in the mirror.

Summerchild, she guessed, and fumbled one of the several mirrors that hung on ribbons around her neck. She caught the light on the gleaming surface, and a moment later saw her friend's face as if reflected over her shoulder. "Dearie," she sighed, "I was going to scry for you the moment things felt safe around here. I hate to make life harder for the poor king, but—"

"After what happened in council this morning," said Summerchild carefully, "I'm not sure you could do that. I think we need both of you back here, as fast as it's possible for you to come."

NINE

The wooden gate into the small adobe-walled pen opened; a man in the rough tunic and coarse cotton pantaloons of a teyn minder shoved an oldish boar teyn through and into the enclosure. The boar stood still, swinging his massive, heavy shoulders as he rocked gently from foot to foot, long arms dangling, heavy head—like a flat blackish-silver rock shorn of its fur—moving a little as his wide nostrils snuffed the air. The minder followed him in and thrust the door shut behind him with his stick. The boar was probably twenty years old, to judge by his whitening fur and wrinkled features: he'd be dead in another five years. Jennies lived perhaps twice that long.

The boar was naked, and his fur had been clipped close. He was sleek and reasonably well fed. There was always a great deal of discussion among the landchiefs about how much to feed teyn, but Lord Mohrvine inclined toward the better-care, less-replacement school of thought.

Watching the teyn over her grandmother's shoulder in the gleaming surface of her grandmother's mirror, Mohrvine's daughter Foxfire felt a surge of gratitude that this was so. Six months ago, at fourteen and a half, she had begun to realize that her father was not the godlike and charming hero she had always believed him, unquestioningly, to be. She didn't know if that understanding had to do with the budding of her abilities in magic, or whether that was just something that happened when girls' fathers tried to marry them off to dreadful old men like Lord Akarian.

But she still loved her father dearly. Now that Lord Akarian was definitely out of the picture, she was glad that her father was a man she could respect: a man who made sure his horses, his dogs, his teyn, and his slaves were well fed and well treated.

Her love for her father—and the respect he'd taught

her for those within her power—made what she was witnessing in her grandmother's mirror all the more difficult to know what to do with. She felt as if she held some alien object in her hand that had to be put away, and she could not find the box or cupboard into which it went. She couldn't even exactly name what it was in her hand . . . anger? pity? shame?

The teyn minder took his charge by the arm, and—though teyn were far stronger than men—shoved him, hard, against the closed door of the pen.

Foxfire saw the teyn strike the rough wooden planks hard enough to rebound into the pen. But the teyn collapsed to its knees, doubled over in pain. It grabbed and clutched at itself, clawing its arm and side where they'd come in contact with the wood. She saw its mouth stretch wide, tusks gleaming in a silent agonized howl. It crawled away from the door, body visibly shuddering, and Foxfire's grandmother shifted her seat on the leather camp cushion before her low dressing table, and said a word respectable ladies weren't supposed to know.

"Looks like the pain is just as bad as the last experiment," she said in her cracked, deep voice, and reached for the tiny glass-and-silver cup of coffee at her side. The Red Silk Concubine, as she had been called at that time, had been the youngest, loveliest, and most formidable woman in the harem of fat old Oryn I; at seventy-five her bones were beautiful still. Even before she'd begun to develop the ability to see distant places in her mirror or to make marks of ill or inattentiveness on walls or bedding, she'd been widely feared in the household of Mohrvine, her son. Foxfire had grown up in terror of her from her earliest recollection.

Now that Red Silk had taken over elements of her education, Foxfire knew her better, loved her profoundly, and feared her more, and differently. Her grandmother, she knew with a sensation of wondering awe, would not hesitate a moment to destroy her—or her father and brothers or the house or anything in the Yellow City—to protect herself from being interfered with. Foxfire trusted the old lady's wisdom and wiliness implicitly. But she did not trust *her*.

"Has Summerchild said anything to you about spells of pain?"

In the mirror's gleaming circle, the teyn minder edged tentatively toward the shut door of the pen, reached with the hooked handle of his stick for the slight notch in the planks that was all the purchase available on the doors of the compounds where the shambling unhuman laborers were kept. At night, or at such rare times during the day when the teyn were returned to their compounds, the gates were bolted from the outside. The man flinched and dropped the stick when it came in contact with the door, stumbled back, clutching his hand.

The teyn, who'd sat up in the center of the pen, hugging itself and rocking in pain, remained impassive, but something in the way it settled its shoulders made Foxfire think it smiled inwardly.

Red Silk swore again.

The minder, a silent tiny image in the mirror, had to yell for his partner outside to open the door.

"I know Summerchild works with pain spells," Foxfire answered her grandmother after a time. "She's taught us the ones that work most often for her, to use in self-defense; to throw pain at another person. She doesn't like them."

"Or says she doesn't," muttered the old lady. "This coffee's cold. Don't you go for fresh, girl—this isn't a Blossom House and I'm not a man. Ring for one of those lazy sluts. She's never spoken of ways to modulate pain, to exercise it in varying degrees? Humph. And she calls herself a Pearl Woman. A Pearl Woman must be perfect in *every* art." Under white brows her turquoise eyes glinted, a shade paler than Foxfire's but clear and deadly as the summer sky in deep desert, when neither water nor help is at hand. "That includes the arts of pain. I suppose that stupid cow Chrysanthemum didn't think to teach you anything about those in that precious Blossom House where your father spent such a fortune having you trained?"

"No, Grandmother." Foxfire shivered at the thought, but kept her voice even, as she had been trained to do.

"And it isn't pain that we need, in any case." Red Silk passed one wrinkled white hand across the face of the mirror, releasing the elements of the glass and the silver from the domination of her mind. Ruby rings half hid old scars on her fingers. "It's fear. We'll look again in an hour and see if the pain lingers any longer in the wall or the gate than it did in the other pens where we've tried it. What sigils went into the makeup of that spell, child?"

Foxfire turned back to the little scribe desk in the corner of the chamber and the box where she kept the note tablets about her grandmother's experiments in using magic to master the teyn. Like most women of the deep-desert tribes, Red Silk had never learned to write, not even in the simple alphabet of city women called Scribble, much less the thousands of glyphs that made up High Script. The morning's heat was growing strong. Even in this tiled pavilion in the gardens of her father's summer villa of Golden Sky, the sun's implacable wrath made itself felt. Foxfire guessed the open pens she'd been looking at all morning in the mirror would be insufferable even for teyn before long.

"Damn that brat Soral Brûl for an inattentive lout," her grandmother went on. "I know there are sigils he never bothered to learn while he was with the Sun Mages." She named the young former novice, hired a few months ago by Mohrvine and currently occupying—under discreet guard—a comfortable chamber in a secluded corner of the lakeside palace. "Has that girl Shaldis mentioned others that we don't know about? I know she keeps her mouth shut, but she's got access to the Citadel library—"

The old woman broke off and sat up sharply, as if she'd heard a sound, then leaned to her mirror again. "Your father," she said, brushing its surface with the backs of her jeweled fingers. Foxfire glimpsed in it a cloud of dust along the road to the Yellow City, the flat roofs and crenellated walls rising in the distance. "And in a hurry at that. Something's happened. Stay where you are, girl," she added as Foxfire made an impulsive move toward the door. "Riding that way, he'll come to us before he even knocks the dust off his boots. A man thinks more of a woman—or of another man, for that matter—who doesn't run to meet him at the gate like a love-struck schoolgirl; the sluts at that precious Blossom House they trained you in must surely have taught you *that*."

Foxfire whispered, "Yes, Grandmother."

The cold turquoise eyes held her, as if runes of power were written in the pupils' tiny pleatings of blue and emerald, so that she could not look away. "But they didn't teach you why you must make others value you," said Red Silk softly. "They didn't teach what happens to women in this world who are not valued. Only life teaches that."

Foxfire thought of her friend Opal, whose delicate beauty had been horribly marred by an accidental fire in the Blossom House. The sixth daughter of a poor laborer in the city, she would have been sold for what she'd bring, to grind wheat or haul water, once she was no longer lovely. In a toneless voice Foxfire said, "Yes, Grandmother." And then, a thought coming to her, "Can you look into the Yellow City and see if there's signs of trouble there? Papa will value us still more, if we can say, 'Ah, yes, the riots . . .' or whatever the trouble is."

A slow grin widened Red Silk's withered lips. "You're learning, girl." She leaned back to the mirror.

To use the mirror took concentration, and when Foxfire felt the strange little stab of sensation in her right elbow that told her someone had crossed the Sigil of Ward at the gate of the tiled pavilion's courtyard, Red Silk did not look up. Foxfire didn't know whether her grandmother was aware of the ward sign's activation or not. Since the mirror had shown Lord Mohrvine's cavalcade still some distance from Golden Sky—just passing the villa's date palmeries on the road to the Yellow City— Foxfire guessed this intruder was Opal, with the coffee she had sent for. Mindful of her grandmother's instruction she reclined a little on the divan and turned her face toward the door with an attitude of hauteur, just in case it wasn't.

But it was Opal, and as soon as the maidservant came into sight in the open doorway Foxfire scrambled to her feet and went to help her with the coffee tray. "Don't!" Opal turned her shoulder to prevent Foxfire from taking the heavy cloisonné vessels from her hands. Her velvety brown eyes danced in the ghastly landscape of scars. "Your grandmother says I'm to serve you whether you want me to or not."

"Yes, but we're not serving *me,* we're serving Grandmother."

Opal set the tray with its tall-spouted pot on the low table; Foxfire held the small clean cup in both hands, kneeling, while Opal poured the smoking coal-black brew. Then both carried the cup, with its tiny attendant tray of sugar lumps, cinnamon sticks, and rose water, to the dressing table where Red Silk sat before her mirror, a withered, white-haired, brown-skinned woman in silk striped green and gold.

Red Silk did not turn her head. Over her shoulder, Foxfire could see, by concentrating, what her grandmother saw: the Golden Court, the great semipublic outer court of the House of the Marvelous Tower. In the heat of the summer forenoon it was usually somnolent, even the vendors of oranges and tea retreating into the shade of the colonnades that ringed it. Now it more resembled the markets of the Circus District, men crowding around the porter's lodge at the gate or into the surrounding workshops of the royal weavers or goldsmiths, gesturing in frenzied dumb show, demanding . . . what? Two of the palace guards emerged from the porter's lodge and were swarmed, like drops of honey dripped into an anthill.

"And we can't get a closer look into the palace itself, curse it," Red Silk muttered. Opal shot Foxfire a glance of worried inquiry—she herself was unable to see a thing but the reflections of the two women's faces in the glass, young and old. Within the mirror Foxfire saw the scene change to the Square of Ean, the still-larger open space between the palace and the city's greatest temple, and the activity was much the same: men running, catching one another, wild with excitement.

No bloodshed. No soldiers. No smoke.

The ward sign jabbed at her elbow again, and this time Red Silk turned from her mirror, straightened her narrow shoulders, and gestured to Foxfire to seat herself on the divan. Without being told, Opal returned to the coffee, poured out another cup for Foxfire, and handed it to her, kneeling, with the respect that less than a year ago would only have been accorded a man. Her beauty may have been destroyed, but the short, curvaceous girl still retained the gracious manners and perfect skills of the most carefully trained Blossom Lady.

Opal was still kneeling when the crunch of boots on the gravel courtyard path announced Mohrvine's approach; and the next second his graceful form blotted the doorway. She sank at once into the deepest of salaams.

"You shouldn't race your horses in heat like this," Red Silk greeted him calmly, and sipped her coffee. "It isn't as if the city's under attack."

Mohrvine did an infinitesimal double take on the threshold, instantly concealed. Six months ago he had learned that both his mother and his daughter held the power of magic in their hands; he was not quite used to it yet. Foxfire rose and performed a very appropriate salaam called Lilies in the Rain—suitable for a daughter to execute for a noble father—with a languor that would have done her preceptors proud.

"Fetch my papa coffee, would you, darling?" she requested of Opal as she sank back onto the divan. "Would you care for pastries, Papa? The moonjellies are particularly delicious today."

"My heart splits open with joy at that news." Mohrvine unslung the silk-fine white wool cloak from his shoulders, hung it on a carved peg beside the door. "Don't trouble yourself with it, child," he added, when Opal would have collected it as she departed with the coffee tray. Then he glanced back at his mother and his daughter, raised one sardonic black brow. "You know, then?"

"That skinny little witch of the king's keeps the palace itself under a cloak of shadow." Red Silk folded her hands. "But I know it would take more than moonjellies to bring you back here at full gallop. What has our nephew done?"

"It's not what he's done." Mohrvine settled himself on the divan next to Foxfire, facing his mother on her cushion of silk. "It's what he'll be required to do at the dark of the moon. That imbecile Akarian's called for a jubilee."

It was, Foxfire observed, her grandmother's turn to be taken aback. The turquoise eyes widened in shock, then narrowed again as the implications sank in. "And Oryn didn't have his head struck off on the spot? That's enough to make me wonder if the man's Greatsword's son or a by-blow."

Amused, Mohrvine shook his head. "Believe me, madam, I've checked. Repeatedly. And he doubtless would have had *my* head struck off, had I suggested such a thing. But that old fool was perfectly sincere—he always is—and everyone in the council could tell it. Word of it was being shouted in the Golden Court before Oryn could get his breath. The High Priest of Ean was sending formal notice to the Keepers of the Sealed Temples as I was riding out of the city. At the dark of the moon, Oryn will face the ordeals of consecration once again."

"Without old Hathmar's magic to pull him through." Red Silk's long, skinny fingers traced the gold rim of her cup. Her pale gaze fixed upon space, as if some invisible mirror hung in the air before her, showing her what no others could see.

Foxfire tried to recall what she'd heard of the ordeals that kings had to pass through upon taking the throne. One of the six Sealed Temples stood near the House of Six Willows in the Flowermarket District, where she'd been trained in all the arts of pleasing men. She'd passed by it any number of times as she ran errands for the ladies whose exquisite entertainments—and other activities— had largely supported the house. Once she'd asked Gecko, the house's old factotum, what that low and windowless black stone fane was, and why no worshipers were ever seen passing through its bronze doors. What god was revered there?

It is the house of Shibathnes the Serpent King, Gecko had replied, and had pulled her dark veils more closely around her face. With the other hand she'd drawn Foxfire to the far side of the small and rather shabby square.

Foxfire had never heard the name before, which surprised her. In the Blossom House, and in her father's house before that, she'd heard tales of the dozens of minor deities, village spirits, and nomad divinities worshiped in addition to the great gods like Ean and Oan Echis and Darutha.

He is one of the old gods who watches over the king, Gecko had said, and would say no more. Foxfire had later traced its low black wall behind the district's taverns and eating houses and had been surprised at the size of the place, but she'd only twice seen a single priest, coming and going from there to the market with food. No one, as far as Foxfire had ever heard, worshiped the Veiled Gods. No cult attached to them, no temples to them existed outside the city. Opal, whose family was from old peasant stock, said simply, *My granny told me never to speak their names,* and Gecko had changed the subject and pretended ignorance when Foxfire'd asked.

Now Red Silk said, "Some of the ordeals are easily fixed—at least your father didn't seem to lose much sleep over them." She shrugged. As a nomad, she'd never performed more than lip service to the gods of farmers. "Nor did your brother, when it was his turn to go through that little comedy. And believe me, a comedy is all it is, to convince the people that Ean and his holy sons have taken the trouble to personally approve one man over another to tell them all what to do. As if they were not all men alike."

"It may be a comedy to you, Mother," replied Mohrvine grimly, "but to those of us who're going to have to go through it, the jest loses a little of its savor. I don't believe any more than you do that BoSaa of the Cows and Rohar of the Flowers and all the rest of that gaggle, whose priests have convinced the general populace to give them food and lodging gratis, will step down to shoo the crocodiles away from me when I go wading in the lagoon in the Temple of the Twins. All I'm saying is that somebody had better."

They expect King Oryn to fail, Foxfire thought, not even shocked at her father's sacrilege—which she'd always sensed, though this was the first he'd spoken it outright before her. *And they expect his brother, Barún, to take the tests, and to fail them, too.*

They expect them both to die.

Grief twisted at her, for she was fond of her cousin the king. Her father was always telling her of the man's foolishness, credulity, and willingness to put the whole realm to unnecessary labor over a situation that was at best temporary, but she liked that tall fat gentle man with the beautiful voice. She knew, too, that Summerchild loved him above her life. Anger tinged her grief, the same anger she'd felt at the tormented teyn, that her father seemed to have already disregarded Oryn's death.

And flooding in after the anger, cold panic, as logic opened the next door, and the next in her mind.

"I know of no spells that will control either crocodiles or serpents," Red Silk said, and tasted her coffee. She made a face, and set the cup aside. "That imbecile Soral Brûl has given me half a dozen to try, and all I've gotten out of it is half a dozen dead teyn. The ones to counteract poisons generally are no better, those that I've tried."

"Then I suggest, Mother, and you, Daughter"—Mohrvine pressed his palms together, his voice steady as his eyes moved from Red Silk's impassive face to Foxfire's frightened one—"that you arrive at some, and soon. Because if Oryn dies, and Barún, I'm going to need those spells very badly."

TEN

"I have to go." Shaldis closed her hand around the white scrying crystal, looked up into her father's worried face.

The worry changed to alarm. "But you can't!" Something told her that his concern was less his father's actual danger than his own fear of what the old man would say—no matter what he'd screamed at her in his study—about Shaldis's walking out of the house with the puzzle unsolved.

Or maybe both. Shaldis had long ago given up trying to sort out what were genuine emotions in this household and what were simply the smoke and mirrors of denial, resentment, and fear.

"I'll be back," she promised. "He is my grandfather."

And that, too, she thought dourly, was a lie masquerading behind truth.

That frightful old beast downstairs was her grandfather, the patriarch of her family, and Shaldis was aware, within herself, of the unthinking reflex: you never abandoned your family. You never said no to them, never cast them off.

But she was aware, too, that her motive in returning to them wasn't that simple.

With the dissolution of the Sun Mages, who for six hundred years had brought the rains to the Realm of the Seven Lakes, there remained eight women—only eight, none of whom completely understood how to make her own magic work—to summon the rains at the end of the coming winter.

The woman who had tried to kill her grandfather would make nine.

If they were lucky.

She passed her hand again over the wood of the outer door in whose opening she still stood, half in shadow, half in light. While she couldn't imagine any reason Mohrvine's mother, Red Silk, would try to murder her grandfather, it wasn't beyond the realm of possibility. According to Summerchild, Mohrvine had connections with most of the wealthy merchants of the city and with a number of the crooked water bosses whose thugs ruled the slums outside the city walls. And Cattail would work for anyone's pay without asking who might be hurt in the long run.

It could be either of them.

Or not. The voice returned to her mind, the voice in her dream.

Help us. Our children are dying. We the Craft women . . .

WE the Craft women.

More than one.

Whoever they were and wherever. And whatever it would take to secure their alliance, to beg their help.

Shaldis took a deep breath. Summerchild had said she

was sending someone with a horse, to bring her to the palace as swiftly as possible.

That didn't sound good.

Behind her friend's face, Raeshaldis had glimpsed the carved openwork walls, the polished wooden pillars of the Cedar Pavilion, where the king held his councils. Another bad sign. Whatever had happened at the council, Summerchild hadn't even waited to return to her own pavilion to call for help.

"When I come back," she said, turning to face her father, "I'm still going to want to talk to every woman in the household. Has there been anyone new since I've been gone?"

"Eight Flower," he said a little numbly. He still looked as if he couldn't quite put together this tall, self-possessed young woman with the spindly, gawky girl who had walked out of the kitchen court that day two years ago.

"And your brother Tulik will be married next year to Vortas Brenle's daughter . . . You remember, the salt merchant Father trades with? She's been in the house a number of times. But surely she wouldn't . . . Surely no one in the household would . . ."

"I don't think so, either," said Shaldis, which was not quite the truth. "But I need to see everyone just to make sure."

It was true that to her magic had meant escape, not retaliation. But whatever else could be said of him, Chirak Shaldeth was her grandfather. A slave woman might see the matter otherwise.

"Your aunt Yellow Hen Woman is still with us," Habnit added, with a half-smiling shake of his head. "Your grandfather tried to sell her last year to Namas the silversmith, but she made such a scandal—spreading the story to everyone in the market and causing such trouble to Namas—that Namas returned her. *And* your grandfather blamed her for being a bad example to you."

"You'd think he'd learn." Shaldis smiled a little in spite of herself at the thought of her aunt, whose crooked back, buckteeth, and ax-blade nose had defeated forty years' worth of Chirak's attempts to marry her off. Legally, of course, he was within his rights to sell her as a slave, but men who did so to their own children without the excuse of direst poverty were held in universal contempt.

And whereas Chirak Shaldeth didn't give a snap of his fingers for any man's opinion of him, he knew that contempt usually translates to a loss of business.

For as far back as Shaldis could remember, Yellow Hen had held on to her position in her father's house despite everything the exasperated patriarch could do, to Shaldis's secret admiration.

"It hasn't made her lot any easier."

"I don't think an easy lot is what she wants."

Shaldis had thought she'd seen her aunt from the gallery above the kitchen court, sitting in the shade with the teyn who spent the day grinding the endless amounts of flour and cornmeal required for the family's food. It would be good to have a few words with her now, while waiting for Summerchild's messenger. With her, with her mother, with Foursie and Twinkle and all her old friends and allies in the kitchen court.

"Father!" bleated Habnit, even at his age aghast at being caught in her grandfather's room.

Shaldis whirled, stifling her contempt for her father's guilty panic—*What does he think Grandfather's going to do, beat him?*—and at the same time bracing for the storm of the old man's wrath. But Chirak advanced into the room with his hands held out and his big yellow teeth bared in what he clearly imagined to be an ingratiating smile. "Well, my dear, I trust your father's shown you everything you need to see in here? I've ordered the girls to make up a room for you, Eldest Daughter, a nice one in the front of the house beside your mother and your aunt."

By aunt Shaldis knew he meant her uncle Tjagan's wife, Apricot. Yellow Hen slept in the maids' dormitory, where Shaldis herself and her sisters—and Tjagan's three daughters—had all slept, listening to the more venturesome of the maids giggling when they let one or the other of the camel drivers in, in the dead of the night.

"It's been too long, dear girl, since we've had the pleasure of your presence beneath this roof."

It was as if the scene in his study had never taken place. Shaldis's eyes darted past the old man to the other figure standing in the doorway behind him. It took her a moment to recognize her brother Tulik, who had been barely more than a schoolboy when she'd gone away. He'd grown in two years, and grown more like her father in appearance. In another year or two he'd fill out with their father's broad-shouldered bulk.

But where her father's face wore an expression of amiable eagerness to please, Tulik's was already settling into lines of watchful intelligence, gauging everything by the standard of how useful it was or could be. Where her father's brown eyes were gentle under their straight, gingery brows, Tulik's were already hard.

"It is indeed good to see you, Eldest Sister." Tulik

came into the room and, like his grandfather, held out his hands to her. "I can't tell you how grateful I am—we all are—that you've come to help us in this terrible time. Maybe—now that you're back with us—we can persuade you to look into one or two other little problems we've been having. With the teyn, for instance. Now that the spells of fear on their compound gates aren't working, we've had a devil of a time with escapes. They've gotten sulky, too. And I'll wager you've learned some really fine good-luck words to put on our caravans." He winked at her. "All in the family, of course."

Shaldis stared at him, first blankly, then feeling the heat of rage climb from her belly to her face, so that she was glad of the shadowy dimness of the chamber. Even her grandfather's earlier fury, down in his study, hadn't been as bad as this.

"You'll have to excuse us if we're not up on how witches would prefer to be treated," Tulik went on with a practiced, conspiratorial grin. "But it's really something nobody's had to deal with before this. You'll let us know— Father or Grandfather or myself—if there's anything else you'd like. Whatever it is, we'll get it for you; we're that glad to have you back. Aren't we, Grandfather?"

"Absolutely," assented the old man with a decisive nod and a glitter in his eye as if he were already planning which caravans to have Shaldis put a good-luck word on—and which rivals to grace with a bad one. "With the Citadel closing down, I hear, it's high time you returned to us. But you could have come before, you know." He ratcheted his smile wider.

Shaldis fought the desire to throw up. In a shaking

voice, she said, "I'm sure I could have, sir. But as you said downstairs, I was afraid I'd be taken for a whore."

And brushing past them, she left the chamber and the gallery, descending the stairs with her father's voice calling her name after her, and walked as swiftly as she could out of the house.

The guardsman Jethan met her where Sleeping Worms Street turned before it opened into the square before the Grand Bazaar. As Summerchild had promised, he led a horse, one of the cavalry's stringy little mounts; he sat his own with the straight-backed seat of a warrior.

"There you are." His voice was accusing. "The Summer Concubine—"

Shaldis caught the pommel and swung herself into the saddle: "Don't you say one word to me." After the unholy trio of her father, her brother, and her grandfather, she was in no mood for the big guardsman's defensive loyalty to Summerchild or his disapproval of females who studied the arts of magic and went running around the streets of the city unveiled and alone. The morning was already hot, and the square with its vegetable stands and its clutter of thatch-roofed booths and barrows seemed to float in a haze of golden dust.

She jerked the reins out of his hand, aware that it wasn't at Jethan that her anger had flowered, but too angry to care. What she really wanted to do was cry—for her father, for her childhood, for the knowledge that she'd have to revisit that house.

So she settled for jabbing her heels hard into her

mount's washboard sides and plunging off at a trot through the red-and-blue kiosks, the makeshift stands selling eggplants and tomatoes and little yellow horoscopes, with Jethan—tall and frowning and, as requested, silent—riding in the cloud of her dust.

ELEVEN

As always, the gardens that were the great luxury of the House of the Marvelous Tower quieted Shaldis's heart. They constituted almost a dwelling in themselves, some great rooms with long vistas, like the Green Court with its lawns and fountains and lines of rose trees, and some small and intimate, like the jungles of jasmine and gardenia that sheltered the Summer Pavilion in a magic enclave of quiet fragrance. When Jethan bowed stiffly at the entrance of the pavilion's garden and would have gone, Shaldis touched his arm.

"I'm sorry. My family . . . does that to me."

He opened his mouth on an unconsidered retort, then closed it and regarded her with eyes whose light jewellike blueness seemed brighter in the sunburned dark of his face.

She added, "I haven't seen them in two years. I wish I could go another two. Or twelve. Or twenty-four."

He gave the matter grave consideration. Shaldis had

seen him smile only on rare occasions, as if his face were unused to the exercise. Then he asked, "All of them?"

She thought of the fragmentary music of her mother's laughter; of Foursie, growing leggy and gawky on the threshold of adolescence; of Twinkle, who'd been so fragile as a child. She was aware that her shoulders relaxed; saw the reflection of the change in Jethan's eyes.

"I haven't seen my family in five years," he said in a quiet voice. "I miss even the horrible ones."

"You're a man." The words were out of her mouth before she could stop them: the accusation and the bitter taste of old despairs.

He had a narrow face that seemed to have been formed by and for disapproval of every innovation to the way things were done in his village. But the look in his blue eyes, for one instant, was simply sad, as if at the recollection of burdens shirked: of a man's part not properly played in some desolate farm village in the far north.

But he only bowed to her and walked away across the sunny green of the rose garden.

"Are you all right, dear?" Summerchild came hurrying down the gravel path among the jasmine to her—she must have heard their voices from the pavilion's terrace. She looked, as usual, breathtaking, though the silk-fine, pale blue linen of her dress was unornamented by anything save the slim straightness of her carriage. When she saw Shaldis was alone she unwound her veils, managing to make them drape in a pleasing pattern over her shoulders. Had her life depended on it Shaldis had never been able to make veils look like anything but washing hung on a line. "Is all well with your family? You said there was trouble there." She slipped an arm around the tall girl's waist.

"There is," said Shaldis. "How bad I don't know, but . . . Have the others come?" Summerchild had told her, through the crystal, that she'd sent for Pebble and Moth, and for Pomegranate as well from the north.

"Not yet. The king's here, that's all. We'd rather wait till the other two arrive before going into what happened at the council, if you haven't heard the news being shouted in the streets on your way over."

Shaldis shook her head, though now that she thought back on it, there had been more men and women than usual, running from stall to stall in the vegetable market in the Bazaar Square, and thicker crowds than one would normally see this late in the morning, milling in the Golden Court. "Is the king all right?" she asked worriedly as Summerchild led her through a pergola of feathery wisteria to the pavilion's door.

"For the moment, yes, though there is trouble ahead. Tell me what happened to your family."

The lower floor of the Summer Pavilion—and of nearly every one of the dozens of similar structures scattered about the rambling gardens—was divided into a reception chamber, whose latticed shade walls had already been put up against the growing heat of morning, and a dining room, with jewellike private baths tucked away among the pepper trees of the garden and a tiny kitchen built as a sort of annex behind. A stairway, hidden by carved screens, led to the bedchamber above and to the terrace that caught the sweet breezes of the lake. Summerchild led Shaldis to the divan in the reception chamber and sat beside her, pouring out lemonade from a stone cooler.

She listened in silence as Shaldis told her first of her dream of strange sounds and strange scents and of a woman's voice pleading for help, and then of the attempt on her grandfather's life. "So I don't know if I've suddenly crossed the path of one, or two, Crafty women unknown to any of us," she concluded. "The magic I felt in the door of his room didn't feel like Red Silk's, though I can't be sure. Inside the room . . . I can't describe exactly what I felt. A very strange magic, ugly. A sense of something sticky. And deadly. Hidden away, waiting, like a poisonous spider under a divan cushion. Just waiting for you to sit down."

"But recent?"

"Oh, yes. Well, you know that it isn't just the magic of the wizards that's failing. It's the magic that they did, the magic that they put into things, like ward signs and the fear spells on the compounds of the teyn. Which my grandfather thinks I should know how to renew," she added distastefully. "I don't think I've ever been so thankful for not being able to make a spell work. I kept getting the feeling that if he could, he'd hire me out to his friends. Or lend me, in exchange for their goodwill."

"At least Cattail gets to keep the money people pay for *her* services," mused Summerchild, and Shaldis raised her brows. She hadn't thought of it that way. "And, yes, Pomegranate told me of some rather alarming complications of failed ward signs. This woman who was calling you . . . you weren't able to reach her in the crystal?"

Shaldis shook her head. "I mean to try again from the scrying chamber in the Citadel. According to Yanrid, back in the days before magic changed, there were some of the alien wizards who could be contacted only through crystals, others only through water or only through ink. He said he thought that was because their magic was sourced differently from ours. And, with those wizards, adepts had to learn their languages; they were taught at the Citadel for hundreds of years. I could hear this woman speaking in another tongue, but because it was a dream I understood what she said."

"Did her language sound like one that was taught?"

"Not even remotely. And I'm pretty sure I wouldn't understand a word she was saying if I was awake. You know what it's like, hearing people speak in dreams."

"And you're sure it wasn't just a dream?"

"Absolutely. As certain as I'm speaking to you now. Yanrid used to set me to watch the ink bowls—as a punishment, I thought at the time, or to keep me out of the way. But I prayed, just once, to see one of them, to see some mage from another land, another place. He'd tell us about them—Yanrid would—outlander wizards from realms where everything was locked in ice, he said, where even the stars were different. Wizards whose skin was black or brown, or whose faces were covered with hair like the teyn. Wizards who'd learned our language the same way we learned theirs, over lifetimes."

She folded her hands around the alabaster cup, thinking of the mages of the Citadel who'd become friends with those alien wizards over the years. Who'd traded news of their families, their kings, their studies of the skies.

Did their Citadels, too, stand empty now? Did they work as librarians or secretaries or teachers, to feed themselves?

Did they kill themselves, as at least one mage here had?

Did they envy and hate the women whose powers had blossomed in the time of the mages' withering?

Power no longer flows from their hands. . . .

"We have to find her," she said softly. "We have to find them both."

"Sooner than you know," Summerchild replied.

And her soft words were answered by the light chatter of voices from the garden and the glimpse of pink silk and sun-paled sensible blue and brown among the leaves. Moth's laugh came sweet and childlike: once over her initial agonizing shyness, the seventeen-year-old concubine of a silk-merchant's son had proved to be as good-hearted, as undemanding, and as uneducated as any other laborer's daughter sold for her beauty. When Pebble had made her way to Summerchild's pavilion almost a year ago, she'd been twenty-three, old for a girl still living in her father's house, but the placid housekeeper for the widowed contractor and caretaker of her half-dozen younger brothers and sisters. Large boned and a little clumsy looking, she'd begun to use her power healing the strained muscles and occasional colics of her father's oxen, horses, and teyn; alone of the Raven sisters, she seemed to have the gift of consistent and powerful healing, though she could seldom describe how it was worked.

Shaldis and Summerchild rose to greet them, the soft little bundle of concubine and the big, slow, fair girl who smelled of soap and milk. The king came downstairs as well. Shaldis had often had occasion to marvel at the big man's tactful good manners in disappearing when she needed to speak to Summerchild alone—and by some signal Shaldis couldn't detect, sent word to the main palace kitchen. In a very few minutes Geb, the king's fat little chamberlain, appeared with slaves, food, freshly cooled lemonade, and carved boxwood caddies of coffee, sugar, and tea. Shaldis thought that under the extravagancies of his cosmetics His Majesty looked badly shaken up. She saw, too, how Geb watched him under his painted eyelids.

Whatever was wrong, even the servants knew of it.

So did Moth and Pebble. "You really gonna have to swim across a pool of crocodiles, Majesty?" demanded the little concubine, finishing her Sun in Splendor salaam and falling like a starving woman upon the quail and couscous before the servants were properly out of the room.

"It certainly looks that way."

Shaldis said, *"What?"* and the moment the servants were well and truly gone—she could hear Geb clucking at them not to linger, all the way down the garden's gravel paths—Summerchild told what Lord Akarian had set into motion in the council pavilion and the horrifying facts that Hathmar and the others had subsequently revealed.

"Damn it," Shaldis cried when the favorite's narrative was done. "I thought Hathmar was just testing me on ward spells, when they took me through all those wards against crocodiles and snakes. Because they really do have a problem with the crocodiles in the fields along the lakefront, you know, and along the Fishmarket Canal, especially with the night carnival going on there till nearly dawn. I've heard of them crawling all the way inland to the Slaughterhouse District, and nothing Hathmar showed me seemed to work when I did it."

"If I could come up with a snake ward I'd sure be the richest kitten in the street," added Moth. She licked honey from a baba cake off her hennaed fingers and readjusted a jade pin in her sable coils of hair. "I hear Cattail claims she got one, but me, I think it's just red pepper dust, like you do for ants. I ain't never heard it worked."

Summerchild and the king traded a glance. "We should prefer," said His Majesty slowly, "that Mistress Cattail be kept out of this for the time being, unless one or the other of you knows for a fact that she can ward against crocodiles or snakes or can undo the effects of poison at a distance and without knowing what the poison is. Her discretion cannot be relied upon, and discretion is of the utmost importance in this matter."

Shaldis saw Moth's huge brown eyes flick knowingly around the chamber, then slide sidelong in unspoken observation to Pebble: neither Foxfire nor Red Silk were present.

"It is an article of faith," the king went on, gathering his flame-silk robes to sink cross-legged to the divan beside his favorite, "among the people of the city, and particularly among the villages, that the king is selected for his position by the gods. I'm sure every member of the great houses—every lord who can command the lesser sheikhs and clan lords and village councils to provide him fighting men—guesses that it's probably magic. But they don't know for certain. And the people want it to be the gods, not simply one more tool of power that any rich man can buy."

He took the coffee cup Summerchild offered him with a bow of thanks, but Shaldis could see he was barely aware of making the gesture. He didn't drink, only turned the delicate nacre and gold cup in his plump, jeweled hands.

"There's no reason, you know, for people to follow the king, except that he is chosen by the gods. In the days when the Zali ruled around the lakes of the Sun and the Moon, the great lords and landchiefs were in fact kings: the Sarn around the Lake of Roses, the Jamornid in the north. And there was chaos, men rising up in rebellion constantly—not that it mattered a great deal then, except perhaps to the warriors killed in battle. It rained reliably every winter, even far out onto what is now the desert, and the most the mages had to do was keep the teyn in line. The houses that lasted were the ones who got the priests on their sides, not the mages; the houses whose lords were adopted by the gods. Even at their most powerful, people never really trusted mages. It is to the gods that people look for comfort and care."

"But it *is* the gods who look after us," said Pebble timidly. "Isn't it?"

"It is indeed," replied the king. "And it is the gods who look after the realm—and the lives of everyone in the Valley of the Seven Lakes—by allowing magic, instead of dying, to pass to new bearers. Bearers whom I hope will assist me in holding the realm together until we can either get the aqueduct built or establish a large enough group of Raven sisters who are capable of bringing the rains."

He folded his hands, the topazes of his many rings flashing even in the pavilion's shady cool. Under eyelids tinted gold and bronze and rimmed with kohl, his hazel eyes were deadly earnest. "Should I die, and should my brother—for whatever reason—not achieve the consecration of the Veiled Gods, the lords of the Sealed Temples who have guarded kings since the days of the Zali, I think that the realm will break apart very quickly. Not only will the armies of each landchief turn against those of other landchiefs rather than against our common enemies the nomad raiders from the desert, but each landchief will seek to hire and control as many Crafty women as he can. Inevitably, that will mean a division in the force of whatever magic we are trying to muster for the summoning of rain."

The women looked at one another again, again silently counting.

Nobody needed a second hand for their calculations.

"What about the djinni?" asked Moth, when Pebble, still looking very troubled, did not speak. The young concubine looked across at Shaldis, who had been the last person known to speak to a djinn. "I know they mostly disappeared, but isn't there one still hid out in that temple in the Slaughterhouse District? The one everybody thought *was* a god?"

"He's still there." Shaldis spoke hesitantly, and shivered at the recollection of her visions of Naruansich, the Sunflash Prince, the foul thing that clung to the gold-sheathed crystal of an ancient spirit trap, feeding on the energies of slaughtered animals and squeezing forth from those energies a tainted and uncertain magic.

"Can you talk him into helping us?"

She thought about it for a time, wondering how or if it could be done, and at what cost. Then she shook her head. "I don't think so. He was three quarters mad when I encountered him—when I went into the crystal matrices of the statue's heart—and the blood and death he was living on were further twisting what was left of his mind. I've been into that temple at least a dozen times since then, sometimes to draw him out with a blood sacrifice and sometimes just trying to communicate through the circles that worked before. Nothing happens."

The brooding darkness of the temple had the taste in

her mind of some vile dream. The image of the hawk-headed war god, unthinkably old: crystal wrapped in gold and ringed with three bands of iron.

And within that image, the bloodied labyrinth of the djinn's mind, created with magic and maintained with the magic that burns on the threshold between life and death.

Maybe, she thought, if she *truly* wanted to return to that place, if she *truly* wanted with all her heart to go back into that insane consciousness that existed—that could exist—only in magic . . .

But she didn't.

And she couldn't make herself truly want to return.

"He's there," she concluded softly. "And he's aware of me. I know it. But he will not speak. Whether he'll speak to anyone else, I don't know."

"Me, I can think of a couple folks I'd rather he didn't speak to," Moth muttered, and selected a vanilla wafer from the plate.

"But what about the gods?" It was the first time Shaldis had heard Pebble question the judgment of anyone, let alone the king. "The real gods, I mean. Ean and Rohar and Oan Echis and Darutha—the ones who made the world and keep it running. Hasn't anyone asked them what *they* want?"

"The problem with asking the opinion of the gods, my child," said the king softly, "is that one cannot always trust the interpretations of those who claim to speak for them. Priests are mortal, when all is said, even priests who speak in holy trances . . . or claim to."

Pebble stared at him, her eyes slowly filling with tears of disappointed shock, like a child hearing that her father has sold her nurse.

Very gently, the king went on. "I don't ask the gods much because I don't trust men. When you're a king, you can't afford to. I can only act, to the utmost of my abilities, as I think the gods would have any man act, to keep the realm together at all costs. And for that I need your help. Do you understand?"

The big girl sighed and wiped her eyes. "No," she said and, reaching across the low table, took his hand and kissed it. "But I trust you, sir. And I trust Summerchild. And I'll pray every day, to every single one of them. Then if the gods ever tell *me* what they want, I'll let you know."

The king smiled. He had probably the most beautiful smile Shaldis had ever seen. "Thank you." With his other hand he grasped Moth's, sticky fingers and all. "Thank you all. Aside from the fact that I really, *really* don't want to go into the water with the crocodiles 'for real,' as the children say . . . if the realm breaks up, we are all doomed. I just don't know how quickly. If the rains cannot be brought this spring—if we cannot muster enough labor and supplies to finish the aqueduct—the lakes will dry. It's ninety days by caravan to the coast, which is rockbound, barren, and without the soil to support a village, as far as anyone has ever traveled. And in all other directions there is nothing. Only sand. If lands lie beyond the desert, no one has succeeded in reaching them. Ever. There is, quite simply, nowhere else to go."

TWELVE

What should I do?" Shaldis asked when Pebble and Moth took their departure. The sun had reached noon, the heat nearly unbearable even in the palace's lakeside gardens. All over the Yellow City, farmers were packing up their vegetable stands and cobblers their lasts. In the villages, wives and slaves were putting up curtains of woven straw over windows and doors to close out the heat. In the fields, men drove oxen and teyn under shade, and lay down themselves to sleep through the worst of the day.

All would start up again an hour before sunset. Even the insects slept.

"There's almost certainly a Crafty woman somewhere in the city that we don't know about; and there's one, and maybe more, somewhere, I don't know where but probably nowhere near the city, or else she'd know about healing with herbs and poultices."

She adjusted the long boxwood sticks that held her hair in a tight roll at the back of her head—there'd been no time, before dawn that day, to braid it into its usual lacquered knot. "Should I concentrate on finding them, or should I put most of my energy into a library search at the Citadel for anything concerning crocodiles, poisons, and snakes?"

"Hathmar and the Sun Mages were good enough to offer to do that." His Majesty padded over to the cooler and fished out the remains of the now-tepid jar of lemonade, which he doled out equally between his own cup, Shaldis's, and Summerchild's. "Cheers," he added glumly, lofting a toast. "To the continuation of the senior branch of the House Jothek. It will be many days before Soth and Mistress Pomegranate return, but neither of them has heard of any Crafty women working in either the City of White Walls or the City of Reeds. It's most discouraging, even without the resurgence of lake monsters that's been reported, the gods apparently being under the impression that I don't have enough to occupy my thoughts."

"Rachnis said that he'd come to the palace and look through the Royal Library," Summerchild went on. "Soth let it get into a terrible muddle during the years when he was not well—"

Shaldis had for years watched her father's accounts deteriorate in the morass of depression and *sherab,* and could only shudder at what the shadowmaster would have to say of the mess the royal librarian's ten-year bender must have caused. Rachnis had little sensitivity but a very instructive line of invective.

"—and though he's been working to straighten them out, he'd barely started when he went north with Pomegranate on his search. The problem is that so many spells need the strength of two or three or four Crafty women working in concert, combining their magic through the

Sigil of Sisterhood. Soth suspects that the problem may be in sourcing our power, because a single mage could work them. And just because a spell doesn't work for one woman—or two or three—does not mean it won't work for four. Which means that we would like your help tonight, when we ride out along the lakeshore to test everything we already know about crocodiles."

"I'd figured that," Shaldis said. "I'll send a note to my grandfather that I won't be back there till tomorrow morning. Which is fine with me—I don't think I could take him and my brother again this soon."

"Otherwise," continued the favorite, "I think," and she glanced across at the king, who inclined his head slightly in acquiescence to whatever her opinion might be. "I think the best use of your time would be to concentrate on helping—and if possible finding—the woman in your dream, and most important, tracking down the Raven sister who attacked your grandfather. Even if, for whatever reason, she will not help us—she will not help the king— I think we need to know who and where she is."

Voices in the garden. The chatter of servants and a child's treble laugh. Shaldis saw the look of joy that flashed between the king and Summerchild as both got to their feet. The next moment Geb, two palace slaves, a plump and well-dressed nurse, and a slim dark girl filled the archway that looked into the gardens. The king cried, "Princess!" and held out his arms, to sweep up the girl as she ran to him.

Rainsong. Summerchild's only surviving child by the king.

The king's only surviving child.

Amid their laughter, the king's inquiries of his daughter,

how she fared at lessons that morning, and Rainsong's dignified protest that she was *much* too old to be picked up, Shaldis blew a silent kiss to Summerchild and took her leave. As she made her way through the jasmine arbors, the fountain courts, and the groves of myrtle and bamboo, she thought about that beautiful, dark-haired child, only a little older than her sister Twinkle, and of what would become of her if His Majesty died.

The great houses married among each other, and the upper levels of their landchiefs actually controlled the vast estates that made up their wealth. Like the children of the wealthy merchants, the sons and daughters of the warrior lords were the bricks and mortar of alliances. The king's brother, Barún, was the first royal heir in nearly a thousand years to actually marry, and in marrying Lord Sarn's niece he'd sealed one alliance for House Jothek and created a dozen potential enemies, whose daughters and sisters and nieces had been passed over.

Lord Sarn, Shaldis guessed, would be the power in the land if the king were to die—and Lord Sarn had enemies, and agendas, of his own. He'd try to hold on to Summerchild and the other Raven sisters, by force if not through loyalty.

The gods only knew where that would end. Hostages, threats, lies. Shaldis shivered as she came within sight of the Red Pavilion, a tiny structure tucked away in the gardens behind the library, which the king had given instructions to be always kept ready for her use. If the king were to die, it wasn't just Rainsong who stood in danger of being used as a hostage for Summerchild's services. It was whoever and whatever were prized by each of the Raven sisters.

Twinkle.

Or Pebble's beloved father and siblings.

Or the child that only a few days ago Moth had excitedly whispered to her that she, Moth, carried in her belly, a little girl-child. She already knew it was a girl.

It was fourteen days until the new moon.

Pebble was right, thought Shaldis as she moved into the cool shadows of the pavilion and climbed the stairs to the little bedchamber above. *We're going to need the help of the gods, and we're going to need every fragment of help that they're willing to give.*

THIRTEEN

Grandmother . . ." Foxfire pleaded in a whisper as she hurried to keep up with the stooped bundle of black rags that hobbled so purposefully on ahead of her. "Raeshaldis already told me, the djinn in that statue doesn't come out! She's tried seven or eight times since the spring, and—"

"And you believed what she told you?" Red Silk turned, and above the edge of her dirty and ragged veil her turquoise eyes shone bright and hard as jewels. Her skinny finger stabbed out, ringless now and crooked with arthritis yet so white and well kept as to give the lie to the whole of her beggar's array—always supposing that there was anyone abroad in the suffocating heat of noonday to

see them. "You're a fool, girl." She turned on her heel.
Foxfire, half smothered under her own set of dirty rags
and veils like horse blankets, had to almost run to keep up
with her, and the goat she was dragging on the end of a
rope didn't help.

As she trotted, she kept in her mind the haze of spells
called the Gray Cloak, that rendered both women—and
the goat—absolutely unnoticed by any who might pass
them by. This, in Foxfire's mind, was a totally unnecessary precaution. The beggars, thieves, and whores who
populated the Slaughterhouse District—a straggly slum
that trailed away outside the city's eastern gate—were all
asleep in the noon heat: she and her grandmother could
have paraded naked up and down the squalid alleyways
with basketfuls of jewels in their hands and come to no
harm.

And in the hammering heat of midday, naked was the
way she wished she was. And while she was wishing, she
wished she was back at the villa of Golden Sky and not
risking death by suffocation through her grandmother's
scheme.

"You don't believe a thing that woman tells you," Red
Silk threw back over her shoulder. "She's the king's min-
ion. They all are, and that skinny-bones concubine of his
most of all. What he says, they do. You don't trust any but
your own. And you keep one eye on *them*."

That, Foxfire supposed, was the reason she and her
grandmother had been brought to the Slaughterhouse
District by three of her older brothers: dour Sormaddin,
fierce-tempered Úrthet, and dandified Zharvine, sons of
her father by his legal wife, Hearthfire Lady (no newfan-
gled dropping of the old name forms for *her*!). Sor-

maddin and Úrthet had been left with the camels among the ruined villas that lay along the eastward road. Zharvine, reveling at the prospect of lurking about in disguise, followed them at a distance with drawn sword, clothed as one of the bullyboys whose violence ruled the slum. Foxfire considered his presence as unnecessary as the spells that hid her and her grandmother. The least he could have done was lead the goat.

She knew what her grandmother intended, and though their success might well save her father's life, she wished desperately that she was home.

The walls narrowed around them, high now though ruinous and sending back waves of heat as if the two dark-clothed women made their way through a bread oven. The reek of rotting meat from the slaughtering yards, of dung and privies, made Foxfire dizzy. Before them the black stone walls of the old Temple of Nebekht rose over the surrounding jumble; six months ago the cult of the Iron-Girdled God had been strong enough to nearly oust the king from his throne, and now, like the Citadel of the Sun Mages, it stood empty.

Empty save for the king's guards and for the statue of gold-sheathed crystal where Raeshaldis said that the djinn Naruansich still lurked.

Foxfire half closed her eyes, stretched out her mind. Let her consciousness pass into the black stone walls of the temple, as Summerchild had taught her—had taught both the mother and the daughter of her lord's enemy, because they, like she, were the Sisters of the Raven. Because they, like she, needed the full use of their magic, for all to survive.

The guards in the lobby were dozing. As who

wouldn't in this heat? Her spells probed at their somnolent, undefended minds, halfway toward dreaming already. One man, the older, had brought a book with him, a compilation of the runes of High Script, which he'd been copying onto wax and studying, along with a simplified version of the *Classic of Kings*. No wonder he'd fallen asleep, reflected Foxfire: part of the training of a Pearl Woman was to learn the thousands of runes of the High Script and how to read the classics of philosophy, scripture, and ancient lore written in them. The younger man was daydreaming about his girlfriend. Foxfire felt the warm tingle of his reminiscent lust, and blushed a little under her veils.

"Two guards, Grandmother," she breathed.

"Can you put them to sleep?"

She drew a deep breath. "I think so."

"Do it, then."

It wasn't difficult. Shaldis had taught them all the Sun Mage spells for easing people over the edge into dreamland, but Foxfire, like all the women, had used these only as a starting point. She realized she'd been making up little songs in her head for years, to make her nurses and governesses—and later some of the ladies in the Blossom House where she'd had her advanced education in the womanly arts—drift off to sleep. Raeshaldis had told her that she'd done the same thing at her grandfather's house.

So Foxfire and Red Silk had practiced, all over Mohrvine's household, without anyone being the wiser. Most times Foxfire could put a guard to sleep, or one of the pages waiting in their little day room. Once she'd whispered a dreaming song that had put the whole dormitory of maids under, but as that had gotten the girls soundly beaten by the housekeeper she hadn't tried it again. Her grandmother, who experienced no such scruples about who got punished for falling asleep on duty, was much better at it than she was.

But in this case, aided by the day's heat, the matter was ludicrously easy. Foxfire breathed a sweet nostalgic air into the younger man's mind, about his beautiful sweetheart, and into the older man's whispered a soft monotony of runes, lulling as the song of spring wind in willow trees. Beside her she heard Red Silk chuckle. "Very good, little minx," the old lady whispered. "You've put half the neighbors down as well. Now come. Let's see how you are with opening doors."

That was another skill Foxfire had practiced under her grandmother's watchful eye. At least that one didn't get the servants in trouble. Foxfire wrapped her hands in the end of her veil before pressing them to the sun-hot bronze of the temple doors, probed into the iron-strapped slabs for the mechanism of the locks. Soth, Oryn's librarian, had taught them that, and mad old Pomegranate, whose brother was a burglar: all the women had studied the construction of locks and latches, to know what to feel for with their minds. Foxfire could see the mechanism in her thoughts, as if she were remembering a dream she'd had, but she couldn't touch the intricate maze of levers. She felt it when her grandmother reached in, and pushed the tumblers aside.

Her grandmother had poured dumbweed down the goat's throat, to paralyze its voice. Still it struggled, rasping hoarsely as they pulled it over the threshold, as if it knew what would become of it in the vast enclosed dark of the temple.

Foxfire shuddered, hating herself as she drew the great doors closed.

The sanctuary that lay beyond the vestibule breathed with the old reek of sacrificial slaughter, of dirty blood and scraps of meat left rotting in corners—the followers of Nebekht had never enjoyed a reputation for cleanliness.

Above all, the statue of the Iron-Girdled One brooded in the dark.

"High One!" Red Silk's voice rang in the darkness like the blow of a hammer on steel. Foxfire clutched at the sleep spells on the guards. "Sunflash Prince, Naruansich, lord of the invisible kingdom of the winds!"

Foxfire winced, knowing that her grandmother had learned the djinn's true name from Shaldis. She wanted her father to survive—she wanted her father to be king, but she knew betrayal when she saw it.

"We call upon you, Lord of the Thousand Lights, we beg of you, show yourself!" The old woman fell to her knees before the idol.

"We seek your council, wisest prince! We seek your aid. Show yourself, we beseech, we pray! Speak with us here!"

Silence, and the reeking weight of the noonday heat, as if the whole of the heavens pressed down upon the black rafters far above their heads. After what felt like hours—but, Foxfire calculated, was probably about as long as it would take to walk a mile—her grandmother cursed, and pulled from beneath her robes a corked gourd bottle of brandy doctored with tiga root, which the no-mads of the desert used to simulate madness. Lohar, to whom the djinn had spoken in the name of the god Nebekht, had been mad; Foxfire privately considered that to "free the mind" in this way was crazy in itself, but knew better than to tell her grandmother so.

Trembling, she led the goat forward, and the two women wrestled it to the dirty floor. It flung its horns up and down, and the broken noises that came from its mouth seemed louder than shouts in the horrible shadowed silence of the windowless temple; Foxfire was hard put to keep her thoughts concentrated on the two men sleeping in the vestibule, on the other spells Shaldis and Summerchild and old Pomegranate had taught her, to turn the attention of passersby aside. She couldn't believe no one would hear.

The goat's hoof slashed her wrist and drew blood. A stone knife glinted dully in Red Silk's hand, a sacrificial implement from the desert tribes among whom she'd grown up. Foxfire draped her weight over the goat's thrashing legs and grabbed at the horns, and Red Silk struck. The flint blade tore through hair and soft flesh; blood fountained out. Pressed to the goat's body, Foxfire felt its lungs and heart work wildly as its life gushed away.

In her heart she cried, *I'm sorry,* and fought not to weep for the animal's soul.

Fought to keep her little songs of sleep upon the guards.

She stumbled back, nauseated by the stink of the fresh blood, her own garments dribbled and blotted. Reeling with the onset of the drugs, Red Silk knelt over the dying goat, slit the body open, and plunged her hands inside. Foxfire looked away, and when she looked back she saw her grandmother standing before the plinth on which the idol rested, her body pressed to the stone. The temple was windowless and the darkness complete, but Foxfire could

see in the dark, as all Crafty ones could. She saw the trail
of blood that led from the goat's body in her grandmother's wake, saw the thin streams of it crawling down,
from where Red Silk's ensanguined hands stroked the
idol's golden feet.

"Come to us and help us." The old woman's voice was
thick now and strange, stammering with the drugs that
disjointed her mind. "Speak, and we will speak for you.
Help, and we will grant you whatever it is you ask for,
whatever it is you need." She pressed herself to the stone.
Flies, that were to be found everywhere in the Slaughterhouse District, began to roar dully in the stillness and to
settle on the dead goat and the blood trail.

Foxfire felt sick.

For almost two hours Red Silk whispered, screamed,
pleaded, and threatened: offered blood, more goats, teyn,
slave children. "Tell me what it is you wish! What price
you demand! You must speak to me! You must give us
your help!"

Sleepy-by, sleepy-by, you're safe in Mama's arms,
Foxfire sang mechanically into the minds of the two men
slumped by their lamp in the oven heat of the vestibule.
Sweat crawled down her face and body and the drone of
the flies filled her mind like the howling of desert winds.
As long as she's with you, you'll come to no harm.

She forced her thoughts to see only that plump little
brown-eyed girl that the younger guard loved, a little like
Opal before the fire, singing the sleepy-by song as she
brushed her hair (*Who is she? Do you treat her well?*); to
shape the one-thousand-two-hundred-and-fourth, the
one-thousand-two-hundred-and-fifth of the twelve thousand specialized sigils of the High Script. *What will you*

do with this knowledge? Write poems about the stars,
read the tales of the ancient kings?

It seemed to Foxfire in her half-dreaming state that
they were not alone in the temple after all, that someone
or something stood quite close to her grandmother beside
the blood-smeared plinth. Something that shined as if all
the stars of the Milky Way had collapsed upon one another into a single column of unbearable light.

Something that looked upon the old woman and the
dead goat with disgust and contempt in its golden eyes.
Around her the air seemed for an instant to buzz and jangle, as if with the sound of a hundred thousand chains
shaken at the far side of the universe.

Then it was gone.

At last her grandmother staggered back to her, tripped
on the dead goat, fell to her knees, and vomited. Foxfire
hastened to her side to steady her, but was shoved away.
"Damn it, girl, you think I can't look after myself? In the
tribes a woman who can't get to her feet again is left behind. Give me my stick."

Trembling, Foxfire obeyed.

"There's nothing here," muttered Red Silk. "Nothing.
Curse them all. Curse them for liars. Let's get out of
here."

She reeled toward the door, leaving the goat's carcass
in a puddle of filth, blood, and flies for someone else to
clean up.

"We'll find a way, though. You mark my words, girl—
my son will be king."

In the doorway she slewed around, dilated eyes staring
into the darkness. Then her drugged gaze swung onto
Foxfire, contempt bitter in her voice. "Just like that hussy

Raeshaldis to lie about him being here. There's no one here. You can't trust her. Can't trust any but your own."

But who, Foxfire wondered, *are my own?*

FOURTEEN

A little before sunset Raeshaldis woke. The afternoon heat broke in the palace sooner than anywhere else in the city; breezes ruffled gently in from the lake, bringing the dry rustle of the date-palm groves along its shores, the creak of the long lines of bucket hoists that these days transferred water across the stretches of what once had been submerged.

She had slept with her crystal beneath her pillow, hoping for another dream. Now she cradled it in her hands, tried to call back anything, any image, that might lead her to sight of the unknown Raven sister who had cried for help in the night.

But nothing came.

In time she set the crystal aside, collected a light robe from one of the wall cupboards, and went downstairs and along the garden path to the palace baths.

There were several of these, dating from the times when kings had maintained dozens of concubines and scores of dancing girls, some of whom had to be kept from encountering one another at all costs. Although in his youth King Oryn had pursued an extravagant course of debauchery, it had been, Shaldis suspected, more to annoy his father than out of any true inclination for multiple liaisons; he'd generously dowried and married off most of those young ladies the moment his father's death had opened for him the way to the woman he truly loved.

To her knowledge, four of those former concubines had asked to remain: one of them worked with Soth in the palace library, two had become lovers and lived contentedly as pensioners in a small pavilion in a corner of the gardens, and the fourth had taken over administration of the palace household funds, invested part of the income from royal lands and lent the rest out at interest, and was making a small fortune for herself and the king. All of them got on extremely well with Summerchild.

At the baths this evening, however, Shaldis encountered only Summerchild herself, who gave her further details of the search Soth and Pomegranate had been engaged upon since late in the spring and the problem of lake monsters which would eventually have to be dealt with. "The odd thing is, Pomegranate says that she encountered marks that felt like ward signs in the City of Reeds and in one of the villages along the shores of the White Lake—both in places where everyone has said there are no Crafties of either sex and have not been since the magic of men faded. She says she isn't certain, but she thinks they're newer than that, and she thinks they were made by women."

"I don't understand." Shaldis moved her shoulders into the powerful massage of the bath woman's hands. She and Summerchild had passed through the soaping and rinsing, the bubbling hot pools and the steam, in small talk and silence; now they lay on towels and warmed marble in the delicious afterglow stage that made actual baths—as opposed to the pan-and-pitcher scrubs with which most people started their mornings—such addictive pleasure. The royal bath women were the best in the realm and had hands like blacksmiths'. "That's what I don't understand about what happened to my grandfather, either. Why would a woman who has magic, who can do magic, hide her skills? I mean, Cattail down in the Fishmarket is practically coining money!"

"Maybe they're afraid of Cattail," surmised Summerchild quietly. "Although to tell the truth I've never heard of her threatening another Raven sister. Her attitude seems to be there's plenty of customers out there for everyone."

"Including the ones she's sold *good*-luck spells to, to counteract the *bad*-luck spells their enemies have paid her to put on them." Shaldis took a sip of the mint tea whose delicate cups stood between their respective massage slabs. "That wouldn't hold in any case for those in the north, when there isn't a jealous and powerful Raven sister trying to corner the market."

"Unless someone was lying to Pomegranate."

"It could be children." Pebble and Moth came in, sweating and pink from the hot tubs and swathed in enormous cotton towels. Before returning to their respective homes at noon—borne in the palace sedan chairs in which they'd been fetched—both junior sisters had promised to return that evening, to ride along the lakeshore and test spells on crocodiles. Pebble went on, "When I was little, my friends and I played games with signs: *You can't walk past this line*, that sort of thing. Could Pomegranate tell what the signs had been made for?"

"No. She said they weren't real sigils or ward runes,

just simple little squiggles imbued with magic." Summerchild and Shaldis exchanged a look as they yielded their places on the massage slabs to the others and retreated to the couches. A junior bath girl brought their tea; two others fetched sandalwood combs and began to comb their hair. Pebble just wound her limp, mousy strands into a knot, but Moth had brought her own maid to execute one of the elaborate braided coiffures that were in such fashion in the city, when the massage was done. "That sounds like children, at that. But surely their parents would know. Would tell someone."

"Maybe they don't know themselves yet," mused Shaldis. "And maybe they come from families like mine, where even five-year-olds know they'd better keep everything to themselves if they want to have any kind of lives of their own."

"Pomegranate say anything else?" asked Moth, wriggling like a contented cat into the massaging hands of the bath woman. "Other than monsters coming out of the lakes and stomping on villages just like in the stories? I always thought monsters in the lakes were just fairy tales, you know, like phoenixes and rocs that fly away with camels in their claws and devils that can put the Bad-Luck Shadow on you when you're asleep." Her dark eyes sparkled with childlike delight that such marvels might come true.

"My father told me he heard a rumor yesterday about a plague among the northern lakes," said Pebble quietly. "One of the men on the lumber boats from the Mountains of Eanit said whole villages were killed off in a night."

"Maybe they got a lake monster up there, too?" Moth didn't sound terribly upset about the prospect.

Summerchild's face was grave, and suddenly tired. "I'll have the king send word to the marketplaces to ask," she said, and sat up on her couch. "Thank you, dear," she added, to the girl who was coiling her hair into its deceptively simple knots. "And it may only be rumor. Sometimes I wonder if the realm won't fall apart simply because we don't have Sun Mages in Ith or the City of White Walls to speak with Yanrid every morning in the Citadel's scrying chamber and let him—and us—know what's happening three hundred miles away. The City of Ith could be destroyed by lake monsters—or by plague or an infestation of locusts or Bad-Luck Shadow—and we wouldn't know it for weeks."

Our children are dying.

"Pomegranate didn't happen to mention anything that might have been the sound I heard in my dream, did she?" Shaldis sat forward on the couch and drew her bath sheet closer around her thin shoulders. "A long soft roaring followed by a crash? Like an avalanche, but repeated, spaced out at about a count of five."

Summerchild shook her head and looked at the others. They both returned blank stares.

Shaldis sighed. "Just a thought."

※

The king joined the ladies for a light supper at the Summer Pavilion just after the sun went down. When full dark came, they all set off from the northern gate of the palace that opened to the kitchen courts, riding secretly in twos and threes under the cloak of spells. Summer nights saw a thousand daytime occupations, and a carnival atmosphere prevailed in the rural suburb that clustered outside the Yellow City's northern gate. From the road through the palmeries and farms of the lakeshore, Shaldis could see the torchlight of the gate and its surrounding taverns and bawdy houses. Not many people, it was true, walked along the wall to the lakeshore itself—if you didn't get eaten by crocodiles, the saying went, you would be by mosquitoes—but everyone who hadn't gone back to work by torchlight was out walking in the evening cool.

They kept the cloaks—of magic or of dark anonymous wool—well wrapped around them until they were clear of all these evening strollers. It wouldn't do for anyone to report that the king had ridden out with his coterie of Raven sisters, to see if by spells they could circumvent the will of the gods. Looking ahead of her at Jethan's broad shoulders and stiff back, Shaldis wondered if that young man had been one of those who'd believed implicitly in the will of the gods.

She wouldn't put it past him.

"The guards on the Temple of Nebekht report that they awoke from deep sleep this afternoon to find the mutilated carcass of a goat in the sanctuary," murmured the king, reining back his tall horse to ride between Shaldis and Summerchild. "There was blood on the statue—were I a betting man I'd wager six pots of first-class ointment and four camel loads of white rose petals that the celebrants of that particular little rite were my uncle Mohrvine's ladies."

"You really think you could find a taker, my lord?" Summerchild raised her brows, exquisite beneath the pearl border of her head veil.

"I'm sure I could order someone to accept my bets. I understand kings have in the past." He glanced away across the fields and pastureland east of the road to where the low black wall of the Place of Kush, the only one of the Sealed Temples to lie outside the city, stretched almost invisible beneath the chilly glow of the stars. "Completely aside from the uncleanliness of it—they could at least have tidied up after themselves—I shouldn't care to think Lord Mohrvine now has a djinn on his side."

"It tells us one thing," remarked Shaldis. "It tells us Red Silk doesn't have the power to make those spells work, any more than we do. Not if she's bargaining with a djinn for goats. We know Naruansich's name," she added, "and we know spells that will hold off a djinn. Or at least they did last time. And personally, I don't think he came out. He was a slave before, doing the bidding of a madman. I think he'll be careful about putting himself in that position again." In a lower voice, she added, "I would be."

In addition to the king, the Raven sisters were accompanied by Bax, the white-haired commander of the palace guard; by Yanrid, Rachnis, and the novice Kylin; and by a handful of trusted guards, who formed a cordon in the darkness among the cornstalks and the tomato vines. By everyone, in fact, Shaldis guessed, who could be trusted with the secret that Crafties, not gods, were to be behind the king's success in his ordeals of consecration. Leaving the king and Kylin to mind the horses, they picked their way through the dark field rows to the spongy stretches of mud where the water had dried away to mazes of pools, papyrus, and desiccating reeds.

Mosquitoes swarmed here, and Shaldis, who eschewed veils with the pride of a young woman who can protect herself, was extremely glad for the gauzy folds

Summerchild had lent her: pride was one thing but there was no need to be stupid. Crocodiles swarmed here, too, not only in the streamlets and irrigation canals but crawling among the islets of dry land and up in among the rows of corn and vegetables onshore. Shaldis and her fellow Raven sisters carried wicker hampers filled with newly killed chickens, to leave Bax and Jethan free to use, if necessary, their crossbows and pikes.

They needed them. The four women tried every spell and combination of spells that the two former wizards could think of—including a dozen variations of Pomegranate's lake-monster spells—individually and with their powers fused by the Sigil of Sisterhood, to drive the twelve- and sixteen-foot reptiles back from the chickens they tossed out among them. Twice Bax and Jethan had to fire flaming crossbow bolts at hungry reptiles for whom a few chickens weren't enough.

In the end, exhausted and frustrated, the little party beat a hasty retreat up the path through the cornstalks, Shaldis and the others stretching out their awareness to listen for the rustle of huge scaly bodies in the dark away from the trail. They found the king and Kylin both mounted again, torches in hand and looking nervously down at the road around their horses' feet.

"No, no, I haven't had any company," the king explained, dismounting gingerly as the party of magic workers emerged from the cornstalks onto the road. "Just a great deal of rustling, which of course could have been rats or foxes as easily as crocodiles. Indeed, it occurred to me that you might have driven the crocodiles away with spells so potent that they rushed ashore and all this distance inland in a panic. . . . No? Well, a man can hope."

FIFTEEN

We command the fire and the serpents and the stinging insects. . . .

Shaldis watched the main party of king and guards turn along the dark path toward the palace's northern gate. The late moon was rising, full and smiling as a young wife carrying a longed-for child.

It would wither away to nothing in fourteen days, leaving the king to face his ordeal in its darkness.

She rubbed her eyes, her head throbbing. That afternoon's siesta and bath seemed years in the past.

Fourteen days.

Ahead of her, Rachnis, Yanrid, and Kylin talked softly about negotiations with the grocer and whether the Citadel should liquidate some of its hard-won investments in order to purchase a collection of grimoires being offered by the widow of a former Pyromancer in Ith who had hanged himself last spring. Behind, she was aware of Jethan riding with a single lantern, in silence.

"Thank you for doing this tonight," said Summerchild softly, riding at her side as they passed through the city's northern gate. "I know it's late."

It was well past midnight. Even the jostling late-night shoppers, the prostitutes and tavern keepers and sellers of horoscopes and silks who livened the summer nights of the Flowermarket District around them, were retreating to their beds. Customers emerged, chattering happily, from the discreet doors of the Blossom Houses; servants waited till they were out of sight before gratefully putting up the shutters.

Dawn would come soon.

"I meant to ask you to help me scry for the woman in my dream this morning," said Shaldis, "only my father showed up instead."

If bath and siesta felt years ago, the morning had retreated into the mists of the legendary past. They reined their horses apart from the king, his guards, and the other two sisters. Like shadows they passed through the gates as they were closing and along the city's silent streets: Shaldis and Summerchild, Rachnis and Yanrid and the novice Kylin, with Jethan riding behind.

"I'm not sure two of us will be able to find her any more than I could myself," Shaldis went on as they came into the night-drowned Square of the Sun, beneath the Citadel bluff. "But just for not having to ensorcel all the implements myself, I owe you more than I can repay."

"You've repaid me already, just by letting me know there are others of us out there," said the concubine. "By telling me we're not alone."

The Citadel's gates had been closed but not barred, for old Hathmar and Hiero the cook had not known whether anyone who was capable of working a bar by magic from the other side would come back with Yanrid and Rachnis. Kylin took the horses to the stable in the lowest court;

Yanrid led the way on foot up the broad sandstone steps to the court halfway up the bluff where the scrying chamber was located. It was a small building, circular and tiled in pale blue. Jethan followed them in, his lantern throwing their shadows huge across the inside of its dome and gleaming gently in the smooth facets of the crystals there, the mirrors in their frames of silver and iron. Shaldis rubbed her eyes again, then went out to the courtyard fountain to dip up water for the water bowls. She paused by him in the doorway and said softly, "Thank you for coming with us tonight. For shooting those awful crocs down by the lake."

"You don't need to thank me for doing my duty."

Shaldis shrugged. "I want to," she said. She had gone past the stage of being snappish with weariness and had passed into a kind of camaraderie of exhaustion. There was nothing she could do about Jethan acting like Jethan. She looked across into the guardsman's eyes. She was a tall woman, but he stood taller, stiff as the wooden image of some primitive northern warrior god. In the months she'd known him he'd always held her at a distance, disapproving of a woman's power, perhaps—maybe just of a woman who walked around unveiled and carried money in her purse like only men were supposed to. He had risked his life for the king, and for her in the king's service; she was fond of him, as of a brother. A brother who wasn't Tulik.

She asked, "You really haven't seen your family in five years?"

His face remained unmoving, but something softened in his eyes. "It's a long way back to my village." His voice was a murmur no louder than the lap of wavelets on the shore of the lake—a deep voice with the flattish far-north inflection to the words, hard to describe but unmistakable. "Three weeks of travel, even to get to the City of Reeds, and from there all the way down through the canals and the Great Lake. I send my mother letters, but I don't know whether my father reads them to her. I have never had a reply."

Not only Ith, Shaldis reflected, could be destroyed by lake monsters unbeknownst to a soul in the south. She glanced over her shoulder into the lamplit gloom of the scrying chamber. Yanrid bent over the ancient stone tablet, grinding ink for the ink bowls (for which she, Shaldis, should even this moment be bringing him water); Summerchild's hands rested on the table, whispering the spells that would strengthen the drawing power of the questing thoughts.

Her eyes returned to Jethan's.

"I don't know whether I'd be able to see to a place that I know nothing of," she said. "I've never seen your village or your family or anyone there. Sometimes I can get an image in spite of not knowing what I seek. I can focus on your mother's name, or on something you can describe or draw, maybe, to give me something to look for. I could at least see if she's still alive, if your family's house still stands."

Jethan closed his eyes. She saw the muscles tighten in his jaw. "Thank you," he said without inflection in his voice. But when he looked at her again, some of the weariness was lessened from his eyes. "I'd like that. Tomorrow, or the day after. When you are rested. I understand from His Majesty that scrying takes a great deal of energy. I know you have more important tasks."

"Some that mean as much to me," she said, "not that mean more." She turned and crossed the dark court to the fountain, its waters glittering where the light of the traitor moon came over the high walls. In the two years she'd lived in this place, she thought, she'd always known that her father and mother, that Threesie and Foursie, Twinkle and Tulik and youngest brother Zelph, were all less than a mile away on Sleeping Worms Street, should she ever really want to go back there.

For weeks she'd spoken to Pomegranate through these very mirrors and crystals. She knew just how long a journey it was along the waters of the lakes and up through the great cross-country canals. Three weeks from the City of Reeds would put Jethan's home somewhere in the parched rangelands of what had, she guessed, once long ago been a single great stretch of water, but which was now the three dwindling lakes called Mud Lake, Sulphur Lake, and the Lake of Slaves.

A land of tiny villages, of meager crops and herds of skinny goats. Of nomad raids and endless work that broke soul and body, with no books, few tales, no time or energy for music or dance. No relief, save what rye liquor could bring.

No wonder he'd fled. Fled and left them to their own devices, she thought. As she had. Like her, he had done the unthinkable—walked away from his family, to save his own sanity.

After her struggles on the lakeshore to make wards work against crocodiles, Shaldis knew she was too tired to attempt scrying spells. On the way through the night market she'd bought a half-dozen candied dates wrapped up in a plane-tree leaf and divided them with Summerchild, for both were ravenous. Whether at another time their combined strength might have been enough to open the closed doors of distance, she did not know.

But after all their spells and concentration, the crystals, the mirrors, the bowls of water and ink, all remained dark. The woman who had cried to her for help was out there somewhere, but as if she stared out the door of a safe fortress into the blackness of a desert sandstorm, Shaldis saw nothing.

In time, Summerchild went up to the Citadel guest room Rachnis offered her. Shaldis walked her to its door, then returned to the scrying chamber in secret. Her mind numb, her body aching with weariness, she refilled the water bowls, remade the spells.

Our children are dying.

Help us.

The lamps had been quenched, only the stink of burned oil lingered in the dark room. Silence lay on the Citadel, but for the murmur of the fountain in the court.

Help us. . . .

Footfalls behind her, a hand warm on her arm. "You've had enough."

She pulled against Jethan's grip. "You don't understand."

"I understand when someone is too tired to help themselves or anyone else."

She wrenched her arm unavailingly. She might just as well have tried to wrench an oak from the ground with her hands. In the thin light of the setting moon he looked older than his twenty-some years, and his blue eyes seemed very light, like the crystals in her hand. "They will die without our help," she cried, passionate with despair. "They may be dead already." And in her exhaustion and her grief, and her weariness at the thought that she had to go back to her grandfather's house after all this, she burst into tears.

The guardsman put his arms gently around her, disregarding it when she pushed at him; he wore the light leather cuirass of palace duty and it was like trying to push a statue. Or like being embraced by one.

"You need to sleep." His breath whispered against her temple, fluttering the straggles of her hair. "The world is a wide place, Raeshaldis. The gods carry the sky in their hands, light as a silken scarf; they don't need our shoulders to keep it aloft. At least not tonight they don't." And he dried her tears with a handkerchief, taken from some hidden purse at his sword belt—tears that in her more rested moments she would have died rather than let him see her shed. "You cannot save everyone."

She whispered, "I can try."

She didn't know if Jethan heard her. He picked her up in her arms—in their six months of friendship it had always surprised her how physically strong he was—and carried her up the steps to her own chamber in the novices' court. There he laid her on her bed as gently as a nursemaid, and drew the sheet over her. "And I'll be sitting right outside your door," he added. "And if you try to stir out of this room again before first light I'll lock you in."

That sounded more like the Jethan she knew, reflected Shaldis, in the two seconds before she dropped into sleep like a dead woman.

SIXTEEN

Oryn knew exactly where he was, in his dream. He'd thought, as a young man, that after he was obliged to pass through the ordeals of consecration himself he'd no longer have to dream about them, but apparently it didn't work that way. Nothing he'd ever heard of or read could alter dreams.

He was seven years old. He stood in a crowd of people in the dense, still heat of the Place of Kush, the Place of the Lion, but because of the rise of the ground—the slight plateau that lifted all around the Dead Hills—the walls of the Yellow City were not visible. They could have been in the midst of the desert, for all the signs of habitation anyone could see.

The Place of Kush stood isolated, as if to remind the people that the desert that lay beyond the hills was Kush's domain. The God of Destruction—the King of Winds—was one of the six ancient Beings whose temples had formed the core of the Yellow City, whose names were considered unsafe to utter by the great majority of its people. The place, like the other five Sealed Temples, was ruinously old and very small, a stone sanctuary not much bigger than a shed, scored and cracked all over with the violence of sun and time, so that whatever carvings had once covered it were barely to be seen anymore. Kush had as little regard for his own dwelling as he had for anyone else's.

That was one of the several very frightening things about Kush.

Oryn watched the door of the temple open, the door that was sealed at all other times. His father stood on the steps before the door, and it was his father who saw clearest what waited inside, the Servant of Kush wearing the mask of a lion. The adult Oryn—the waking Oryn—knew this from having stood on those steps himself. Two lesser priests stepped out and removed from Taras Greatsword's broad shoulders the crimson military cloak he wore.

They dropped it on the steps, where it lay in the sunlight like a pool of blood, while everyone walked around the side of the temple to the enclosure behind it. Many brought boxes and stools to stand on—some even carried folding ladders, having lugged them the three miles from the city on their shoulders, knowing the crowd would be deep around the Place of the Lion. In his dream the child Oryn didn't know what was happening in the temple; he clung to the hand of his tutor, Soth, whose long hair was still red, his blue eyes sharp and bright.

In his dream Oryn didn't know that the Sun Mages, whose blue-and-gold robes stood out like flowers among the dull clothing of the other spectators, were there for any other purpose than to witness the king's trial before the gods.

In his dream, Oryn didn't know that his father would survive.

The enclosure was huge, far larger than even in waking life, where it stretched six hundred and seventy feet from the temple's bleached stone pillars to the small locked door at its farther end. It was like a great courtyard, dug down into the earth to the depth of twenty feet, and the walls of it were faced with cut stone. When the winter sandstorms filled this pit, sometimes five and seven times in a month, teyn belonging to the temple were put to work digging it out at once: this had been the custom, time out of mind. It was as if the Veiled Gods said, *There is no telling when the king will die.*

Taras Greatsword stepped from the temple, walked down to the enclosure alone. He was naked but for a thin white shift, and his brown hair, short cropped like an ordinary soldier's, glittered with sweat. He stood a head taller than nearly any man in the realm and his body was like hewed oak, marked with the scars of lances, of arrows, of swords. He was thirty-two years old.

Oryn's hand tightened pleadingly on that of his tutor. Only a few months before his father had returned from war against the last Akarian pretenders to the throne at the news of the death of Oryn's mother: poisoned, some said, by other concubines jealous of her position. Greatsword had lingered only long enough to report to his own father and to order Oryn taken away from his nurse and put into the charge of tutors, with strict instructions that the nervous, sensitive boy should be no more picked up or cuddled or have his hand held. *Men do not cling to other men's hands,* he'd said.

It was the last Oryn had seen of his father before his grandfather's death had brought Greatsword back to the Yellow City, to claim the kingship as his own.

As he looked down into the vast pit, Oryn had hated his father, hated him as much as he'd loved his mother and his gentle and lively nurse. He knew his hatred was wrong and that evil would come on him for feeling it—the tales his nurse had told him were full of evil, selfish, hate-filled people who'd come to dreadful ends—but he could not help what he felt. He was glad that Soth disregarded orders and risked a beating by closing his long cold fingers tighter around Oryn's groping hand.

And in his dream, Oryn's hatred had power.

When Taras Greatsword began to run the length of the pit, a door beneath the temple opened and a lion sprang forth. It was red maned and tawny, of the breed that haunted the rangelands beyond the White Lake, and could run down and kill the great long-horned cattle that roved there. Greatsword ran, not looking back, and the lion bounded after him, the crowd all shouting as if they were watching a game or a contest, the men screaming his name. Oryn's heart was in his throat with panic and terror, but in his heart was also anger: for his mother's death, for his nurse who had been sold to another master because Oryn had cried for her.

It was his anger that made his father trip and fall sprawling on the sand.

When he'd dreamed this, even as a child, he'd been able to smell the lion's feral stink, to feel the grinding pain in his father's palms and knees as he struck the sand. The scraping of hot pebbles and abraded flesh before the overwhelming agony of claws, teeth, and slamming weight. In his dream he was unable to hide his eyes or cover his face, but watched the lion tear his father to pieces—heard his father screaming.

Heard himself screaming, *No! Papa, no! I didn't mean it!*

Because, of course, that had never happened.

Oryn jerked awake, trembling, gasping, the stink of the lion and of his father's blood burning his nostrils.

In terror of power, and of what power could mean.

Lamplight made speckled patterns on the tile work of the Pavilion of Lilies. The gauze curtains shifted a little in the garden's scented breeze. On the fountain's edge in the moonlight, one of the palace cats cleaned her white-tipped paws.

Oryn sank back to the pillows of his bed, almost sick from the hammering of his heart. It did no good to tell himself that he knew perfectly well that his father had survived the test, had beaten the drugged lion handily to the second door, and had gone on to rule for seventeen years before he'd died of a stroke after a gazelle hunt and a hot bath.

Nor to reflect that this particular dream hadn't been as bad as others he'd had, concerning the fire or the snakes or the crocodiles. Even when he dreamed about his own experiences of the ordeals, there was always something— some voice in the back of his mind that whispered that he didn't really need to fear. That he'd passed through them safely after all. That the Sun Mages wouldn't *really* let him come to harm.

But the power of the Sun Mages was spent. And there was nothing to take its place. He was like a child again, he thought, staring up at the patterns of the lamplight, the shadowed glimmer of the painted beams. Like that child, watching the one most powerful in his world step into the hands of the gods without protection.

And be devoured.

Knowing that he would be next. And because of his own sins, he was unfit to survive.

※

"Do you see him?" asked Soth, above the soft splashing of the oarsmen's strokes. Pomegranate angled her mirror to differently take the last of the full moon's light, trying to summon Hokiros's fearsome image in its depths. After half the night of walking along the banks where the King's Canal was too shallow now to take a boat, it was good to get into the re-dug section, to feel they were making progress. To feel they were at last returning home.

And to be outrunning the mosquitoes that infested the morass of shallows behind them.

Pomegranate shook her head. "I see something," she reported after a moment. "Moving shapes. The water's murky that deep in the lake, but I think there are several, of different sizes."

Soth muttered a curse.

Pomegranate raised her brows. "That's what you said yourself had to be the case. And at least as far as I've been able to tell, the old boy hasn't come ashore again."

"So far." The king's librarian turned his face from her, rested his arm along the light deck rail, his chin on his wrist.

Pomegranate settled herself against the willow work of the backrests provided for the vessel's passengers, let her mirror fall back among the tangle of her beads, and for a time watched the dark shapes of the banks in silence. Their little cabin was in the barge's stern, barely more than a sunshade of woven straw. The beat of the coxswain's drum was soft, more a heart tap than demanding thunder. The rowers were men, not teyn, and took it turn and turn about to time the strokes.

After a time she asked, "What's that?" and pointed. Soth adjusted his spectacles, the lenses rectangles of reflected silver on either side of the long curve of his nose. After a frustrating evening of negotiating broken shallows and long stretches where the narrow vessel had to be carried, they'd come to one of the canal's newer reaches just after midnight, where Pomegranate could scry for whatever news she could of Hokiros's movements. By midmorning they should see the wide waters of the Great Lake open before them.

Even to the old woman's magical sight there was little around them here to see. The banks stood high above the sunken channel, walls of velvet black on one side, of etiolated pewter on the other. But along the southern rim a greenish light glowed, less bright even than the starlight. Even as she pointed it faded away.

"Did you see it?"

The beaky profile dipped in assent.

"What is it? I used to see something like it from time to time last winter, when I'd sleep in the ruined villas out past the Slaughterhouse District. Sometimes it looked like spots of greenish fire in the Dead Hills, sometimes like a little greenish mist moving along the wadis. I thought it might have something to do with the djinni."

"It could," said Soth slowly. "The king says he saw it, too, far out on the desert when he was trying to contact the djinni. . . . But, no, I don't know what it is." He hooked one elbow over the rail, turned his head to watch the place on the high banks as it retreated behind them with the boat's silent speed. "Any more than I know what those things are in the Lake of the Moon or what Hokiros was or is. I looked through over a hundred volumes in the palace library, and quite a few of the Citadel's as well, for anything about those lights, and there was nothing. That fact alone troubles me."

"That you can't find any record of such a thing?"

"That it's . . . unprecedented. Like our friend Hokiros." He faced her again and drew the thin white mosquito veiling over his face and ears as the boat followed the new-cut channel closer to the shore. His bony hands were perfectly steady; whatever new hope and purpose he had found in his inclusion in the circle of the Raven sisters, it seemed to be proof against the murky memories of his years of drink.

"At one time I thought that my losing the power to do magic was the worst thing that could happen," he said. "I was one of the first whose powers failed. I didn't understand then that it was going to happen to *everyone*, to every single mage I knew. Or that the rains would fail. Or that the djinni would disappear. Or we wouldn't be able to heal with our hands or ward against mice and locusts . . . or lake monsters. Or that the realm would be endangered. Or what else? What comes after that?"

He looked down at the moonlight glittering on the arrow of the bow wave that lapped the hull, on the slick, glassy crests where the oars cut the water and the wet black blades as they lifted free. A tiny craft like a folded leaf, skimming the ebony surface of an unknown universe below.

"That's what worries me," he said. "The fact that we think we've seen the worst of it, and maybe we haven't."

The night was far spent; the air like warmed syrup, scented already with the coming day. Oryn knew better than to sleep again so soon. He groped for the robe of yellow silk that lay over the foot of his bed, slipped from beneath the mosquito bar, and padded to the stand where his harp gleamed gently in the night-light's glow. Moonlight made checkered patterns on the floor, glittered on the waters of the lake.

There was an old love song his nurse had taught him on her wooden flute. He picked it out, sweet fantasies of embellishment, then simple phrases of that ancient tune: longing and love, hope and delight. *This is for my Summerchild,* he thought, *dreaming her dreams. May they not concern crocodiles.*

This is for my Rainsong Girl.

He started through it a second time when lamplight joggled among the jasmine. A moment later the stout little form of Geb emerged from the garden. Oryn put the harp aside.

Someone was with Geb. A young man, dark and bearded and wearing the striped coat of a small-time merchant, a traveler in goods from one settlement to the next.

Oryn thought, quite calmly, *Damn.*

Nobody ever came into the gardens of the king in the middle of the night bearing *good* news.

"My lord," said Geb, "this is Poru, of the merchant clan of Brûl. He's come from the village of Three Wells, in the rangeland out by the Dead Hills, a day's ride east. They're dead there, my lord." The chamberlain's sweet alto voice shook a little; in the light of the lamp he held, his round, ageless face was like collapsed suet under its layer of cochineal and kohl, and his eyebrows stood out like two strokes of black paint. "They're all dead."

SEVENTEEN

When Shaldis woke, very late in the morning, Jethan was gone. Despite the fact that he was managing, disapproving, and old-fashioned enough to believe that even a woman who had the powers of magic needed protection from the rough world, she was conscious of disappointment.

Either Kylin or Hiero the cook had left a kettle of scrub water simmering over the coals of the outdoor oven in the kitchen yard for her. When she entered the refectory, shaking her wet hair through her fingers to dry it, she expected to find the immense stone chamber empty and hoped to find at least that Hiero the cook had left her some bread and the dregs of the teapot. Instead she found, a little to her surprise, both Yanrid and Rachnis still at the single small table in the corner. The rest of the chamber, where close to a hundred and fifty Sun Mages and novices had once been served, echoed softly with the murmur of their voices in the rich yellow sunlight from the windows.

"A messenger came for the Lady Summerchild before daybreak," said the crystalmaster, beckoning Shaldis to join them. "Your boy Jethan escorted her to the palace. I gather they would be riding out of the city at once."

"There was a plague in a village called Three Wells." Her fellow novice, Kylin, draped in a kitchen apron over his robe, dropped onto the bench at her side and poured a cup of tea for himself, before Shaldis could comment on the fact that Jethan was not "her" boy. "They say everyone died." He sounded both excited and scared; all thought of Jethan vanished in a stab of sickened shock.

"Of plague?"

Our children are dying. . . .

I can't be too late! Not having come so close!

"If they died of plague it was from unclean dishes." Hiero the cook appeared in the pantry door, tall and slightly stooped, his wise, kindly face luxuriantly bearded and radiating serenity. He looked exactly like every wizard in every story Shaldis had ever heard, far more so than the two rather sleepy old ruffians across the table from her. "Or from a lethargy caused by laziness."

Kylin gulped down his tea and got to his feet, darted back into the kitchen.

Yanrid, of whom Shaldis had spent her first eighteen months at the Citadel absolutely terrified, grunted. "Disaster struck Three Wells the night before last," he said. "Had the woman in your dream been there she would not have said *Our children die,* but *We all perish.*" He smeared a little goat cheese on his bread, studied the result in a shaft of sunlight that was already growing hot. "And in any case there is little you can do. And nothing that you could have done."

Shaldis knew he was right—knew it down to her bones. Why then, she wondered, did bitterness and anger sicken her so? She pushed her own bread away, her hand shaking, and sat for a time gazing into the shafts of sunlight, the shadows beyond. *Did I leave the scrying chamber too early? If I hadn't let Jethan talk me into abandoning it then, would I have heard from her?*

Did I really destroy our only hope through my weakness, my carelessness?

She looked across at the craggy-faced man opposite her, saw the dark eyes that had always seemed so unfeeling still on her, filled with an understanding concern.

"How did you *do* it?" she asked softly. "How can you do it still? Knowing the outlander mages, knowing they have to be going through something just as terrible as we're going through here, if their magic has faded. Friends, people you've known for years. You know what's happening and you can't do anything! She could be dying—she could be dead already."

"If she is dead, there was nothing you could have done." Yanrid's voice was like granite, unmoving. But not, she realized, because he didn't feel. "If she is alive, there is nothing that you can do to keep her from dying tomorrow . . . or not dying. I think no one who has our powers—your powers," he corrected himself gently, "ever loses the feeling that we owe it to everyone to help them. And until we find a way to step past that, there is no end to the harm we do ourselves and others. We do what we can. And we come to understand the things that we cannot do. You don't know whether this woman is alive or dead. It isn't necessary to hurt yourself thinking she's dead when, in fact, you simply don't know."

"It comes with age, child," sighed Rachnis, giving his white hair a single deft twist onto the back of his head and skewering it into place with a stylus. Then amusement glinted in his black eyes and he added, "Or anyway I hope it will to me," and they all laughed.

"As for what you can do," said Yanrid, "since this woman seems able to communicate through dreams rather than regular scrying—a method which has been written about but for which no spell of control exists—I suggest that each night before you sleep, you meditate on the healing herbs that will bring down fever and the spells to be written over them that add to their strength. With luck these things will enter your own dreams, and she may read them there."

"But what if she lives in the deep desert?" asked Shaldis. "Or the mountains—she has to be somewhere far away, not to have heard of healing with herbs to begin with."

"That only means you must meditate on as many different varieties as you can. I'm sure"—here he glanced beside him at Rachnis—"that we can come up with enough herbals in the library to keep you and your unknown sister busy."

Shaldis drew a deep breath, as if the old men had lifted some great weight from her shoulders. It hadn't even occurred to her that others had communicated in this fashion before. "Thank you. I'll do that. And if there's anything else you think of that I can do . . ."

"Yes," said Yanrid firmly. "Take care of yourself, so that when you do sleep, your own dreams will be clearer. As I said, no one has ever come up with a method of opening this dream communication at will, but if it happens again, any notes you can take on the subject will—"

Kylin swept back into the refectory, a towel slung over one shoulder and sand all over his apron, with which they scoured the pots. "This came for you." He fished in his belt satchel and brought forth a tablet of the sort that merchants' accounts were tallied on. The two wooden leaves were tied together with green string and sealed with the seal of the Clan Shaldeth.

Another attempt last night. Grandfather well, though shaken. A maid killed.

How like Tulik—Shaldis recognized her brother's textbook-neat hand—not to bother to say which of the maids had died.

She closed the diptych, slid it into the purse at her belt, and snagged an orange to eat as she walked. "I don't know when I'll be back."

"That can't possibly be Three Wells, can it?" Oryn shaded his eyes with his hand against the horrific glare of the forenoon sun. The morning's warm cerulean had burned out of the sky: the Hero Sun, the mages called this strengthening, nearly vertical heat. The province of Ka-Issiya, the god of the golden noon.

The rangeland beneath it was a gilded anvil, still as death.

The wheeling vultures were too distant to be more than minute specks swimming in blue emptiness, but Oryn thought there were a lot of them.

"You said the village lay due east and a full day's ride,

did you not?" Oryn turned in the saddle as the young salt merchant Poru reined his horse up beside the king's.

"I did, my lord. There are vultures there right enough, or at least there were when I passed through it yesterday. But we'd not be seeing them yet." Like the rest of the cavalcade the young man's face was wrapped in gauze veils against the sun, and the skin around his dark eyes glistened with sweat and ointment.

Numet— captain of the first company of the king's guard—joined the little group at the forefront of the line of guards, remounts, and provision mules, and squinted against the blazing light in the direction of Oryn's worried gaze. "That'll just be a dead steer, is all, sir." Since they'd ridden out of the city in the darkness before dawn, they'd seen more than one picked-over skeleton. He urged his horse forward, then turned back when the king made no move to follow.

"That's a lot of vultures for a single steer, isn't it?"

The captain looked again. He was a broad-shouldered young man from one of the cadet branches of the House Jothek, chosen like many officers of the guards for his good looks. "It could be two or three steers," he offered. "Maybe there was a stampede, and several fell down a wadi all together."

"Hmn." Oryn untoggled the spyglass from his saddle horn, rose in the stirrups to get a better look. Behind him, Elpiduyek—master of the king's parasol—unfurled the white-and-gold rooflet, and the first company closed ranks around the little knot of captain, merchant, royal mount, royal concubine, and parasol bearers. Geb and Elpiduyek had both pleaded with Oryn to travel by litter as befit the king—and to bring along a second litter for

Summerchild rather than have her ride horseback like some trooper's moll—to little avail. Oryn had spent the first dozen years of his reign lolling in a litter on those few occasions when he went out of the Yellow City at all, and he knew exactly how long that sort of elegant transport took to even get out the palace gate.

Much as he loathed jolting over the rangelands on horseback—not to mention the weeks it would take to repair the sun's ravages on his complexion, ointment, veils, and parasol notwithstanding—he understood in the marrow of his aching bones that there was no time to lose.

Maybe no time at all.

In the sharp circle of the spyglass the vultures made a wheeling black column, like a dust devil. He thought, but he wasn't sure, that its base was far too wide for even two or three dead cattle.

He turned in his saddle, scanned the horizon toward the east, though Three Wells would be far too distant yet for any trace even of a vulture column to be seen.

"Poru, my dear boy, is there a wadi there where the vultures are circling? Were they there when you rode past this place yesterday afternoon?" He passed his spyglass to the salt merchant.

The young man studied the column for a time, then said, "That looks about where Black Cow wadi should lie. It's true cattle or goats sometimes fall over the edge and kill themselves, but it's also true that bandits, or rogue nomads, will sometimes ambush caravans there. The edge of the wadi overhangs and makes good cover. Everyone who makes the rounds of the villages knows about it."

"Do they indeed?" Oryn took the spyglass back and

passed it to Summerchild. She looked through it for a time, then folded it up, handed it back, and drew from the reticule at her belt a silver hand mirror. This she gazed into for so long that Numet began to fidget and look pointedly at the angle of their shadows and off in the direction of Three Wells village. Oryn paid him no attention—he knew perfectly well that if he said they were going to camp for a week exactly where they were, the captain would be required to acquiesce no matter what his opinion was—but kept a close watch on Summerchild's topaz-blue eyes.

He saw her brows draw together in puzzled distress. "There's at least a dozen men dead there," she said at last. "They look like nomads, the an-Ariban tribe, I think. They're not one of the warlike groups—mostly sheep stealers and tomb robbers."

"If they met a bad end, serve 'em right." Numet laughed. "Thieving beggars. Why we should make ourselves late to the nooning site over it—"

"Heaven forfend that we should," agreed Oryn affably. "Still, I *am* the king. And I'd like to have a look."

He could feel the glares of his chamberlain and parasol bearer like knives sticking in his back as he reined in the direction of the vultures.

On her way to the Bazaar District along the broad Avenue of Gold—with its handsome houses, beautiful temples, and even-more-beautiful public baths—Shaldis ran through in her mind the women of her grandfather's household. Her father had mentioned the addition of one maid, whose name would inevitably be Eight Flower and who would almost certainly be a child, knowing her grandfather's habits of domestic economy.

But in spite of Pebble's surmise yesterday evening in the baths, Shaldis would have been surprised to have little Eight Flower turn out to be the Crafty behind the murder attempts. A child old enough to do the heavy housework required even of very young maids would have been old enough to recognize the potential of her own power and, depending on her nature, either offer it for sale to the head of the house or use it to flee.

A child young enough to be utterly dependent on adults, her grandfather would not have bought.

Her sisters? Magic had generally appeared in boys at age four or five, then vanished again until puberty. Shaldis wasn't sure whether this pattern held true for girls as well. Foxfire, the youngest in the circle of the Raven sisters, had been fourteen when she had consciously begun to use her full powers, but that had been at a time when all over the Yellow City, such powers had begun to stir in the hearts of those who later became crafty.

Foursie was twelve, Twinkle eight.

Shaldis was almost positive that had there been another Raven sister in the household in the months preceding her departure—if her mother (difficult as it was to even think about picturing that!) or Aunt Apricot or old Yellow Hen had begun to develop power—she would have known. She would have felt it in the walls of the house.

And she was almost—though not quite—certain that they would never have left her to suffer and be cast out alone.

If they had developed such power after her departure, they almost certainly would have gotten word to her at the Citadel.

That left the maids.

She considered them, one by one; considered the world in which they lived. The world that, but for her propensity for sneaking over the courtyard wall in Tulik's clothes, would have been the whole of her own world until her marriage to sulky Forpen Gamert.

A world of gossip and hard work, of hair pullings and whispered secrets after the lamps were out. Early on, she'd fled from the chattering hive of the maids' dormitory to sleep and study in one of the attics above the kitchen—the heat was ghastly in midsummer and the rats worse—but she'd still grown up in their world of horoscopes and astrological almanacs, of petty thefts and pettier rivalries, of shirked tasks, love notes from camel drivers, and the vital importance of who knew what about whom.

A world of soul-killing smallness, thought Shaldis with a qualm of bitter memory. And yet, not nearly as bad as that desolate northland village Jethan had fled. Most were illiterate. Cook, Four Flower, and Aunt Apricot spent their evenings drinking cheap *sherab* and smoking hemp, and who could blame them? When One Flower— Old Flower, everyone called her (out of Grandfather's hearing)—had grown too old even to grind corn with the teyn, Chirak had tried to sell her: Shaldis's father had paid the small asking price through an intermediary, and the old woman shared the cook's tiny chamber behind the kitchen, a secret the whole household kept from its head. Two Flower—Cook's older sister—was nearly that feeble as well when Shaldis had last lived in the house, and was going blind.

None of them—with the possible exception of her uncle Tjagan's concubine the sharp-witted Nettleflower—had ever impressed Shaldis as imaginative or outward looking, qualities she associated with magic. And yet, she reflected, as she crossed the Avenue of the Sun and plunged into the lively string of open-air marketplaces that led toward the Grand Bazaar, Pebble was of nearly the same mental makeup as the maids: simple hearted, even a little simpleminded, shy in the presence of adults and loving the animals and birds with which she surrounded herself.

Nettleflower—a slim woman whose beauty always reminded Shaldis of first-quality honey—had the sly intelligence that probes for secrets. Shaldis remembered her as the troublemaker in the stifling little world of the maids: always prying out information and carrying tales to Chirak Shaldeth, whom she seduced within twenty-four hours of coming into the household, to the deep distress of Shaldis's grandmother.

Chirak had grown bored with the girl within a year and had, according to Habnit, passed her along to Uncle Tjagan shortly after Shaldis's grandmother died. The other maids hated her. Nettleflower might not want to murder Chirak, reflected Shaldis, as she peeled her breakfast orange with her fingernails and edged her way through the narrow Lane of the Blue Walls. But her services might easily be bought by someone who did.

Rohar God of Women, she prayed, *don't let her be the Crafty in the household!* She caught the prayer back guiltily, knowing how badly the Raven sisterhood needed every woman of power. But the thought of working with Nettleflower, the thought of the havoc she'd cause, turned her stomach.

In any case, Rohar of the Braided Hair must have been feeling in a benign mood that day, because her wish was granted. When she stepped through the gate into the kitchen court and dropped from her the Gray Cloak of illusion that she'd assumed, almost automatically, to pass through the dusty chaos of the outer court of the camel drivers, the first thing she asked old Yellow Hen was "What happened? Who was killed?"

"Nettleflower." The old lady spat without missing a beat at her grinding quern. "Good riddance to the little slut. Tulik wants to see you."

EIGHTEEN

S he was killed in the passageway that leads past Grandfather's study, out to the alley." Tulik lifted back the sheet that covered Nettleflower's body, where it lay on a worktable in the kitchen storeroom. Shaldis winced at the sight of the contorted, blue-lipped face, the blood-dabbled disorder of the honey-blond hair. "Grandfather was awakened by the sounds of someone moving in his room. Before he could cry out for help, someone rushed at him in the dark, slashing and clawing at him. He thrust his attacker off and heard him—or her," he added with the air of one making a concession, "flee. So bruised and shaken was he that it was several minutes before he could follow, and when he did, he found poor Nettleflower lying dead on the floor of the passageway and the alley door standing open. He then came back upstairs and awakened me, and we both tried to revive her, but, alas, were too late."

He drew the sheet back over the girl's face. Through the open archway into the kitchen court, the grumbling scrape of the grinding querns made a soft background of sound, and with them came the stinks of dust, of woodsmoke, of indigo boiling in the dye cauldron. The house had always been a place of violence, thought Shaldis, looking down at the threadbare linen that outlined the dead girl's sharp nose and curving breasts. Never a day had gone by here, in her recollection, that had not been rendered hideous by her grandfather's screaming rages and hissing rod.

Though it came from the outside, this murder seemed to be of a piece with all those recollections, all those days of sickened fear.

"What was Nettleflower doing down in Grandfather's garden in the middle of the night?" she asked. "Had she been with my uncle Tjagan?"

Tulik hesitated, and from the doorway, Foursie—who was leaning in the arch with Twinkle—replied at once, "No, 'cause Uncle's gone out to Kamath to look at camels."

"Foursie, take your sister upstairs and get to work on your sewing," ordered their brother. "She shouldn't see something like this—nor you, either." He turned back to Shaldis. "I can only assume that she'd left or . . . or had forgotten something in Uncle's room and went back to get it." More confidently, he went on, "In fact I think I heard her in the gallery—I have the room up there between Uncle's and Father's now, you know. I wasn't sleeping well, and I *did* hear her walk past."

"But you didn't hear her being killed?" Shaldis pulled the sheet aside again, revealing the whole of the body in its torn and rumpled red dress. The dress she recognized as one of Aunt Apricot's. Nettleflower had probably talked Tjagan into giving it to her, the way she'd gotten most of her grandmother's jewelry. "Looking at the state of her clothing and the blood in her hair, she fought. She wasn't just strangled, she was battered to death against the walls of the passage. You didn't hear this?"

Tulik's eyes shifted. "If a wizard did it, he could have kept anyone from hearing."

Shaldis's skin prickled, as if tiny lightning bolts had run up her spine.

Before she could speak, a shadow darkened the archway and her grandfather snapped, "Of course a wizard did it, imbecile! How else could he have undone the bolts in the passageway door by the study? And I know what wizard it was, too! It was that poisonous charlatan Ahure—"

Shaldis said, "What?"

At the same time Tulik corrected, in the voice of a man correcting a child, "Of course that's only a guess, Grandfather, since your room was *pitch-dark* and you *didn't see* your attacker—"

"Nonsense!" Chirak Shaldeth thrust his grandson aside as Tulik attempted to ease him back into the courtyard. He pushed his way into the storeroom and caught Shaldis roughly by the arm, as he had when she was a child living in this house. "I always thought it was that scoundrel Ahure and now I'm sure of it! A stinking leech and a liar! He's sought to cheat me and steal from me for years!"

Shaldis said nothing, only stared at the old man in shock. He had clearly been battered by someone, his cheeks and forehead marked by the parallel scores of claw marks or nail scratches, and bits of dried blood still stained his unkempt white mustache. He wore only his bed robe, though it was late in the morning. Shaldis looked down and saw his wrists and hands, too, marked as if someone had tried to tear something from his powerful grip.

"Grandfather . . ." Tulik stepped between them, closed his hand over the old man's wrist, and stared hard into his eyes. "You're not feeling well, remember. You're still quite shaken up."

"Balderdash! I'm well enough to know—"

"You're not, Grandfather." With their faces close together—and within a few handsbreadths of Shaldis's own—she saw again how similar they were, not in shape or coloring but in expression. It was hard to recall her brother was only sixteen, his cheeks innocent of any trace of down. "Trust me, Grandfather," he went on, emphasizing the words. "*You need to rest,* probably for the remainder of the day. You've had a terrible shock."

For a moment Shaldis saw the old fire glint in Chirak's eye, as if he were going to lunge forward and bite his grandson's face off.

Then the fire died. It was like watching a lion go down under a hunter's spear. Shaldis felt shock and dismay at her own flash of pity.

"You're right, my boy," muttered Chirak. "I . . . You're right." His shoulders slumped, as if all strength had gone out of him, and he made no protest as the youth led him away across the hot sunlight of the court. Shaldis heard him say, "It was Ahure," but his tone was that of a petulant child. "He's a thief. He wants to rob me of what's mine."

"Yes, Grandfather, I know he is But you mustn't say so to just anyone."

Why not?

Shaldis turned back to look again at Nettleflower's body. The nails of both hands were broken, as if she'd torn and clawed at her attacker's face and wrists. When Shaldis looked more closely, she saw blood and skin clotted up under them, and lodged in that blood, a stiff white hair from a beard.

The sun was high and blisteringly hot when Oryn and his cavalcade reached Black Cow wadi. The horses were beginning to labor in the heat; the men bowed down under it. They would soon have to break their journey and set up even the minimal shelter of army shades, to hide through the worst of the burning noon. With this detour—as Captain Numet and Geb both pointed out on several occasions during the ride—they wouldn't reach Three Wells until almost twilight.

Yet his instincts told him that whatever had destroyed Three Wells, it would be best to know if it was capable of reaching out this far beyond that doomed village and killing again.

He glanced sidelong at Poru as they rode, remembering the young salt merchant's description of what he had found when he and his men had ridden into the village the morning before. *They all died at once, my lord, for 'twas clear none had tried to bury any other or even drag them into the houses from the streets. The birds were just beginning to come down as we made the town, the sky just growing light. Wolves must have been there in the night, I think, for I saw pieces of bodies in the streets as well as bodies still whole. It was as if a battle had passed over the place, yet there was no blood. We stood only at the edge of the town and looked. If it was sickness that had done it, we wanted to carry none away. It was clear none moved about alive.*

Oryn wondered whether Poru and his camel drivers had thought about the possibility that some survivor had lingered, incapacitated, in one of the houses. If that had been the case, he reflected, that survivor was undoubtedly dead now. And another quick look at the thin dark face of the merchant, the exhausted mouth and haunted eyes, told him that yes, Poru had thought about it, probably many times on his ride to the Yellow City to deliver the news.

Did you look into the teyn compound? he'd asked as Geb had fetched them coffee and the palace pages had darted away with orders to fetch Summerchild from the Citadel of the Mages and to ready a cavalcade and guards.

Poru had shaken his head. It was true, Oryn knew, that teyn suffered the same diseases as humankind. A teyn could take a disease like smallpox from a man, or pass it to him, much as a man could take a cold from a dog.

Still, if the teyn had been closed into their compound

before the disease struck, he didn't like to think of them shut there, without food and probably without water, for the day that it had taken for Poru and his men to reach the Yellow City and for this second day that it would take for help to return. *We heard the cattle lowing in the byres,* Poru had said, *the asses complaining and the camels in their stables. Yet we dared not enter the town.*

At least they all had that much sense, Oryn reflected, his glance going beyond the merchant to Summerchild, and to the baggage ass led by her most faithful maid Lotus, bulging with packets of herbs and books of healing. He edged his horse to Summerchild's side, asked her softly, "This woman Raeshaldis sought for in the scrying crystals, the Raven sister who called out for help. You say she spoke of sickness?"

"She did, yes. And of healing 'no longer flowing' from wizards' hands. Yet if she was from Three Wells, she'd be close enough to the Yellow City to have heard of healing with herbs, which indeed nomads and midwives have been using for centuries without benefit of wizardry."

"That may be so," murmured Oryn. "But it's also true that I've never heard of an herb or a nomad or a midwife who could cure madness. Or indeed, of any sickness that produces it to the degree that it would wipe out a town."

Vultures stretched out their naked heads at the intruders as the king and his guards came up on the dry deep crevasse of Black Cow wadi; opened bloody beaks to squawk curses and spread their soot-dark wings. The nomads lay, not in the wadi itself, but about a dozen yards from its edge, crumpled among the summer-yellowed bunchgrass. Their dark hair was wet with blood, their eye sockets stared sightlessly at the hard colorless sky. All men, Oryn observed. A cattle-stealing or tomb-robbing party almost certainly. All were small and lithe, their swarthy cheeks, chins, foreheads marked with the black tattoos of the an-Ichor tribe. Summerchild's guess at an-Ariban hadn't been far wrong—both tribes wove a cloth dyed red and indigo, only the pattern of the stripes differing.

"They at least didn't die of sickness," murmured Jethan, stepping from the saddle and turning one of the bodies over with his foot. The man's throat had been slit with some rough weapon, a blunt-edged tool or a chipped stone. "Yet their tracks lead back toward Three Wells."

"Teyn did this." Captain Numet raised his head from an examination of the scuff marks around one of the bodies. Oryn himself had already seen the flat, crooked, splay-toed tracks lacing everywhere, interspersed with the marks of dragged knuckles. He dismounted cautiously, gathering the fluttering golden silk of his robes to keep it from snagging in the ubiquitous camel thorn, and picked his way among the corpses. Small hoof gouges, torn-off bridles and saddlecloths, huge gouts of splashed blood clearly announced that the an-Ichor had had at least a couple of their tough little desert ponies with them. Wilding teyn—the untamed bands that roved the near-desert preying on insects and lizards—would kill a straying goat or sheep if they thought they could get away with it, but it was unheard of for them to attack men.

Or at least it had been, up until that spring.

"I don't like this," Oryn murmured as Summerchild returned to his side. He patted under his veils at the sweat rolling down his plump cheeks. "I don't like this at all. Before last spring you never heard of teyn attacking men at all, not even the deep-desert nomads who hunt them for the market. I didn't know they could organize themselves for an attack, for one thing, much less cut throats with edged weapons. How can they coordinate an attack, if they don't speak among themselves?"

"Nor do wolves," pointed out Summerchild. "They seem to do all right." She followed the scratched and bloody marks where a horse had been dragged toward the wadi's edge. Dry wind lifted the ends of her veils like a silken flag. She shaded her eyes as she looked up at Oryn. "But the teyn who turned on their masters at Dry Hill last spring were mingled with wildings, when you caught up with them, you and Bax and his guards."

The brush was thicker closer to the wadi's edge. Oryn held up the hem of his robe, knowing Geb would kill him—or kill himself—if the green-embroidered saffron silk ended up snagged. "You don't suppose the teyn in the Three Wells compound—"

The teyn that erupted out of the brush around and in front of him emerged so fast, and so close, that Oryn could only gape in shock in the split second between their appearance and being thrown to the ground, seeing the rocks in their hands, the broken-off spikes of sharp bone. With an inarticulate yowl of fright he rolled in time to avoid having his skull smashed; felt huge hands—hands with the startling strength of animals'—clutch at him; smelled the musty, sweetish stench of their flesh. Then the air above him exploded in a searing burst of white fire and the teyn jerked back in shock, and the next second Summerchild strode forward, hand uplifted to cast a second spell. At the same instant Jethan waded into the midst of them, sword flashing bloody in the sun.

Oryn tried to scramble to his feet and got kicked over

again as more teyn came pouring out of the wadi, silent—
silent as horrors in a dream. Numet and his men charged,
either afoot or on horseback, swords glinting in the hot
noon light; and teyn rose up out of every thicket of
mesquite and camel thorn in the landscape, brush that
Oryn would have taken oath couldn't have sheltered rabbits. Jethan waded in among them, striking at the hairy
faces, the massive hands, and tusked, gaping mouths.
Oryn rolled out of the way of a cavalry mount's hooves,
the teyn who held him breaking and fleeing only to re-
assemble and charge. They hurled rocks, sprang in fives
and sixes at the charging horses, dragged and clutched at
the riders. More white light exploded in the air, and a
horse screamed as it was brought down. Oryn gasped,
"Dear gods!" and it seemed to him that teyn were everywhere, rising from the wadi and the brush and converging
on the little knot of horsemen from all points of the
compass.

"Back!" he heard Numet's voice shouting above the
din. "This way back!" At the same instant Jethan dragged
his horse to a foaming halt almost on top of Oryn, two remounts on lead.

"Summerchild!" yelled Oryn as Jethan heaved him
onto one of the remounts. Three teyn tried to swarm them
from the other side, grabbing bridle and stirrups, slashing
with their splinters of bone; and the young guardsman
laid about him with his sword, cutting off hands and
heads as the horses reared and thrashed.

"Back that way!"

"Summerchild!" It wasn't at all like battles in songs
and Oryn hadn't the slightest idea where Summerchild
was or if she was alive or dead; and with the dust kicked

up thicker and thicker around them like a fog and horses and guards and teyn pouring in all directions around them, he couldn't imagine how he'd find out if she was all right until after it was over and it was too late.

"Ride!" yelled Jethan, slapping the flank of Oryn's horse hard.

The horse leaped, Oryn looking wildly around him. A thrown rock hit him in the back with an impact like a club and another half-dozen teyn were around him. More rocks rained; a bone dagger ripped into his boot and his leg, then Jethan came charging out of the choking yellow curtain of the dust to grab the horse's bridle.

A trumpet blasted shrilly, signaling in which direction everyone was to go. Overheated and tired as they were, the horses galloped full tilt for nearly half a mile before Numet shouted, "Pull up!" and the whole stampede slowed to a milling circle.

Only then did Oryn see Summerchild, safely mounted nearby.

The next thing he saw was the line of settling dust they'd just fled, jagged and dotted with the silent, crouching teyn.

Numet—transformed from a slightly foppish princeling to a battlefield commander by a liberal coating of dust and blood—was already counting his men. Oryn picked out Jethan's sable mane, Lotus clinging gamely to young Poru's horse's crupper, and Geb and the servants clustering together with the spare horses and the baggage asses. Elpiduyek was sobbing in frustrated rage at the loss of the royal parasol, which lay like the broken corpse of a gilded bird, halfway between the royal party and the crouching line of teyn.

The king rode back to Numet's side. "What in the name of the gods was that all about? Has there *ever* been an attack by teyn on mounted troops?"

"You know there hasn't." Jethan and Summerchild joined them. "You would have been told."

"Never, my lord," affirmed Numet with the crossed-hands gesture that called Ean to witness his oath. "And, by the gods, they'll be taught a lesson. Firmin."

A boyish trooper near them urged his mount closer, dipped a quick salaam to the king.

"Ride back to the city at once. Notify Commander Bax that we were attacked by a major force of wilding teyn and that we need reinforcements, a hundred riders at least. Are you all right, my lord?" the captain added as Firmin trotted to the knot of remounts to switch horses before riding away. His own mount, Oryn saw, was stumbling with heat and weariness. It would be a terrible ride back, through the desolate country in the hammering heat of the noon.

"I'm well." Oryn wiped his face and winced, then looked with surprise at the blood on his hand.

"I told you you should have remained in the city." Geb urged his horse nervously into the group. "What on earth will it serve for you to put yourself into danger like this?"

"They're not advancing on us." Jethan's quiet voice rode effortlessly over the chamberlain's shrill despair. The young guardsman circled back to the little group around captain and king, and gestured with one arm toward the teyn. As the dust was settling they could still be seen, squatting in a ragged line perhaps three-quarters of a mile long, stretched across the direction in which Three Wells lay. The ground behind them was dotted with the slain and with dark splashes where blood soaked into the ground. The vultures were beginning to come down again. "They seem to be waiting."

"Insolent beasts," Numet fumed. "They'll be taught a lesson for them to carry to their kinsfolk . . ."

"But what lesson will they be taught?" wondered Oryn softly. The cavalcade grouped again and moved back in the direction from which they'd come through the brutal shimmer of noon heat. The teyn did not follow, but neither did they disperse. They only waited.

For what?

"Captain—Jethan—Was it my imagination or were there both wilding teyn and escaped domestics in the band that attacked us?"

Numet looked nonplussed by the question, but Jethan said, "Both, Lord King. I'm guessing the domestics escaped from the compound at Three Wells. The wildings probably moved in the moment they could see the villagers dead."

"Good heavens," gasped Numet, "you don't think the wildings killed the villagers?"

"Poru said specifically that the majority of the corpses were unharmed," said Summerchild quickly. "Only a few, he said, seemed to be dismembered. The teyn would have butchered the cattle in the stalls as well, and he said he heard them alive." Even in the chaos of battle she'd kept herself demurely veiled— Oryn supposed that was something Pearl Women were taught to do—and her delicate brows stood out dark against her face. "I understand that the people in other villages—and in the cities as well—need to be warned that the teyn must be more closely guarded. But I think we need to take care how we warn, lest teyn who hadn't the slightest thing to do with this suffer the consequences of their masters' fears."

"But there's no way of telling which teyn have nothing to do with rebellion," pointed out Numet. "You can't know what's going on in those thick skulls of theirs! God of war, I've never seen so great a band of them! Never heard of more than a dozen together in the wilds!"

The riders had drawn up in a sand flat where not even clumps of rabbitbrush would offer shelter to a creeping assault; the men were beginning to set up shades for the nooning and to string out into a perimeter guard. With his spyglass Oryn could still see a teyn or two, only dark specks now, but sitting precisely where they'd left them, across the line of march toward Three Wells.

"We cannot allow this to continue," Numet went on as Oryn was helped from his horse by Geb and the other camp servants and guided toward the single small tent that had been set up. The captain leaped down from his horse and followed, gesturing as he walked. "Surely Your Majesty can see that that must be your first consideration, the first consideration"—he didn't so much as move his eyes in Summerchild's direction—"of the . . . the persons of power under Your Majesty's command."

Oryn stopped and stood, shading his eyes, looking quietly at the captain. Around them, the little band of guards was unpacking waterskins and field rations of curds, dates, and boiled rice. Though the teyn were no more than distant dots now among the rocks and scrub, no man's hand was more than a few inches from his sword; and as the cavalry mounts were unsaddled, the tack was put at once onto the fresh horses, picketed under guard in their lines.

"I agree that the matter must be my first consideration," said Oryn. "Oh, stop fussing, Geb, do, and look after the men who were genuinely wounded; I'm not going to die of a bruise. And I do hope we'll be able to find a way to keep this sort of thing from occurring again . . . once we figure out exactly what this sort of thing actually is and what it means."

NINETEEN

It didn't take Shaldis more than a few moments to ascertain that whoever had opened the door that led from the passageway—where Nettleflower's body had been found—it hadn't been the former Blood Mage Ahure.

Shaldis knew Ahure. In addition to having worked magic at his side in the spring, when both had participated in the great rite that had attempted to bring the month-late rains, she had at one time suspected him of murdering three of her fellow Raven sisters and had visited his quarters when he'd still been Lord Jamornid's court mage. She was familiar not only with the characteristic feel of his spells imbued in the walls there but with the calculated charlatanism by which he'd maintained his position for months—perhaps years—after his powers were utterly gone.

Someone had used magic to move the latch on the

passageway door. Shaldis could feel it when she put her hand on the iron-strapped mountain oak, the wrought-iron bar. But she didn't think it had been last night. Two nights ago, or three. The same magic she'd felt in her grandfather's room, she thought, her long fingers tracing the Sigil of Deep Awareness, her eyelids half closing in a listening trance.

But it hadn't been Ahure. It didn't feel like the magic of a Blood Mage at all. The magic practiced by that order had always filled her with disgust and unease, its obsessive intensity repelling her as much as the Blood Mages did themselves. Those she had met had been, for the most part, a dirty and frightening group, their tongues, lips, and earlobes pierced with ragged scars and holes where they drew thorned strings through, to concentrate their own power through blood and pain. Many had cut off fingers when they needed to source great power or had gashed open their shaved scalps.

Shaldis wondered what her own reaction might be, if she were to learn that such mutilation was the only sure way to raise power these days.

Let's not think about that right now.

She stepped a few paces back along the plastered walls of the passageway, traced again the Sigil of Deep Awareness, and breathed her mind into the mud brick underneath.

The queasy reek of rage and violence rose through her, the stink of blood and perfume. The shouting horror of rage so blinding, so unreasoning, that it amounted to madness. Shaldis jerked her mind back from it: *Was the killing like THAT?*

Insane fury like the screaming of trumpets?

And no magic at all. Not last night. Not in connection with Nettleflower's death.

She stood for a time in the narrow passageway, looking along its shadowy arch to the hot greens and flower spangles of the garden. As she watched, Tulik came down the stair, hastened through the archway at the far end of the garden into the kitchen court—looking for her, she supposed.

Her brother was sixteen. It was hard to remember that, seeing how he spoke to the servants, to the teyn, to their father, even. He had spoken casually about having a room off the gallery above the inner court, a privilege accorded only to the men of the family, her father and Uncle Tjagan.

A room, she guessed, that had been taken away from her father's modest suite.

For at least two years before Shaldis had left the household, the boy had been checking their father's bookkeeping—which grew less reliable as each day drew on—and assisting their grandfather in the trading end of the business, while Chirak filled his post as proctor of the Grand Bazaar. As proctor, she knew, Chirak had a great deal of power, and they had already begun to discuss Tulik's taking over their grandfather's position as soon as the other proctors would permit it—or, alternatively, marrying into one of the other big merchant houses and taking over *their* proctorial seat. Then the Shaldeth clan would have two votes, not one.

But Tulik was, when all was said and done, still only sixteen.

And if their grandfather died—or was found to be mad and removed from his post—that would leave the

Shaldeth without any voice in that inner council. The seat in the red-draped inner court of the Grand Bazaar would be given to some other family who would *never* turn it loose.

With a quick glance in both directions, Shaldis emerged from the passageway and crossed the garden, climbed the steps to the gallery outside her grandfather's room. She moved with the soundlessness in which the wizards had for centuries been trained and cast her thoughts before her, probing toward her grandfather's room. Listening for the sound of his breathing, for the quick angry stride that would tell her that he heard her coming.

But there was nothing. Only the snuffle of an old man sliding into sleep.

Breathless with fear—the fear she'd felt as a child of this all-powerful, terrible man; the fear of that mad, screaming rage she'd sensed in the passageway where Nettleflower had died—Shaldis crept to his door and laid her hands gently on the handle.

No magic had worked its latch last night.

Her grandfather's story of an attack in his room last night—the story Tulik had corroborated—had been a lie.

Had he suspected Nettleflower was going to the passageway beside the study, to open the alley door? For whom? A lover? Or a business rival to whom she was selling information?

Ahure, perhaps?

Snaldis shivered as she descended the stair. She'd always known her grandfather was an arbitrary man, one addicted to his own rage; a man who loved to get angry, to exercise the power that law and custom gave him over his family and slaves.

But that hysterical paroxysm, that shrieking fury she'd felt like a dark stain in the walls of the passageway . . . that was the stuff of madness.

On her way through to the heat and noise and indigo stink of the kitchen court, she passed the door of the storeroom and, glancing within, saw Tulik there, washing the blood from Nettleflower's stiffening hands.

In the kitchen, Foursie, Twinkle, and Yellow Hen were chopping bloodroot for a dye bath while Cook and Shaldis's mother plucked chickens for dinner. Shaldis asked, "What's really going on?" and her mother turned from the worktable and laughed.

"My darling, for two years now I've wondered—I've worried—if the wizards would have changed you, made you into someone else that I maybe wouldn't like so much." Her brown eyes twinkled as she crossed the sweltering little room, embraced Shaldis with chicken blood and feathers all over her plump hands. "And now I see how foolish that worry was. Have you had breakfast, dear? Not enough, I'll wager—I understand those poor old men up there are starving to death and getting jobs sweeping floors to feed themselves."

"Hogwash," said Shaldis cheerfully, and pulled up a tall stool to perch on while her mother went back to work. Her mother and Cook, she noticed, still wore half a dozen amulets apiece—copper, malachite, glass—although the wizards who'd made them undoubtedly had no power to ward off anything anymore. Foursie and Twinkle were the same. Only Yellow Hen seemed to have accepted the fact that talismans were a waste of money. But then, Shaldis recalled, her aunt had never had much use for purchased luck.

She went on. "The king sends us whatever we need. The masters are all his old friends, for one thing, and even if they weren't, they're still teachers who know all the old spells, even if they can't do them."

"Exactly what I was saying," declared her mother triumphantly.

"Nonsense, Barley Sugar," retorted Yellow Hen, "you were telling me only yesterday that the king had deserted the mages."

"That isn't what I meant," explained Shaldis's mother with a slight scolding note in her voice, as if her elderly sister-in-law had willfully twisted her words. She turned back to Shaldis. "As for what happened last night—Foursie, darling, get Old One some bread and butter, because whatever she says, they really *are* starving her to death. The first thing any of us heard last night was shouting and thumping down in the garden. The girls heard it, that is, since the dormitory looks onto the garden and your aunt and I sleep farther away."

"We all saw Grandfather rush out of the passageway and up the stairs to Tulik's room," breathed Foursie, her thin cheeks flushed with excitement where a few moments before they had been deathly pale. "At least, later on we knew it was Grandfather—it just looked like a white blur because he was wrapped up in a sheet. Tulik came out of his room and ran downstairs with him and into the passageway, and then after a little while he came back up and told us Nettleflower had been killed."

"He looked sick," put in Twinkle, carefully placing a handful of dripping red shreds into the smallest of the dye pots. "Sick and scared." Like Foursie, the youngest of Habnit and Barley Sugar's daughters was dark and delicate boned. She'd braided up her hair—or more likely gotten one of the maids to braid it for her—in a killingly fashionable tree-of-life style, and in addition to fifteen amulets wore a whole collection of cheap bright-colored beads of marketplace glass around her neck that clinked and clattered when she moved. Clearly, she was already on her way to becoming as style-conscious as Moth. She swallowed hard, asked timidly, "Did it— Do you think it hurt her to die?"

Shaldis thought about the broken nails, the bloodied hands. Her grandfather's scored face.

"Oh, I don't think so, darling," said their mother.

But Shaldis said, "Yes, I think it did. That's why I'm going to catch the person who did it and see that he's punished."

The words flaked over her tongue like ashes.

No, you're not.

Tulik will lie himself black in the face, to keep anyone from suspecting that Grandfather killed someone in his own household in a fit of madness.

At least until he's eighteen. She'd never heard of anyone being permitted to take his seat as a proctor so young, but wouldn't put it past Tulik to manage it.

At eighteen.

Sixteen, never.

She took a deep breath. "So why does Grandfather think it was Ahure the Blood Mage?"

Foursie looked nonplussed at the question. "Wasn't it?"

And Twinkle said decisively, "It was." She looked up at Shaldis again. "We saw them—Foursie and I—when we went with Mama and Aunt Apricot to the milk market yesterday morning. We went to get a horoscope, and we both saw Nettleflower standing talking to this horrible man with a bandage on his hand and cuts on his head and dried blood and flies, and Foursie said, *That was Ahure the Blood Mage.* You don't have to cut your fingers off to make magic, do you?"

"No," said Shaldis.

Her mother interpolated, "I should say not! I've always said, it's the most unsanitary—"

"Are you sure it was Nettleflower?"

Both girls nodded. "She was wearing the silk veil she'd got Uncle to give her just before he went to Kamath village," provided Foursie. "Green with pink flowers, and bells at the corners. She was always getting permission to go out and go shopping. When she couldn't, she'd tell old Two Shoes that she had it anyway and he'd let her out. Once he wouldn't, and she told Uncle he'd stolen from her and he beat him. After that Two Shoes let her out whenever she wanted to go."

"Ahure gave her something," added Twinkle, "in the market. We saw him."

Foursie nodded. "And anyway Ahure and Grandfather hate each other," she said, her eyes sparkling at the recollection of the dramatic scene. "Last time he was here in the house Ahure said he'd put a curse on Grandfather."

"What?" said Shaldis, startled. "Why? What was he doing *here*? I didn't even know Grandfather *knew* Ahure."

And at the same time she thought, *Why didn't Tulik tell me that? Why keep Grandfather from bringing up his name?*

"He knows him, all right." Yellow Hen sat back from the hearth, where the kettle of water was just beginning to boil for the first of the yellow dye baths. "Noyad the jeweler—"

"You girls get on out of here, now," broke in Shaldis's mother with a sharp look at Foursie and Twinkle. "Go on, now. This is grown-up talk."

"It wasn't grown-up before," protested Foursie. Her mother gave her the Look that Shaldis so well remembered. Foursie resignedly took Twinkle's hand. Twinkle pulled loose and carefully lifted the largest and most elaborate of her amulets off over her coiffure. She held it out to Shaldis—cheap beggar silver with a garish pink-glass bead.

"This will protect you," she promised breathlessly, "from Ahure's evil spells."

Shaldis knew the only way it would protect her from Ahure's evil spells was if she hit the old Blood Mage over the head with it and knocked him out. But she put it on at once and said gratefully, "Why, thank you, Twinkle Star." Since Ahure hadn't been able to cast a spell, evil or otherwise, for probably a decade, the fact that the amulet was worthless scarcely mattered.

"What about Noyad the jeweler?" she asked as her younger sisters scampered away.

"Your grandfather has a number of—of associates, whose names are best not bandied around the town," her mother said. "Not that he has a thing to be ashamed of, except his disgraceful language. You aren't eating your bread and butter, dear."

"One of 'em's Noyad the jeweler." Yellow Hen stood up from the hearth, dusting ashes from her hands. "Your grandfather got him a pitch in the best part of the Grand Bazaar—a place other jewelers have waited years for—in exchange for a cut of his profits. And Ahure works for Noyad these days."

"Doing what?" Shaldis had seen the haughty old Blood Mage's elaborate peep shows of illusion and machinery, designed to keep Lord Jamornid believing in his ability to do magic. She couldn't imagine Ahure coming down to do anything so mundane as keeping a jeweler's books.

"He won't say," replied Yellow Hen. "And if anyone asks him he merely looks haughty and denies it. But word's spread around the town that Ahure's found a way to imbue gems with good luck or ill."

"That's silly." Shaldis obediently tore her bread into pieces and consumed it, the butter dripping down her fingers. "Ahure couldn't imbue a sponge with water. No mage can."

"You sound awfully sure of that, dearest."

"I *am* awfully sure of it, Mother. And I'm certainly awfully sure of Ahure."

"Be that as it may," said her aunt with her crooked, toothy grin, "by looking wise and tapping the side of his nose and raising his eyebrows when anyone asks him questions, Noyad—who swears Ahure only 'does him favors' and won't say what—is charging three crowns for turquoise pendants that no one in their right senses would pay three dequins for . . . and is getting it, and getting it so fast he can barely keep up. What he asks for real jewels that have 'passed through Ahure's hands,' I'd hate to tell you."

"Oh, *please*. And Ahure and my grandfather fought?"

"Ahure came to the house three or four days ago," temporized her mother. "Of course no one heard what they said, but Nettleflower—who was up in your uncle's room on the gallery over the garden—said that she saw Ahure storm out of your grandfather's study, shouting back at him that he would put such a curse upon the house that it would crumble to the ground. Of course," she added with a glance sidelong toward the storeroom where Nettleflower's body lay, "though she was quite a . . . a good-hearted girl underneath, I'm sure, sometimes Nettleflower wasn't entirely truthful."

That, reflected Shaldis, as she licked the butter from her fingers, was putting the matter mildly.

Whatever had actually happened between her grandfather and the former wizard, Nettleflower was the only possible witness.

And a few days after that, the girl had met the old man in the marketplace.

Money? With a promise of more, if she'd let him into the house by the alley door?

And before the next day's sun had risen, Nettleflower was dead.

"What is it?" Oryn rolled over on the loose bed of cushions laid out for him on the ground, propped himself on one elbow, and immediately wished he hadn't. The bruises that had seemed minor a few hours ago had stiffened and he felt as if he'd been racked. *Dear gods, I never properly appreciated what the guards go through. I really must raise their pay, give them a special liquor allotment, have a special baths built for them in the palace, or something.*

Summerchild was sitting up beside him already. Even within the shelter, the heat was like being slowly roasted to death. No wonder he'd dreamed about being bricked up in a furnace. . . .

"What's burning?"

She pinned her veils over her face and hair again and crouched her way to the tent flap, Oryn hobbling behind. He noticed that Summerchild, who had taken just as many blows in the battle as he had, still moved with the lithe unconcern of a dancer.

Jethan and two other troopers were also out of their shelters, talking to the pickets around the camp. A column of smoke stood in the eastern sky.

Summerchild asked, "Is that Three Wells?"

"It's the only habitation in that direction, lady."

"Can you call up the image of the place in your mirror?" asked Oryn, looking down at his ladylove, and Summerchild's brow puckered.

"I'm not sure. I've never been in Three Wells, but I could try focusing on the smoke. I'm not sure how much I would see."

"Try it," said Oryn softly. "If the town is deserted, and all there are dead, I am most curious as to who set the fires. And why."

TWENTY

At no time of the day or night did the Dead Hills appear welcoming. There were those who said that the broken badlands east and south of the Lake of the Sun had earned their name from the tombs that honeycombed them—those of the kings more isolated, those of nobles or the wealthy merchants dotting the dry wadis that could be reached from the Yellow City in a few hours. But those who looked on the hills, or rode through them, quickly came to the conclusion that the name had come first, the tombs, after.

Summer or winter, they had the appearance of a land the gods hated, or at least those gods who had the good of humankind at heart. The bleak waste of pale-brown stone was like a dream landscape of half-buried skulls, riven with twisting canyons; a world whose parched shade offered no coolness. Dusty precipices and blank stretches of broken talus flung back the day's heat even in the deep of night. Even where the King's Aqueduct pierced them, a gray finger pointing toward the distant Oasis of Koshlar across two hundred miles of desert, the hills seemed dead, waiting silently for some night when they might silently swallow up the work camps of men and teyn and camels.

In the Valley of the Hawk, twelve miles from the aqueduct and fifteen from the walls of the Yellow City, the silence and the waiting seemed more perilous.

Foxfire climbed stiffly down from the litter in which she'd swayed, suffocating with heat, since the previous night and asked, "Who in their right mind would build a house in this place?"

The villa lay before them, the same dusty brown as the surrounding rock. At one time the pylons on either side of its gate had been painted with scenes of lion hunts and crocodile spearings. At one time there'd been sycamore trees in front of the pylons. Their desiccated trunks remained, behind which the flaked eyes of hunters and prey stared hopelessly across the desolation of dust.

"What did they teach you in that school of yours, girl?" demanded her grandmother, swinging down from the horse which she'd insisted on riding, knee to knee with her son. "A hundred and fifty years ago there were springs in a dozen places in the foothills, and the lords of House Jothek hunted lions in the desert from here. If she's to remain under your roof," she added, regarding Mohrvine as he dismounted, "that daughter of yours had best put in her spare time here studying the lore of her own House."

"I shall mark it down as a future course of study for her," replied Mohrvine smoothly, crossing to Foxfire's litter and putting a gentle hand on her shoulder. "Let us use the time here to the better purpose of making sure our House remains the House of Kings. Then she shall take her place in its lore"—he smiled down into her eyes— "rather than merely reading of the deeds of others."

Foxfire looked around her, hating the place. Hating the sense of being watched by something just out of sight in the shadows of those sun-blasted arroyos. She was deeply grateful for Opal's little veiled shadow in the second litter she'd insisted her father provide for her maid.

"Must I stay here?" Her voice was barely a whisper. "Won't you need someone in your household in the city who can communicate with Granny at a moment's notice? I'm much better at it than I was."

The hopeful eagerness as she brought out this fib warmed her father's eyes, turned his coldly handsome face gentle and human. In that moment she would have done anything for him. Anything except remain here, if given a choice.

But her father did not believe in choices. Not when the advancement of the cadet branch of House Jothek was the prize. "My child, your grandmother has more need of your powers than I do. Pigeons can carry a message from the city in a matter of hours. They will have to do."

Behind them a baggage camel groaned. The caravan that had accompanied the litters moved forward as the villa's gates opened between the pylons. Foxfire looked through them into a courtyard as dust-choked and brown as the hills.

Beside the camels a line of teyn walked, chained neck to neck. The lead boar balked at the sight of the hills; and Foxfire's brother Zharvine, who was in charge of the baggage train, tapped him with the end of his six-foot rod. "Don't start giving us trouble now, Dogface; you'll have worse than the sight of those hills to think about, believe me." The teyn only looked around them in silent anxiety, not understanding a word.

Her least-favorite brother, Úrthet, emerged from the gate, squat and stocky. He walked up the little rise to where Foxfire and their father still stood beside the litter. Even the litter bearers—teyn matched and trained to respond to the commands of the human team captain—clustered together, swaying fearfully from foot to foot as they gazed at the parched wadis, the sharp columns of grayish-buff rock.

"Well's dry as a crust, sir." Úrthet practically spit the words out. Twelve hours traveling in the blistering heat, with only the shortest of noon halts, had done nothing for his temper. "We've put the waterskins in the cellar. We'll have to ration."

"We'll send out for more tomorrow," promised Mohrvine with the casual ease of one who has at least three of the city's gangster water bosses in his pay. "Is there enough for Belial?" He glanced with a kind of affection at the tall-sided wagon that had been nursed and lifted over nearly fifteen miles of rutted path, the wagon whose black felt canopies and tarred sides glistened with damp and smelled of murky wetness and filth.

"Should be, sir. Though he'll need more soon."

"He'll have it." Mohrvine's smile widened as his green gaze followed the wagon down through the courtyard gate. Still affectionate, but all gentleness had disappeared. Then he turned back to Foxfire and laid his gloved hands on her shoulders again. "Be a good girl, and do exactly as your grandmother says," he admonished and leaned down to kiss her forehead. "Don't leave the compound for any reason. These hills shelter nomad raiding parties in the summers and bandits—they pass through the wadis to have shelter in attacking the rangelands around the city."

Foxfire looked out past him at the hills, reflecting that

the warning was hardly necessary. He could have given her a million gold pieces and a written promise from Deemas, the patron god of thieves, attesting their nomadless state and she still wouldn't have gone anywhere near them. There was something within them, among them, that watched her and waited. She knew it.

"Learn all you can from Soral Brûl," her father went on, naming the young adept, formerly of the Sun Mages, who was even now walking back to the gateway with Úrthet. "And from Urnate Urla." He nodded at the crabbed and skinny little man who, after his powers of earth wizardry failed, had gone to work as secretary for one of the Slaughterhouse water bosses. "But don't tell them anything, don't trust them, and don't let yourself be alone with them. Understand?"

"I understand." Her grandmother's horse appeared from around the corner of the compound wall, and Red Silk leaned down from the saddle to address the two former mages, young and middle-aged. She made a sweep with one arm, as if describing a barrier, and Foxfire heard Soral Brûl hoot with laughter.

"Why don't you hang straw dollies on the walls while you're at it?" He named one of the old peasant cantrips against the Bad-Luck Shadow. "Or plant marigolds around the walls to chase ghosts away? *Poqs,* I mean." He spoke the nomad word for the thing the wandering people claimed was responsible for every ill from dead sheep to cross-eyed babies.

"Don't laugh at the Bad-Luck Shadow when you stand so near his abiding place," responded Red Silk drily. "You need not believe in the warding spells that guard you from him for them to work." She reined her horse away.

Foxfire shivered. As a child she'd half believed in the Bad-Luck Shadow, as something that "got" bad little girls, though she'd never heard or read of anyone who'd ever actually been "gotten." Unlike the djinni, who had been attested to by sightings and periodic contacts for centuries, there was nothing real called a *poq*. Yet out here in this utterly silent land—this exile where she and her grandmother were to come up with spells to deal with crocodiles, cobras, and whatever poison it was that the Priest of Time concocted for the test of the king—she felt the presence of Something.

Anything seemed possible here. She stretched out her hand to the other litter; Opal emerged through the curtains, gave her a protective hug.

Her father's voice called back her thoughts. "You won't be here for long, my little vixen," he promised. "Indeed, the quicker you find an answer to our problem, the quicker you can return home. But for good or ill you will be back in the Yellow City in forty-three days."

Foxfire started to say, *but it's only thirteen to the Moon of Jubilee,* and realized that her father wasn't thinking of Oryn's tests.

He was thinking of his own, to be held under the new moon that succeeded Oryn's death.

Late in the afternoon, with the gold sun lying two handsbreadths over the scraggy sagebrush to the west, Jethan's voice said, "My lord king?" outside and Oryn pushed up the light inner curtain.

"I suppose Geb will have a stroke when he learns I've

acted as my own porter," sighed the king, beckoning the guardsman inside. Even on its downswing the sun was a power to be reckoned with, and the evening wind had not yet begun. "But goodness knows where we'd put a porter inside here with us, and bringing along a lodge for one to sit outside would have meant another baggage ass, and that sort of thing can get out of hand very quickly. Any sign of the reinforcements?"

"The pickets have just sighted a dust cloud in the west," reported Jethan, kneeling upright under the tent's low roof. He had, Oryn observed, washed his face before presenting himself; water still glistened in his hair. "That isn't why I've come, Lord King. The teyn appear to be gone."

"As of when?"

"Not long ago, I don't think, my lord. I've been watching with a spyglass all afternoon. I could see half a dozen of them most of that time, just sitting."

"That's odd in itself, isn't it?" remarked Oryn. "I mean, they can usually hide under pebbles, it seems. Why sit in the open?"

"To let us know they were there, perhaps?"

Oryn raised his brows. "That isn't behavior one usually hears of with teyn—that kind of planning ahead, I mean. But, then, up until last winter one never heard of them attacking men, either. If they're no longer in evidence I suppose Numet should send out scouts."

"I already went, sir," said Jethan. "When I didn't see any teyn I took a horse and rode two or three miles in the direction of Three Wells. I was unmolested."

"Good heavens, my dear boy, you didn't need to do that!" cried Oryn, really distressed. "You could have been killed." He could see, beyond the edges of the bandages on the young man's arms, the blackening bruises of rock hits. "The gods bear witness that just getting on a horse at this point would kill *me*."

Jethan didn't smile. Oryn suspected he considered grimness part of his job. "I was mounted, sir, and could probably have outrun them. When I wasn't attacked I checked for tracks. There were hundreds, dispersing in all directions. As if they'd all decided that they no longer needed to hold us here."

"Or as if someone had decided for them." Oryn heaved himself to his knees with a gasp. Jethan helped him to his feet and supported him to the tent door. As they both straightened up outside, Oryn untoggled his spyglass from his belt again and scanned the eastern desert, the thinning column of smoke that was now almost extinguished in the pallid sky.

"I don't like this," he said softly. "I don't like it at all. They're behaving like soldiers—soldiers under some central command. Why murder the nomads who'd been through Three Wells? Why block the way to the town from us until it could be burned?"

"You make it sound as if there's someone controlling them," said Jethan. "Using them as tools. How?"

"I think at this point," murmured Oryn, "*how* doesn't matter as much as *why*."

"My lord!" Captain Numet appeared between the low shelters as men began emerging, pouring out slim field rations from waterskins, preparing their horses for another ride. "Reinforcements are approaching; we should be able to deal with the teyn now." He saluted sharply. "My advice is to press on as soon as you can be ready, my lord, so that we can be through them before dark."

"Or we could, if they behaved like men and stayed put," remarked Oryn. "Thank you, Captain. Yes, I shall be ready in a few minutes. Geb, darling— Yes, there you are. No, I don't think I shall have time for you to shave me. . . . No, what I'm wearing is quite all right. Thank you," he added, with a smile to dispel his chamberlain's disapproving pout. "Just have them make a horse ready for me and for my lady. I'm rather curious," he added as captain and chamberlain went striding away in opposite directions, "as to whether the teyn have actually dispersed, or whether this is simply a trap of some kind. And I'm even more curious as to what we shall find in Three Wells that someone would rather we didn't see."

TWENTY-ONE

With the evening's first cool, Raeshaldis made her way through the southern gate of the city and took one of the brightly decorated water taxis down the canal that led to the Fishmarket District on the lake's edge. This was still a pleasant trip of a mile or so through the relative coolness of palmeries and gardens, although the ward spells that had once kept the mosquitoes from the canal had—like all other wards—failed.

Mostly, the Fishmarket District was concerned with the fleet of big reed canoes that sailed each sunset out into the deeper waters and brought in netfuls of silvery trout, flopping bass, and millions upon millions of tiny, oily sardines—the staple food of the city's poor—and with the barge traffic from across the Lake of the Sun. Corn and dates and rice from the Jothek and Jamornid clan lands around the White Lake and the Lake of Roses came in here, and pigs, goats, cattle from the richer Sarn farmlands along the shores of the Great Lake to the north. As they approached the lake, Shaldis was interested to see how the canal had been deepened, to allow for the gradual retreat of the shoreline over the past decade. On either side of the canal, land that up until a decade ago had been lake bottom was now a dispirited-looking tangle of reeds, ponds, and brush, alive with birds and crocodiles in the last red glow of the retreating sun.

This was the first year that the shoreline hadn't retreated still further. Without the Sun Mages to sing the rains across the desert from the barren coasts of the distant ocean this spring, Shaldis wondered, watching the back of her veiled but otherwise nearly naked boatman dip and bend with the stroke, how soon would it be before the waters retreated too far for the distance to be traversed with canals and bucket lines?

Eight women.

The gods help us.

And one of them, the gods help us, Cattail.

Cattail had had a new house built this year, on the site of the modest dwelling she'd shared with the long-suffering little nonentity who'd been her husband. The big, dark-haired woman liked to proclaim in her deep voice how nothing could induce her to abandon her friends and neighbors in the Fishmarket; the uncharitable (Shaldis among them) suspected that Cattail so loved the worship of the coterie of neighbors whom she had dominated for years with advice and favors that she simply couldn't stand the thought of living elsewhere.

In either case, thought Shaldis, the house looked like exactly the sort of thing a laundress would have built if she should suddenly happen to have several hundred thousand gold pieces thrust upon her by merchants, land-chiefs, and wealthy gentlemen desirous of love potions or curses with no questions asked.

Cattail was sitting on her little roof-garden terrace, enjoying the cool breezes and the sight of the wharves below. As Shaldis was shown up by an extremely comely young serving man, Shaldis noted that reeking smudges of lemongrass and pitch burned everywhere: Cattail hadn't figured out a mosquito ward, either. And the doors and windows of the little kiosk through which the stair from the house below opened into the garden were defended with massive shutters and bars, so Cattail hadn't had any more luck with the problem of thieves, despite her reputation. The Fishmarket was a poor district.

"Raeshaldis, my dear child!" Cattail rose from her short-legged couch and crossed the garden to meet Shaldis, her jeweled hands held out. "So good of you to call." In the heat of noon, just before the dead hours of siesta, Shaldis had gazed into her crystal and spoken Cattail's name. When the swarthy, heavy-featured countenance of her sister Raven had appeared, she had asked if Cattail would do her the favor of receiving her that evening.

There'd been four other people in Cattail's downstairs waiting room when Shaldis had come in. They'd all glared daggers at her when the handsome young steward had heard her name and taken her up before them.

"Leopard, go fetch us coffee," Cattail commanded with a wave, and the steward bowed deeply and departed. Shaldis had to admit she felt a little shock, since even slave men were *never* given the descriptive pet names that women—and, she reflected, teyn—went by. Even the lowest male slave was named by his father with one of the names that appertained to their clan, and that was that. Men kept their names, even slaves or entertainers like the graceful Belzinian who danced in the Circus District before scandalized crowds. Everyone Shaldis met was shocked, in one degree or another, that she'd taken a male clan name when she'd left her grandfather's house; it had never occurred to her that a woman would arbitrarily rename a male slave she'd bought, the way men routinely renamed women.

For that matter, she'd never heard of a woman owning slaves in her own name, and guessed that Cattail had a mud husband tucked away somewhere, the way the madams of the Blossom Houses and brothels did: a legal spouse contracted with and supported by a small stipend, who legally owned the woman's house and slaves and who knew better than to *ever* put forward his claim. Most of the Blossom Mothers and madams worked through gangsters contracted to murder the mud husband out of hand in the event of funny business.

Shaldis didn't envy Cattail's spouse.

Then she was embraced in a great wave of expensively perfumed flesh and guided to a chair. "Dearest child, is it true about the King's Jubilee? Is he really going to go through with it? It will make it excessively awkward for poor Summerchild if he fails, and her without a son. Awkward for us all. I wonder she hasn't done more about getting herself to conceive by the king. It's really a fairly simple matter."

She regarded Shaldis with those heavy-lidded dark eyes, and Shaldis's mind went back over the two or three attempts that had been made, over the past year, by various landchiefs to introduce new, youthful concubines into the king's harem. It was generally supposed that Summerchild used spells of her own on the king—which Shaldis didn't think was the case, though she'd never asked—and that she had placed some sort of spell ward on him to keep him proof against other women's love potions, something else Shaldis had no information about but which she considered only logical.

Maybe their love was simply beyond all that.

Three of the clients in Cattail's opulently decorated chamber downstairs were women, anonymously veiled in extremely costly silks. Spells of fertility, thought Shaldis, or spells of love, despite the fact that even when the men had been working magic, spells of fertility were dangerous things and as often as not killed the mother or produced a dead or deformed baby. Summerchild was keeping a record of such things, now that women were either trying to work men's spells or inventing their own. Despite Cattail's claims, there was little reason to believe they'd gotten any safer.

"I'm glad to hear you say that," said Shaldis, watching her hostess's face carefully. "The Lady Summerchild keeps her own counsel, the way she always does, but I was asked recently by one of my grandfather's household about a spell to make her conceive, and since that's not in my line, she asked me to come to you."

The plucked brows arched up. "Asked *you* to come to

me? Dear child, and you agreed to run errands for a *concubine*? With that kind of attitude I can see why the Sun Mages ran into trouble. No one respects even a Crafty who'll run their errands for them. Be advised by me, dearest, don't let yourself be imposed upon again in that way. Why didn't the poor thing come to me herself?"

"If you'd ask that question, you can't know my grandfather Chirak Shaldeth."

Under the layer of cosmetics there wasn't the smallest change of expression in Cattail's face. Only a small puckering of the brows—carefully executed so as not to wrinkle the paint—as she tried to place the name.

"One of the Grand Bazaar proctors?" Shaldis prompted.

"Oh, of course! Silly of me. I knew the Shaldeth had a proctorship, and I should have realized with the name you'd chosen that you were one of them. Your grandfather is a proctor, dear? The only proctor I know is Merj Glapas."

Leopard appeared with the coffee, and Shaldis sipped it—it was thickly laced with sugar, vanilla, milk, and cinnamon—and chatted with Cattail as the rose-amber globe of the sun sank itself, burning, into the lake and all the yellow-sailed fishing craft slipped out over the glowing water, borne on the hot whisper of the desert breeze. The time of Sunrest, the mages had called it, sacred to its own god Ka-Theruabin. Every spell performed during that hour had a special formula attached to it, to take account of the particular magic of that time.

As far as she could tell, either Cattail had never had the slightest thing to do with her grandfather's house or household, or she was a consummately clever actress—

something Shaldis was certain that she was. It wasn't, of course, easy to casually bring up anything in a conversation so overwhelmingly dominated by her hostess's insistence on telling her every detail of everyone else's business in the neighborhood and what she had paid for the coffee service, the embroidered cushions, Leopard, or her hairdresser, but Shaldis persevered. When she slipped into the conversation the mention that one of her grandfather's maidservants swore she'd seen Cattail herself in the house at night, Cattail's eyes widened with credible-looking startlement and she said only, "Good heavens, what an extraordinary idea!" instead of, *Who says this?* or *When?* "How on earth would the girl have known what I looked like?"

Shaldis shook her head. "I have no idea. But I think that's what gave poor Ten Flower—the girl who asked me about the fertility spell—the idea that she wanted one. She says when she heard this, she thought one of the other maids was trying to get herself with child by my uncle Tjagan, to get special privileges, and Ten Flower, who is also sleeping with my uncle, wanted to get in there first."

"Good lord, these poor silly children." Cattail shook her head. "As if any man—though I'm sure your uncle is a very paragon of virtue, my dear—is going to treat any woman better if she bears him a brat. Still, wait here for a few minutes and let me see what I can make up for her. Shall I bring Leopard back and have him sing for you? Or have him read to you? He has a ravishing voice, among other things," she added slyly.

"No, thank you, I'll be fine. The silence here is lovely, this close to the lake."

"I should think that after living up in that ghastly Citadel for two years you'd give your thumbs for the sound of a little music, but to each her own. More coffee? A gazelle horn?" She moved the gaudily cloisonnéed plate of cream-stuffed pastries closer. "My cook is a marvel—I don't think even the king has one as fine. He cost a hundred gold pieces from Lord Nahul-Sarn and worth every dequin of it, I assure you. Not a woman in the realm can cook as well as a man who is truly an artist. Well, help yourself, my dear."

For a few minutes after Cattail's departure Shaldis did simply sit where she was in the protective ring of stinking mosquito smudges, drinking in the lakeside quiet. The noises of the wharves were transmuted by distance to a musical murmuring, like wind in trees. The evening breeze passed with a gentle *hrush*ing among the forest of dried-out reeds that had grown up between the old wharves just below the wall of Cattail's house and the lake's current shoreline a hundred feet away. Swallows veered and darted over the pools, and even the sewery, fishy stink of that intervening stretch of reeds didn't seem so bad, brushed over by the movement of the night air.

The magic light of Sunrest lay upon the world. Soon it would be gone, and dark would come.

When she was sure Cattail had retreated to her workroom elsewhere in the house, Shaldis got to her feet and went to the door that led back into the rooftop kiosk that contained the stair down into the rest of the house. It stood open, veiled in gauze to keep the mosquitoes at bay, and through the pinkish layers she could see the pierced lamps of the tiled stairwell. The elaborate tile work—brilliantly colored like everything else in the house—went around the opening of the door, breaking only for the heavy iron hinges of the folded-back leaves of the door itself.

Shaldis spread out her hands, brushed them lightly across the doors, the tile, then knelt to touch the threshold, and stippled her fingers over the curtain of gauze.

The sigils of protection, of warning, of ward leaped out at her as if they'd been shrieked. Beneath them lay other sigils still, glyphs tinkered together from both High Script runes and from the hasty letters of Scribble into signs of cursing, scrubbed into the wood and iron, written in salt and blood. Shaldis sensed those evil signs were inactive, but they'd been activated, then put to sleep again, recently and often—probably every night, she thought. To whoever forced or opened those doors at night, terrible things would happen . . .

There were no limiting spells on those curses, which shocked her deeply. It meant that the evil would take any form, disproportionate to the act of burglary and striking those for whom the cursed one cared, as well as the offender himself. They would also, eventually, have an effect on the inhabitants of the house, not only Cattail but the handsome Leopard and the talented cook.

One of the first lessons Shaldis had been taught as a Sun Mage—and in fact one of the first principles taught by any of the organized systems of male wizardry—was that all spells must be specifically limited in their duration, in their strength, and in their effect. The carelessness of Cattail's defenses both horrified and disgusted her. The former laundress didn't care, evidently, that the generalized curse placed on a burglar might take the form of a contagious disease spread to half the neighborhood, or the maiming of his innocent wife or child by a crocodile's bite.

You touch my house, something AWFUL will happen to you, was all she cared about.

Had she been taught by a responsible mage, who'd been taught responsibly by his master, would she have done differently? Shaldis knew that the house had been built—and therefore these curses laid on the doors—after Summerchild had pointed out to Cattail that spells must be limited, even though there were many spells that did not work nearly so well that way.

Almost certainly, no one burgled Cattail's house. Not anymore, anyway.

Shaldis couldn't be sure, but she felt that the magic that had made those signs was different from that used to put sleep spells on the guards in the gallery outside her grandfather's room. The faint residue she'd sensed in the wall of the gallery had a different color to it, a fundamentally different quality, as if she were differentiating Summerchild's sweet tones from Cattail's throaty purr.

Which was just as well, she thought, returning to her chair as she heard her hostess's rather heavy tread on the stairs. Confident as Shaldis was in the strength of her own counterspells, she wouldn't have wanted to risk one of Cattail's curses sticking to her by breaking in and having a look at the woman's account books some night.

"It's odd," she said as Cattail handed her a little pottery bottle (*Pottery, good gods! And after Summerchild told her that ensorcelled substances* must *be contained in glass, which has its own special properties with regard to magic!*). "I'm remembering what Nettleflower said"—

she watched Cattail's eyes again but saw no reaction—
"about thinking she saw you in Grandfather's house. She
said it was a Raven sister, so I think she assumed it was
you. But is there someone else working in the city that we
don't know about?"

Cattail sniffed. "Other than that poor frump Pebble?
Good lord, I swear the child puts sheep fat on her face for
ointment. And her clothes! And if I have to hear one more
time about that dreary 'papa' of hers or her tedious batch
of sisters."

Shaldis wondered what Cattail said about *her*, behind
her back. "I thought so, but it was on a night when I know
Pebble and Moth both were at the palace with Summerchild. In fact I'd thought that you were there, too," she
added hastily, seeing Cattail's eyes narrow with slighted
anger. "But I know sometimes you're busy and don't go."

"Well, *some* of us have to earn our living and don't
have our bread handed to us by men—"

Shaldis broke hastily into what she guessed was a
coming tirade with "Do you think there's someone else
working in the city? Another Raven sister?"

And saw Cattail's mouth harden to a slit. "Nonsense."
There is.

"I know you hear everything." Shaldis hoped her
widened eyes and the slightly worshipful note in her
voice—copied from Nettleflower's best efforts with
Uncle Tjagan—would eradicate the memory of her earlier expressions of distaste for Cattail, her clientele, and
her methods. "I thought you might have picked up a
rumor—"

"Rumor?" The older woman spit. "It wouldn't be a matter of rumor, my girl, with the king and that concubine of

his holding out as much gold as you care to think about to any woman with the smallest wink of power to come over to their side. A woman has only to be able to call birds to her hand or charm the fleas off her papa's donkeys for Summerchild to take her in and start telling her how to conduct her life. Why would you think I'd know?"

"Because you're independent," said Shaldis, taking the pottery phial, *very* carefully, from Cattail's hands. "Summerchild is the one who has access to the royal library, after all. Just because some of us seek to learn what Summerchild has to teach doesn't mean we think her way is the only way."

She waited, but Cattail only regarded her with hard suspicion in her dark eyes. "You owe me half a royal," she said after a moment. "Let me know when your grandfather's girl conceives."

Shaldis nodded and produced the coin with a friendly smile. "I will. And thank you."

She followed the handsome Leopard down the stairs, holding the phial wrapped in a corner of her mosquito veils and reflecting that she'd be lucky if she wasn't pregnant by the time she got home. There were seven clients in the waiting room by that time, drinking coffee and chatting as if they were at a bathhouse. Shaldis didn't recognize any of the veiled women, but one of the men— corpulent, pockmarked, overdressed in pink and purple satin, and studying the room with the sharp attention of one who could price the embroidered cushions to within a dequin of their value—she recognized as Xolnax, the thug who was water boss of the Slaughterhouse District. And, according to her aunt Yellow Hen, a frequent visitor to her grandfather's study.

She boarded a water taxi and returned to the torchlit walls of the Yellow City in a thoughtful mood.

TWENTY-TWO

A column of a hundred riders reached the king's camp just before sunset, with the first whispers of the cooling evening breeze stirring their banners and the captain's plumes. These, like Numet's company, were levies of the House Jothek, loyal to the king and his family and paid, now, from the royal treasury. Watching them approach, Oryn reflected not for the first time that there ought to be some other way of policing and defending the boundaries of the realm. All the great landchiefs had their private armies, whose loyalty to the king was less real to them than their duty to their clan chief.

A dozen of his minor chiefs—and all the sheikhs *they* ruled—were in fact originally vassals of House Akarian, who had gone to the banner of Taras Greatsword in protest against the decadence of their former lord. What they would do in the face of the jubilee, thought Oryn, watching the tired horses, the sweating and heat-sick men ride up to the little camp, was anyone's guess.

The tents were packed up, the horses watered, the saddles of the newcomers changed to fresh mounts. In spite of Geb's near-tearful declarations of humiliation, Oryn, with only minimal repairs to his coiffure and eye paint, looked as kingly as he ever did, though he suspected he more resembled a two-hundred-and-fifty-pound bouquet than a king. *Where is Barún to look noble when I need him?* The captain of the column saluted and agreed that his men press on, at least until they were well past the point where the teyn had attacked before. Having passed that point with no sign of further trouble, at Oryn's suggestion they halted for an hour's rest. "We're not going to reach Three Wells much before dawn in any case, and if we encounter teyn closer to the village I'd so much rather have rested men around me than tired ones."

Numet looked a little surprised at this consideration. It wasn't, Oryn reflected, very like the warrior heroes in ballads, wherein everyone simply leaped on their seemingly inexhaustible horses and pounded away at full gallop for fifty miles whether it was midsummer or not. But having lost half a day, there didn't seem much point in dashing madly to what he was almost certain would be a smoking ruin.

His father would have, of course.

They rode through the night, ringed by scouts and prickling with wariness, but no attack came. "They're near," Summerchild whispered, riding beside him, her eyes half closed in a listening trance. "There are dozens of them, moving along beside us through the sagebrush, far more than any band I've ever heard of."

"Only the teyn?" whispered Oryn. "No one else?" And, when she shook her head, "That's unheard-of."

"Who knows what the teyn are truly like," Summerchild replied, "when they're free to act without wizards to keep them afraid. To keep them enslaved."

Oryn glanced down at her, this beautiful woman, this

Pearl Woman, the mother of his daughter and the delight of his life. Now all those things and something more. It had seemed completely natural to him, when he'd learned that Summerchild's perfections included the abilities of a worker of magic. As a Pearl Woman, she had been trained from babyhood to be a perfect weapon, a perfect tool, in the hand of the man who owned her.

But he knew that she felt responsibilities to magic itself, which outdistanced her love for—and duty to—him.

And in her voice he heard, as he had heard before, that she did not feel that the gods had given her magic to enslave or terrify anyone.

Not even those whose unwilling service meant the difference, now, between life for the people of the Seven Lakes or slow death.

He didn't know what to do about this. As king, he knew that the time would come very soon when he would have to do *something*.

And he feared what it might be.

※

After her visit to Cattail, Shaldis felt that her next call of the evening had better be the Slaughterhouse District. By ancient decree, the gates of the Yellow City were closed at nightfall, only opening again for the market-going farmers an hour before first light. But in fact, during the summer months the Fishmarket Gate remained open until well past midnight. Heat-sickened families would stroll out together along the canal's high banks, and the wealthy would float along its tepid waters in lamplit barges. Around the Fishmarket Gate, and the square pool at the head of the canal, a small night fair operated through the summer months, jugglers and singers and tent-sheltered taverns selling date wine and beer. It wasn't considered safe to stray too far from the torch-light—thieves and crocodiles alike waited in the dark-ness, the one species occasionally providing a late-night snack for the other—but it was a cheerful and beautiful scene nevertheless, torchlight and color warm against the cobalt darkness.

Shaldis reached the head of the canal, and paid off her water taxi, not much more than a half hour after full dark. She bought a bag of raisins from an old sweet seller, and a packet of dried apples soaked in honey. To these she added a jar of wine, reflecting with a certain amount of pleasure on Tulik's probable expression if he were to find out where the money he'd given her was going. There was plenty of time, she knew, to walk.

A well-worn path stretched along the outside of the city wall to the Slaughterhouse District, and there was little dan-ger of crocodiles once one got away from the basin at the canal head. The inhabitants of the Slaughterhouse District were no more averse than anyone else in the city to carnival sweets and cool breezes—in fact most of the pickpockets at the night fair commuted along that footpath to homes in the Slaughterhouse when their evening work was done. As Shaldis made her way along the wall she breathed deep of the rich scents of the orchards and gardens that spread all around the city on this side, though she didn't neglect to keep a listening ear on the undergrowth. The Gray Cloak of illusion worked only on humans.

As she came around the eastern side of the city the ground grew higher and drier, the beds of tomatoes, beans, eggplant giving way to the harsh dryness of the rangelands. Southeast the Redbone Hills shouldered against the sky, a rough outlier of the Dead Hills and, like the Dead Hills, the province of tombs and tomb robbers. The dry wind brought her the stink of the slaughterhouses that lay outside the East Gate, and mingled with that stink, the greater reek of the squalid suburb where dwelled the city's lawless poor.

No clan had jurisdiction in the Slaughterhouse and there was, in effect, no law; even the city guards came to the district only in groups, and never at night. Mud hovels crowded up against the sides of what had been handsome villas, once upon a time, now crumbling and crowded hives in which whole families occupied single rooms and let boarders sleep in the corners. Those too drunken, too uneducated, too lazy, or too unconventional to find work with the guild artisans in the city made their homes here. Shaldis herself had roamed its filthy alleys in boy's disguise as a child, and last spring had hidden here from a murderer of Raven sisters. There were still a dozen people here who knew her by the name of Golden Eagle, her pseudonym at the time.

Little Pig Alley ran down one side of the shut-up Temple of Nebekht, and Greasy Yard opened off that, into what had formerly been the stable quarters of a large house. Shaldis ducked through the red-painted adobe archway into the yard and saw the familiar sight of children darting wildly around the dusty space playing moonlight ponies; saw Vorm and Zarb, the two local drunks, lounging in the doorway of one of the little rooms engaged in their endless slurry-voiced yarning as if they had neither moved nor come to any conclusions since spring. On the opposite side of the court, a rawboned dark-haired woman was making couscous over a dung fire in the doorway of her room. Shaldis let the Gray Cloak dissolve around her and the woman looked up and said, "Hey there, girl. Come to see how your old friend Rosemallow's doing?"

"Come to gossip." Shaldis dropped her night-fair purchases on the ground beside the fire and seated herself on the remains of an old camel saddle next to the house wall.

"I thought Crafties could just draw pictures on the ground and blow chicken feathers over them and find out everything they need to know." Rosemallow looked at her across the pot with a glinting, gap-toothed smile. Like most of the women of the Slaughterhouse District she didn't bother wearing veils unless she was going into the city and wanted to look elegant. Certainly, few inhabitants of the Slaughterhouse bothered to divide their dwellings into *seryak* and harem, the domains of men and women.

"I did," Shaldis replied. "And that chicken feather fell into the corner of the picture labeled *Go ask Rosemallow.* Don't touch that," she added, setting the veil-wrapped jar in the corner by the step.

"What is it?"

"One of Cattail's fertility potions."

Through the open door of the room next to Rosemallow's a woman's voice could be heard, moaning "Oh, my darling—oh, my beloved! Ah, ecstasy! *Ecstasy!*"

Rosemallow dumped half the raisins and half the apples into the couscous and blew on the steaming spoon. "Then for the gods' sakes set it on the other side of the door so our girl Melon won't even *pass* it when she's done with this one. That's all we'd need around here, and if it's Cattail that made it, the dear gods only know what she'd birth. What is it you need to know, dearie?"

"Where does Ahure the Blood Mage live these days?"

"Lord, girl, you don't need chicken feathers and honeyed raisins to find that out. He's got a house south of here at the foot of the Redbone Hills by where the Carpenter's wadi comes out."

"What, that scraggy old mortuary temple?"

"The house just beside it. Reach through the door there, honey, and get me some cinnamon. That box there just inside."

Shaldis obeyed. Rosemallow's room was, unexpectedly, spotlessly clean, her own bedding and that of her children unrolled already over the divan and floor and her gray cat, Murder, solicitously nursing a litter of kittens. "Isn't that dangerous?" she asked, re-emerging into the courtyard. "You get wilding teyn and runaways in the hills. Bandits, too."

"His magic protects him." The older woman dusted a pinch of spice into her stew. "Of course, Noyad usually sends a couple of his boys out to keep watch over the place, but to hear Ahure tell it, he'd be fine alone."

"Noyad the jeweler must value him, if he keeps bodyguards out there."

"Why not, if he's making money for Noyad hand over fist putting luck wards and passion spells and what have you into those trinkets of his."

"Do you have one?"

"Melon does." Rosemallow nodded toward the dark doorway of her friend's room. "She'll be out in a minute," she added unnecessarily, since matters were audibly approaching a conclusion within. "She has about a dozen. Me, I'll stick to Starbright's horoscopes." She patted the half-dozen brightly beaded leather amulets strung around her neck, each containing advice for those born within her year, sign, phase, and aspects. Men's horoscopes, which were keyed to the sun, were much simpler.

Shaldis settled her back against the camel saddle again. "You haven't heard rumors around town of any new Raven sister working, have you?" she asked. "One that maybe the water bosses out here have control of and aren't telling anyone about?"

"Funny you should ask that."

She looked up uninterestedly as a young man staggered from Melon's room, a half-drunk camel driver who smelled worse than any self-respecting camel Shaldis had ever met. He leaned back through the doorway, mumbling words of endearment. *Does Tulik make a fool of himself chasing the Melons of the world?* wondered Shaldis contemptuously.

She couldn't imagine it.

Does Jethan?

The thought was like accidentally rolling over onto a thorn branch, but before she had time to sort out why, Melon appeared in the doorway, casually draped in a half-dozen veils of assorted hues and not very much else. Her hair—a towering confection of braids and blossoms whose general style Twinkle had obviously been trying to achieve—hadn't even been mussed. "Pig," she remarked, as the camel driver disappeared through the gate into Little Pig Alley. She produced a mirror from goodness knew where on her person and checked the state of her eye paint (unimpaired). "Piglet, I should say. Hey there,

Golden Eagle," she added, with a wave at Shaldis. "Are those apples? *Darling!*" she added when Rosemallow produced the wine, and bounced over to give Shaldis a hug that reeked of camel driver.

She looked around for her cup and moved in the direction of the veil-wrapped parcel. *"Don't touch that!"* the other two chorused. "Tell her what happened to Murder," added Rosemallow, when Melon sat back with the wine.

"Oh, yeah." The girl nodded, her round face with its bright-pink cheeks growing grave. "Poor Murder got caught by two of the dogs over in the next street—by the time I got them off her I could see it was too late. She ran and hid in a crack in a wall, and before I could get her, that thug who owns them came out and gave me grief for whacking them—he's one of Xolnax the water boss's thugs, who guards the wells around here and charges five coppers apiece to let anyone draw water. By the time I'd dealt with him Murder had dragged herself away. I knew she couldn't live—her leg was nearly torn off and her skin ripped back and bleeding."

Tears filmed the girl's eyes as she drank her wine; Shaldis glanced back at the door of Rosemallow's room, through which Murder could clearly be seen, calmly nursing her brood.

"We couldn't find her for days," Rosemallow went on, "and we had to feed the poor kittens ourselves—their poor little eyes weren't even open! Then two days later I wake up one morning and there she is, healed. She hopped back in among her kits and started nursing them again like she'd never been away. She has a big fresh scar on her leg and another one on her back where the skin was ripped away, and she was hungry and skinny."

"It was magic," said Melon. "That I swear. She wasn't gone above two days, and she couldn't have lived. Here, I'll show you." She went into the room and re-emerged a moment later with the gray cat in her arms. The scars on Murder's body were fresh. When Shaldis touched her, she felt the echo of the magic that had saved the cat's life. There were echoes there of the sweet simplicity she'd felt on her grandfather's door latch, on the walls of the gallery where his camel-driver guards had been put to sleep. She stroked Murder's head, traced the huge scars with her fingertips.

It had to be the same Crafty one. Yet why didn't it feel more similar?

There couldn't possibly be two unknown women working magic—hidden magic—in the streets of the Yellow City.

Could there?

"That isn't all," said Rosemallow. "I heard someone found an ill-wish mark—*fresh*—on the house of one of Xolnax's goons—"

"Which one?" asked Shaldis. "Who?"

"Don't know. This is just something I heard thirdhand in the baths. But Xolnax has been asking all around the town—not just in the Slaughterhouse but everywhere—about who might have made it. Cattail's been asking, too. And she's been coming down here, touching the walls like you do." She mimed the brushing gesture Shaldis had made in her grandfather's study and gallery, in Cattail's garden, everywhere she sought the whisper of another's magic. "She's looking for her, all right. From the questions she's asked, it sounds like she thinks it's a child. . . ."

Nonsense, Cattail had declared, with that hard suspicious glare. *Why would you think I'd know?*

The king and that concubine of his holding out gold . . .

Resentment had glinted in her voice like the raw rash of nettles.

She had withheld herself from the circle that Summerchild had formed, disdaining to have others tell her how to use her power.

But now she was seeking to make a circle of her own. To control others and to draw on and drink their power through the Sigil of Sisterhood, as she fancied Summerchild did with Pebble, Shaldis, Pomegranate, and Moth.

"If it wasn't a child," put in Melon, her mouth full of couscous and raisins, "she'd already be selling passion potions down in Hot Pillow Lane and making a fortune," a piece of logic with which Shaldis could not argue.

"If it's a child, may the gods help her," said Rosemallow grimly. "Because Xolnax—or Cattail, whichever of them finds her first—is going to buy her from her parents and raise her as their own, so that they'll be able to control her magic for their own ends. And then the gods help us all. Oh, show Shaldis your pendants from Ahure, honey," she added as a couple of young men—brothers by the look of them and obviously thugs in the pay of some one of the local water bosses—appeared in the archway from the street, leaning slightly on each other and calling out Melon's name.

Melon smiled smugly and preened herself a little. "Gotta go, kittens. Thanks ever so for the wine—you be here when I get back?" She stood, and unfastened one of the several pendants from around her neck. "Take good care of that," she added in a whisper. "It's brought me I don't know how many good customers." And she took each bedazzled young thug by an elbow and guided them both into her room.

The pendant was cheaply made, as Yellow Hen had described. Inferior bronze set with a bad-quality topaz and chips of blue faience. A circle of what looked like earth-wizard runes were inscribed around it. There was no more magic in it than in an adobe brick.

TWENTY-THREE

Shaldis turned them over and over in her mind as she walked back along the path by the city wall to the Fishmarket Gate, and from there along Great Bazaar Street and so home in the darkness as the city settled toward sleep:

Cattail.

Ahure the Blood Mage.

A woman calling out in despair in the rhythmically booming darkness.

A skinny gray cat who should have been dead and wasn't.

Echoes of magic that were almost the same but not quite.

A child would use those simple spells to heal a cat.

Would a child use her magic to assist an assassin?

Shaldis had seen too many five-year-old pickpockets and housebreakers in the streets of the Slaughterhouse District to have any illusions about what the innocent could be coaxed, tricked, or blackmailed into doing.

And Cattail was seeking to buy herself that extra power that domination of a Raven child would bring.

Shaldis ghosted among the blankets of the sleeping camel drivers around the embers of the courtyard fire at her grandfather's house, slipped through the silent kitchen court, and up to her own room above it, between her mother's and her aunt's. Bedding had been made up for her, under one of the new mosquito-net tents. As she lay on it she pictured the healing herbs as Yanrid had instructed her, meditated on each one: scent, taste, bark, and leaves.

Fever tree and hand of Darutha, emperor root and chamomile.

After that she stretched out her senses through the house, listening to the sounds in each chamber and gallery. At any other time or place she would have sniffed as well, but at the moment even the senses of the Crafty could not penetrate past the ammonia reek of the dye pots in the kitchen court.

Still, she heard nothing but the night sounds of the house: the snuffle and sigh of her parents' breathing, the thready whisper of Twinkle telling Foursie stories in the dark of the maids' dormitory: "So the evil queen said, 'You must agree to become my slave, and to do my bidding forever. . . .'"

Then she slipped over into sleep, an hour before first light.

The king and his company reached the village of Three Wells about an hour before first light. "Best we camp, my lord," said Captain Numet quietly, when they came within the ring of dusty cornfields that surrounded the town. "As you said, an hour won't make much difference. The scouts say there's not a sound, either from the village itself or from the teyn compound."

"Is it safe?" Oryn rose in his stirrups, looked around him at the dark sea of cornstalks, shoulder high to the mounted troopers, in places head high. Beyond them, rough ground rose to the east, a stretch of badlands that the merchant Poru had called the Serpent Maze, separating the village oasis from the true desert beyond.

"We'll keep back of the cornfields, where we can get a clear view, Your Majesty. Anything that comes from the badlands, we'll be able to see before it gets to us."

Something flickered in the corner of Oryn's vision, something that was gone when he turned his head in the direction of the hills. He nudged his horse over to Summerchild's as the men dismounted and began to set camp. She, too, was gazing at the hills.

"What's there?"

She shook her head. "Something . . . I don't know."

"Teyn?"

"No," she murmured. "They're everywhere but there."

Shaldis jerked awake. *Voices crying out—*

The rags of dreams flicked from her mind. What she thought had been strange music on the edge of hearing, scents and sensations of strange sweet poison, dissolved into the peaceful stillness of the time the Sun Mages called the Sun at His Prayers, the hour at which even the rowdiest camel drivers slept.

Yet she was certain she'd heard or smelled or felt something.

What WAS that? Not the Crafty woman crying for help. Something else.

Her mind quested through every chamber, every gallery: kitchen, gardens, the compound of the teyn.

But all she encountered was the night silence of the sleeping house.

With the coming of first light, the king and his party rode through the cornfields to the village.

Vultures were everywhere. The high corn, parching from two days without irrigation, rustled with activity: coyote, kit foxes, and, Oryn saw, the village cats and dogs.

Within the ring of the cornfields lay the vegetable gardens, the charred maze of low walls visible beyond. As they passed the gate of the teyn compound he saw that it stood open, and vultures perched on its blackened walls and on the bodies that lay both within it and outside the gate. It seemed to him that only a few lay outside.

After two days, the town was enveloped in a cloud of flies, and the stink was enough to knock a man down.

A woman lay on her back near the edge of town, face—or what the vultures had left of her face—to the sky. It was hard to tell the state of her clothing now, but Oryn didn't see any obvious wounds. A round-bellied kitchen pot lay as if she'd carried it in the crook of her arm; Jethan sprang from his horse and tilted the pot with the handle of his quirt so he could look inside. "Eggplants, my lord." He tilted the pot over, spilling the contents on the ground, stirred the smooth white-and-purple globes to see if there was anything of value—or interest—among them.

There wasn't.

"Over here, sir."

Numet stood over a detached arm, the limb protruding from a bundle of green-and-white cloth that looked like a man's work tunic. "Looks like there's been grave robbing here."

Oryn dismounted. The arm was almost black, the desiccated flesh collapsed onto the bone, slick as long-dried leather. He straightened, looked back toward the broken hills of the Serpent Maze, visible now above the burned walls of the village.

"That's a mummy's arm, surely," said Captain Numet, and turned to Poru as the salt merchant emerged from the charred shell of a house. "Are there tombs back in the badlands?"

"Absolutely," Oryn said, and, though he looked a little surprised that the king would know this, the young merchant nodded.

"The hills are rotten with them, Majesty. Some quite big ones. Every now and then the young men of the village will dig through them—especially nowadays—but they've all been looted clean centuries ago."

"The kings of the Zali Dynasty had tombs out here," provided Oryn, kneeling gingerly and poking at the arm with a stick. "Here, and north by the Lake of Roses, hoping, I suppose, that the more trouble they made for tomb robbers the likelier they were to be left in peace—the more fools they. I have one or two pieces of Zali jewelry—which are interesting but not very pretty—and a tremendous collection of burial texts: I suspect most of the Zali jewelry was melted down centuries ago. But why would a tomb robber steal a mummy, much less bring it into the village? They mostly just strip them and dump them on the floors of the tombs."

"Whyever they did it," said Jethan grimly, looking into a house nearby, "it wasn't just one."

After the fourth time she woke, heart pounding, positive that she'd heard a singing that proved on waking to be illusory, Shaldis gave it up. The house was still shadowy, and the silence now profound. The few hours of relative coolness snatched from the jaw of the ravening lion of midsummer.

Birds in full song in the garden.

She slipped from beneath the mosquito net and dressed again in her white novice's robe, made her way unseen down the stairs and through the kitchen court where Cook's dark form could be glimpsed beyond the kitchen archways just making up the fires, then out to the street.

Every alley was a canyon of shadow, the vegetable market in front of the Grand Bazaar a world of luminous blue. Pigeons pecked the dirt in quest of grain dropped the day before.

The first of the farmers were setting up their stands

there, so Shaldis knew the Fishmarket Gate was open, after being closed barely two hours. This time she followed the path along the wall only halfway, and turned off it onto the smaller but still well-worn track that led toward the Redbone Hills, where the landchiefs and the great merchant princes had been buried, time out of mind. Around them, closer to town, were interred everyone else who could afford it: each wadi and hillside honeycombed with tombs great and small. In the clear dove-colored light the tablelike marble tombs, the small sharp markers, looked like bits of broken bone, scrawled all over with ancient formulae and curses and protective wards to keep forgotten forms of evil away. Deeper in, Shaldis knew, the rich were buried in crypts dug in the hillsides, painted doors at the backs of caves like the hollowed sockets of skulls.

From the top of the rise where the dry rangelands began, she could see the house Ahure had taken. Like nearly everything else in her world she'd known of it most of her life. It stood alone on the brow of a little knoll half a mile or so from the start of the Redbone Hills proper, just where the old burial road from the city twisted around. There'd been a mortuary temple there whose ruins still stood under the back of the hill. It was too far to easily walk, though Shaldis could have done it had she had nothing else to do that day. It looked frighteningly isolated against the yellow hills, the brown-stained plaster long unpainted and crumbling, the dull-green cacti half shielding it like an ugly forest.

So that was where Ahure had taken refuge, after Lord Jamornid had politely let him know that he had better uses for his money than supporting a mage who could no longer work magic.

Lord Sarn, at least, had taken in his brother Benno, who'd once been rector of the Citadel of the Sun Mages—though, naturally, thought Shaldis, as she watched the first sunlight stream across the Redbone Hills, Lord Sarn hadn't offered Benno back his birthright of elder son, and erstwhile heir, of the great House Sarn.

Gold streamed across the high harsh domes of the Dead Hills, the lower labyrinths of the Redbones, those bitter badlands that divided the rangelands of goats and cattle east of the Yellow City from the true desert, the deadly desert. The realm of Kush the Destroyer. The light struck the isolated little house among its cacti, turned the dirt-colored walls to molten amber.

She turned her steps back toward the city.

✳

As they moved through the narrow streets of Three Wells, Oryn and his party found withered fragments everywhere among the bloated and vulture-torn corpses of the villagers. Sometimes those blackened arms and legs were found separated from bodies, sometimes—gruesomely—they were attached to coal-dark leathery lumps that proved upon inspection to be bodies that had shrunk and contracted to the size of contorted children. "Is that an effect of the kind of mummification they used then?" asked Summerchild, wincing back from a particularly shocking specimen. "What would cause that?"

The face—what there was of it—smiled up at them from the collapsed head in an expression of unnerving bliss.

Oryn drew her away, sickened. In a way it was far

worse than the unwounded modern corpses that lay in the doorways around them.

Tracks of teyn were everywhere, though only a single corpse lay, badly hacked, in the street. "Look how they superimpose every human track in the dust," murmured Jethan. The new gold sunlight streaming across the desert threw his shadow over Oryn as king and concubine knelt to examine the single dead subhuman outside the teyn compound gate. "They go from house to house."

"It couldn't have been they who burned the town, though," said Oryn, groaning as he got to his feet. "Teyn are afraid of fire."

"Teyn used to be afraid of the walls of their own compounds, Your Majesty." Jethan reached out significantly and flicked the old fear runes on the compound door with the back of his hand. "And if someone's controlling them . . ."

"They couldn't have got here from where they held us off in time to burn the village," protested Captain Numet, emerging from the burned ruins of the overseer's house. "It was half a day's ride!"

"If someone *is* controlling them," responded Oryn gently, "he—or she—may be giving instructions to two separate bands."

The captain looked thoroughly nonplussed at this idea. It was not one that Oryn particularly enjoyed either.

"I think," said Jethan, "that the tracks I've seen here are mostly domestics. They're bigger and heavier than the wildings, and they walk more upright, without leaving hand tracks in the dust."

"You mean they escaped," said Numet with an edge of panic in his voice, "and then returned to burn the town after . . . after what? You don't think it could be a curse? A curse that fell on the town because of someone's bringing in a cache of mummies from some tomb in the hills?"

Summerchild shook her head at once. "The curses that lay on the tombs have all failed." Her voice was sad. "Like the spell wards against mosquitoes and mice, and grasshoppers around the fields—"

Like the wards of dread around the teyn compounds, Oryn mentally added.

"—the magic of the wizards that held curses into the stones of the tombs has dissolved. I think that's what our friend Poru meant," she added with a kindly smile, "when he said, 'especially nowadays,' when we spoke of the village men helping themselves to the tombs. Haven't you heard the same thing about the tombs in the Dead Hills?"

Captain Numet seemed a little reassured. "That's a fact, lady. But seeing this . . . it makes you wonder."

"What *I* wonder," said Summerchild, returning to Oryn's side, "is whether this plague—this madness or fever that caused everyone to run out into the streets like this to die—can have come from the mummies themselves?"

Oryn winced. "I suppose that means a quarantine. Perhaps we can make it last until after the Moon of Jubilee, to buy ourselves a little more time? Captain," he added, "you might want to tell your men not to touch anything here in the town."

Numet, who'd wandered a few paces to watch the men as they gingerly entered the broken houses, raised his brows. "I'll tell them, sir. But, by the gods, what on earth in this village would there be for anyone to want to take?"

Walking back toward the city walls through the swift-rising heat of the new day, Shaldis turned over in her mind what she knew of Ahure. A charlatan now, yes, but like many mages a man of intense pride, the birthright pride of one who has known from tiny childhood that he was special. Like the djinni, who were composed entirely of magic, magic was what Ahure *was*, his sole perception of himself. He couldn't imagine himself no longer being special.

Couldn't imagine existing—as the djinn Naruansich had learned to exist—in any fashion other than the one he had known all his life.

The charlatanry was a way of hanging on to what he had been, she reflected. To what, in his heart and his mind, he still was.

How long would it be, Shaldis wondered, as her boots scuffed the hot dust of the roadway and lizards flicked out of sight before her shadow, before Noyad the jeweler concluded that Ahure's powers were all fake and ceased to send him the protection of his hired bullyboys?

To whom would that sour old man turn then?

Healing no longer flows from their hands. She heard the voice of her unknown sister whisper in her memory, out of the depths of those dreams.

What had the wizards of *her* acquaintance done when they found that magic no longer flowed from their hands? Did they stew in rancor, in hatred, in envy of those who for reasons unknown now exercised the powers the men had lost?

Or had it been one of them who, like Yanrid, had taught the unknown Raven sister the means of reaching out for help, with spells that he himself could no longer perform?

The morning sun heated her shoulders under the thin white wool of her robe, and before her she could see the dust-clouds already rising, where farmers brought their produce to the city gate.

✴

It was true, reflected Oryn, that, as Captain Numet had said, there was very little in Three Wells worth stealing. "If there *was* looted tomb gold anywhere in town, cursed or otherwise," he murmured to Summerchild, "whoever burned the place while we were being held at bay by the teyn did a *very* good job of collecting it."

She slipped behind him through the door of the largest house in town, just off the main square. The overseer's, probably. Jethan had insisted on preceding them around every corner, sword drawn as if expecting to encounter a hostile army. Oryn had the feeling that the young man was slightly disappointed when he didn't.

"Do you think that's what happened?" Summerchild asked. "That someone killed them to retrieve something from the village?"

"No." He paused in the middle of the roofless room, looking around him at the fallen beams, the burned body of a man crumpled in a corner, the broken dishes and cups. The new-risen sun of morning heated his shoulders through the silk of his robe, warmed the air even under the roof beams' broken shadows. "No. Too many of those people in the streets too clearly killed one another."

The guards at least all seemed to be giving the corpses, modern or ancient, wide berth.

Could sickness cling to gold? For that long? Over a

thousand years? Oryn cursed himself for not knowing. If some guardsman found, among all this ash, one or another of those big crude-looking gold Zali pendants set with obsidian, or one of those smoky balls of green-and-silver glass, would he leave it alone?

Or would he bring it into the Yellow City to sell?

"So what do you think happened?" Summerchild wrapped the end of one of her scarves around the handle of a mirror and picked it up from the ashes on the floor. She turned it over. Both sides were blackened with fire. It had been broken, Oryn saw, by being struck on the corner of the wall bench beside the door. Glass sparkled, half buried in the ash.

"I can't imagine. Everything we're seeing should be clues, but they don't seem to add up to anything." He held out his hand to pick up a shard, and Summerchild touched his arm stayingly.

"I put spells upon myself, on my flesh and my clothing, against infection," she said. "If something must be touched, I'll do it."

"I do need to be in good shape for my jubilee, don't I?" Oryn dusted his hands, though he had handled nothing. "If that mirror was burned on both sides—and under the glass bed, too, I see—that means it was broken *after* the house was first burned, doesn't it? Or at least picked up and moved.

"By the teyn? You say their tracks are everywhere, Jethan, dear boy." He turned toward the tall guardsman. "Have you seen any tracks that look like they shouldn't be here? New boots, or better boots than the villagers would wear? Even horse or camel prints superimposed upon the ash from the second fire?"

"I've been looking, my lord king," replied the young man rather stiffly, as if even long familiarity with the king hadn't inured him to being called *dear boy*. "And I have seen nothing but the marks of the teyn."

"It should mean something," said Oryn worriedly.

For a moment they stood, looking at each other, the tall king and his slender concubine in the hot latticework shade of the house's broken rafters. Hazel eyes looked down into blue, sharing speculation and fear.

Outside the city gates, Shaldis joined the jostling line of asses, camels, farmers bearing yokes, bringing eggplants, tomatoes, onions, sweet bunches of purple-black figs to the city's markets. Sheep and goats bleated, chickens flapped against their wicker crates. Shaldis left off her cloak of inconspicuousness and smiled at passersby as she edged among them, wondering whether Summerchild would be back today, and what she herself might find in the Citadel library. She should probably contact Pomegranate.

Then pain hit her.

Pain, and the frantic summons, instantly cut off.

The sense that her magic was bleeding.

Shaldis gasped, staggered into the corner of the gate. Terrible cold, as if her very life were draining away, and the magic bonds of the Circle of Sisterhood twisted and strained.

For an instant she thought she heard music, unknown yet half recognized, veering through her brain.

Then an avalanche of darkness. A fading scream.

Shaldis thought, *Summerchild.*

Her vision cleared; she was still clinging to the side of the Fishmarket Gate. A friendly-faced man had run to support her, yokes of spinach baskets still on his shoulders. "Are you all right, miss?"

By his face she must be white as a sheet. She managed to whisper, "I'm fine."

And shaking off his helpful grip, she started to run.

※

"All the glass is broken," pointed out Summerchild. "Goblets and what looks like a bowl as well. I wonder if there's anything in the Citadel records about the teyn fearing it. I know people say they're not to be trusted with it, out of clumsiness, but there are at least a dozen of the palace teyn who carry glass vessels back and forth to the storerooms daily without problem. I'll be curious," she went on as she set the mirror down, "to see what we find in those tombs."

She spread her hands out and rested them, and her forehead, lightly against the blackened adobe of the wall. Closed her eyes, sinking once more into her listening trance. Probing, seeking within the mud-brick of the walls the echoes of whatever had been in this room. Reaching inward to touch it with her mind. Oryn knelt near the bricks of the hearth, keeping his hands well clear of the colored shards of the bowl but studying them where they lay.

There were certain magics, Soth had told him, that could only be held in glass, but glass had to be specially ensorcelled to be used for purposes of magic. Did that still hold, now that magic had changed? But in any case, all the glass in the village couldn't have been—

Summerchild screamed. Oryn swung around, sprang to his feet in horror to see her body arch back, her hands still pressed to the wall, her blue eyes staring for a blank second at the hot morning sky. Then she screamed again, as if flesh and mind were being sliced apart in one excruciating second, and crumpled backward into Oryn's arms.

TWENTY-FOUR

Shaldis was halfway to her grandfather's house when she knew someone was trying to speak with her. *Pebble, Moth, Pomegranate* . . . Shaldis was inclined to simply ignore the urging in her mind until she could reach the privacy of her room, sink into a trance, and look for Summerchild herself, but the thought that one of the others might have already done so made her stop and perch on the low plinth beside the Grand Bazaar's brass-studded doors and fish in her satchel for her crystal.

She had barely drawn two breaths and let her mind relax when Pebble's homely, frightened face appeared in the central facet.

"What is it, what's happened?"

In the background Shaldis could glimpse the vine leaves that shaded the inner court of the house of Pebble's father.

"I don't know. I was walking in the street, I haven't had time to put myself in trance. It's Summerchild, isn't it?"

"I think so," replied Pebble. "I—I feel that she's the one in danger or the one who's been hurt. It was just a horrible flash that came and went, as if it were dying away in a long corridor. Now I feel as if she's drawing on my power, my magic, but it's very weak. It comes and it goes. I tried to speak to her through the water bowl at once but nothing happened." Tears streaked her face. In addition to hero-worshiping Summerchild—as Cattail had so scornfully remarked—she loved the concubine dearly. "But I'm not that good with it. More than half the time, nothing happens. But you felt it, too?"

You felt it? As if the pain wasn't like being hit over the head with an ax. Shaldis almost laughed. But she said only, "I felt it."

"Do you think she's all right?"

Shaldis was hard put not to snap *How the hell should I know?* But Pebble's terrified eyes stopped her. "I'm going to see what I can learn by going into a trance at home," she said, keeping her voice steady with an effort. "But if I don't find anything quickly I'll go to the palace. You meet me there. If you talk with Moth, tell her to meet us both there." She could already feel the urgency rising and pushing at her mind again.

"And don't tell anyone what's happened. For one thing, we don't know if the harm came to just Summerchild, or to the king and his party as well—"

"Oh, dear gods, I didn't ever think of that! Do you think—?"

"I don't think anything," said Shaldis. "And the last thing we need right now is rumors flying all over the town. Don't tell anyone *anything*. Just meet me at the palace."

"All right." Her image faded—Shaldis marveled that she'd let go that quickly rather than hang on asking for reassurance—and was immediately replaced by that of Moth. It was the first time Shaldis had seen the young concubine with her long brown hair hanging completely undressed and with no makeup.

"Where you been!?"

Buying candy and having my nails painted, where do you think?

Stop it. She's just scared. People lash out when they're scared.

"Talking to Pebble. Were you able to learn anything? To feel her mind in trance?"

"No, but it's Summerchild, isn't it?"

"I think so, and Pebble thinks so. . . . Neither of us could tell what happened."

"It was magic," said Moth. "I felt . . . awful. Like a spear in my heart. Then it faded away, fast. You don't think Red Silk got her, do you? Her and Foxfire? I hear they left Mohrvine's villa Golden Sky the night before last, sneaked out with a huge train of baggage, nobody knows where."

Oh, good. Just what we need. A wizard war. The rains don't come, the lakes dry out, and what's the best thing we can think to do? Fight among ourselves.

Shaldis took a deep breath. "I don't know what happened. Can you—?"

"Or what if Cattail's selling her services to somebody like Lord Sarn? And she put a hex on Summerchild, to make sure the king dies, so that stupid brother of his can take over and that new concubine he's got will lead him around by his—"

"We don't know what happened," Shaldis nearly shouted, and resisted the temptation to add that the idea of Cattail being able to defeat Summerchild in a battle of magic was ludicrous. She already knew that such an observation would only open the door to endless—and pointless—discussion and speculation. "I've asked Pebble to meet me at the palace. Would you meet us there, too? I was out in the street this morning when it happened, but I'm going to go home and see if I can learn anything by going into a trance."

"I did that and didn't get nothing. Do you think maybe—?"

"Then I probably won't get anything, either," said Shaldis. "But I'm going to try. Then I'll head straight for the palace as well. Please don't speak to anyone of what happened, or of what it could mean. The last thing we need is all kinds of rumors flying around."

"No, absolutely!" Moth made a peasant sign of averting evil. "Besides, I never spread no rumors nor gossip."

"I know you don't," Shaldis assured her, hearing as she did so her mother's stricture that her tongue would turn coal black at that magnitude of lie. "I'm relying on you, Moth. But I must go." And with that she closed her hand around the crystal and looked away. Breathless, dream-like thoughts swirled through her mind.

Look in the crystal. Please look in the crystal.

After a moment she looked.

Foxfire, her face running with tears.

Am I NEVER going to get home and have a chance to see what's happened for myself?

"What happened?" Foxfire was in some dark place, a storeroom or a cupboard, Shaldis thought.

"You tell me."

"Is it Summerchild?"

"We think so. Nobody knows. She and the king rode out early yesterday morning to investigate the report of a plague in some village. Where are you?"

"I . . ." The girl swallowed, trying to collect herself. She was the youngest of the Raven sisters, though her training in the most expensive Blossom House in the city had given her the deportment of a much older lady. That deportment was gone now and she was a child again, a child alone and scared.

"I'm not supposed to say," she whispered at last. "But I dreamed a dream, a terrible dream. My grandmother would never let me join with you by the Sigil of Sisterhood, but Summerchild and I did work together, when I was learning healing. And I know it was her I heard cry out. It was her I felt, that awful wave of coldness." She swallowed, wiped her eyes. Her hair, like Moth's, was unbraided for sleep, and she wore a striped linen bed robe pulled hastily around her slim shoulders. "It woke me up, and it didn't fade, like dreams do, but got stronger."

"Did you try to reach her in trance?"

"I . . ." Foxfire glanced around her, as if hearing the sound of approaching feet. "I couldn't. I can't. I have to go."

The image faded.

Shaldis thrust the crystal into her satchel, and strode as fast as she could across the vegetable market toward the house on Sleeping Worms Street.

✳

"And what do you think you're doing, girl?"

Foxfire stopped at the sound of her grandmother's voice, turned with the most profoundly innocent expression she could muster. "I was just listening to the birds on the terrace."

"You're a liar, girl, there hasn't been a bird within a hundred miles of this place since the Akarians were kings." Red Silk's cold eye passed over Foxfire like the edge of a knife, taking in the unbound hair, the too-baggy bed robe, the bare feet on the cracked red floor tiles, the half-open door of the wardrobe room a few yards down the gallery. "Give me what you have in your hand."

Foxfire held out the mirror. Her grandmother's lined, beautiful face was unreadable and absolutely terrifying.

Red Silk passed her hand over the little circle of silver-backed glass, reading the magic that had passed through it as if it had been a lingering heat. Her turquoise eyes seemed to pale as they grew cold.

She said, "So." Foxfire didn't think she'd seen her so angry since she'd caught one of the maids plucking feathers from one of her pet finches.

She'd had a servant pull the maid's fingernails out, and had set her to washing floors.

Her hand flicked out like the striking head of a snake and she caught Foxfire's hair close to the scalp, pulled her forward with a brutal grip.

"I see you're going to have to trust Opal from now on about how your hair looks, and if your eye paint is on straight." Her voice was as level as a marble floor, and as chilly. "We're rationing water as it is: I'll just give orders that you're not to have a cup or a basin left in your possession—you'll have to ask, to drink or to wash or to clean your teeth. I thought I could trust you."

Foxfire made herself whisper—made herself not cry out as Red Silk's grip tightened excruciatingly on the handful of hair—"You can, Grandmother."

"You'll have to show me that on another occasion. To whom were you talking?"

Through gritted teeth Foxfire replied, "Shaldis, Grandmother."

"And you said?"

"Only that I was lonely. That I'd had a bad dream which frightened me."

"And you didn't come to me?" As she spoke Red Silk pulled Foxfire down toward the floor, Foxfire struggling not to scream with pain, tears pouring down her face.

"I went into your room and you were gone." A lie, but Red Silk was dressed and booted and had come from the direction of the main house, not from her room.

The horrible grip pulled her steadily down until Foxfire was kneeling on the tile, then down further, so that she bent over, her face nearly touching the floor with Red Silk crouched over her. Foxfire began to sob with pain. "And Opal was where?"

"Sometimes Opal doesn't understand. Sometimes there are things only someone like me, someone with magic, can understand. Please don't hurt Opal, Grandmother, don't have her beaten."

The grip on her hair released. Foxfire collapsed to the floor, crying in earnest now, burningly aware of the folds of her grandmother's black linen robe lying over her hand.

"Have her beaten until her understanding improves?" Red Silk's voice crackled with amused irony, and that cold, strong hand touched Foxfire's head. "You're the one whose understanding needs improvement, girl. But until your father is king—until my son passes safely through the hands of the gods—the stakes are too high to leave our hopes supported by a pillar that has so much as creaked once. Do you understand?"

Foxfire nodded wretchedly.

"Sit up, girl, I'm done with you. You shall have ample opportunity to demonstrate to me how sorry you are, and how trustworthy. For my part, I am sorry that you're lonely. I did what I could to obviate that. But women born under the shadow of the Raven to some extent will always be alone."

And women born under the shadow of the Raven, thought Foxfire, with a sense of falling into a gulf of infinite despair, *will always be sought after by those who want to control them for their own ends.*

Even Father.

The knowledge yawned in her, a black wound. Mortal. She made herself say, "Yes, Grandmother."

"What we do here is too important to risk discovery," said Red Silk. "And that concubine of the king's can charm the birds off the trees, let alone charm information out of someone who's lonely. Habnit's Daughter is no more than her handmaiden—and why shouldn't she be? She owes her the bread on her plate, these days. You cannot trust them, either of them."

"No, Grandmother." Her lips only formed the words; no sound came out.

"Next time you're lonely, come to me. You haven't broken your fast, have you? We're starting the first of the test spells with the cobras in an hour. You have just time to get yourself washed."

"Yes, Grandmother."

Foxfire raised her eyes as her grandmother strode away up the gallery, following that small black figure as it passed through the muzzy shadows of the columns that surrounded the bare central courtyard, the clear shadowed morning light. Seeing in her mind those scarred white hands, strong as an eagle's talons and scented faintly with attar of roses, dripping with goat's blood in the Temple of Nebekht. Hearing that cracked ancient voice screaming the trapped djinn's name.

She felt a kind of dizzy shock at the wound of knowledge. *The only reason Father hasn't married me off already is that he wants to keep my power at his own beck and call. It is all I am to him.*

Is it all I am to him?

She didn't know, and didn't know how to go about finding out.

If I ask him, will he lie?

Of course he will.

She wondered how she could possibly feel that much pain and not bleed. She had been trained in the arts of a Pearl Woman—the perfect courtesan, the perfect concubine, the perfect tool and helper of whichever man she was given to—and had delighted in her skills, for they had won her father's praise. Pearl Women did not cry. Not for themselves, anyway.

She dried her tears.

Is that what it does to you, that knowledge? Makes you like Grandmother?

Foxfire walked back to her room, feeling more alone than ever in her life.

TWENTY-FIVE

Shaldis slipped back into the house through the camel-drivers' courtyard, keeping the Gray Cloak about her. As she walked she felt the hammering of her heart, the frantic fear that grew in her with every step. What the *hell* had happened?

Summerchild had tried for one instant to use magic, to defend herself with magic . . .

And had been swallowed up.

Dear gods, let her be all right!

As Pebble had described, Shaldis felt the dim tugging of the Sigil of Sisterhood in her heart. As if another member of the circle were trying to draw upon her magic. She dodged up the stairs from the kitchen court and into her room. The tug of the sigil dissolved into the urgent demand that she look in her crystal again. She shot the bolt, dropped cross-legged onto the bed. It was Pomegranate. "I think she's still alive," said the old woman, who by the look of it was in the latticed shade of some lakeside village square, presumably waiting for the next boat. "I listened for her, listened deep, and heard nothing. But Pontifer Pig says she lives. I think he's right, because I looked for the king and couldn't see him. That means he's still with her."

Shaldis wasn't certain of that. Summerchild had sought last spring for two of the sisters who'd been killed, and had not even been able to see their dead bodies. As for Pontifer Pig, Shaldis wasn't entirely sure what to think. For ten years, Pontifer had been merely a figment of Pomegranate's deranged imagination: at one time the beggar woman had actually owned a white pig, but the original Pontifer had long ago met his destiny under the wheels of a cart.

At least, thought Shaldis philosophically, it was her pet pig she imagined, and not her equally deceased husband, Deem. And she wondered briefly, with a smile, how her friend Soth had made out, traveling with a four-footed invisible companion that only Pomegranate could see.

When Pomegranate let her mirror fade, Shaldis tried to summon the king's image first in the crystal, then in the hand mirror she sometimes used, with equal lack of success. That might, as Pomegranate had said, mean he was close to Summerchild, and that Summerchild was alive.

She glanced at the room's latticed window. The hour of the Bird Sun was passing. Brazen light crept inexorably down the wall on the other side of the courtyard.

She drew a few deep breaths. Three Wells was a day's ride, everyone said. Had they been delayed there or trapped, or had they met something on their way back? But what would they have met? She knelt beside the bed, and with white chalk and red drew on the tiled floor the wide ring, the curving power lines, of the Sigil of Sisterhood, the mark that bound the minds, and the power, of the Sisters of the Raven together. She fashioned the sigil five times, linking the marks with a pentagram. In the midst of this star she lay down and folded her hands on her breast.

Are you there?

What happened?

Where are you?

Deep breaths, and the meditation on the sigils.

Concentration on the faint pull of magic, following its tugging down into darkness.

Singing, very far off. The beat of drums and the mingling of voices. *Human?* Scents. Of what? The glimmer of green light, blowing like mist across . . . across what?

Don't try to understand. Just listen, and breathe, and see what you see.

She thought she saw Summerchild, or sensed her in the distance. As if she, Shaldis, were swimming down a long well of glowing blue water and saw her at the bottom, sleeping on the floor of the lake. Sleeping in a halo of green light. But the Sigil of Sisterhood was traced around her in the sign of a pentagram, as it was on Shaldis's bedroom floor. The green light hemmed her in but did not touch her.

Then darkness. The sound of rain on leaves. A sweetness in the air that bordered on ecstasy.

That other sound, the slow booming sough that had troubled her dreams. Infinitely distant, like a heartbeat in her blood.

Suddenly, shockingly, she was looking out over a lake of fire. The rock underfoot trembled, and burned her feet through her boots. The air scorched her lungs as she breathed. All things appeared blindingly distinct: dull-red crusts of mud broke to show fiery liquid beneath, liquid that glowed like the molten gold in a smith's crucible, a lake of it, bounded by dim black cliffs whose riven walls caught the ruddiness when the flames shot up. Darkness lay over the cliffs and the burning lake, darkness thick with steams and smoke, but through the darkness moved something that looked like curling snakes of green mist, mist that clung together and did not disperse.

Mist that probed among the rocks as if hunting something.

Shaldis called out, *Summerchild?* She couldn't imagine what this place was. The dreamworld of a djinn, such as she had entered before?

The world of Summerchild's nightmares?

The green mist glowed as it moved closer to her through the rocks around the lake's black shore. Outcrops of rock glinted, black and shiny, like nodules of inky glass, and Shaldis thought the music she heard, the voices, were coming out of the mist.

Summerchild?

Fear filled her, and a terrible longing. *It knows the answer. The mist will be able to tell me anything. And everything.*

Do not let the mist touch you, said a voice in her thought. The words were foreign, but through their musical tones she felt the mind of the woman who had cried out to her, who had begged her for help. *Flee it. Flee this place.*

Who are you? Shaldis asked. *What happened to my friend?*

But it felt to her as if hands seized her, or a mind seized her mind. Force flung her into darkness and she grasped for the hand, the mind. She cried out, "Who are you?" and Pebble's voice replied,

"It's Pebble. Are you all right?"

Shaldis opened her eyes, annoyed. "Of course I'm all right. Why did you—"

She realized it was dark in the room. Lamps burned in the niches on either side of the bed, and the air had the rank dusty taste of night.

The Sun's Dreams.

The SUN'S DREAMS? The hours after midnight.

She stared up at the other girl in shock. Pebble swallowed, her eyes red with tears and fright. "We tried and tried to wake you." Shaldis realized the other smell in the room, even stronger than the indigo in the court below, was burnt feathers. She couldn't imagine how she could have remained asleep with one of those waved under her nose.

"With what Jethan told us about Summerchild—" began Moth, who Shaldis now saw was sitting on the bed at her feet.

"What?" Her mind groped, still trying to deal with the fact that she'd closed her eyes—for a few seconds, it seemed—toward the end of the hour of the Bird Sun and now it was the hour of the Sun's Dreams. A whole day gone. "Summerchild? I thought Jethan was with the king."

"He was. He rode in about an hour after sunset, when I was still at the palace, but I'd sent Pebble here and she found you on the floor and couldn't wake you up. You want some coffee?" Moth leaned over to pick up a cup of it that was resting in a lamp niche. "Jethan said Summerchild couldn't be waked neither, and sent more guards out with a litter, to bring her back from Three Wells. By that time Pebble sent me word you was out like the dead here, and Jethan said one of us had to come back with him."

"Is Jethan here?"

"Downstairs, and I think if we don't get him out of here soon he's gonna kill that grandfather of yours or that grandfather's gonna kill him, or at least bite him and give him rabies. What an old baboon! He says—"

Shaldis scrambled to her feet, and nearly fell, her stiff muscles cramping from long inaction. It had seemed to her that she'd only skimmed the edges of dreams, had only shut her eyes moments ago. A vision flickered through her mind of the smell of rain, of a lake of fire.

That sound. That distant crashing.

And a woman's voice warning her. Warning her of what?

She was halfway to the door when Pebble caught her sleeve. "Did you find her? Did you . . . did you touch her?"

Shaldis stood for a moment, trying to remember. She thought she'd glimpsed Summerchild ringed by the sigil, but had lost sight of her. And though the successive vision was curiously vivid, nothing in it fit with anything she knew.

She said softly, "I don't know."

"Should we look? Moth and I? One of us can find her."

"No!" Shaldis looked back at the dark-haired concubine, who was tucking her veils back around her face and hair preparatory to going downstairs where strangers could see her. Moth drew back, startled, from the frightened vehemence of her voice.

"Don't either of you try this," said Shaldis. "I *never* get lost in trance; *never* get so deep that I don't know where I am or how long I'm under. I don't know what happened, or whether it has anything to do with Summerchild or not, but until we know more about what happened to her, *none* of us is trying this again. All right?"

The other two nodded, and—silently acquiescing to the takeover of command by a girl their own age—followed her down the stairs.

※

"Don't be absurd," snapped Tulik when Shaldis announced she was going with Jethan to meet the royal party on its return to the Yellow City. "I forbid it."

"There's been murder and mayhem in this house," added her grandfather, who'd been—as Moth had related—in the midst of a furious argument with Jethan in the long *seryak* parlor when the three Raven sisters entered. "Damn it, girl, someone is trying to—to murder me, to use magic to bring this whole house down about our ears, and you rush off with some good-looking soldier because he beckons you?"

If Jethan's back could have gotten stiffer than it already was, it would have—and, Shaldis reckoned through a burning flush of anger and embarrassment, he probably would have snapped in two.

"I am 'beckoning' your granddaughter, *sir*"—Jethan could barely get the words out—"because her skills in the craft of magic render her assistance to the king imperative." In the golden lamp glow of the *seryak* his own dusky skin had flushed darker.

"Nonsense! You have other Crafty girls." Chirak's thumb jerked rudely at Moth and Pebble. "Take one of them, if the king wants a wench so badly."

"Don't you call me a wench, you moneygrubbing old counter jumper!" Moth whirled like an enraged lapdog.

"Hold your tongue, girl, if you don't want to be sent

back to your master with every thread of his stock in the bazaar, so he can sell it and you in the streets!"

"Grandfather—my lady. . . ." Tulik and Jethan nearly bumped into each other getting between Chirak and Moth.

After a moment's silent mutual regard, Tulik said, "Of course we are most gratified that His Majesty values my sister's skills as we do here—she being the only formally trained woman of magic in the realm. But as my grandfather says, there have been two attempts on his life here, attempts made by magic, and he must be protected at all costs."

"I'll stay," volunteered Pebble.

"Which of 'em's stronger?" demanded Chirak, his glare going from the big fair girl in peasant blue to the pink-and-gold spitfire beside her.

"It don't matter which of us is stronger because, me, I wouldn't stay to keep you from being chewed up by magic mice and spit back out three times a day for a week! And if somebody wasn't already trying to kill you with magic, I'd do it!"

"My lady." Tulik raised placating hands, then turned to Pebble with a deep salaam. "Thank you, my lady. Guardsman, how long will His Majesty require my sister's services? If it's no more than a day or so, yes, thank you, we will accept this young lady under our roof, providing her husband is agreeable."

"Father," corrected Pebble.

"Father. And he shall of course receive ample compensation for her services, as well as every assurance that his daughter shall be accompanied and looked after by my mother and aunts at all times that she is beneath the Shaldeth roof."

These formalities dispensed with, Raeshaldis ran upstairs, changed as fast as she could from the white robe of her novitiate into the boy's garb of pantaloons and tunic she'd brought here yesterday, and ran down the stairs again, to meet Jethan in the courtyard. By the light of torches borne by the stablemen—the teyn had long since been locked up for the night and in any case weren't to be trusted with fire—Jethan's face had a wooden look as he held Shaldis's horse for her. He said nothing as he led the way through the gate and back along the Avenue of the Sun, where every temple and town palace now slumbered in shuttered silence.

Only after Jethan showed his written pass signed by Bax, the commander of the guard, to the guards on the Eastern Gate and they were clattering along through the mostly somnolent squalor of the Slaughterhouse District did Shaldis say, "I'm sorry that I . . . that I kept you waiting so long. I couldn't help it. I'd meant to just see if I could reach Summerchild's mind, touch her thoughts, just to see if she still lived."

Jethan's broad, stiff shoulders relaxed and he said, "I'm only glad you *did* come out of it. That you're all right." Embarrassed awkwardness lingered in his voice.

Her grandfather was right, Shaldis reflected, considering Jethan's profile by the light of the gibbous moon. He *was* good-looking.

But she couldn't imagine him "beckoning" her to run away with him, nor that she'd do so without a whopping good reason.

TWENTY-SIX

I wish there was some way we could have let you know what had happened, so you wouldn't try to follow her into trance."

"I'd have tried anyway. I had no idea I'd be trapped, too, if that's what happened."

"*Does* she still live?"

Shaldis was silent, trying to make sense of what she'd seen. And failing. The moon drenched the range with liquid silver, turned the flatlands to ivory velvet, the jumbled hills to monsters sleeping in shadow.

At length she said, "I think so. Pomegranate thinks so, too, or at least she informs me her imaginary pig told her so."

Jethan rolled his eyes.

"Don't dismiss what Pontifer says, Jethan. For a figment of an old woman's imagination he's right a good deal of the time. You say she's on her way back to the palace?"

"She should be. His Majesty left guards around the ruins of Three Wells. Some of the houses in the village were burned three nights ago, when the people were all killed, and then someone—it may have been teyn—came in and burned the whole village."

"Teyn? But—"

He held up his hand against her shocked protest. "Burned it while a band of several hundred teyn kept us away."

"Several hundred? Acting in concert?"

"Burned it," he concluded grimly, "and broke every mirror, everything made of glass, in the place."

For a few moments she only stared at him, baffled. Then she began, "What on earth?"

"That," he said, "is what His Majesty says the Summer Concubine was trying to find out."

After a moment she asked doubtfully, "Will the guards be all right out there?" For some reason Ahure's lonely little house came to mind.

"They have instructions to touch nothing. Not walls, not debris, not the water in the wells. The caravan taking the litter out to bring the Summer Concubine home includes a hundred waterskins. His Majesty hoped, after you had seen the lady, that you would ride back to look at the village yourself and see if anything there can give a clue as to what happened there. Not," he added, his voice turning a shade more dry, "that I would suggest a course of action so likely to produce an apoplexy in the head of your clan."

Shaldis shot him a glance that he either didn't see or pretended not to, but she felt herself relax. As they followed the worn pale trace of hoofprints across the range to Three Wells, through the remaining hours of night and on into the heartbreaking beauty of the rangeland dawn, she outlined to him the events of the past three days: the accounts of the first attack on her grandfather and her certainty that she was being lied to about Nettleflower's death.

"I'm guessing it was Ahure she went downstairs to let in, two nights ago," she said while they rested their horses in the shade of a withered mesquite. "I think Grandfather followed her down and killed her in a rage."

"Over what?"

"I don't know. I need to find that out. Someone definitely attacked him in his room the night before Nettleflower's murder, though, and if it was Ahure he had someone else working with him, someone who can do magic. And my brother's trying to cover it all up," she added with an effort to keep her bitterness, her sinking sense of being used by her family, out of her voice.

"What does your father say?"

Shaldis had to turn her face aside in anger and shame. "Mostly, *Isn't it time for another cup of* sherab?"

"Ah," said Jethan. And then, "Your brother must be scared to death."

Shaldis glanced back at him. It hadn't occurred to her that Tulik was feeling anything but anxiety that the proctorship would slip out of his grip.

"If it's an attack on the House Shaldeth in general, he'd be in danger as well, wouldn't he?" He pulled his own veils back up over his face—crimson, the royal color. Shaldis didn't even want to think what it had cost to dye that much gauze. Above them, his blue eyes seemed brilliant as the desert sky.

Shaldis nodded. She hadn't thought of that. "He is only a kid," she said at last.

"He's probably been taking care of everyone in sight

all his life. Like you." Jethan got to his feet, held out the
waterskin to her. "You want any more of this?"

When they emerged from their shelter they could see,
hanging above the harsh yellow wasteland to the east, the
dust column of a moving company. They changed saddles
on their tired horses and rode toward it, and reached the
slow-plodding line within an hour.

Shaldis was shocked to see the haggard grayness of the
king's face beneath ointment and cosmetics, the stricken
look of his sleepless eyes. "I hope we did well in moving
her," he said as he raised the outer curtains, then the inner
gauzes of the ten-bearer litter where Summerchild lay.
Around them, though it was only midmorning, the guards
and camp servants began to pitch camp, the king's tent
erected around the litter itself. Two of Summerchild's
maids stood by, with water to wash her and clean linen
for her to lie on when Shaldis was done.

"No, you did right. I think," Shaldis added, looking
down at her friend's still face and trying not to remember
that this woman had gotten her into the College of the
Mages of the Sun in the first place. Had cared for her and
stood by her in days when Shaldis had not known to
whom she could turn and had in fact believed that she
was not able to turn to anyone.

She tried to think of Summerchild as only a patient, a
subject of healing, and not someone she loved.

It crossed her mind, as she felt the rustle of apricot-
colored silk and smelled the musky languor of extremely
expensive perfume at her side, that the king must be
struggling, too.

In a very careful voice, Oryn asked, "Can you do anything?"

Shaldis knelt, as the tent's shadows dropped down around them, and felt Summerchild's wrists and face. "Will she drink? Swallow anything?"

The shake of his head was barely a movement at all. "We're keeping her as cool as we can, and moving with the best speed we can manage. We should be back at the palace sometime tonight, and the doctors there can do everything that they usually do, for those in . . . in coma, like this."

"Moth's at the palace already," said Shaldis. "Pebble will get there as soon as I return to the city. Pebble and I both felt her trying to draw on our magic. I tried to reach her"—her fingers moved slightly toward the still form on the litter—"tried to touch her mind in a trance, to find her and bring her back. I think . . . it looks like I slid into trance myself, for nearly the whole cycle of the sun. As if whatever harmed her, when she opened her mind to seek for it, got or tried to get me as well. They couldn't wake me, Pebble said." She looked up into those dark-circled hazel eyes, saw them widen with shock. "I'll try again, if you want me to, sire. But I don't think it's safe."

He swallowed. "No, my dear," he said gently and took her hand. "You must not put yourself in danger. I have my doubts about you riding back to Three Wells as it is. Something very strange is happening out there, as Jethan may have told you. If someone is controlling the teyn, using them as a weapon, they may very well attack you, either on your way there or once you leave the place. It's a few hours' further ride and there's no way you can make it back to the city by nightfall. Jethan can describe the state of the village to you."

"He did, on the way here," said Shaldis. It had occupied several miles, as they'd ridden through the stillness of the rangeland dawn. "But I'll still need to see it. There's always something a—a nonmage won't see." She barely stopped herself from calling him an Empty, as the novices had referred to men born without the power of magic, when the masters weren't in hearing. There had been no word, of course, for women born without those powers, because at that time there had been no word for women born *with* them.

Though she was tired from the ride, Shaldis elected to press on to Three Wells, a decision with which Jethan concurred. Oryn insisted they take a bodyguard of ten riders, with which Jethan also concurred. "We have no idea what's happening out here, Shaldis," he said when she protested that she could deal with any trouble that arose. "We'd be fools to lessen our odds of dealing with it because we feel silly about taking an army on what might turn out to be a simple scouting mission."

The killing heat of noonday had well and truly settled on the land by the time their little cavalcade reached the watch camp of guards that had been left posted beside the parched cornfields. A sentry, emerging from shelter, sent word to the corporal in charge, and Jethan and his riders set up their rough military shelters, the one assigned to Shaldis modestly hung with a half-dozen crimson riding veils to mark it as harem. Even that brief exertion of pitching the shelters left Shaldis sweating and dizzy from the heat. She crawled inside and lay down at once.

But sleep eluded her. The heat was like a goldsmith's furnace, and every pinhole in the shelter's weave seemed to admit a searing needle of vertical sunlight. The deep silence, the desert silence, was like the implacable consciousness of Khon, the veiled god of death. She felt no trace, now, of Summerchild's distant touch on her power.

Please don't let her be dead.

Footfalls in the gravel. Jethan's voice outside her shelter. "Shaldis?"

She crawled through the veiling over the entrance. A man never entered a place that was harem, save within his own household.

He held out a gourd of water to her. She drank, sparingly. It was hot and tasted like sand. "Can we go to your tent?" she asked, groping back through the veiling for her satchel. "I want to try something."

In Jethan's shelter, she had him sketch in the sand what the hills looked like around the village that had been his home. "What was the name of the place?" she asked, and he had to think about it for a moment. It had been, she deduced, so far from any other village that even its own inhabitants had trouble remembering that other places existed.

"Goat Slough," he said at last.

"And your mother's name?"

"Gray Rabbit Woman."

She cupped the crystal in her hand, angled its central facet to the harsh brazen hell of the noon sky visible through the shelter's open end. "I'm seeing a house," she whispered at length. "It's one story, brown adobe; there's a dead tree near the front door and wards painted around the windows in white and indigo."

"Yes, that's ours."

"There's a pine-pole ramada at the side. A gray-haired woman is grinding corn there—there's a younger woman beside her with a baby, working a loom. They're both tall, I think—it's hard to tell—but the younger woman has a white streak in her hair."

"My sister," said Jethan softly. "Anyone else? A boy . . . he'd be sixteen now."

Shaldis gazed for several more minutes in silence, then shook her head. "No. No one else." And, when Jethan sighed, she added, "Just because I don't see them doesn't mean they're not just indoors or down at the village well or something."

"It's a day's walk to the village," said Jethan curtly. For a moment he looked out, into the wavering yellow mirages of the noon heat. Then, "Go back to your shelter, Shaldis. I think we both need to sleep."

When the sun had gone over into the hour called the Mercy Sun, and she and Jethan and the other guards in the camp emerged from their shelters to drink a little water and make their afternoon patrols, Jethan did not speak of what she'd seen in her crystal or what it might have meant to him, and she did not bring the matter up.

"Nobody's been near the village that we've seen," reported the corporal, a dark young man named Riis. "Coyote and jackals, but no teyn. Certainly no nomads."

"So it smells all right to coyote and jackals," remarked Jethan as he and Shaldis walked the hundred yards or so that separated the guard camp from the first of the burned-out clusters of walls.

Shaldis swallowed hard as the lukewarm shift of breeze strengthened the stench of rot. "Yum," she said.

Jethan looked like he was about to frown, then broke into the first grin she'd ever seen on his face. He sobered almost at once, as if he were afraid someone would catch him smiling. "If they were staying away," he said, "I'd worry more about going in."

"With what you've told me about teyn attacking in groups and maybe burning the place, I'm not sure I *can* worry more." Shaldis looked around her at the black, empty walls, the swollen corpses, the green-black clouds of flies, and the glitter everywhere of broken glass. "Where'd they get the fire?"

"The merchant Poru said several of the houses were burned the first night. There'd be coals still alive under the ashes. Domestic teyn would know that."

She stopped, drawing back from a half-dozen vultures and a whirling column of flies that amply indicated another corpse lying among the drooping bean plants. "This is weird," she added, pushing with the snake stick she'd cut at the tangle of pumpkin vine that grew among the beans, showing where the blackened leg of a mummy protruded. "Why haul a mummy—or part of a mummy— clear out here?"

"I wondered that myself," said Jethan. "So did the king."

She poked a little among the vines. "I don't see any wrappings or any dropped trinkets. And in the dark, with all the confusion of the village being massacred and at least a couple of houses burning, it's odd that scavengers would get *everything*. I wonder how deep out there the tombs are?"

She straightened and turned her eyes to the low red-brown masses, the striated shadows, of the Serpent Maze badlands, the edge of the true desert. She briefly considered riding out to look at the tombs themselves, but the sun was westering. It would be well into the night before they reached the Yellow City, and she wasn't sure that whatever she might learn in several hours spent wandering through the Serpent Maze was worth the danger to Summerchild that her continued absence would cause.

And somewhere in the Yellow City, someone—a child?—was being forced to use her magic for the petty machinations of gangsters and water bosses, when the realm and its king stood balanced on the brink of death.

Without touching the walls here—without opening her mind to whatever residue of spells had struck down Summerchild as she opened hers, without fingering the broken glass that glittered, she now saw, everywhere among the bean fields and pumpkin vines around the dead town—she could learn no more. "We'd better go back," she said.

As they mounted fresh horses by the little watch camp, Shaldis turned to Corporal Riis.

"I know it isn't much," she said, "but I promise you, I'll look at your camp—or get one of the other Raven sisters to look at it—through a mirror or a scrying crystal at sunrise, noon, and sunset. If something happens out here, something you can't cope with, tie one of your red sun veils onto a stick in the middle of the camp. I swear we'll get someone out here as swiftly as we can."

Riis inclined his head. "Thank you, lady."

As Shaldis and her bodyguard trotted away from the camp in a huge cloud of amber dust, Jethan remarked quietly, "You know that's not going to do them any good. By the look of the corpses, death took every one of those people at roughly the same time. It's a day's ride from the city. Even if you saw whatever it was, swooping down on the camp—"

"The village was taken asleep and unprepared." She glanced sidelong at the guard. Only his eyes were visible above his veils, and there was a trace in them that could have been anger or could have been only concern. "Riis and his men are watching for trouble."

"Do you think that will save them?"

Shaldis was quiet for a few minutes. Then she said, "No. But it might. I have no idea what it is that will come out of the desert, if anything. And if it truly makes no difference one way or the other, there's no harm in letting them know they're not simply being abandoned without a thought."

"And does it help to know you're being abandoned *with* a thought? I'm sorry," he added almost at once. "You're right, of course; it is best to know that someone at least hasn't forgotten you, even if there's nothing they can do to help. Anything that even sounds like a promise raises the hair on my nape. I shouldn't have spoken."

"You sound like you had a father like mine," said Shaldis softly, remembering all those assurances of treats, of books, of a tutor who'd teach her. And hard on the heels of memory, the thought, *It wasn't his fault he never came through with them.*

Jethan drew rein a little, his gaze moving unceasingly over the pale wastes of the rangeland, dyed now with the molten colors of the sky. A moment later Shaldis saw a small pack of coyote trotting toward Three Wells.

"As a child I spent a lot of time with animals," he said, as he rode on. "Hunting wild goats or looking after my uncle's sheep. I remember realizing very young that animals don't understand what you say, only what you do to them. And by the same token, they never tell you one thing and then do something else. If your dog loves you he lets you know it, without worrying about what you're going to do with that information later. I love that about them."

And who told you they loved you, wondered Shaldis, *and then turned around and acted only for themselves?*

She didn't know how to ask. Instead she said, "Maybe I shouldn't have spoken. Because you're right, and Riis has to have known there's nothing anyone can do. But there's something out here, something deadly."

She turned in her saddle. The burned walls and circling vultures were no more than a dark spot in the distance, alone in the empty land.

"No argument there." Jethan's voice was dry. "And if someone has found a way to control the teyn, to make them attack and maneuver as an army, it's going to be more than deadly. Every village has its compound of workers, every house in the city, practically, its sweepers and water drawers. If someone can command them to kill, it will be disastrous."

He was right, of course, thought Shaldis, reining her horse after his down the arroyo, westward toward the Lake of the Sun.

But that wasn't what she'd meant.

She didn't know what she'd meant. Again and again she paused, turning to look back at the circling vultures that marked the dead village, until even that column was lost in the vast spaces of the oncoming desert night.

TWENTY-SEVEN

"Don't be a ninny, girl." Red Silk's hand closed around Foxfire's arm as the girl tried to turn away—she had a grip like an eagle's claw. Chained to the post in the midst of what had been a small temple at the back of the Valley of the Hawk compound, the half-grown teyn doubled over and began to spasm in the horribly familiar convulsions of wild arum root poisoning. It was the seventh that had died that day. Like the others, even in its agony it didn't make a sound.

"If this was my father's household, we'd be using men and not teyn. I'm not sure that we shouldn't be using them as it is." And Red Silk glanced across at Soral Brûl.

"As I've said, my lady," replied the young former Sun Mage, "a spell that protects a teyn will usually protect a man."

"Sun Mage spells." She waved a dismissive hand and turned back to watch the teyn as it sank to its knees, vomiting and clawing at its belly and mouth.

Foxfire closed her eyes. *I will not faint.*

"According to everything in the Citadel's library, that

held true for all systems of magic. Blood Mages, Earth Wizards, Pyromancers . . ."

It's only a teyn. How would I like it if it were Father? It will be if we don't find a spell that will protect against all poisons. I WILL NOT FAINT.

How can they talk so calmly while something, anything, is dying in front of them in that kind of pain?

The jangle of the chains, the sound of retches and gasps, filled Foxfire's mind and drowned her grandmother's discussion of male and female magic. The fight not to cry made her almost ill.

Seven. None of the spells Soral Brûl had guided the two women through since dawn had had the slightest effect. Nor had the earth-wizard magics taught by Urnate Urla, though the bitter little man was seldom sober. Some enchantments would protect against a single poison, but it was guessed—no one knew for certain—that the Servant of Time mixed two and three poisons together in the cups that the kings found within the maze there, and there was never any telling which cup the king might drink from. The Sun Mages had always used a spell of general protection.

A spell that could not now be made to work by either a woman or a man.

Foxfire wished with everything that was in her that she knew a spell that would kill at a distance. That would end those desperate, awful noises.

Not that her grandmother would let her use one.

And since Red Silk had forced her to bind herself with her into a Sigil of Sisterhood, there was probably no way to do it secretly.

I WILL NOT FAINT.

Silence. Her grandmother said, *"Grzh,"* a foul curse indeed in the language of the deep-desert nomads. Foxfire felt tears track down her face.

"Well, bring in another one." Red Silk's voice slurred. She'd taken tiga root in brandy to work the spells on the previous two teyn, in larger and larger doses. On this last one she'd had Foxfire drink it, too. "To open her mind," she'd said.

Foxfire heard Soral Brûl go to the door, call for Garmoth, the captain of the guards. "Grandmother," said Foxfire carefully, "could we wait and start again tomorrow? I don't think I have your head for brandy. I think maybe the last one . . . didn't work"—*It died! I put everything of me into protecting it and it died, it died in agony*—"because I might have been dizzy from the brandy and couldn't concentrate." Not to mention being half-crazy with tiga.

"Nonsense." The old woman was already stirring the silver pitcher that contained the decoction of madness. "Don't get squeamish on me, girl. I expected better of you."

"Grandmother, please."

Red Silk grabbed her arm again, shook her hard. Soral Brûl caught Foxfire as she staggered.

"Perhaps she's right, lady," he said in his most unctuous voice. "She looks very pale."

"Garmoth!" yelled Red Silk as the guardsman came in with two others, leading the old jenny teyn the keepers called Eleven Grasshoppers. "Fetch coffee for my granddaughter and be quick about it." The hard turquoise eyes were dilated so that only the thinnest rim of green showed about the swollen pupils. "You'll be more pale watching your father die of what's in that cup, girl. Or do you want him to die? Is that it?"

Foxfire whispered, "No." Wanting to die herself.

Soral Brûl stepped back, clearly not about to cross Red Silk's will. As he did so he gave Foxfire a wide-eyed gaze with eyebrows tweaked in what he obviously meant to be sympathy: *You have all my support.*

As long as it doesn't mean going against your grandmother.

Foxfire took a deep breath, her knees trembling. "Please. Grandmother, please. I . . . I don't want us to disregard a spell that doesn't work, if maybe it is the right spell, and it's only not working because I'm too tired to concentrate." Between exhaustion, hunger, terror, tiga root, and the sickened horror of watching those seven lingering deaths, she almost couldn't get the words out in anything resembling a sensible order.

The guards yanked the manacle pin from the dead teyn's shackle, fastened the old jenny in his place. She sat at once, hugging herself and rocking, nostrils snuffing fearfully, pale eyes wide. Foxfire felt as if she, too, were shackled in this terrible room.

Please, PLEASE, let me go!

Red Silk's eyes narrowed, and she shook the girl again. "So if I let you go today at sundown, are you going to find yourself 'too tired' to go on at noon tomorrow? You think magic is something that will wait until you're feeling happy and your hair's combed? Brûl, was it part of your training to work spells when you were tired or had a bellyache?"

"Yes, my lady, it was." The young man gazed with great earnestness into her face, hands clasped before his breast, brown eyes wide. A lock of his light-brown hair trailed down over his forehead. "We were put through sword drill until we were too tired to go on, and then . . ."

Yes, but that was after you knew which spells would work!

Foxfire knew if she started to cry, her grandmother would keep her in this suffocating, lamplit box of a room, putting protective spells on teyn and then murdering them, until midnight—and would probably slap her, too.

And, no, she didn't want her father to die. She didn't want her cousin Oryn to die, either, or her cousin Barún.

Red Silk shoved her away with drunken strength that almost knocked her to the floor. "Lazy slut," she said. "Get to bed, then. Garmoth." The dark-featured guard had just reappeared with coffee. "Tell the cook to send food to my granddaughter's room. Brûl, come with me. We need to talk about this mess here." She gestured to the dead teyn, the old jenny chained to the post, the whole dim chamber's reek of death. "Have this cleaned up." She took the coffee cup from Garmoth's tray as she swept through the door.

Soral Brûl paused beside Foxfire as he started to follow her out, put his arm protectively around the girl's shoulders—protective, she thought, as long as there wasn't anything there that he'd actually have to protect her *from*. "You were most brave today, my lady. You have such extraordinary power—it's rare that I've ever seen such strength to match such beauty."

Foxfire pulled away from him, trembling with disgust. "If you think I haven't heard you flatter Grandmother with those same words, think again," she said. "Do you think I'm more desperate than she is, or just more pleasant to kiss?"

She pushed past him into the colonnade, where the desert twilight was just beginning to settle on the barren courtyard, tears running down her stony face as she walked to her room.

"Sweetheart!" Opal caught her in her arms as she stumbled through the door. "Are you all right? I kept some of my food for you at lunch."

Foxfire shook her head, weeping now in earnest as she clung to the smaller, plumper girl who guided her to the bed. Opal sat her down, went at once for a basin of lavender water. "They're sending something," Foxfire managed to say when Opal returned with cold barley tea as well as the lavender water and a dish of rice and chicken. "No, don't light the lamp. I want you to lie in bed here with the curtain down and the sheet over you. When the slave brings it in you just say, 'Set it on the table . . .'"

Opal's eyes widened in apprehension. "What are you going to do?"

"I'll be back soon," Foxfire promised, sitting up and clasping her friend by the shoulders. "I promise I'll be back soon. Grandmother's been taking tiga in brandy all day—after she's done talking with Soral Brûl and Urnate Urla she'll probably just fall asleep. I just . . . I can't . . ." She shook her head again, her long black hair trailing loose from its pins, her hands trembling as she snatched up the little dish of her maid's humble lunch. "I have to get out of the compound for a few minutes. I won't go far. . . ."

"There are bandits in the hills," whispered Opal. "Bandits and wilding teyn." She sounded scared—maybe less of the dangers outside the wall than of her ladyship's wrath if Foxfire was discovered missing.

"I won't go far." Foxfire wiped clean the shallow dish from Opal's lunch with the end of an old veil, used another veil as a makeshift sling to carry the dish and a bottle of water. Wrapping herself in the Gray Cloak's shifting spells of misdirection, she bestowed a quick kiss of farewell and encouragement upon Opal, then stepped out into the colonnade again.

The gates of the compound were marked with Red Silk's Sigil of Ward, but there was a low place in the kitchen wall, near the compound where the teyn were kept. Standing in a corner of the kitchen court, Foxfire laid a little whisper of spell on the hearth that sent the cook and his assistant darting back into the rickety shed in a panic.

Three strides took her to the wall. Something moved in the shadow of the water barrels and Foxfire swung around, her heart leaping in alarm.

It was the old jenny teyn, Eleven Grasshoppers. White furred, and a little bent with the effects of a lifetime of carrying water and grinding corn, the jenny still moved surprisingly fast, darting on all fours as teyn did when in a hurry, reaching out one long arm to grasp Foxfire's wrist.

"Let go!" Foxfire whispered, pulling against the clutching fingers—useless, of course, given the power of teyn hands. Foxfire said, *"No!"* in her firmest voice. "Off."

Eleven Grasshoppers released her at once. Those were the first commands beaten into the tiniest teyn pips. She pulled back her lips and bared her teeth in conciliation, but the pale blue eyes regarded her anxiously from beneath the overhanging brow. When Foxfire moved toward the barrels that would give her a footing over the wall, the jenny caught her wrist again. She released her immediately when Foxfire turned. Then she said hesitantly, "No." Her long pale arm, the dark flesh seeming to shimmer where the white hair had been shaved close, swept in the direction of the wall. "Off."

After one startled second, Foxfire relaxed into laughter. She stepped close to the old jenny and hugged her, and ruffled the cropped white hair of her head. "You're as bad as Opal, you silly old girl," she said affectionately. It flashed across her mind how nearly this stooped, white-furred creature had come to being poisoned that evening, and she wondered if this was her way of thanking her: trying to keep her out of what she perceived as danger.

Foxfire took her hands, stroked her arms the way she'd seen the teyn do to one another, when one of them was frightened or hurt. "I'll be all right," she said, looking into the blue eyes. "All right— You understand? How'd you get out, anyway?" And she led her to the door of the teyn compound, slipped back the bolt, and steered her in again. As she moved to close the door, Eleven Grasshoppers caught her hand again—very lightly this time—and stroked her arm.

Climbing over the wall after shooting the bolt, Foxfire wondered how she could go about making sure the old jenny wasn't among those Red Silk would pick to poison—or feed to the crocodile—for the remainder of their stay in the Valley of the Hawk.

TWENTY-EIGHT

Although darkness was settling over the desert, Foxfire kept the Gray Cloak spell wrapped around her until she reached the broken jumble of immense pale rocks at the foot of the valley wall, about a hundred feet from the compound. Behind the rocks a wadi twisted back into the hills, and this she followed, keeping to the stony track in its center in the hopes of avoiding being trailed or, nearly as bad, being found out. All it would take would be for Red Silk to come out here and find her footprints, to know she'd slipped out over the wall.

In recollection of her grandmother's tales, she cut a piece of brush from the wadi wall, and dragged it over her tracks. Not, she reflected, that the old lady wouldn't identify the tracks of a dragged branch on sight.

But her errand really would take only a few minutes. Once out of sight of the old hunting lodge, Foxfire was more than ever oppressed by the deadly silence of the hills. She'd stayed up as long as she could last night, leaning against the thick stone wall of her room and listening through it to the sounds of the hills. She wasn't really good at reaching out with her senses yet, but at least she'd been able to tell that there weren't troops of bandits everywhere, as Opal feared. She had heard neither voices nor the clink of horses' hooves, nor the groaning complaints of camels.

There had been the soft stirring of animal sounds, sounds she couldn't identify. But if worse came to worst, she thought, she could always frighten animals or wilding teyn away with fire—though to do so would run the risk of betraying her to Red Silk, after which being carried off by bandits would seem a tame fate.

By the same token, she knew she had to retreat a considerable distance into the hills to keep her grandmother from being aware of magic being worked in her immediate vicinity. As she'd climbed over the wall—and sneaking her pale-blue linen dress into the laundry undetected would be another task for later in the night—she'd seen the crude little bundles of dried grass, ashes, and broken glass that hung from the line of spikes there, an old nomad defense against the Bad-Luck Shadow. A reminder, if she'd needed one, of her grandmother's listening presence.

So Foxfire worked her way up the wadi and over a barren shoulder of red rock and dust turning colorless in the fading light, then along another gulch for some distance before she knelt and filled the pottery dish with water. It didn't make a good mirror and she was afraid to call more than a tiny seed of light over her shoulder for fear that, even far off, her grandmother would see. The moon was rising over the hills, just past full and golden as fire. As her mind traced over the power lines she'd drawn in the dust, the spells she'd sketched invisibly on the inside of the bowl, she thought, *Please be there. Please answer me.*

Somewhere a coyote howled, the voices of the rest of

the pack picking up the cry. Foxfire shivered, trying not to remember that there were tombs all through these hills, even here so far from the city. Trying not to remember the poor teyn, dying in convulsions at the stake.

Please be there! Let me know what's happening!

Don't let me be all alone with Grandmother!

She was aware that the ghostly reflection she'd thought was her own white face was that of Raeshaldis, Habnit's Daughter.

"Are you all right?" was Shaldis's first question, and Foxfire almost wept again, at the older girl's care.

"I'm fine," she said, because you never betrayed your own, even by a word. Besides, to wail, *My grandmother is holding me prisoner and I'm tired and scared!* would be to brand oneself a ninny indeed. "How is Summer-child? What happened to her?"

"She tried to scry the walls in a village where all the people died of . . . of something that everyone's saying was a plague, but I don't think it was. I don't know what it was." Behind Raeshaldis's head, Foxfire could see the blazing starlight of the desert sky. She wondered if Shaldis was in one of the high places of the Citadel or out in the desert herself.

"She was unconscious when I saw her just after noon," Shaldis went on. "I tried to find her mind, to go into trance and look for her, right after it happened. I was nearly lost myself. Where are you?"

"I can't say." Foxfire looked around her sharply, wondering if the noise she'd heard was a fox or something worse. "I'm—Grandmother and I are looking for a way to get my father through the tests of kingship, if His Majesty should . . . shouldn't survive the jubilee." She added desperately, "Please don't be angry at me. Grandmother—"

"God of Women, Foxfire, I've met your grandmother! She's like my grandfather in veils. Is there anything I can do to help you?"

"Nothing," Foxfire whispered, nearly weeping again at the kindness in her voice. "Just be there. I may not even be able to do this again. She took away my mirrors, and I had to sneak out . . . sneak out of the house tonight." She glanced over her shoulder again. It *was* a noise. But she dared not take her concentration from the water bowl, to listen into the darkness to be sure.

She swallowed another qualm of panic. "Is there anything I can do, to help *you*?" she asked after a moment. "To help Summerchild?"

"I don't know yet. I know you can't tell us whatever you and your grandmother find out, but if . . . if you hear anything against the king . . ."

"She isn't—Grandmother isn't—planning anything *against* the king," said Foxfire. "She's just not going to help him. She wants him to die."

"Well, excuse me while I dust off after falling down in surprise," said Shaldis drily, and Foxfire laughed. "Let us know what you can," she went on. "If you can't . . . I know you're in a bad situation. You do what you have to, sweetheart, to take care of yourself. That's the most important thing."

"I will." Maybe creeping out into hills crawling with jackals and wildings didn't sound like taking care of yourself, thought Foxfire, but the alternative—staying behind walls unable to speak to someone whose first ques-

tion had been *Are you all right?*—would have been infinitely worse.

"You haven't heard anything about a Raven child in
the city, have you?" asked Shaldis. "Or rumors about a
Crafty nobody knows about?"

Foxfire shook her head. Something *was* in the wadi
behind her. She knew it, felt it.

"Listen, I have to go," she whispered. "I've been here
too long. I'll speak again when I can."

And let the image fade.

Wilding teyn. Her mind reached out, picked out their
musty, sweetish smell, the rustle of their breathing—God
of Women, they were all around her! In the rocks, creeping stealthily behind the shouldering curves of the wadi.
Foxfire hastily gathered the spells of the Gray Cloak
around her, dumped the water back into the bottle. Her
hands were shaking so badly that the liquid dribbled onto
the sand.

She heard them coming closer. The grit of bare horny
feet on pebbles, too soft for the hearing of any but a
woman of power. As softly as she knew how, her heart
thumping hard, she got to her feet, stole off down the
wadi. But she could hear them follow, stealthy as the
jackals that followed after them for the scraps of their
kills.

Foxfire's night-sighted eyes scanned the shape of the
hills, seeking the way back to the compound. But she'd
gotten somehow turned around, and now the whole of the
barren landscape looked the same. Just stones and other
stones, close-crowding hills, bare eroded slots where
water had flowed centuries ago. The rising of the moon
had changed the appearance of the shadows. She risked

releasing her mind from the wildings long enough to listen more widely, to sniff for the smells of horses and camels, water and smoke that would bring her back to the Valley of the Hawk.

And could detect nothing.

Dear gods, she thought. *Grandmother! Grandmother put spells of ward on the whole place! Not just against the Bad-Luck Shadow but against anyone traveling these hills!*

This way. It was this way.

I think it was this way.

Panic filled her and she struggled to keep to a silent walk. *Didn't a Gray Cloak work against teyn?* She realized she'd never tried to cloak herself against their notice. Why should she? She'd have to ask Shaldis. . . .

Something—some preternatural rustle to her keyed-up senses—made her turn in time to see the dark rushing shadows of two wilding teyn spring from the crevasse of a rock barely ten yards away. Foxfire gasped, bolted like a gazelle, stumbling and skidding over the rough stones and broken ground. Her mind groped at fire spells but fear numbed her thoughts—the glint of tusks in the starlight, the flash of eyes within those rushing shadows. She could only flee, terrified, expecting any second to feel those huge hands grabbing her, those horrible tusks. She plunged down the rocks, fell, skinning her hands.

Which way is the compound?

What am I going to—

Her foot caught in a hole and she fell hard, rolling down the rough gravel of a talus slope, choking on dust and fear. Pain slashed her, knees, palms, head.

I have to get up, I'll have to fight.

Fire! How do I call fire?

Sobbing, she sat up, threw back her long hair.

They were gone.

She saw the dust hanging in the moonlight where a moment ago they'd been. Smelled the dust.

And felt the silence that watched her. Silence that lived.

Trembling seized her, from her flight and from that silence. She saw something—some flicker of greenish light, far off among the rocks—out of the tail of her eye. But when she looked it was gone.

It scared them off.

Panic, pure and icy, seemed to seal her thoughts.

Or something scared them, anyway. And whatever it is, it's still here, it's coming for me.

She managed to get to her feet, but when she turned toward where she thought the compound had to be, she saw—she thought she saw—that greenish flicker there, too.

And in her heart, in the marrow of her bones, she felt a sudden wave of weariness, of weird sweet sleepiness, as if everything were going to be all right. All she had to do was lie down and rest, and all would be well in the morning. Her grandmother would be kind again, and her father would love her without asking anything of her in return.

Music whispered, deep in the hollows of her brain.

Then the scratch of bare feet on the rock behind her startled her nearly out of her skin, like a drench of icy water, icy fear.

A teyn . . .

Eleven Grasshoppers?

The jenny appeared around the rocks, pale as a ghost

in the light of the blazing moon. Her silvery hair glimmered as she hurried toward the girl, running like a wilding on hands as well as feet. "No," the old jenny said, in the hoarse, flat voice that all teyn had when they spoke the few words of which they were capable. "Off." And coming near Foxfire, she caught her torn sleeve, tugged her to follow, then let go immediately, obviously fearing the slap that was the inevitable result of a teyn laying hands on its master. Her eye slits were dilated so that they nearly hid the pale blue rim of iris; her strange narrow face between its thickets of hair seemed very human.

She gestured around her at the dark landscape, the unseen sense that there was some terrible thing there, something that the wildings had fled. Something waiting. "Off."

"I think you're right, sweetheart," agreed Foxfire, and gave the jenny a quick, heartfelt hug. "Let's get *off* right now."

It never crossed Foxfire's mind that Eleven Grasshoppers might be leading her into some danger, and in fact it was only minutes until they emerged from the mouth of a wadi to see the rear wall of the compound in the Valley of the Hawk. It wasn't the same wadi Foxfire had gone up but one on the other side of the compound. She couldn't imagine how the old jenny had navigated in these hills, where, to Foxfire's knowledge, she'd never been before. "Wait a minute," Foxfire whispered, "wait a minute," as Eleven Grasshoppers tried to pull her toward the walls. Foxfire took a deep breath, steadying herself, then—despite trembling exhaustion, terror, exertion, and a ravenous hunger headache—called around them both the concealing cantrips of a Gray Cloak.

She would have liked to stretch out her mind to the

guards on the wall, breathe into their thoughts the spell of inattention and daydreams that had worked so well at the Temple of Nebekht. But such a spell might have been strong enough to impinge into Red Silk's consciousness. Moreover, all the way here she'd been aware that Eleven Grasshoppers was in a state of growing fear, looking around her and now and then plucking Foxfire's sleeve to get her to hurry. Whatever had frightened away the attacking wildings, it was still in the hills. Though Foxfire could hear nothing of its approach, and even by extending her senses she could neither scent it nor see it, it was there.

It was close.

And it had to be fearsome, Foxfire thought, for Eleven Grasshoppers to be ready to return to captivity—and for all the others to remain behind the walls rather than slip out by whatever means she had used—rather than to face it by trying to escape.

Not good.

Despite her growing sense of urgency, Foxfire paused long enough to listen one more time, casting her senses toward the compound—and couldn't hear a thing. *Oh, thank you, Grandmother, for those spells of concealment.* With pounding heart, not knowing what waited for her, she put one arm around Eleven Grasshoppers's shoulders, fixed her mind on the Gray Cloak, and led the old jenny across the moonlit sand toward the low place in the kitchen wall. She could see the silhouettes of the guards on the walls passing before the torches. One of them called another and pointed, not toward Foxfire but past her at the wadi from which she'd just emerged. Turning, Foxfire saw something move, a whisper of greenish mist, the reflection of greenish light on a rock.

She quickened her step and glanced back several more times as she scrambled over the wall. Eleven Grasshoppers followed her with monkeylike nimbleness.

Standing in the darkness behind the water barrels, Foxfire probed the compound with hearing and scent.

No shouting. No weeping from the direction of her own room, only Opal's soft, steady breath. Not even sleeping, it didn't sound like.

And like heaven, the smell of salted lemons, chicken, olives, rice.

God of Women, thank you. Thank you.

Foxfire slipped open the bolt on the door of the teyn compound, gently guided Eleven Grasshoppers in again. (*For all the good that's likely to do!*) She'd have to come up with a story that accounted for her torn dress, bruised knees, and lacerated hands that both took place within the compound and would give her a good excuse to ask for Eleven Grasshoppers as a personal slave, exempt from the stake and the poison cup.

As she pushed the door closed she chopped her hand down in front of the opening, whispered, "No! No."

Eleven Grasshoppers regarded her with those round pale-blue eyes beneath her tufted brow. Foxfire would have sworn they glinted with irony.

"You know what I mean," she said.

Eleven Grasshoppers only blinked and bared her teeth good-naturedly. Beyond her, the other teyn slept huddled together in each other's long arms, scratching and now and then snuffling in their sleep.

She knew they didn't understand. Nevertheless, Foxfire whispered, "I'm sorry. I'm so sorry."

And closed and barred the gate.

Though she was shaking with fatigue and hunger—
and running the risk of being spotted by Red Silk in her
torn dress and wild, dust-covered hair, if her grandmother
was still awake and prowling—Foxfire climbed one of
the pine-pole ladders up to the battlement. She stole
along the compound wall, passing unseen within inches
of the guard on that side, and made her way back to the
western wall, the direction from which she and Eleven
Grasshoppers had returned to safety.

For some time she stood in the darkness at the corner
of the parapet, gazing out at the hills in which she'd stumbled, searching for some glimpse, some hint to what it
was that had frightened away the wildings. For whatever
scared the teyn in the compound so badly that they'd risk
certain death by remaining.

Had one—or some—of the djinni in fact survived?

She didn't think so. She'd felt none of the jangling,
horrible electricity in the air that she'd experienced near
the djinn Ba, the djinn from whose blind hunger Shaldis
and the king had rescued her last spring. The tingling sensation she'd sensed like a whisper across her skin in the
shut-up Temple of Nebekht.

And she'd never heard anyone mention the djinni in
connection with greenish mists or lights.

Only where the westering moon threw inky shadows
did she see that the dust, all along the feet of the hills,
glowed in patches, a faint but distinct green, as if a low-
lying vapor were very slowly exuding from the earth.
Now and then it seemed to her that the mist stirred,
though the night was profoundly still. Once a stream of it,
no thicker than Foxfire's finger, appeared to drift toward
the compound walls—she could hear the guards calling

to one another, pointing and asking—only to dissipate as it drew near.

If she were a better person, a truer Craft woman, Foxfire thought, she'd remain, to watch it and see what it did. Shaldis certainly would. But she was trembling with hunger and fatigue, and her cuts were smarting as if her skin had been filed. Moreover, the longer she stayed away from her room, the greater grew the chances that Opal would be discovered as a conspirator in her absence.

So Foxfire tore herself away from the sight of that strange glimmering phosphorescence and ghosted down the ladder again and along the colonnade to her room. There she let Opal bathe her cuts and brush her snarly hair, and while she devoured her now-cold dinner like a starving wolf they devised a tale of an expedition to the walls ("Because we heard the guards calling"), a fall from the ladder, and selfless assistance from Eleven Grasshoppers ("What was she doing out of the pen?" "You knocked over a water jar and let her out to help clean up.").

But though she knew she'd have to wake at dawn and face another day of exhaustion and horrors, once she lay down, Foxfire could not sleep. Every time she closed her eyes, she saw the faint glow of green mist, curling across the sands.

When she dozed, she heard it sing.

TWENTY-NINE

Oryn was sitting beside Summerchild's bed, where he had been since they'd brought her back at midnight, when word came to him that the priests of the Veiled Gods were waiting for him before the palace gates.

The thick sweet-scented night had seemed endless, like a dream from which he could not wake. Now and then throughout the small hours, Moth or Pebble would tell him to go get some sleep, and he'd politely agree that he needed it and would do so presently. But he knew—and they knew—that he would not and could not leave her side.

He literally could not imagine continuing to live if Summerchild died. He supposed he must—and supposed he must make the attempt to do so, serpents, crocodiles, and poison notwithstanding. Rainsong. He was far too well acquainted with what befell the underaged children of deceased kings to entertain even the slightest hope that his daughter would not perish in the mess of rebellions, power grabs, and infighting that would follow his death.

So he knew in an academic sort of way that he had to

go on living. He had to survive the ordeals of consecration somehow.

And when he thought about it, he shuddered to contemplate the mess Barún—or Mohrvine—or whoever *did* succeed—would make of the realm for the short time before the lakes dried and everyone perished of thirst.

But without Summerchild it all seemed pointless, like trying to make a song after one's tongue and heart had both been cut out.

"Lord King?"

He looked up. Moth was standing beside him again in the speckled light of the lamps in the niches, her beautiful brown hair braided back like a servant girl's. She'd been saying something to him. He replied, "Yes, my dear, I'll go along to bed in a moment."

Fear and grief had wiped away the brisk bossiness that usually so amused him, but she wasn't a girl to lose her head. With great gentleness, she said, "Sir, they're asking for you. They say the priests are here from the Sealed Temples, and you better go out and see them."

Oryn whispered, "Ah," and got to his feet. He almost staggered. His whole body ached from having been in the saddle since daybreak. He realized only then that he was still in his riding clothes, his face and hair covered with dust.

But one did not keep the housekeepers of the Veiled Gods waiting.

Ever.

Pebble handed him a wet towel. He wiped his unshaven face and smiled his thanks, but his eyes remained on the woman who lay within the golden ring of the lamplight. The two Raven sisters had done what they could for her body, but her eyes were already sunken from the dehydration of a day in the baking desert heat. After what had happened to Shaldis, neither Moth nor Pebble had dared go seeking her mind in the gray world of trance-bound dreams. Nor would Oryn have permitted them to do so, had they asked.

Death was one of the Veiled Gods, to be sure, but no one prayed to those strange archaic deities for favors. No one even recalled these days what their rites had been, if any, or how their servants were chosen or trained. They were not, strictly speaking, true gods at all. It did not matter to them whether a man was reverent or rude.

Still, reflected Oryn as he crossed the gardens toward the lamplit gate beneath the Marvelous Tower, it was self-evidently not a good idea to even consider the possibility of not being scrupulously polite.

Even Geb, trotting faithfully at his heels, was silent.

At this blue hour the first vendors of ices and fruit were usually setting up their pitches in the Golden Court outside the palace's gate, and the shutters were being taken down from royal workshops around the court. Housewives of the neighborhood, slaves, and occasional well-trusted teyn would be making their way with water jars through the dark streets to the great fountain house at one side of the square. Lights glowed deep within the Temple of Oan Echis, and on its steps the horoscope ladies would be setting out the day's wares. There were few hours of the day or night when the Golden Court wasn't a cheerful buzz of talk, movement, life.

It was empty now, as if in a continuation of his nightmare vigil at Summerchild's side. Lamps burned in the colonnade which surrounded it, and the dim amber outlined the crowding shapes of vendors, housewives, horoscope ladies, and teyn, all pushed together behind the pillars, watching. In the center of the square, just beyond the glow of the gate's lamps and just outside the circle of brightness from the sconces on the fountain house, the seven Veiled Priests stood, black robes seeming to drink up what little illumination there was.

Ean of the Mountains, greatest of the gods, had created the world and had devised the laws by which the world existed. All the other gods—Darutha of the Rains, Rohar who protected women, stingy Niam, and cheery BoSaa the Lord of Cattle, and all the rest—were Ean's children, as humankind was his grandchildren.

Those things that dwelled in the Sealed Temples were not gods as mankind understood gods.

Death.

Change.

The desert that stretched in all directions and did not end.

Fire that was both life and destruction.

The sightless abyss of the mind, from which both wisdom and madness spring.

Time.

At least they'd stayed out in the court this time, reflected Oryn as he stepped through the gateway to meet them. Twelve years ago, in the time of the waning moon immediately preceding his coronation, he'd woken in the deeps of night to find them standing in a circle around his bed.

The rite was a silent one, quickly performed. The six priests of Khon, of the twin gods Pelak and Drenan, of Kush, Zaath, and Shibathnes, came forward in turn to touch Oryn on the face, shoulders, and hands; the nameless representative of the nameless God of Time did not move. As with most matters pertaining to the Sealed Temples, no one really knew the purpose of the rite, though Oryn suspected that it was so the priests could get a good look at the candidate and make sure the prospective king didn't send in a substitute drugged to the hairline with powdered coca leaves. When they turned away, still in silence, and melted into the final shadows of the dawn streets, he remained kneeling for a long time, fearing that if he tried to rise too soon his knees would not support him.

It was one thing to think, *I cannot live without Summerchild.*

It was quite another to realize that without her assistance, he *would* die a terrible death in ten days.

And his daughter and his brother would die, too, very shortly thereafter.

And then every one of his people.

Dawn transformed the palace gardens into a world of birdsong. Oryn walked back along the paths with Geb fussing at his heels; and even in his shock, his grief, and his fear, he was conscious of, and cheered by, the beauty of the flowers. If there had been the slightest change in Summerchild's condition, he knew a messenger would have been waiting for him in the porter's lodge with Geb, so he detoured his steps to the Porcelain Pavilion and was just in time for his daughter's breakfast tea.

"Is Mama better?" asked the girl as Oryn poured out cups for her, himself, and Rabbit the nurse. Radiant Dawn, the doll who up until a year ago had been Rainsong's inseparable companion ("I'm too old for dolls now, Papa"), had made a reappearance at the breakfast table. Oryn made no comment. Neither did his daughter. It was sufficient, evidently, that this link with her childhood was there—as Soth's hand had been, closed tight on his own during his father's consecration.

Instead, Rainsong conversed in a very grown-up fashion about tea ("I like mountain green-tip best, don't you?") and her lessons. Anything but her fears. Only at the end did she say, "I hope Mama will be all better in time to watch you be crowned king again."

"As do I, my dear." Oryn stood and enfolded his daughter in a rather dusty embrace. "As do I."

"Really, Your Majesty, you *must* get to the baths," a flustered Geb insisted as Oryn rejoined him under the arbors that surrounded the pavilion. "A king is never seen in such a state! I don't know—" He broke off as Oryn turned down the path among the jasmines that led back toward the Summer Pavilion. He reached out and plucked his master's sleeve, and in a gentler voice went on, "It will not change things, you know, in the next hour, for you to go starved and dirty. She . . . she seems to be quite stable as she is. And I have ordered the baths to be got ready."

"Have you?" Oryn paused and looked down at the little eunuch with a smile. "That was very kind of you, Geb." He half turned back toward the pavilion, the shape of its cedar lacework eaves blending artfully with the sycamores and palms set all about it. Lamps still burned in its upper chamber, but the paintwork of gold and blue, the multiple hues of its gardens, were beginning to emerge into their daytime hues with the swift flood of the coming light.

He took a deep breath. *I have to live,* he reminded himself. *I have to live at least long enough to make sure Rainsong is hidden away before the fighting starts.*

"Yes, thank you, I will bathe. Please lay out . . ." His voice stumbled. The choice of robe, earrings, accessories—the usual preoccupation and delight of his mornings—seemed suddenly beyond him. Peacock and turquoise? Blue and bronze with the antique amber necklaces? Silver summer tissue with the parures of ancient rubies? He didn't think he could have picked between a red robe and a blue.

Summerchild.

In his mind he saw the black-robed shadow of Khon—Death—standing before him as it had stood before him in the square, barely as tall as his shoulder, reaching out to touch his face with a long-fingered white hand.

I have to live. Living involves bathing and breakfast. . . .

"Bring me whatever you think is best," he said, keeping his voice steady with an effort. "And send . . . send . . ." *Dragon-eyes tea from the slopes of the Eanit Mountains or lowland black? Sweet green sugarmouse fruit or bananas?* "Send some breakfast up to the pavilion afterward for me. Anything will do. Ask the ladies what they will have."

Geb whispered, "Yes, Majesty," clearly aghast at this indifference.

"I will see her, though, for a moment. Yes, it will really only be for a moment," he added, with a wan flicker of a smile at his valet's expression. Geb clearly expected him to sink into lethargy at Summerchild's bedside again, and for the life of him, thought Oryn, as he entered the pavilion's blue-and-golden shadows, he could come up with no real reason why he shouldn't. An hour in the baths was a long time. If something happened, would they interrupt him in time for him to come here before—?

Desperately, he tried to slam shut the doors of his imaginings. Of coming back to this room to find them waiting for him at the bottom of the stairs, looking at each other, asking, *Will you tell him or shall I?*

Pebble was at the bottom of the stairs with three men. For an instant Oryn only saw the tall girl's shape against the dawn shadows, and his heart seemed to lock into immobility in his chest. Then one of the men snapped, "And I tell you that after what happened last night we cannot wait! The teyn—"

Oryn's heart sank. *Not here!* Those slumped, hairy forms returned to him, erupting from the wadis, driving the men back. Waiting in the hazy heat, clearly at the command of some unseen ruler. *Please, not in the city!*

"What about the teyn?" he asked quietly. "What's happened?"

The smallest of the men turned, and despite the dimness and shadows of the pavilion's lower chamber Oryn recognized Lord Akarian.

"What's happened?" The old man jabbed a skinny finger up at him. "Fifteen escaped from my compound at Dunwall village last night! Twenty more from my villages at Deepditch and Skipfarm! I *demand* that you send your Crafty girls out to put marks of fear on the walls of my compounds that will keep the teyn inside at night where they belong! This girl of yours"—he jerked a thumb at Pebble, who still stood at the foot of the steps, looking doubtfully from his lordship to the men with him—Akarian's sons, Oryn now saw—and back to Oryn—"doesn't owe allegiance to the royal house anyway! My sons have checked. Her father is of the Url Clan, which is a dependent of House Akarian. I am within my rights to demand that she—and that other girl, whose master also appertains to the House Akarian—be sent now, today, to deal with this problem, before we are all of us impoverished!"

I'm going to be eaten alive by crocodiles in ten days, and you want me to send the women of power out to mark your teyn compounds.

Summerchild could be dying, and you want me to send the only ones who might save her to keep your field labor from escaping.

Oryn drew a deep breath. "I understand that there is an increasing problem with teyn escapes, but so far, no magic has been evolved to prevent them."

"That's nonsense! The Sun Mages were able to ward the compounds for a thousand years!"

"Then I suggest you go speak to the Sun Mages on the subject," replied Oryn in his most reasonable voice. He made a discreet finger sign to Pebble to return upstairs. "They will tell you that the magic of men and the power that women are now able to wield work differently, and many of the spells that worked for mages are simply inert when performed by women who otherwise have power."

Oryn could see by the way Akarian was looking at him that his lordship didn't believe a word of it.

"You owe it to us," the old man insisted stubbornly. "As king, divinely appointed by the gods, you owe it to us to share with us the power of these women you've taken under your command."

It took Oryn the better part of half an hour to disabuse Lord Akarian of the notion that he was going to be able to leave the palace with Moth and Pebble that morning and get them to keep his teyn from escaping. When his lordship and his lordship's sons finally departed, they left a petition the size of a short novel explaining why the levy of teyn demanded of House Akarian for work on the aqueduct was unfairly large and should be reduced. As their voices died away across the garden—still arguing with Geb and with the guards who'd been called to escort them to the main gate—Oryn turned to the stair that led up to Summerchild's chamber.

But it was as if his knees had been paralyzed, as if leaden boots had been fixed to his feet. His hand on the corner of the tiled wall, he stood for a moment, absorbing with weary gratitude the silence of the first solitude he'd had in over a day. Then he slowly sank to the steps, leaned his head against the wall behind him, and began to laugh, huge racking sobs of laughter while tears ran down his face.

"My lord, what is it?" Moth came hurrying down the stairs, sat on the step at his side. "You all right?"

"Quite well, my dear," Oryn whispered, aware that for some time he'd been weeping, not laughing. "Quite well. When this is all over I must ask Soth if there didn't used to be Eight Veiled Gods, not seven—there seems to be one immutable force besides Death and Time and Change that they've forgotten."

The concubine looked up at him with worried brown eyes, clearly concerned that he was either hysterical or had gone insane from his contact with the priests in the square. "What's that?"

"Stupidity," said Oryn. He wiped his eyes, looked out past Moth to the garden archway, where beyond the lattices the sun already burned bright and hot, as if the night's coolness, the dawn's birdsong, had never been. "Has Raeshaldis come? She should have been here by this time."

"No, my lord." Moth sounded scared. "We been trying to reach her since dawn, Pebble and me. She don't reply."

THIRTY

I t had been a coyote that delayed them—a spooked horse and a man and horse falling together over the edge of an arroyo, not a serious injury but an annoying delay in the empty rangelands at night. Shaldis had been waiting while Jethan and the others twisted his friend Cosk's dislocated shoulder back into place and tracked the horse, when Foxfire had called her from somewhere in dark hills in the night.

It was almost dawn before they saw the walls of the Yellow City rising before them.

"Will you stay in the Yellow City?" Shaldis reined in, gazed west through the thinning darkness. "If something should happen to the king?"

The baroque pearl of the moon stood a finger's breadth above the formless jumble of land in that direction: hills from this side but in actuality the pink-and-yellow bluffs that backed the Yellow City where they drew near the Lake of the Sun. That flat-topped shoulder of rock, she knew, was the high point of the Citadel, the Ring where for six hundred years the Sun Mages had sung for the coming of the rains.

Even at this distance—three or four miles—it seemed to her that she could hear the echoes of the magic that had been raised there year after year, a whispered comfort in her heart.

In the predawn stillness the rangeland hummed with insect life and sang with birds. From here she could smell the lake and the cook fires in the city that lay invisible beyond the hills.

"You mean if he should die?" Jethan was always relentless, but his voice now was quiet and sad. He owed his life to the king, and though as they jogged slowly through the night he'd treated Shaldis to his opinions of His Majesty's foppish wardrobe, curled hair, painted eyelids, and red-lacquered fingernails, at other times behind his stiff protestations of gratitude and duty she had heard the echoes of his genuine love for Oryn Jothek. "I would remain, of course."

"To serve Barún?" Shaldis had no great opinion of His Majesty's brother. She kept her voice low, to exclude the tired band of Jethan's colleagues who clustered around the injured Cosk—any one of whom, she reminded herself, could have been one of Barún's short-term paramours. "Do you think he'll survive the tests, if Oryn doesn't?"

"I don't think Barún will even take the tests." Jethan's voice, though without inflection, was cold. "Not from cowardice, for His Majesty's brother is as brave a warrior as any man I've encountered. But simply because he does not understand why he can't be king—accepted by the priests and the nomads and the people of all the countryside—simply because he has the largest army and holds the widest lands."

Shaldis was silent for a time, reflecting that for all his appearance of blockheaded obstinacy, Jethan understood the king—and the realm—surprisingly well. After a time she remarked, "It's hard to find grounds on which to argue with him. As long as he *has* the largest army, and some of his captains or landchiefs—or even merchant lords—don't decide that they have as much right to rule as he does."

"Only one man has the *right* to rule." Jethan reined away from the rise of ground where they'd halted their horses back toward the trace that wound toward the gap in the hill concealing the city wall. "And that is the man who has laid his life in the hands of the gods, for all the people to see. It's like when I used to ask my grandmother, 'Can I take my brother's bow and go hunting?' Because I was the older and stronger than he. And she'd say, 'You *can*, dear, but you *may* not.' And I would be ashamed to have acted like a bandit, only because I was strong."

Shadow of that shame still lingered behind his rueful half smile.

Shaldis had seen no woman old enough to be Jethan's grandmother in the striped shade of the ramada beside that isolated adobe house. *A boy*, Jethan had said. *He'd be sixteen.*

There is nothing we can do, Yanrid had told her.

She sighed. "Do all mothers say that? Mine did."

"I think it's a thing that rises into women's minds with their first milk." He drew rein a little and pointed to where a doe antelope and two fawns, barely larger than hunting dogs, melted briefly into view from the sagebrush, their vast ears swinging nervously as the dusty little cavalcade rode past.

For all her instruction in the ways of beasts and birds, Shaldis was at heart very much a city girl. During the past day and a half, she had acquired a profound respect for the simple earth craftiness that set Jethan apart even from his fellow guardsmen. He had a primitive sense of kinship with animals, insects, birds, and sky, a quiet harmony that Shaldis—raised in the crowded Bazaar District—had learned only with great labor and thought.

The other riders, warily alert or joshing Cosk about what he'd do for a day in bed and an extra brandy ration, seemed to lack even that.

After a time Jethan went on, "Without the right to rule, it will come down to whoever is the richest: who can buy the loyalty of the most men and who can buy the loyalty of the greatest number of the Raven sisters. I think that's what the king fears most," he added, seeing Shaldis open her mouth to protest even the thought. "That Lord Sarn will offer one of you the thing that she most treasures— and that thing may be as simple as her family's life—and that Lord Jamornid or Lord Mohrvine will offer another something else: money, perhaps. A lot of money. Don't sneer at it," he added, seeing the flush of disgust rise beneath the thin skin of Shaldis's forehead. "Money buys freedom. Ask any dirt farmer. Or any dirt farmer's wife."

Shaldis thought of Cattail in her elegant house. Of Yellow Hen and Foursie with nowhere to live but under

Cirak Shaldeth's roof. Of that brown adobe house, a day's walk to the nearest village.

"Then, too," Jethan went on, "if one woman stands out against the blandishments of one or another lord, that lord may take it on himself to kill her rather than see her in the employ of his enemy. And that is the road to death indeed."

Shaldis was silent as they passed around the shoulder of the hills and saw the shadowy bulk of the city's walls outlined in the glow of dawn and the tasseled green velvet of cornfields and palmeries all tipped with gold. At length she said very softly, "There are times when I hate men."

Streaming over the Dead Hills to their backs, the long light of morning tipped the palace roofs, the exuberant horns and scrollwork of the Marvelous Tower, with glittering gold. The tower's chimes rang out to greet the morning, vying with the hum of insects, the far-off crowing of the city's cocks.

Stooped, hairy teyn jostled in lines along the cornfield pathways closer to the city, slow moving and deliberate, and lifted their heads to watch the dozen riders as they passed. The other guards called out jocular obscenities to the silent creatures, but Shaldis heard at least one of the men mutter to another, "They got to do better than that, keeping them in line."

News of the attack in the desert would spread, she knew, no matter what orders the king gave to keep it quiet. Garbled and magnified into a threat that every teyn owner would react to. The thought that some Crafty was able to control teyn—to command them to murder their owners—would expose thousands of perfectly innocent, good-natured creatures to massacre at worst and at best ever-harsher methods of incarceration and control.

Yet as the little party rode through the glazed-brick passageway of the Flowermarket Gate, she thought of the empty compound on the outskirts of Three Wells and of the crooked tracks in the dust between those burned walls.

Did the voice that cried to her for help in her dream have anything to do with any of this?

Or the whisper of magic in the walls of her grandfather's house?

She didn't know what to think or what it meant, and moreover, now there did not seem to be anyone to ask. Through the night she'd felt the slow draw on her power through the Sigil of Sisterhood, as Pebble and Moth sought by whatever means they could to hold Summerchild with spells of strength and life. Her instincts shrieked at her to search for both the unknown mages, but deep in her bones where her power lived, she sensed Summerchild poised to slip away.

And with her would go, almost certainly, any hope of saving the king.

And maybe the realm as well.

They emerged from the gate shadows into the Square of Rohar, facing the god's brightly painted temple, and heard men's voices shouting and a woman's screams.

Trouble in any of the city's squares spread very quickly. The donkey trains of market-bound fruits and vegetables, the boys who hawked milk and ointment door to door, and the water sellers with their huge clay jars slung before them and behind panicked first, trying to run without knowing where they fled or from what, stumbling and crashing into barrows of fruit and flowers in the square. Housewives and teyn fetching water dropped their jars and leaped for safety. Shaldis's horse shied violently and one of the guards' mounts reared. Dogs barked and voices rose, shouting; and above the sudden din Shaldis heard a man shrieking, shrieking in rage and agony such as she'd never heard before.

From her vantage point in the saddle she saw him as he ran out of Little Hyacinth Lane, naked as if he'd just leaped from his bed. He carried the remains of a chair and in his other hand a gardener's machete; and he slashed with both all around him—Shaldis barely saw these details, so horrified was she at his face. His mouth hung open, howls pouring out of it like water from a bucket.

His eyes bulged. Windows into hell.

Shaldis flung herself from the saddle, threw the reins to Jethan. The crowd had separated them from the other guards; she ran forward alone, hearing them shout behind her. The howling man plunged through the crowd in the square as if he were running a race, lashing, stabbing, lunging now at one person, now at another; but Shaldis could tell—she didn't know how—that what he saw had nothing to do with the reality around him.

A woman stumbled, fell in a tangle of horoscopes and almanacs as she tripped over her own blanket; the howling man struck her with the chair, bent to rip with the knife. Shaldis yelled, summoning a spell of pain with all her strength and flashing it at the man's guts; and though she saw him buckle—saw blood splash out of his mouth—still he fell on one knee beside his victim, cut her throat, and ripped her body open before Shaldis could get there. In rage Shaldis blasted him with a spell of pain again, and when he sprang up, leaped at her in spite of it, she flung a burst of light at him like the sun exploding before his eyes.

He didn't stop, came at her with eyes wide and staring. Shaldis grabbed the first thing that came to hand, an awning pole off a tipped-over vegetable barrow, and jabbed it straight at him, ramming it in his belly with the force of a thrown spear. It would have knocked any man to the ground breathless and vomiting, but it didn't. He struck at it, lunged at it, striking now at her, swinging the wooden chair like a vicious club and forcing her back with such violence that she stumbled.

He never ceased to scream, never altered his expression, blood pouring out of his mouth now and trickling from his nose and his ears. Face distorted, eyes staring, he struck at her, and she held him off with the pole like a boar with a spear, frantically hurling every spell she could think of at him—of pain, of blindness. What else?

It seemed to take hours and it was probably only a handful of moments before men swarmed him from behind. One instant Shaldis was staring into those frightful eyes, separated from her own by two yards of bending, splintering pole . . .

. . . the next instant steel flashed, and she saw Jethan's face beyond the howling man's shoulder and blood fountaining up from severed arteries as the madman's head rolled forward and lolled on a strip of tendon and skin. The body thrust and rammed and swung its weapon at her for several seconds before it collapsed on the ground.

Shaldis stood shocked, gasping, her face and clothing splattered with blood.

Jethan stuck his sword tip down into the dirt of the street to catch her. "Are you all right?"

She managed to nod.

"It's Gime," someone said in the crowd. "Gime the tomb robber."

"He isn't either a tomb robber."

"He is. He works for Noyad the jeweler, and if Noyad gets his jewels honestly, I'm a—"

Someone handed Shaldis a cup of water. She found herself sitting on the toppled barrow, Jethan beside her wiping off his sword on the hem of his tunic. The other guards came crowding up. "Good cut, Stone Face," and "You all right, lady?"

A man's voice yelled, "What's going on here, then?" and looking up, Shaldis saw two of the city guards thrusting through the crowd.

Voices layered over each other like the baying of a dozen hounds. "Been acting strange . . . hear him shouting at night . . . come crashing out of his room—his room's next to mine at the tavern—screaming fit to wake the dead . . . killed Flower the kitchen wench . . . No, didn't hear no words, just screaming."

One guard bent over the dead horoscope seller, the other moved off down Little Hyacinth Lane in the midst of the knot of gawkers. Both then turned and converged on Jethan, shouting questions at him as if he'd seen the whole thing and knew who the dead man was. The royal guards pushed back, defending their own. The crowd was already jostling away up Little Hyacinth Lane. Using her awning pole for support Shaldis stumbled after them. The track of Gime the maybe tomb robber from the Square of Rohar to the tavern where he lodged was horrifyingly clear, like the trail of a sacking army: blood splashed on the whitewashed walls, broken fragments of the chair, doors and window shutters gouged and splintered, a dead dog with its head twisted nearly off its body. Gime's neighbors—other single men who roomed at the White Djinn Tavern—clustered around her, along with the tavern owner himself.

Yes, Gime worked for Noyad the jeweler. No, there'd been no trouble with him before, a very quiet sort he was, went early to his room and to sleep.

"Dear gods!" The tavern keeper, a stout graying man with a scar on his cheek, stopped in the doorway of his tavern, staring about the room. As Jethan and the two constables pushed through the crowd, the rest of Jethan's guards in tow, the tavern keeper whirled on them. "Look at this place! Look at it! Gime never did all this! Just raced on through."

"My glasses!" wailed his wife, shoving into the room from behind him. "All my glasses! And my mirror, too!"

Shaldis looked through the door at the ransacked common room. Gime's whirlwind progress from the stairway to the outer door was marked by overset tables and shattered chairs, and in one place by the body of a kitchen maid lying with a broken neck against the wall. But someone had clearly entered the room after everyone had rushed out in the madman's wake, opening cupboards, smashing every glass bowl and vessel in the place.

"Did they get the cashbox?" the innkeeper was yelling, and his wife rushed to one of the wrenched-open wall cupboards. "If whoever did this got the cashbox, I'll hold the city proctors responsible!" he yelled at the city guards. "You should have been here protecting my place!"

"Deemas be thanked," gasped his wife, clutching the

little locked box to her bosom. In addition to being the god of thieves Deemas was the god of innkeepers. "But who would do a thing like this?"

Who indeed? Shaldis stepped back as the city guards and what seemed like several hundred other random citizens all crowded into the common room. Hesitantly she put her hand to the doorpost, fearing that if she touched it—if she listened into the wood and adobe as Summerchild had done—she herself might disappear into a coma, her mind vanishing down into sleep that spiraled to death.

Very quick, like an eyeblink, she touched it.

Magic.

It was only a breath, and she didn't dare sink deeper to look for more. There'd been a simple little spell worked here recently—but she didn't think as recently as that morning.

She couldn't be entirely sure, but it felt like the same magic she'd felt on Murder the cat and on the wall at her grandfather's house.

THIRTY-ONE

For four days after that, Shaldis remained almost constantly at Summerchild's side in the blue-and-gold pavilion, weaving and renewing, over and over again, the spells and sigils of life that covered the floor around the bed. When she wasn't doing this she was poring over the books

Yanrid brought her from the Citadel library, searching for
further magics that might be turned to use by the power
of women, to bring Summerchild back from wherever it
was she had gone.

Or, failing that, to simply keep her from dying.

Pebble very practically rigged an arrangement of a
hollow reed lacquered for strength and a bulb of pig in-
testine—of the sort she'd used to give drenches to her father's horses—by which they were able to force water
down the unconscious woman's throat. Sometimes
Shaldis suspected that this, rather than any magic, was
the principal reason her friend didn't die of dehydration
in the grilling summer heat.

She felt utterly helpless and exhausted beyond anything in memory.

"Is there anything I can do to help you?" whispered
Foxfire again, late on the first night of watching at Summerchild's bedside. Shaldis had had a quick scrub after
returning to the palace and a hasty meal, after reassuring
Moth and Pebble, who'd been trying to reach her. Most of
the remainder of the day she had spent patiently feeding
spells of life and energy drawn from her own strength
into the Circle of Sisterhood, and as a result was so exhausted she could barely sit up. But when she'd felt the
mental tug of summons to her crystal, she'd woken Moth
to take over the spell-weaving and had gone out into the
garden—exquisitely cool with the lake breezes—and had
let the images come.

Foxfire looked as bad as she herself felt, her eyes red
with weeping.

"Just keep me informed of whatever you can without
getting yourself into trouble." Shaldis rubbed her aching

forehead. She could see little of the girl's surroundings—
it looked like she was bending over a water bowl in a corner of a bare adobe room, but there was a glimpse of a
window behind her, looking into a waterless courtyard
full of bull thorns and scrub. When she'd spoken to her
last night—it felt like years ago—she'd seen behind her
the jagged shoulders of desert hills.

"I wish I'd joined the circle—gone through the rite of
the Sigil of Sisterhood," said the girl. "Can Pomegranate
send her energy to help you from far away?"

"Yes, and it's saving all our lives. But I don't know
whether what your grandmother's doing would be more of
a drain on us than a help, if you were part of the circle now,
so maybe it's just as well." Shaldis glanced briefly aside at
Moth, sitting on the edge of Summerchild's bed. Moonlight
flooded in from the gardens, where Gray King, the biggest
of the palace cats, sat on the edge of the fountain, gazing in
with enigmatic eyes. "We'll be all right, baby. We're splitting watches now to work the spells to keep her alive, and
when Pomegranate gets back—maybe as soon as the day
after tomorrow—we'll be able to go back to throwing
chickens at crocodiles and teasing snakes."

Foxfire put her hand over her mouth at that and shuddered at some terrible memory. Shaldis felt the flare of
burning anger, guessing how the more brutally practical
Red Silk must be testing her spells.

"Shaldis, it's awful here," Foxfire whispered. "Grandmother . ." She stopped herself, swallowed hard, no
more able to betray her grandmother's doings than
Shaldis, exhausted as she was, would contemplate remaining here rather than returning to her grandfather's
house later that night.

"Listen, there's something terrible happening here, something I don't understand. There's a—a mist, something that rises out of the desert sand. I saw it last night, like a green glow in the hills. Tonight when I walked on the walls I saw it again, before the moon came up. The guards say it's Bad-Luck Shadow and hang all kinds of charms on the walls and on their doors, but it's more than that. The teyn have figured out some way of getting out of their pen, but they won't go past the walls to escape. So it has to be something frightful. Do you know? It's nothing Soth or Hathmar ever told me about."

"I don't know, but I've seen it, too. Usually far off in the desert or around the wadis in the Dead Hills. Pomegranate's seen it near the City of Reeds." *And moving along the shores of a lake of fire in my dream.*

"It couldn't be the djinni, could it? Magic has turned into something else. Could the djinni have . . . have transformed? Shaldis . . ." Her voice sank. "It *sings* to me. I hear it in my dreams. Music, like a buzzing insect, or sometimes bells or voices."

"Voices?" Shaldis sat up. "What do they say?"

"I don't know. I don't understand them, but they sound far off and sweet."

"No other sound? Not like a crashing or a rushing?"

Foxfire shook her head.

Do not let the mist touch you, the woman's voice had whispered to her in her dream. *Flee it. Flee this place.*

"It isn't the djinni," said Shaldis slowly. She had her own theories about what had happened to the djinni and where they were hiding, but could prove nothing. She knew she'd almost certainly be regarded as a madwoman if she spoke about it. "I don't know what it is. But keep away from it. And let me know if you hear things in your dreams again."

The girl murmured, "All right." She glanced aside, as if at some noise, then back. "I have to go."

Her image faded at once.

Shaldis closed her eyes. It was midnight, the hour of the Sun's Dreams. She had left her grandfather's house the night before last at this time, leaving poor Pebble, whose release the king had negotiated on his return to the city, by the simple payment of an enormous bribe.

For a man who seemed to think of nothing but playing the harp and collecting antique jewels, he displayed a keen ability to size up her grandfather's priorities.

But a promise was a promise, and if for no other reason, Shaldis knew she had to go back to the house on Sleeping Worms Street. Moreover, she was virtually certain that the unknown Raven sister would return there on her own or in the service of whomever she worked for. So she sent for one of the palace litters and rode through the lively night markets, past torchlit taverns that remained open until almost dawn. By the time her grandfather had dressed her down about leaving him alone to his enemies for so long—"That fat cow you left here was worse than useless!" he stormed, and didn't mention the king's bribe at all—it was only a few hours till first light. Shaldis fell asleep in the middle of her meditation on healing herbs and slept like a dead woman. Fifty unknown Raven sisters could have danced in a ring around her without her being aware of it or anything else.

Three more days passed, in which Shaldis felt as imprisoned, and as worn, as the teyn who ground corn all day in her grandfather's kitchen courtyard. With Moth and Pebble she patiently renewed the spells of life around Summerchild's bed, while Summerchild's maid Lotus and as often as not King Oryn himself kept her body clean and as cool as they could with constant application of damp cloths, to slow the deadly process of dehydration that was the true killer in wasting sicknesses. The energy Shaldis put into the spells left her drained and shaky, but her anxiety prevented her from eating the meals and sweets Geb sent up: she slept instead, when she could.

Between times, while she was supposed to be resting, she read the scrolls Yanrid sent over, of ward-magic theory or the staggering variety of plants that could be used for healing and the spells that would strengthen their effects. Or she went downstairs to the lower chamber of the pavilion and worked with Rachnis on formulating protective spells and cantrips to be used when Pomegranate returned or when it became clear that the spells of life had at least stabilized Summerchild as she was. As the only one of the three trained in the formal manipulation of magical power, Shaldis could not put this aside. The moon was on the wane. She saw it from the galleries of her grandfather's house as she walked them in the darkness, her senses stretched for the whisper of magic, the creak of some anomalous sound.

And she heard again Jethan's quiet voice against the birdsong of the desert morning: *Only one man has the right to rule . . . that is the road to death indeed.*

In those days Jethan was almost her only comfort, though the strict rules of the guardsmen on duty in the harem gardens meant that she could speak to him only if she walked down the path to his little kiosk by the ornamental gate. And being Jethan, he would not converse on duty. Still, it was profoundly comforting to know he was there.

On her second night of sleeping in the chamber above her grandfather's kitchen court, she was wakened by someone passing the ward sigil she'd put on the alley door. By the time she ran downstairs there was no one there, and the latch was still in place. Opening the door—it was nearly the hour of the Sun at His Prayers—she looked into the black silence of the alley and thought she saw a dark-robed figure slip around the corner. Though it was difficult to tell, in the warm night this close to the garbage middens, she thought the smell of old blood and dirty, lacerated flesh lingered in the air.

Back at the palace on the following afternoon, Geb the chamberlain, nearly spitting with indignation, stormed into the lower floor of the Summer Pavilion where Shaldis was reading with the news that Cattail—"Only she's calling herself *the Lady* Cattail now!" sputtered the little eunuch—had come to the palace offering her services to the king.

"She asked him—she *dared* to ask him—how much he was willing to pay for spells that would guard him from any poison whatsoever!" Geb's round face was pink with rage as he set down the tray of sweet dates and plums and savory chicken and lamb with rice on the low table among the piled books and scrolls. "After coming up to the gate in a litter that I'll *swear* was the one Lord Jamornid had made for his wife the year before last, and I wonder what *she* had to say when he took it and passed it along, *with* its matched team of bearers, to that . . . that *fishmonger's* widow!"

"I hope he didn't pay?" Shaldis was torn between concern—the gods only knew what the spells would actually do—and a desire to laugh.

"Great gods, no! She then said she was quite willing to lay aside her other concerns—*for a consideration*—and take over the efforts to arrive at the other spells needed. 'It is quite clear no magics invented by men are going to be the slightest use to women of Craft,' she said. 'Those who try to force their own power to flow through channels not designed for it are only wasting their time. From the beginning I have made my own spells, wrought and honed my unique methods.' As if what you're doing here is just nursery rhymes to amuse children!"

Shaldis shook her head in agreement and let Geb bully her into eating, but she was uneasily aware that while Cattail's made-up spells frequently did not work, they often did.

It might be, she thought, as she mounted the stairs to the upper chamber again through the breathless heat, that they would come to needing even Cattail's power added to their own, to save Summerchild and the king. She hoped not. Summerchild's prestige as the favorite of the king had kept in check Cattail's fondness for running things. Without her, Shaldis suspected that the woman's inclusion would harm more than help.

If indeed her only motives were money and power, and not something more sinister. Shaldis wondered if the dark-faced Raven sister still roved the alleys of the Slaughterhouse District, seeking the Raven child.

That same afternoon, when she summoned as usual the image of the guards' camp outside Three Wells village in her crystal, the first thing she saw was vultures and jackals fighting over the corpse of a man. Tiny and distant as the scene was—as all things were, scried from afar—it hit her like a blow beneath her heart. She sank back onto the divan and whispered, "Damn it!" and Oryn, kneeling beside Summerchild's bed, looked up sharply from the reports he was reading from the aqueduct camp.

"Something's happened at Three Wells." Shaldis angled the crystal: sometimes, scrying a scene far away, she could look on many angles at once as if she stood in several places in her mind. Her hands shook and she fought to keep her concentration. This time, no amount of angling the crystal showed her any but that single view. "I see a body, fresh—and at this hour of the day if there were any alive in the camp they'd have dealt with it." She looked up, striving to step past, as Yanrid had said, the sense of obligation to help everyone—the nagging guilt that if catastrophe happened, it was due to her failure. But all she could remember was how Corporal Riis's shoulders had relaxed with relief when she'd said she would check on the camp daily.

A lot of good that had done them.

Jethan had been right.

"They were well, when I checked on them yesterday evening. The last of the bodies from the village was buried the day before without any sign of ill effect. I can't imagine there was a man of the company that would have gone into the ruins after that."

"Then something may have come out of the desert and fallen upon them." The king's voice remained reasonable and steady, but in his face Shaldis could see her own thought reflected, and her own guilt. The side of his face still bore the fading bruises left by the teyn attack near

Three Wells. He picked up the silver bell that stood in a lamp niche by the bed, shook it sharply. As Lotus's footsteps vibrated on the stair he went on, "Raeshaldis, my dear, would you be so good as to look in your crystal at the aqueduct camp? It's only a half-day's ride from Three Wells. Ah, Lotus, my pearl of light, could I possibly prevail on you to fetch Bax here? It looks as if we're going to need another expedition out to Three Wells. I kiss your hands and feet, my dear."

Shaldis heard the girl go, heard the silky rustle as the king turned back her way. But he did not speak, and her own thoughts were tangled deep in the half-tranced state that scrying sometimes demanded. It had been months since she'd ridden out to the face camp at the end of the stone-lined canal that now stretched beyond the Dead Hills, and the image within the crystal was slow in forming, as it was for all places where Shaldis herself had not been. Indeed, her reasons for riding out to the camp had been so that she would know at least some elements of it—to focus on the shape and color of the tents, the faces of the foreman and chief teyn minder, the way the aqueduct looked now that its channel was no longer a line of tall stone columns but a deep, straight slot in the earth.

Even so, it took all her concentration, all her power, to summon the image of the camp. Weary as she was, it was as if she stood some distance off in the desert, looking toward the gaggle of tents and pens, the towering haze of dust; and she could not seem to bring herself closer.

Her voice sounded thick in her ears as she spoke. "I see movement—gangs of teyn going to the ditch—lines of camels and asses coming into camp. Kites at the camp dump. Dogs."

"But all looks well?" The king's words seemed to come to her from some great distance away.

"All looks well."

She heard him sigh. She closed her eyes, her tired head throbbing; Yanrid hadn't been speaking lightly when he'd urged her to take care of herself. When she looked again at the whitish-lavender shard of stone, it lay clear and empty in her hand.

"Thank you, my dear," said the king softly. "You have much relieved my mind. May I fetch you some coffee and a baba cake? Summer—" He stumbled on the name. "Summerchild is always rendered ravenous by scrying, she says."

She whispered, "I'll be all right."

He got clumsily to his feet at the sound of voices in the chamber below. Bax, commander of the palace guard; Lotus answering a question, replying, "He's upstairs."

Oryn stood for a long moment looking down at Summerchild's still face. His long chestnut hair hung lank with sweat around his face in the afternoon heat, and his eyepaint was smeared over lids that had the bruised look of too little sleep. Lotus said, "My lord?" from the doorway, and Oryn closed his eyes like a bone-weary soldier hearing the command once again to form up ranks.

Shaldis got soundlessly to her feet and gathered the billowing masses of pale-blue over-robe from the divan; held it behind him, as she'd seen Geb do. After a moment the king roused himself enough to glance back at her and smile. "Thank you." He slipped his arms into the robe and gathered his rings and necklace from the low table where he'd cast them aside: masses of diamonds with an inner fire like the sun. "You're very good."

And pressing her cold hand between his two fat moist ones, he ran with surprising lightness down the stair.

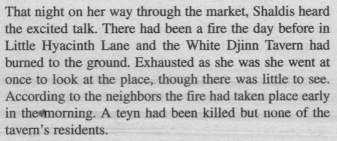

That night on her way through the market, Shaldis heard the excited talk. There had been a fire the day before in Little Hyacinth Lane and the White Djinn Tavern had burned to the ground. Exhausted as she was she went at once to look at the place, though there was little to see. According to the neighbors the fire had taken place early in the morning. A teyn had been killed but none of the tavern's residents.

Standing in the ruins of what had been the common room, Shaldis looked back into the narrow yard, where the kitchen—the only place in the compound where a fire would reasonably be burning in summertime—stood intact. Broken glass glittered in the dust in the light of the waning moon.

THIRTY-TWO

The woman may provide useful information from the palace but she can't scry-ward worth a beggar's curse." Red Silk shaded her eyes against the midmorning glare and the thick dust raised by the caravan. "Thank the gods all the king's girls are still clustered around that concubine's bed wasting their energies on a lost cause. I hope your father remembered to include ointment."

Foxfire said, "Yes, Grandmother," in what she hoped was a matter-of-fact voice.

"That doesn't look like a great deal of water," the old lady added, running a critical eye over the huge wheeled butts as the ox teams dragged them through the compound gate. "Belial's pool is so low the stink's enough to kill those stupid creatures before he even gets to them."

"Yes, Grandmother." Foxfire swallowed hard. The searing white brilliance of the sun made her head pound. All yesterday, and through the morning, they'd been working with various drugs in combination with spells to "open the mind" or increase the strength of their magic. Every death—every pair of terrified, nearly human eyes, every frantic scrabbling to escape—sickened her as badly as the first, though she dared not admit it, dared not let herself faint or be sick.

Red Silk assured her she'd get used to it.

Glancing sideways at that implacable profile, swathed in veils of black and crimson, Foxfire wondered if there had ever been any time when her grandmother *hadn't* been able to look upon death—and death that she should have been able to prevent—with stony equanimity.

The last of the water carts—marked with Cattail's very expensive scry wards—rumbled into the courtyard. Though Foxfire hadn't had a scrub in days, she didn't even notice them, could not really care, through the grief and horror she felt as the line of teyn were herded in. Forty of them, dear gods! She closed her eyes, fighting the sobs that strangled her throat beneath the concealment of her veils.

Big strong shoulders, heavy shaven heads slumped forward, long arms touching the ground with weariness. Some of the jennies carried their infants—pips—in their long arms, pressed to their chests. One big boar had a half-grown pip clinging to his back, thumb in mouth, staring.

Forty. And each one, she'd have to watch die in the knowledge that there was something she could do to save it, if only she could be strong enough, clever enough.

If only she didn't fail, as she'd failed again and again.

And watched them die one by one.

She could hear the wildings in the hills, if she reached out her senses to them beyond the stink of dust and oxen and men's sweat. Smell them, crouched in the wadis all around the compound, silent and motionless as the rocks. Pale slit-pupiled eyes watching under those overhung brows, heavy pale-furred limbs pulled together with animal economy, now and then breaking off a twig of mesquite or camel bush and chewing slowly as they watched. Sometimes Foxfire could scry them. Sometimes, wrung with exhaustion and the various drugs that her grandmother relied on more and more, she couldn't.

Did they know what was happening in here to their big domestic cousins? What did they think of the bodies that were hauled out every morning and buried in the wadis, under shoveled layers of lime to keep the vultures from giving the place away to the king's spies?

What are they waiting for?

When Red Silk hobbled off to speak to Foxfire's half brother Úrthet, who'd been in charge of the caravan, Foxfire slipped away to her room. She closed the door, barred it. She'd seen Soral Brûl on his way across to her with that look of soulful sympathy in his eyes. The room was like a slow oven but she didn't care. She curled up on the bed and lay shivering, sick and frightened and more wretched than she could ever remember being, even last spring when she'd been in danger for her life.

How can I feel this bad when I'm in no danger?

Every time she closed her eyes she saw her grandmother's face and the faces of the teyn as they died.

Already she could hear her grandmother's voice in the courtyard. "Where is that girl? Opal, go get your mistress."

And Opal saying something about rest, making some excuse.

Foxfire wept, quickly and guiltily, trying to do so without letting her eyes and nose swell. A few quick sobs, like stolen kisses. And Eleven Grasshoppers crept from her bed of blankets in the corner, clambered up on the bed—where she wasn't supposed to be—and gently stroked her hair with her big heavy gray-palmed hands, as if Foxfire were her own pip.

"Can you see anything more than you did yesterday?" asked Oryn softly, and Raeshaldis shook her head. Within the central facet of her crystal, the small band of guards rode through the gathering twilight, still several miles distant from Three Wells. Before they'd left the palace the previous day, Commander Bax had taken Shaldis down to the barracks and introduced her to those guards who'd be sent out, under the command of Captain Numet. Now she called their images without difficulty.

They would reach the little town just before full dark.

She knew already what they would find there, and in the charred remains of Corporal Riis's little ring of shelters. She'd scried there several times that day already, and seen the horror of the vulture-torn bodies scattered on the ground.

Above the hills within the crystal she saw what she knew to be outside the archways of the Summer Pavilion where she sat: the moon shrunk to a half circle in the cobalt sky.

※

The following day, just before noon, Soth and Pomegranate returned to the Yellow City. From the upper chamber of the Summer Pavilion, Shaldis could look out through the trees and see the royal barge coming down the lakeshore; a long walkway had been built out from the palace's original landing stage over the vast stretch of mud and reeds to where the water was now. She watched the king walk out along it, shaded by his bullion-tasseled parasol and trailed by his honor guard in gold and crimson. She picked out Jethan among them by his height and the way he walked.

Knowing the king would ask, she unpouched her scrying crystal and looked in it for Captain Numet and his men, though she'd scried earlier that morning and had seen them digging a mass grave near the burned shelters outside Three Wells. Now that the day was hot, they were retreating to their own shelters in a clearing hacked out among the dead cornfields a good hundred yards from both the village and the burned camp. A few vultures still perched on the ruins of the town, but the bodies of Riis and his men were gone.

"Would you be willing to ride out to have a look at the place, Soth?" The king's velvet-rich voice drifted up to her from the garden path. "I'd have said it was another attack by the teyn, except Raeshaldis was watching the desert as well as the camp and saw no sign of teyn within miles. And then, there was something very odd about the original devastation of the village. According to Poru, there was simply not enough blood on the ground. Many of the dead bore no wounds at all. Raeshaldis says Captain Numet has been burying the guards who were killed, poor fellows, and I really suppose between vultures and jackals it would be pointless to do otherwise, particularly since it will take you a day to get out there."

"Either of the other girls scried the guards' camp?" came Pomegranate's scratchy voice. "Here, Pontifer, those are the king's roses!"

"They've tried but haven't been able to see much, they say. They are both quite tired, of course. All three of them have been heroes, since . . . for the past five days. Jethan here was in Three Wells."

The voices became indistinct as they entered the lower floor of the pavilion, saying something about lake monsters and wards. Shaldis slipped the scrying stone back into her satchel, leaned forward to feel Summerchild's pulse, to brush her fingertips along the energy lines of the face, hands, throat. Nothing had changed. Within its frame of dull-gold hair, her face was like wax.

"Here!" Pomegranate came bustling up the stairs, long untidy trails of gray hair flying loose over her shoulders and all her beads clanking. "My dear Shaldis, has that boy Oryn been starving you? And him a king!" And she swooped Shaldis up in her arms, the two women clinging to each other, Shaldis finding herself suddenly shaken with sobs of exhaustion and relief.

"Now, you go downstairs and get some sleep, dearie. I'm here, and Pontifer, too." She patted the side of her leg, to summon the invisible porker back from wherever she conceived him to be wandering around the room. "We'll find a way through this, see if we don't. But you're no good to Summerchild or anyone else if you wear yourself into a ghost. And that goes for you, too," she added, swinging around to jab a finger at the king.

Shaldis did sleep, rather to her own surprise, on the striped linen cushions of the divan downstairs, which Summerchild's maid Lotus had made up into a bed. Her sleep was deep and free of the sense of profound wrongness that plagued her nights in her grandfather's house. She dreamed she was in the unburned kitchen of the White Djinn Tavern in Little Hyacinth Lane, trying to make a tisane of the healing herbs on which she still meditated diligently before lying down every night. Only every pot and basket she opened was, annoyingly, filled with mice, weevils, and grasshoppers. They were written all over with wards, of course, and the wards had all ceased to work. There was a lake monster in the water jar that looked up at her with wise golden eyes and seemed about to speak.

After that, she gave up and walked out to the courtyard—hoping, perhaps, to find a fever tree growing there—and saw before her the burned ruins of the inn. The dead members of poor Corporal Riis's company lay strewn in the courtyard, covered with vultures. The dust at her feet glittered with broken glass.

Only it wasn't glass, she thought, it was jewels: jewels that came from tombs.

Jewels inscribed with curses. *But the curses no longer work,* she thought, bending down to pick up a ruby like a drop of blood at her feet. *Any more than the mouse wards do. That's what happened to Riis and his men—mice killed them. A lake monster came up out of the village well.*

She woke with the lake breeze drifting across her face and the sunlight making sharp-edged golden trapezoids all over the wall above her. She went upstairs and found Pomegranate still beside Summerchild's bed, but obviously Geb had been there in the meantime. A spindly-legged table had been set up beside her bearing coffee things and a dish of heavenly morsels, and the old lady was feeding fingerfuls of whipped cream to three of the palace cats.

"Any change?"

Pomegranate shook her head. "Moth came for a time—you were out like you'd had a draught of poppy, dearie. She'll be back this evening, if you wish to go home and get some real rest." She broke off, looking sharply over her shoulder as if at some sound.

"What is it?"

The old woman listened for a moment, then shook her head. "Nothing, I guess. His Majesty's down at the wharf, seeing off his daughter. He's sending her away across the lake to one of the small estates in the Eanit country. As if he doesn't trust us to get him through his consecration!"

"I'm sure he's only concerned for her health in this heat," said Shaldis. She scooped a fingerful of cream from a pastry. "Would Pontifer care for some? Or doesn't he eat cream?"

"Oh, Pontifer's very particular," said the old woman, "even about the king's kitchens. But Pontifer isn't here."

"Where's he gone?" Shaldis paused, startled, in the

midst of offering the cream to the cats. It was the first she'd heard of Pomegranate's illusionary companion leaving her side.

"To look for Summerchild, of course. Since he isn't a real pig"—Pomegranate's voice dropped to a whisper, as it always did when she didn't want to hurt Pontifer's feelings—"he should be able to go where she is. I hope he'll be all right," she added worriedly. "It's a long way for him to travel, and . . ."

"And what?"

"And there's something amiss here," whispered the old woman. "Something amiss in the city, I mean, some evil going forward. I just hope he doesn't come to harm."

✳

The sun was setting. The guard had changed in the kiosk near the ornamental gate that led into the Summer Pavilion's maze of jasmine and pepper trees; Shaldis quickened her steps to a run, to catch up with the three red-clothed forms of the guardsmen on their way back to the barracks. The Akarian kings had staffed the entire harem area of the palace with eunuch guards, a system that had led to scandalous corruption. As generalissimo, old Oryn the First had sent most of these fairly useless watchers away and had replaced them with men from the regular guard units, rotated frequently and keeping watch in threes. Jethan was with his friend Cosk, his arm already out of a sling despite obvious remnants of pain, and with the boyish-faced Firmin. Through him, Shaldis was finding herself on a first-name basis with half the warriors in the palace, something that would give her grandfather a stroke if he knew.

"I thought with Pomegranate back, the four of you would be out tonight testing spells for the consecration," said Jethan when Shaldis told him what she wanted him to do. They'd fallen back a step from the others, to keep their voices low.

"Well, the first thing the four of us are going to try to do in concert is bring Summerchild out of her coma," retorted Shaldis. "Pebble's going to be here tomorrow morning. *Then* we'll start throwing chickens at crocodiles again. Tonight's the first night I've been able to leave Summerchild's side."

"So you're going to spend it riding out into the desert until all hours." He stopped on the graveled path; the other two halted some distance away, waiting in the dappled shade. They'd removed their helmets and the leather caps beneath them, but Jethan—never one to be less than regulation at all times—still wore his; and his face, framed in gold, had a stripped-down look, as if the structure of its bones had been laid bare.

"I'm going to do something I needed to do six days ago," said Shaldis. "Which is go out to the Redbone Hills and pay a call on Ahure the Blood Mage. Something about our friend on Little Hyacinth Lane the other day is starting to remind me a lot of what we saw out in Three Wells, and both he and Ahure work for Noyad the tomb robber—excuse me, Noyad the respectable jeweler. But if you don't want to come along to watch my back, I can take care of myself."

"I'm sure you can," said Jethan, falling into step with her as she started up the path again toward the gate that led to the guards' court and, beyond it, to the stables, where she meant to beg a cavalry mount from Bax. "Up until the moment that you can't. Riis could take care of himself, too," he went on. "I've seen him do it in more taverns than I'd care to tell you about. The men of his squad were tough, and now they're buried in a cornfield. Do we need those two mangy dogs with us as well?" he added, raising his voice to include Cosk and Firmin, who promptly began to howl, yip, and scratch their ears.

"Good heavens," said Shaldis, more startled at the question than at the behavior of Jethan's friends. "I can't imagine why. I only need someone to keep an eye on things in case a problem comes up. It isn't as if Ahure can do any magic."

"No," said Jethan, pausing again as they reached the square gray block of the barracks' gate. "But someone can. Someone was controlling the teyn, who held us away from Three Wells while they burned the village. And someone has, at least once, used magic in your grandfather's house. You don't know what we'll find out there, once we get to Ahure's house. I agree that we probably don't need four of us, especially considering the difficulty in concealing four riders, but I'm glad you're taking help. Get changed into riding clothes," he added, nodding back in the direction of the Red Pavilion. "I'll talk to Bax about horses."

"Thank you." She turned to stride back toward her palace quarters, then paused and said a little shyly, "I may be too proud and unruly for a woman, but I'm not stupid, you know."

Jethan pulled off his helmet and smiled at her from beneath the sweat-soaked mop of his hair. It changed the whole of his face. "I never thought you were."

THIRTY-THREE

Though the last daylight had barely faded from the sky the house of Ahure was dark. As Shaldis turned her horse toward it, from the wider track toward the necropoli deep in the hills, she wondered in a whisper how many clients Ahure got in the summer's heat. "I mean, Cattail's patrons have the option of visiting in the early hours of the morning or in the evenings when it's cool enough to be out but the streets are still crowded."

"If he's making amulets for Noyad," objected Jethan, narrowing his eyes against the shadowy distance, "surely Noyad would insist he not work for others."

Shaldis grinned. "*Ahure* pass up a chance to impress someone with his greatness?"

And Jethan let out a crack of laughter. "I had an uncle like that. He—"

Then something rustled sharply in one of the clumps of sagebrush that dotted the hillslope before the house: "Jackal," said Shaldis. "After the garbage." By the smell of it there was garbage in plenty, and none of it buried or burned.

Her horse snorted and shied, and Jethan said, "No, it's

too—" And there was a sudden, murderous whine in the air between them. Jethan's horse reared and twisted aside with a scream.

Shaldis saw blood on its shoulder, a long rake, like a knife slash. The same instant her own horse leaped sideways, and Shaldis kicked her feet clear of the stirrups as she was pitched out of the saddle, curling her shoulder to take the impact of the ground. She heard Jethan curse, and the thud of an arrow hitting the sand near her. She lunged for the nearest clump of sagebrush and something moved in it: the glitter of eyes under a teyn's overhanging brow.

Then it was gone, and between Jethan's cursing and the pummel of her horse's fleeing hooves on the earth, she couldn't tell where. When she rolled into the sagebrush and sat up, she glimpsed another teyn darting from cover a dozen yards away, heard men's voices shouting from the house. Ahure's, shrill and harsh, cried, "Kill them, I tell you!"

Shaldis cried, "Ahure, no! It's Raeshaldis!"

"I knew it!" the Blood Mage screamed. "He sent her! Kill them both!"

Jethan dropped from the saddle beside her, keeping firm hold of the reins of his thrashing mount. Despite his efforts to pull her out of arrow range—and the men with Ahure must be using longbows, thought Shaldis, they were too far for crossbows—she called out, "Ahure, my grandfather didn't send me!"

An arrow buried itself in the ground a few feet away. Jethan hooked an arm around her waist and dragged her back down the rise on which that small brown adobe stood. Ahure could be heard howling something, and

Shaldis whispered the other half of the ward-and-retrieve spell she'd taken the precaution of putting on her mount. As she and Jethan retreated toward the main road the brown-and-white gelding came trotting back through the starlit sagebrush, reins trailing.

"He was watching for us," panted Jethan as they cantered away in the direction of the faint sprinkling of the Yellow City's lights. "Or watching for *someone.*"

Shaldis muttered, "Damn my grandfather," and summoned the wards of a Gray Cloak around them, as soon as she judged they were too far to be seen clearly in the starlight. Then she drew rein. "He's afraid of something."

"*I'm* afraid of something," retorted Jethan. "I'm afraid of being shot by a madman."

"Why, Jethan!" Shaldis gave him her most dazzling smile. "I thought the king's guards weren't afraid of *anything*." And she drew her horse near his—he'd stopped a few feet farther down the road than she—and signaled to him to lower his voice. "Sometimes mages can still hear at a great distance, if they go into trance," she whispered. "That's why I think we need to go on foot." And she slipped down from her gelding again.

"Go on foot *where*?" He did remember to whisper. "There were teyn circling that house—I saw three of them. Whoever was controlling the teyn out near Three Wells must have sent them against Ahure as well. The place is isolated enough."

"Unless it's Ahure who's doing the controlling," replied Shaldis softly. "And if it is, I think we'd better find that out."

Soth Silverlord heard the harp playing in the Summer
Pavilion as he returned across the gardens from bidding
Moth and Pomegranate good night at the gate of the Marvelous Tower; the music filled the air like the sweetness
of jasmine and roses. Lamplight glimmered through the
trees, though the hour was very late. He nodded to the eunuch guard in the little kiosk where the pathway curved,
climbed the blue-and-gold-tiled stair to the upper chamber, where the king sat playing, and the woman Pebble
swayed in a trance over the Sigil of the River of Life,
chalked on the floor beside the bed. As Soth reached the
top of the stair the song concluded, and he heard Pebble
say, "Thank you, Your Majesty. That was beautiful."

"Yes," replied Oryn gravely, "all my courtiers agree
that I'm the premier harpist of the land." And Pebble—as
Oryn no doubt intended she should—dissolved into giggles. Oryn chuckled, too, but his face sobered as he saw
Soth step around the lattice screen. As if he read Soth's
expression he inquired, "More good chickens perished
for naught?"

Soth took Oryn gently by the elbow, led him out onto the
garden terrace. "You should get some sleep." Oryn had
promised to do so when he'd walked Soth back to his quarters behind the palace library at noon. By the look of him
he hadn't.

"Why, do you think my dreams are going to be that entertaining?"

Soth said nothing.

"I'm sorry," said the king immediately. "It's just
that . . . I'm sorry."

And Soth squeezed the surprisingly muscular arm that
he held. "Moth tells me the four of them are going to

combine their powers tomorrow morning, to try to bring Summerchild out of her coma," he said. "It may be indeed that spells that do not work with three enchantresses may work with four. If we can try the same some evening with these warding spells—"

"I won't have Summerchild left alone."

Not even to save your own life? Looking into his former pupil's eyes, Soth didn't say it; in the naked glance he already read the answer.

The true answer, not the one Oryn knew he must make for the sake of the realm.

The next moment Oryn looked away, the muscles clenching suddenly in the heavy jaw. In an almost inaudible voice, the king said, "Yes, I know you're right." He took a deep breath, looked back at Soth with weary resignation. "Tell me, dear friend, were there any kings who didn't survive the tests of their consecration? Or who refused, when it came time to pass through the renewal of their relationship with the gods at the jubilee?"

"There are only ten kings, in all the records of the Later Hosh and Durshen dynasties, whose reigns lasted forty-nine years." Soth settled himself on a bench beside the pool, where the fat crescent of the waning moon's reflection floated on the water. "Before that, the records are incomplete —mostly because the Hosh made a practice of burning anything that didn't agree with their version of history. As far as I can make out, in the time of the Zali kings, the entities whom we know as the Veiled Gods were the only deities of this land—only then, as now, they weren't exactly gods. And in putting himself into the hands of the priests of each temple in turn, the king gave each of the local groups the power of veto in his ascension.

Only when the kings of the House of Hosh aligned themselves with the Sun Mages—who did start out as a priesthood themselves—were the kings able to supersede the lesser magic of the Veiled Priests and break themselves free of their control."

"And I don't suppose there's a chance the magic of the Veiled Priests is still active, is there? I didn't think so." The king sighed and plucked a strand of jasmine to trail across the moon's reflection in the water. "It was just a thought. Where did you learn all that, Soth? It wasn't part of the histories that you taught me as a child."

"Ironically, in this past year I've been able to study the inscriptions in the Zali tombs and on the jewelry that's been taken from them. And a great deal of it has been showing up on the market lately."

"I know." Oryn shook his head wearily. "The thieves aren't even bothering to melt it down anymore. Yet another thing my successor will have to deal with."

"And it's all quite common magic." Soth kept his tone matter-of-fact, as Oryn had kept his when, in years past, Soth had been in the grip of his own demons. "Once the curses and wards ceased to work one can go in and out with impunity. Even the inscriptions we don't understand—the precursors to those standard formulae you still find in tombs about 'corpse walkers' and 'dream eaters'—are sourced the way ordinary magic was, for all the years of its history, from the earth or the sun or whatever."

"Corpse walkers I understand." As Soth had hoped, his former pupil's shoulders straightened a little at the prospect of a puzzle of scholarship. "At least, according to Raeshaldis, when the djinni began to lose their magic they apparently *did* take refuge in corpses, some of them, to keep from dissolving completely, the gods only know where they are now. If they did that in times past, no wonder the old priests put spells on tombs to keep it from happening."

"I think it likelier," said Soth, "that some of those formulae were written to prevent the mages of the Black Cult from sourcing power from the energies released from human minds at death. Which, whether we like it or not, was a very strong source—for those who could manage to use it without going mad."

The king raised his gaze from the reflection of the moon in the water, the half circle whose inner edge showed the faintest concavity, and met Soth's eyes. The question hovered for a moment between them, palpable and deadly: *Would it work?*

Not to save his own life, thought Soth, *but to save Summerchild's.*

Instead he shook his head. "Well, let's hope Mohrvine's frightful mother doesn't think of that one. She's dangerous enough sane. And thank goodness all records of the Black Cults were destroyed. What were dream eaters supposed to be?"

Soth removed his spectacles, polished them on the end of one of the sun veils looped around his neck. He was dressed and booted for riding; if the two men listened, they could hear the far-off sounds of horses being assembled in the Golden Court for the ride to Three Wells. "Mortuary spells have been almost standard for thousands of years," he said. "The formulae written in Zali tombs are almost exactly what you'll find today, allowing for the change in the style of the runes. I know along the northwestern shores of the Great Lake there's a belief that the dead continue to dream—that your dreams *are* the world to which your soul returns after death."

"I can see why the idea of Ean's paradise superseded *that* one." Oryn shivered. "Or even the transmigration of souls, if Tsocha's followers are to be believed. On the other hand—" He smiled a little, as if recalling the more delightful dreams of his childhood. "I suppose if one generally dreamed of the happier parts of one's life, one *would* be a bit peeved if something came into the tomb like a maggot and chewed them all away, leaving you with . . . what? Continually reading and rereading the rest of the mortuary formulae written on the inside of your coffin? How ghastly dull! You'll see to it that there's something more interesting pasted in mine, won't you, Soth? A good novel or a couple of volumes of poems?"

"Since the point of all our work tonight is for *you* to outlive *me*," retorted the librarian, "I'm not going to answer that." He got to his feet. "According to Bax, his riders will be ready to accompany me to Three Wells at midnight. It's nearly that now."

"You don't mind? What a silly thing to ask; of course you mind, you've just journeyed five hundred miles after slaying a truly fearsome lake monster, or at least convincing it to stay in its lake. Speaking of problems my successor is going to have to cope with. But truly, I'll feel a great deal better when a trained observer has had a look, not only at Three Wells but at the aqueduct camp as well." Oryn got to his feet, walked a short distance into the scented shrubbery of the terrace garden. "It's growing harder and harder to keep provisions moving out to the camp, you know. Everyone keeps asking me what's the use? And I must say

I'm becoming quite offended by the universal assumption that I'm going to be eaten. I understand the wagering on the subject has reached proportions previously reserved for theoretical mathematics. I do hope Raeshaldis is investing the Sun Mages' money thus."

"I hope so, too," replied the tutor mildly. "Since without your support, those three old men up at the Citadel are certainly going to starve." Above the cobalt stillness, the jewellike lamps of the palace, the chimes began to sound from the Marvelous Tower, bronze voices and silver mingling.

The king held out his hand in farewell. "Make sure everything's all right out there, Soth," he said quietly. "I daresay it's a foolish hope, but if I am going to die, I should like to do what I can to make sure everyone else in the realm isn't going to die with me."

"There's no way that you can do that," replied Soth. In the scented darkness he remembered his own pain, the hideous sense of helplessness when he'd first realized his magic was failing. It still came over him, that awful darkness that even the strongest *sherab* would not lighten. It was like a dagger in his heart, that the man he'd met as a curly-haired child, this tall, fat, sybaritic harpist whom he loved as a son, had to face that dark alone. "But I'll certainly do what I can."

Oryn frowned a little, straining his eyes at some movement among the reeds and mud of the lakeshore visible from the terrace. "What is that?" he asked. "That greenish light. It's gone now, but it was there a moment ago. See? I've seen it before: sometimes it looks like a light and sometimes like a mist."

"I've seen it before, too," agreed Soth, and his quiet

voice was grim. "Twice, recently, as we came down from the Lake of Reeds. And it glimmered over the lakeshore tonight when we were testing spells, Pebble and Moth and I, about where you see it now. A glowing mist among the dead papyrus, maybe a thousand feet?—fifteen hundred?—to the north of where we stood. Since there were about a thousand crocodiles in that space I still didn't get a good look at it, though it's the closest I've ever seen it."

He glanced at Oryn, and in the moonlight his thin face was grave. "It used to be I'd only see it in the desert. This is the closest it's come to the walls of the city."

"That we know of," said Oryn. "So far."

He turned and walked back to the golden lights of the pavilion, where Pomegranate waited for him beside Summerchild's bed.

THIRTY-FOUR

Shaldis kept herself from saying *I thought so* out loud, and simply pointed to the line of ruined pillar stumps, barely visible among the tangle of camel thorn and mesquite along the sides of a flat rectangle of land below the hills. Though Jethan had not a mage's night-seeing eyes, he'd been following her in the clear desert starlight for long enough that now, with the waning moon just showing over the hill's rim above them, he nodded and signed to her that he understood.

Logically, if this level ground had been the rear court of a mortuary temple, it would have connected by tunnel to the main temple on the other side of the hill—on which Ahure's house now stood. Shaldis could see where a niche had been carved into the red rock of the hill itself, and though the niche was choked now with the more stubborn varieties of rangeland foliage, she could see the beam holes where a second floor had been.

The entrance to the tunnel was covered with a curtain of interwoven tumbleweeds and, behind that, a door that looked new. When Shaldis probed at the latch with her mind she encountered not only the usual levers and tumblers but also a wire connected to a bell. This she stilled as she moved the mechanisms of the lock.

Interestingly, it was in the niche near the tunnel entrance that she found the slight trace of magic on the stone. It was so faint that it didn't even feel entirely like that which she'd detected near her grandfather's house, but it certainly was similar.

She touched Jethan's hand, signing him to follow.

There were three more booby traps in the tunnel, none of them serious, warning bells only. A Crafty—man or woman—could see and avoid them in the dark. The last, on the narrow stairway up to what Shaldis guessed was the house itself, she felt as she passed it: a ward sign.

Cattail's.

She heard a bell ring somewhere in the dark at the top of the stair.

"Curse," she said. "Come on, fast. . . ."

She heard footsteps approaching the door at the top of the steps as she dragged Jethan behind her by the hand. Probed with her mind at the bolt and slammed it open, shoved against the door as a man's stride reached it and a man's weight tried to slam it shut against her.

Jethan heaved on the rough planks and thrust them back. After the moonlight and darkness, even the dim orange flicker of a grease lamp in the room beyond seemed bright.

"My grandfather didn't send me!" shouted Shaldis as she slithered past Jethan into the room. "We're here for advice!" She stumbled a step or two, then realized it wasn't Ahure who stood with his shoulder to the door but a wiry little bald man in rough clothes whom she did not know and two young men whom she vaguely recognized as the two men who'd come calling on Melon the harlot at Rosemallow's place in Greasy Yard.

"Damn, I tried to tell him that, miss." The wiry little man shook his head. "I got my orders from Noyad, 'Do as he says, Ghru'; and teyn is one thing, but, bless it, teyn don't ride horses." He spit. "Mad, he is. Lord Ahure, I mean, though these days Noyad— Was he always mad?"

"It's a little hard to tell." Shaldis looked around the room, a rock-cut cellar from which a further stair mounted the far wall to a door hidden in shadows some fifteen feet above the floor. "Have teyn attacked the house before this?"

"I told him," said the taller man in a disgusted voice. "Like I was sayin' to my brother, Dupy, here, only today." He jerked his thumb at his chubby brother. "Teyn won't attack a house. Not even wildings'll attack a house, 'less they see there's only kids there or something."

"He says they have." Ghru scratched his scarred nose. He was also missing the tips of both ears—a frequent penalty for theft—and had been branded on the hand for manslaughter. "He says they come after him ten feet from the front door one night, and another night tried to break into the place, hammerin' at the doors and the shutters with rocks. And you can see where the wood's fresh splintered, that's for sure. We've had 'em snoop three or four times, since the boys and me came out, and we managed to kill one or two with lucky shots. But attack? Nah. You really Chirak Shaldeth's granddaughter that's the Crafty, like he says?" And he looked past her at Jethan, sizing up the crimson tunic and trousers.

"I am," agreed Shaldis. "Though I'm here to ask advice—" She'd made sure she had some genuine questions to ask, though in fact she had no expectation of getting a word of truth or help out of the Blood Mage. All she really wanted was a look around the house. "What *is* the quarrel between him and my grandfather, anyway?" she added in the voice of one puzzled and exasperated about a matter of ultimately little moment. She looked from Ghru to the brothers, whom she guessed to be simple and good-natured souls at heart, a bit like Jethan's friends in the guards but not so wellborn. "One of my aunts told me there'd been a shouting match of some kind ten nights ago, but it's a long way from a shouting match to ordering you to kill me."

"By BoSaa's boots, more than a shouting match, missy—lady," Ghru corrected himself. Then he shrugged. "What do you expect, bringin' in outsiders to the tomb-riflin' game? Two men take a fancy to the same bit of glitter and think that gives them claim over the rules of division."

"Rules of division?"

"Of course, rules of division!" Ghru drew himself up

proudly. "What you think we are, street brawlers? Smash-and-grab thieves? Tomb riflin's a game that's been goin' forward as long as kings been plantin' their daddies. If there wasn't rules, hard rules, about who gets what, and what happens to them that doesn't like it, we'd all have killed ourselves off inside the first year. *They'd* all have killed *their*selves off," he added. "I only knows this from hearsay, of course."

Yeah, right, thought Shaldis. *And I bet you got your ears clipped in a terrible accident at the barber's, too.*

"Drupe, Dupy, let's get these folk upstairs and see if his lordship's still awake. Come along, now."

He shifted his lamp to his other hand, and led them wide around the lines of baskets that occupied most of the center of the room, a precaution that would have served well in the cellar's darkness had Shaldis not been able to see perfectly clearly in the dark.

Some baskets, she saw, contained jars of alabaster and onyx of the sort that royalty and nobility had buried with them filled with the highest-quality ointment and wine. Other baskets held jewelry, sorted by size: pendants, earrings, bracelets. The amulets that had been wrapped in the bindings of mummies, to call down curses on those who robbed them.

Only of course, those curses had no power now, any more than the curses written around the doors of the tombs. At one end of the cellar a couple of hampers brimmed over with coils of stiff and friable linen, glinting with the sullen gleam of gold.

"Now, I hope you understand me to say Noyad doesn't buy a single jewel or ounce of gold if he thinks it's from a tomb," Ghru went on with a self-righteous glance at

Jethan. "Mind the steps here—we had to fill 'em in with adobe, they was so worn, and it don't hold up so well to traffic. And I'm sure it's just a misunderstandin' that some has accused Noyad of dealin' with robbers, for he'd never do such a thing in his life. But the fact remains that with the city guards pickin' and pryin' into his affairs, and Ahure not bein' able to vouch for every single piece that he trades for, they had to bring your grandpa into it, missy, him bein' proctor of the market and all."

The long stone stairway debouched into a storeroom cut into the living rock of the hill and raftered in pine poles and brush. One wall was built up of adobe: a low door let them through into a tiny chamber, furnished with two solid plank doors, remarkable in so humble a house. In most poor dwellings, especially away from the wood port on the lake, a pantry or a closet like this one would have been equipped with a curtain or a lattice screen.

"As I understand it," Ghru went on in a hushed voice as he guided them through one of the doors to the house's rather bare front hall, "Noyad made your grandpa a gift of a choice piece, to thank him for all his help, one that Ahure wanted to keep for his own. Now me, I could care less about that old stuff." He held the lamp higher and tapped one of the several figures that its light revealed, standing in plastered niches of the adobe wall. "Crude, it is, and who cares if it's two thousand years old? The Dur-shen had a way with jewels and gold that nobody's had since, if you ask me, though I like a lot of the Interregnum pieces. But these? Pish."

Pish indeed, thought Shaldis, politely putting her hands behind her and studying the image. It was crude, with its distorted face and lumpish body, yet the glass it was molded of was exquisitely colored, pale greens and browns like water, with a chain of trapped bubbles twisting through it. She glanced back at the scar-faced bodyguard, who displayed such a surprising streak of connoisseurship, and said, "This is Zali Dynasty work, isn't it?"

"Supposed to be." Ghru shrugged. "We're gettin' a lot of Zali plunder now. Trash, I call it, and half of it glass. You, Drupe! See if his lordship's awake. The piece his lordship got into such a lather about with your grandpa was just glass. One of those glass balls they find in the Zali tombs—pretty, I suppose, but nuthin' to make yourself sick angry over, walkin' the floors at night and carryin' on."

"You'd think if Lord Ahure was a mage," said Shaldis, knowing she was rushing things but keeping a wary eye on the taller brother as he disappeared back out the door through which they'd come, "and he wanted something that badly, he'd take steps to get it, wouldn't you?"

"You'd think." Ghru ran a hand over his pink scalp. "I thought he would, myself. And after all his pesterin' and cursin' to Noyad, I was ready for there to be no end of trouble, if he tried anything. You know." And he made twiddling gestures with his fingers, in a layman's imitation of a mage casting a spell. Then he frowned, puzzled and a little pitying. "It's like it took everything out of him, that fight with your grandpa, miss . . . m'lady. I thought we'd have trouble after that. But since that time—and it was just a night or two before that that the boys and I started coming out here—seems like he just crumples up, come nightfall, and falls asleep like a child. Like havin' it took away from him is burnin' him up inside. Noyad's right peeved about it, I can tell you."

"He must be," remarked Jethan sarcastically, turning back from his examination of a beautiful Durshen statue of Darutha God of Rain that stood in another niche. "Considering it's the custom to—er—*meet with the traders* from whom he gets all these pieces by night, isn't it?"

"That it is." Ghru winked. "I tell you, other than one night when he went into town on business, it's quiet as tombs out here. But he insists he's in danger from the teyn, so who am I to contradict?

"Who are you, Ghru," whispered a harsh, sibilant voice from the shadows at the far end of the room, "to speak of me and my affairs to anyone, much less to a demon brat in the pay of my enemy?"

Except where niches broke the wall, most of the front chamber of Ahure's house was curtained floor to ceiling in black, which Shaldis had guessed already concealed one or more doorways as well as any number of the scorpions and spiders inseparable from desert living. Thus Ahure's seeming materialization didn't surprise her. As she'd spoken to Ghru she'd walked about two thirds around the perimeter of the room brushing these curtains with her hand—albeit gingerly—and had found no trace of magic, not even Ahure's.

Which didn't mean that he wasn't holding the unknown Raven sister in some kind of thrall. Or wasn't simply paying her, as he'd clearly paid Cattail to come and mark his house with ward signs—and, for that matter, had clearly paid poor Nettleflower, either to steal back his coveted trinket or to let him into the house to steal it himself.

She'd already ascertained what she'd come to the

house to learn: namely, whether the unknown Raven sister had worked magic inside his house as well as just outside the connecting tunnel, and if so, how much. But she stood for a moment, shocked at Ahure's appearance. Burning up inside, his bodyguard had said, and Shaldis saw by the lines around the deep-set pale eyes that this was true. He was wasted and haggard, his long hands uncontrollably trembling. Behind her she heard Jethan's swift intaken breath; the Blood Mage had clearly been trying to raise power in the old way, and his shaven scalp, mutilated hands, and scarred cheekbones were crisscrossed with lines of fresh scabs.

Beneath those wounds—and by the smell of old blood and poultices he was cut all over his body under the filthy black robe he wore—lay a horrible palimpsest of older injuries, some self-inflicted, others crude and jagged in a yellow-green mottling of three-week-old bruises.

Shaldis gasped. "Did the teyn attack you, sir?" Somebody certainly had.

"*Did the teyn attack you?*" mimicked the Blood Mage through his nose. "You know that well enough, witch, for it was you who set them on. Have you come to gloat? To take word back to your grandfather, may the maggots devour his bones."

"It was not me who set them on," said Shaldis, thinking fast, and she executed the deepest and most elaborate salaam she could think of. "Rather, I came to you in the hopes of ending this quarrel, for your curses have brought sickness and ill fortune to my grandfather's house."

"And they will bring worse!" declared Ahure, clearly under the impression that he still did have the power to curse. "He will find—"

"Sir, we *are* finding it so!" Shaldis had to shout to be heard against the Blood Mage's impassioned shriek. "I want to end this! Tell me what it is you're looking for and I will see what I can do."

"Don't—you—touch it!" Ahure strode toward her like a monstrous bat, black robes billowing, white face inhuman with rage. He seized Shaldis by the shoulders, shook her like a child shaking a doll. She heard Jethan swear and the clatter and shuffle of a struggle behind her with Drupe and Dupy, even as Ghru darted forward.

"Now, my lord, now, my lord, no call to lay a hand on the young lady!"

"Slut!" Ahure screamed as Ghru pulled his grip away from Shaldis's arms. Ahure's hands had the strength of a madman's, but like most Blood Mages he'd cut off a number of his own fingers in the raising of his particular style of magic, and his clutch was easy to break. "Witch! Demon! Keep away from it! It is not for the likes of you!"

He twisted in Ghru's grasp, and both Drupe and Dupy released Jethan and hastened to their chief's aid. Jethan caught Shaldis against him, drew her away as the Blood Mage began to spit as well as howl and claw at her with his few remaining hooked and grimy nails.

"You tell that senile cheat that it's mine! Tell him that the evil that has befallen him is *nothing* to what will happen unless it is returned to me! Tell him—"

The door shut behind the struggling group of guards and Blood Mage. Shaldis stood, shaking a little with shock, in the circle of Jethan's arm. She realized she could have, and probably should have, used a spell of some kind to hurl Ahure back from her but wondered if one would have worked on him, any more than it had worked on poor Gime, who had died howling in Little Hyacinth Lane.

Ahure's screams could be heard through the adobe walls, gradually subsiding into silence. A moment later Ghru slipped out through the door of the little room from which the stair led down to the tunnel.

"Damn me, miss, I'm sorry." The bodyguard had a bruise on one cheek and claw rakes from Ahure's nails on the other side of his face. Shaldis hoped he'd douse them with the strongest brandy he could find, fast. "He's been bad since that quarrel with your grandpa, but never this bad. I hope you understand—you seem an understandin' kind of girl—lady—that he's not in his right head when he gets so. My boys and me"—he jerked his thumb toward the back room where Drupe and Dupy were no doubt putting the wizard to bed—"we do the best we can, and if you was to put a bad mark on the house, or even on him personal, we'd be the ones would suffer. I doubt *he'd* notice."

"No, I think you're right." Shaldis stepped forward and laid her hands on Ghru's muscular arm. "In truth, I came out here to see if Ahure had the power to do the harm that's been done to my grandfather, and having seen him, I don't think he has. You say he's been here every night but one since his quarrel with my grandfather. Which was what? Two nights ago?"

Ghru counted back on his fingers. "Night before last it was, miss. Now, I tell a lie, he was in town twice since his little set-to with your grandpa: first time was the last night of the full moon. He came back late that night, and cursing."

The night of Nettleflower's death, thought Shaldis.

Presumably, because he'd gone to the alleyway door at the back of the house to meet her, only to find the household in a hubbub over her death.

"Then, yes, he did go in night before last, to meet the boss, Lord Noyad, I should say, and he come home in a foul mood. He'll be fine during the day," the bodyguard went on, "or as fine as ever he is, at any rate—seein' those who come out from the city to have spells or curses, or sometimes goin' out into the hills with . . . er . . . to meet them as *trades* in old gold." And he gave her a wink at the euphemism. "But he'll get restless with the coming of night, and then as soon as it's dark, it's like he's had a draft of somethin', and he's off to bed, sometimes before the light's out of the sky. Me and the boys stand watch here, to guard him from the teyn he says are after him, but it's a lone and dismal stand, let me tell you."

"These visitors who come," said Shaldis, determined to take advantage of Ghru's eagerness to placate her out of cursing the house. "Who are they?"

"Folk from the city." Ghru shrugged. "Some rich, some not so rich. Noyad don't like it—he says it takes away from the sales of them 'enchanted amulets' he sells—but Lord Ahure just agrees with 'im and sees 'em on the quiet. Myself, I hear tell wizards don't got no power no more—that only Crafty ladies such as yourself can work spells—but there's many and many that don't believe it and will come to them as claim the power still. And I must say, his lordship puts on a good show, with his colored lamps, and them levers he's got behind the curtains. Whether his spells really work, well, the feller who used to watch here with us—Gime was his name, one of Noyad's boys—he said those were poisons Ahure brewed up out of the herbs in his garden. Poisons and healing drafts both. Who's to say the words he lays on 'em don't make 'em stronger to their tasks?"

"Are any of those who come to see him Crafty women themselves?" asked Shaldis.

Ghru considered. "That Cattail from down the Fishmarket's been here once or twice. She's supposed to be a Crafty. The gods know she talked enough about how she was."

"Any others?"

The sparse eyebrows pulled together for a moment; then he shook his head. "If they was, they didn't say so. It might be as some of the nomads was Crafty. They don't come inside, just meets him by the gate or halfway up the path."

"Nomads," said Shaldis thoughtfully.

"Rangeland tribes," agreed Ghru as he showed them to the outer door. "Though now and then there'll be a couple from the deep desert. You see more deep-desert tribes coming in these days than you used to when the rains were more regular. It's the deep-desert tribes that know the ways to the truly old tombs, the Zali tombs far out in the desert itself that ain't been opened till now. Not, like I said, that I'd give a snap of my fingers for Zali ware, myself, but it all melts down the same. Will you be all right, gettin' home? It's a long ways. We have horses here, but they'd need to be returned, and if word got to Noyad we'd lent 'em . . ."

"It's all right." Shaldis pressed her palms together and whispered again the spells of ward and retrieve, which summoned the animals she and Jethan had turned loose far enough from the house that no wizard, listening within, could have detected their approach.

"This glass ball that he's so angry about," said Shaldis, "did he get that from the nomads?"

"I don't know where he got it from, m'lady, and that's a fact. It came out of a tomb for sure." He shrugged again as he opened the door to the blue-and-ivory stillness of the desert. "There's no mistaking that old work. They do say the curses that were writ on the old tombs have no more strength nowadays, but this piece seems to be doin' not so bad, if it's turned his brain this way. Not that it had far to turn, if you ask me. And maybe it would have happened, glass ball or no glass ball. You watch out as you ride to the city, now, miss. It may not have been teyn, but something attacked him out there, and it's a fact we've had wildings close around the house."

Like faithful ghosts materializing from moonlight and shadow, the dun gelding and the paint trotted up the path, snuffling and evidently pleased about their little holiday of rambling the hills at night. Shaldis listened for a moment before she swung to the saddle, probing the night for the sound and scent of intruders.

Ghru was right. There were wildings within a few hundred yards, invisible in the still landscape of sagebrush and mesquite. Jethan started to speak as they rode away, but she signed him quiet, listening behind her. The teyn made no attempt to follow as they trotted their mounts back toward the road, then broke into a gentle hand gallop back toward the city under the silver light of the waning moon.

THIRTY-FIVE

Shaldis returned to her grandfather's house too weary to do more than make a single, listening patrol along the galleries, and heard only her mother and her aunt Apricot rising and going downstairs to get the kitchen fires started and start the teyn grinding the day's corn. It was the hour of the Sun at His Prayers; she dropped to the bed in her own room and formed up the images of fever tree and willow before crashing into dreamless sleep.

When she woke it was broad light, and her head and body ached with the scraped weariness of too little rest. *Now, this is a good way to be going into a major effort of spell-weaving,* she thought bitterly, and hoped Jethan— who could barely have returned to the barracks in time to change his clothes before going on duty at the hour of the Bird Sun—wouldn't think too harshly of her for obliging him to be up all night. One of the maids had, Rohar be thanked, left scrub water for her outside the door of her room. She used it, and stumbled downstairs to the kitchen court in time to watch her father have three cups of wine with his simple breakfast before going up to doze over the clerical work that Tulik would check in the evening.

Tulik himself was already in their grandfather's study, deep in conversation with one of their corn-brokers, with two caravan chiefs waiting outside. He would not, Shaldis reflected, welcome an interruption on the subject of why the head of the household might have murdered one of his son's concubines.

The camel drivers who acted as guards on the gallery outside her grandfather's door during the night had gone back to their mates in the front court. His door was still locked.

On her way to the palace, Shaldis turned aside from the route she normally took through the Gem-Cutters' District and passed through a small square close to the city wall. The houses there were very old, and one side of the square was bounded by the black stone wall of a tiny temple whose rear was set into the city wall itself.

Shaldis had seen the square, and the silent black stone temple, hundreds of times in her years of childhood ramblings around the city. It had always appeared deserted and half forgotten, though she'd always known that a single servant of the god dwelled there, performing unknown rites behind its sealed door. The laundresses who lived around the square might drive spikes into the wall for their clotheslines, but they made signs of aversion when asked about the nature of the god whose house it was and would not speak his name.

Today, the clotheslines were gone. Instead, every laundress who used the square had already marked out her own little pitch of ground with stakes and rope, each pitch occupied already by a half-grown child. In five days, Shaldis knew, those laundresses would be able to charge a crown a person for standing room in that square. And they'd get it, from people who'd come to watch the king go into the Temple of Khon—the House of Death.

Always supposing, she thought, quickening her steps almost to a run along the alleyway toward the Golden Court, he made it that far.

"He says he's found her." Pomegranate cradled the small cup, alabaster delicate as blown glass, between her callused palms. Her eyes looked hollow, as if she hadn't taken her own advice about unsleeping worry wearing one to a ghost.

Moth and Pebble, seated on the divan with the remains of an excellent palace breakfast before them, exchanged a glance behind the old woman's back. Shaldis dropped to her knees beside the bed on whose corner Pomegranate sat, and looked up into her face. "Is he all right?"

Pomegranate nodded, looking relieved. *To have been asked?* Shaldis wondered. *To be believed?*

"He says he can't reach her, can't get her out. He says he doesn't understand that kind of magic."

Moth looked like she had a number of comments to make on the subject of the conversation that must have taken place between Pomegranate and the imaginary pig, but from the corner of her eye, Shaldis saw Pebble squeeze her hand. Shaldis asked, "Did he say where she is?"

"He said, *Don't go there,*" replied Pomegranate quickly, twisting the chains of beads around her neck. "He said, *Don't even try to go there.* It's deadly, he says.

It will devour the body through the mind. He says it's only what we're doing here—what we've been doing—that's kept that from happening so far. Otherwise she would have been gone."

The old lady frowned and took another sip of her coffee. "I'm glad Pontifer's back safe," said Shaldis. She added, looking down at the floor, "Pontifer, sweetheart, thank you. That was a brave thing you did."

Pomegranate smiled, clearly touched. "I'm glad he's getting out and about more. He didn't used to take an interest in anyone but me, and I suspect—" She glanced around, as if to make sure her unseen pet wasn't in earshot. She lowered her voice. "I suspect it's not good for him, or for anyone, to have such narrow interests."

"Did he say what the place looked like?" asked Shaldis, sitting back and clasping her arms around her knees. "Was it a lake of fire? Molten metal, or molten rock even, surrounded by black glass. Green mists drifting among the rocks."

Pomegranate looked startled, and shook her head. "It's . . . it is rock," she said. "The rock of the earth, deep in the earth. He didn't say anything about rock melting. *Can* rock melt?"

"*Sand* certainly melts," spoke up Pebble unexpectedly. "That's how they make glass."

"Look, where she is, that's not important," said Moth. "What's important is we get her out, we get her back. Then we can *ask* her where she been."

Not having experience with this kind of ailment, the Sisters of the Raven dared not sponge out the Sigil of Sisterhood or the Sigil of the River of Life that surrounded the bed, to draw them anew. But standing in a circle around the bed—a circle that now could stretch to include holding Summerchild's cold, inert hands in theirs—Shaldis guessed that this did not matter. The sigils united them. The circle gave each the power of the others, power that they channeled into the River of Life; power that filled her heart and mind, erasing her weariness, flooding her with strength. Shaldis felt her fellows, as acutely and intensely as if they were truly her sisters, raised in the same household, or that she had been raised in theirs. Understanding and loving Pebble's sunny kindness, Moth's acerbic humor, the tragedy and madness masked by Pomegranate's humble exterior. What, she wondered in some corner of herself, did they see in her? Through Pomegranate's mind she even glimpsed Pontifer Pig, sleeping at the foot of Summerchild's bed with his nose on Pomegranate's discarded sandals.

But of Summerchild, she felt nothing, as if she were not even present.

And when, at last, drained of energy, they each emerged from the deep trance of healing, the room was filled with the first shadows of evening.

And Summerchild lay as she had lain that morning, a wasted little wax doll in the pale rivers of her hair.

Geb brought them food. The others ate in silence; Shaldis could only curl up on the divan in the corner, numb. Only after the others left, at the chamberlain's invitation, to avail themselves of the palace baths, did Shaldis sit up and creep to the table to pick through the remains on the serving platters.

"My dear child, let me send for something fresh."

She looked up, startled, and saw the king, standing in the garden doorway.

"You don't have to."

"It's sheer selfishness on my part, my dear," he went on earnestly. "Word gets out, you know. It's bad enough knowing half the city's betting on the crocodiles without hearing them hiss at me behind my back, *And you made that poor girl pick at leftovers, too.* I hope you're investing in wagers?" he added as Shaldis burst into laughter. "Besides, Geb loves to fetch and carry. My dear," he added in distress as he saw that her laughter had flowed into tears of near-hysterical weariness. "Here," he said gently, and, sitting on the divan beside her, gathered her into his arms. He said again, simply, "Here," and then just held her, offering neither a comfort in which she could not believe, nor mitigation that she would have despised.

He was only there, big and solid and surprisingly strong, the deep blue silks of his robes smelling of musk and vanilla.

When she was finished crying, he gave her a clean linen handkerchief and brought some water for her to wash her face. To her astonishment she felt better, and hungry; and together they devoured the leftovers, quibbling like dogs over the best bits. To his questions, Shaldis told of her ghastly stay in her grandfather's house, and from there went on to speak of her grandfather's quarrel with Ahure, Nettleflower's murder, and her own visit to the Blood Mage's house the previous night.

"Ordinarily I'd question Ahure's story about being attacked by teyn near his house," she said, picking the remainder of the meat off a chicken bone. "Because that bodyguard Drupe was right: the teyn *don't* attack adults, as a rule, and never if they have open desert to flee to. But that's all changed now. We don't know what they'll do.

And they *were* watching the house. Does it look to you as if the teyn are being controlled by a nomad Raven sister—or Raven *sisters*, since sometimes the traces I've found feel like they were being left by different people? It would explain why she's never been seen in the city. The nomads come and go."

"Dear gods." Oryn passed a tired hand over his face. He had lost flesh, despite Geb's obvious efforts to tempt him to food; it was one of the few times Shaldis had seen him without eye paint, and she saw now with surprise the gray at the roots of his hair.

He went on, "For more than a year now I've been waiting in dread to hear that the nomads had Crafty women among them. There have been nomad mages, over the years, but without proper training their powers were always limited. Are you sure?"

"No." She dipped her hands into the washbowl, dried them on her napkin. "But it might make more sense than a Crafty child or children roving the city's streets. Someone would surely have noticed. Did the Zali wizards use glass to work magic? Or to store magic power in, the way the Sun Mages did with crystals?"

The king shook his head. "Not that I've heard of. Surely they taught you the history of thaumaturgy at the Citadel, didn't they?"

"They did. And certain kinds of magic *can* be stored in glass, which is why so many amulets are made of it. But except for a few small wards, the magic came unfixed from most amulets around the same time men ceased to be able to work it—at least all those I'm familiar with. But if it's the Zali, I don't know. I wish Soth hadn't left so soon."

"Oddly enough, he spoke about Zali magic only a few nights ago. And it seems to have been perfectly ordinary magic and, in fact, somewhat less powerful than that used later on. And yet there's quite clearly power of some kind coming out of the tombs, enough to curse the whole village of Three Wells—and then kill those poor guards simply because they were camped nearby—not to mention sending that tomb robber mad. A pity Ahure isn't talking about what it might be." He frowned. "I never did like the man or trust him. But he seems to think he knows enough about this power—whatever its source—to think he can use it."

"If it was a nomad Raven sister he paid to try to get that glass ball away from my grandfather," said Shaldis softly, "she may be trying to keep him from doing so. And she's used the teyn to keep you out of Three Wells long enough for her to . . . to find something there?"

"Or do something there." The king's face grew grim in the soft blue twilight of the darkening pavilion. "And when she refused to work for Ahure anymore—or possibly sent the teyn against him—he was reduced to bribing your uncle's concubine to steal it. It makes sense, though of course there could be other explanations. Do you think our nomad Raven sister will have another try on her own?"

"I'm almost sure of it. I've been listening for her, walking the house—" She broke off, hearing herself say it, and rolled her eyes in self-disgust. "Walking the house and scaring her away."

"Is there a place nearby where you can watch, not in the house itself?"

"The alley," said Shaldis promptly. "That's the way she came in the first time anyway. The wheat broker next door dumps broken baskets and things into the alley—there's always a pile of them back there. You could hide a couple of camels in there, let alone a person." She glanced through the archway, past the garden trees at the luminous sky. "There's a night market in the square in front of the Grand Bazaar—it'll be hours yet before the place quiets down."

"Then I suggest you get some sleep," said the king, and rising, helped her to her feet. "I shall have Geb wake you an hour before midnight. And when you catch her, *if* you catch her"—his voice grew grave—"make an ally of her, at any cost. Offer her anything. Whatever she wants, I will honor it, somehow. And I hope you understand this isn't simply because I have a constitutional aversion to crocodiles."

"The thought of motivation so petty had never crossed my mind, my lord."

"I'm glad." The king took her arm and escorted her down the stairs. "By the by, have the dreams of healing herbs you mentioned borne fruit? Do you know? I'm assuming that this isn't the same woman . . ."

"I'm almost positive it's not," said Shaldis. "But in ten nights I haven't heard her—whoever she is—calling for help."

Not, Shaldis reflected, that she'd gotten much sleep to speak of in that time.

"That may mean that you have already succeeded," said the king. "And even though it would be nice if this lady suddenly appeared to resolve all our woes—and send us rain next spring—if she lives, and her children live, then that should be enough. And at the moment, only the gods know that."

THIRTY-SIX

Wrapped in the Gray Cloak, Shaldis slipped past the main gate of the house on Sleeping Worms Street. Even at midnight, torchlight flared in the arcade around the court where the camel drivers were unrolling their bedding. At other merchant houses, women from the night market would come in and dance for those illiterate but loyal ruffians, and afterward bed them in the fodder of the stables; there was none of that, under her grandfather's roof. The women were there, of course, but they spoke in whispers; she heard their giggles as they shared the messy feast of supper leftovers with the men.

Shaldis passed around the corner to the alley, settled herself behind the scratchy and mouse-smelling baskets. When she closed her eyes and extended her mind into the house, she could hear the women in the main court still, the coarse relaxed murmuring of lovers who knew each other as friends.

Did such women visit the courtyard of the palace guards?

Of course they do, she told herself roughly.

And then, when something squeezed tight and angry in her chest, *Did you expect Jethan was a virgin at HIS age?*

She pushed the thought away and tried not to ask herself why she felt pain.

Don't be a schoolgirl.

And anyway you're not here to think about Jethan. You're here to find this woman, this nomad Raven sister. Not just to save Summerchild, to rescue the king from being eaten by crocodiles.

To save us all.

Half in the dozing trance of meditation, Shaldis picked out every voice, every sound, every clattering trail of footsteps, as the house settled into sleep. For five nights—since Summerchild had been brought back from Three Wells—Shaldis had been too exhausted and drained to listen so, over a long period. She had checked for the whiff of magic and had fallen at once to sleep.

Now she listened to her father's querulous singsong as he rambled on to someone—Tjagan, by the sound of it—about a lovely dream he'd had; to her grandfather's deep, slow breathing in sleep. To Tulik, demanding irritably where Shaldis was and why wasn't she back yet. *We are her family, it's to us she owes her loyalty. . . .*

The camel drivers talked endlessly of gambling, of women, of a thousand petty altercations with the city guards or with other camel drivers. Their friends came in, with the latest information on how the betting stood on the king's surviving one or all of the tests of consecration and which gods would see him through and how to tell it.

Then in time their talk, and the soft whispers from the fodder stacks in the stables, faded, and the house sank into silence. Shaldis's head began to ache from concentration. Rats crept through the piled baskets, and now and then a drunkard came staggering into the alley to relieve himself.

The stars moved overhead and the crescent moon made fragile shadows on the roof edges. In the house, Foursie cried out frantically in her sleep, and Three Flower gently shook her, held her while she sobbed.

The city slept. The sun dreamed, deep in the bottom of the night.

Then sudden and clear as the note of a harp, Shaldis felt it. A sleep spell, sliding off her but palpable, like silk slithering over her face. It startled her so that her concentration broke, and only with greatest effort did she keep still behind her wall of baskets. At once she focused her mind again—after a split second's burning desire for several platefuls of dates and cheese—on the sounds of the alley before her and not only heard the stealthy whisper of footfalls but smelled the unmistakable musty sweetness of teyn.

Her mind tried to grope deeper, but the strong animal smell—not unpleasant, as many claimed—drowned whatever other scent there may have been. And, in fact, Shaldis realized, if the nomad Raven sister could control teyn from a distance, there was no reason she had to be close at all.

A moment later she heard the dry scrape of the bolt on the inside of the alley gate slide back, felt the tickle of the spell that operated it.

Either she's here after all, or she's able to work it at a distance—something no mage or Crafty woman of Shaldis's acquaintance had ever managed to do.

She held her breath, then, as the teyn slipped through the gate, eased herself to her feet, slithered past the baskets and into the alley. As she'd ascertained, no one waited there. Though if this woman was strong enough to work a door bolt from a distance, would she be able to cloak herself even against another Raven sister's sight? Shaldis didn't know. She was used to thinking of women's magic being weaker and less reliable than men's had once been. How strong *could* women's magic be?

Soft-footed as she could manage, she crept down the passageway to her grandfather's garden, the passageway that still held, for her, dim ragged echoes of Nettle-flower's murder. She could see the dark trees, the white-starred shrubs ahead of her through the narrow archway; glimpsed movement. Glimpsed something else and quickened her stride—the glimmer of greenish light, of what looked like green mist, rising from the grass. *Do not get near it.* The Crafty woman's voice had spoken in her mind, on the shores of the lake of fire. *Do not touch it.*

Though the garden was enclosed and the night windless, it seemed to be moving, spreading up the stairs.

What in the name of the GODS is it doing HERE?

Shaldis ran, and skidded to a stop at the end of the passageway as the smell of teyn suddenly filled her nostrils. She was starting to leap back even as one teyn came around the corner and sprang at her, so that it was unable to seize her. She called a spell of bursting light between them, but that didn't stop it. It knocked her down, then fled across the garden like a silent, misshapen shadow, to where a second teyn, a jenny, waited in the kitchen passageway's dark.

Shaldis cried, "Stop them!" and scrambled to her feet,

dashed in pursuit. One of them slammed the grilled gateway to the kitchen court. Shaldis saw them flee across the court as she scraped and fumbled at the latch—which stuck and jammed under her fingers. "Stop them!" she yelled again, and heard the camel driver wake on the gallery outside her grandfather's room and begin to clatter downstairs toward her. By that time the teyn were nearly to the gate of the main court and from there would vanish in the dark streets.

Wildly, Shaldis lashed forth with her mind. She meant to slam the gate that led to the main court, and when she saw that didn't work, thrashed forth another spell that knocked the vat of indigo from its tripod, dashing the contents over the second of the fleeing teyn.

The next instant the grille's latch gave under her hand, but before she could dash in pursuit, the camel driver who'd been on guard by her grandfather's door caught up with her, grabbed her, yelled, "Got you, you sneaking bitch!" and slammed her against the tiled wall of the passageway.

Shaldis ducked his blow and her shout of "It's me, the Old One, you idiot!" was drowned in his cursing as his hand connected with the tiles. She had to shout it two or three times, dodging another slap and being shaken so her teeth rattled. Only when Tulik came panting into the passageway with a lamp did the driver seem to realize his mistake.

"What's going on?"

"An attack—I don't think they got up the stair." Shaldis looked past her brother and the bodyguard into the garden court. There was no sign of the green mist, but after an instant's hesitation she ran back to the stairway, raced up it to pound on her grandfather's door. "Grandfather?" From above, looking down, there was no sign either of the mist. Her mother and her aunt Apricot appeared on the other side of the gallery, clinging together with sheets wrapped around them, not willing to come into range of the head of the household's wrath.

"Grandfather?"

Shuffling. "Who is it, damn you?"

"It's Raeshaldis— It's the Eldest Daughter," she corrected herself. "Are you all right?"

A bolt scraped, then another. The door opened a crack. "What the hell do you mean, pounding on my door and waking me?" He looked absolutely ghastly, unshaven, filthy and naked, as if it was past his thought even to look for a sheet. He didn't seem to have shaved since she'd seen him last—six days ago now, that was—and the room behind him reeked of bedding unwashed and unaired.

"You asked me to come to this house to protect you, so I'm protecting you," retorted Shaldis. "Two teyn broke in, tried to get up the stairs. . . ."

"You're crazy, girl. Teyn—"

"No one came in? Let me in."

"Go to hell." He slammed the door in her face.

She heard the bolts scrape.

She could have slammed back the bolts and confronted him—and while she was at it demanded to have a look at the glass ball that was the focus of the trouble—but she knew that every second, the teyn and their mistress would be heading for whatever bolt-hole had let them through the city wall. Tulik and the camel driver came dashing along the gallery, and Tulik called out, "Grandfather!"

"Let him be," said Shaldis. "If that's the way he wants

it, I have other things to do. Get me a horse, a remount, a groom, and two days' food and water and get them fast. I'm going after them." She'd already pushed past her brother and was striding back along the gallery toward her room to change clothes. "And tell Grandfather that when I get back, I'm going to want to see whatever it is that he's got hidden in his room."

THIRTY-SEVEN

*T*wo laborers insane in two days, rumors of others. Please send someone to advise. Ykem.

Ykem was the foreman in charge of the aqueduct camp.

Oryn turned the curled scrap of parchment over in his hands. "Get some horses saddled, if you would, please, Geb." Geb started to protest—probably that it was already midmorning and no cavalcade was going to get far by noon, and besides it did not suit the dignity of the king to ride horseback and look what had happened last time.

Oryn simply lifted his hand and shook his head. Moth—who was on duty at Summerchild's side that morning, stylish as ever in pink gauze and topazes—did not even look up from her meditations. "Is the messenger who brought this still in the palace? Please find out, and, if he is, have him meet me in the Golden Court to ride out with us. Jethan!"

The young guardsman, who had brought the message from the front gate to the Summer Pavilion, came swiftly to the bottom of the stair as Oryn raised his voice. Palace custom dictated that whatever commands Oryn had for a guard would be taken by Geb, or preferably by a page, but Oryn simply descended the stair, to the chamberlain's scandalized twitters.

"Would you be so kind as to go back to Chirak Shaldeth's house and ask Raeshaldis to join us on the road to the aqueduct? This is all becoming . . . very disquieting."

"Yes, my lord." Jethan salaamed.

"And send another guardsman here at once!" added Geb as the young man strode away up the garden paths. "My lord, you can't simply—"

"I'm the king, my squash blossom," said Oryn with a faint smile. "As I keep telling you, I can do whatever I want."

Except save the life of the woman I love.

He looked for a time down at Summerchild's face. In the hot morning sunlight she seemed terribly pinched and wasted. Yesterday evening, after the four sisters had made their sigil and their circle, he'd thought she looked better and had dared to let himself hope.

Silly, he thought. His father would have had a few words to say to him about *that.* Not to speak of what he'd have said of a king letting a silk merchant's granddaughter cry on his shoulder and pick through leftovers with him.

He wondered what, if anything, had been the result of the tall girl's ambuscade last night. Nothing useful, he thought. If she'd actually found this nomad Raven sister, she'd have brought her here to the palace early that morning. Or brought word of her own defeat.

Dear gods, don't let the battle between them have harmed her.

If Shaldis had been injured or killed . . .

He looked down at Summerchild's face again, and thought once more, *I can do whatever I want, except save the life of the woman I love.*

Or the lives of my people.

Or my own.

The messenger was indeed awaiting Oryn when the king's guards, packhorses, and Elpiduyek the parasol bearer—*honestly, Geb!*—assembled in the Golden Court. He reported that both men were simple laborers on the aqueduct, part of the small gang in charge of roofing over the finished section behind the main diggers. One man had come running out of his hut with a knife in hand just after sunset and had thrown himself into the midst of a band of teyn just being brought back to quarters from the ditch. They'd killed him before the minders could whip them away.

The other man was still alive, tied hand and foot, alternately screaming and singing in a language no one could recognize.

Had the villagers sung, Oryn wondered, as they'd run among the burning huts of Three Wells?

Though the cavalcade assembled with a swiftness unheard-of among kings, still crowds were gathered along the Avenue of the Sun to watch them ride away.

There was something speculative in their silence, though when Oryn raised his hand to them they cheered, like a sun patch breaking through winter clouds.

"They don't imagine I'm running away, do they, Bax?" he inquired, leaning a little in the saddle to speak to the commander, who rode at his side.

"Course they do." The stocky soldier spoke without turning his head, his pale-blue gaze scanning each side street and temple; Oryn wished he didn't suspect the white-haired commander of marking out possible sites for fortification should street fighting break out in the wake of a bid for power by Sarn or Mohrvine or Akarian. "I expect before noon there'll be odds offered at every café in town as to whether you're coming back."

"So nice to know my people take an interest in my welfare."

"Don't you think they don't, sir." Bax nudged his mount to a hand gallop, deftly avoiding Elpiduyek, who determinedly cantered close by, silken canopy flapping up and down with the jogging stride. "There's hundreds in the city doing just that—betting the gods will carry you through. Will carry us all."

Betting Raeshaldis and the others will come up with the appropriate spells, perhaps. Oryn wondered again what that tall, shy girl had encountered last night that had prevented her from either coming herself that morning or sending word. The events at her grandfather's house and those at Three Wells—not to speak of the madman in Little Hyacinth Lane—had a suspiciously similar ring. And whether the advent of the lake monsters—thankfully uncomplicated so far by a reappearance, according to

Pomegranate—was part of the puzzle or merely the gods' attempt to prod him into nervous prostration before his consecration, only the gods knew.

He'd sent another messenger posthaste to the ruined village, with a message to Soth to make all speed for the aqueduct camp.

But as the cavalcade passed through the east gate square, with the harsh sun bright now on the gate's green tiles and the dust like a golden fog, Oryn happened to turn his head. And though he knew that the Veiled Priests never left their temples, he could have sworn he saw them, seven black figures almost invisible in the shadows of the alleyways nearby.

Watching him as he rode out the gate.

"She movin' over rock, miss." The camel driver Tulik had fetched for Shaldis as a groom was an elderly man named Dhrosas, whom everyone in the caravanserai called Rat—Shaldis had known him from her childhood. He now pointed with his quirt at the streambed, decades dry but paved with smooth stone and gravel and dotted with the gray desiccated mounds of camel bush. The noon sun sent up waves of heat from that impermeable pavement already, flung harsh glare into the pursuers' eyes. "We not find her tracks before, we sure not find her here."

"I thought nomads could pick up the tracks of birds an hour after they'd flown past."

The little man grinned and leaned forward to pat the neck of the lean bay mustang he rode. "I'm only half nomad, miss, so I only track that one halfway to where she goin'." He did look like a rat, too, reflected Shaldis, with the tip of his long nose—pink with sunburn—sticking out through the dark gauze veils that protected his face and eyes, and below it his bristling white mustache. His skinny hands on the reins had the look of a rat's forepaws in their tattered gloves. Most camel drivers didn't live to be old—their lives were too harsh, and most of them that weren't killed by bandits and nomads died in bar fights. But she remembered Rat telling her stories of the djinni, when she was a child.

She sat back in her saddle and closed her eyes. As she'd suspected, she wasn't able to scry the fleeing teyn in her crystal, which meant she was with the Crafty who controlled her. But half in a trance of seeking, Shaldis could still catch the acrid pungence of indigo, clinging to the rock of this parched Dead Hills streambed, hanging in the air. Scanning the dun slopes above the banks of the wadi, eyes narrowed against the blazing sun, it seemed to her that far off, she saw the moving dot of blue.

She had followed that scent through the night, among the tangled wadis and steep-walled canyons of the Dead Hills, moving south from the Yellow City, then bending east. In the darkness her ears had sifted through the scuffle of hunting jackals, the yips of foxes, and the scrambling whisper of rabbits, searching for the steady tread of fleeing bipeds. But those sounds, like her scrying, had been masked by cloaking spells. Now and then she'd stopped to look up and to gauge by the stars burning white and steadily above the matte-black cliff faces where they were.

And sometimes, in those cliffs, she'd seen the faint

glow of greenish light, outlining the mouths of the ancient tombs that dotted those withered valleys.

Keep away from the mist, the voice had whispered in her thoughts. *Flee it. . . .*

She wondered if, in some nomad legend forgotten by Rat's father, there was mention of a lake of fire.

Or of something that crashed and boomed, again and again, with the regularity of breath?

They'd ridden through night and morning. Now with the sun straight overhead they had come to the end of the hills, and before them the desert stretched, north, east, and south. Far away to the north Shaldis was aware of the tiny glittering cloud that marked the construction face of the aqueduct, but beyond that there was no sign of habitation, of human passage at all. Even the salt caravans that crossed the distances to the oases and the migratory camps of the deep-desert nomads, who navigated by the stars and by the far-off shapes of the land, knew well that to go beyond the farthest oasis was suicide.

She opened her eyes and saw Rat kneeling on the descending bank of the failed wadi, making a cairn of stones to guide them back. He'd done this half a dozen times already, through night and morning. In the desert, one did not take chances.

Even behind the protection of the veiling he shaded his eyes to look up at her. "Nothing out there," he said. "That direction—one oasis, ten days journey, and the Rai an-Tzuu camp there this time of year. They hunt teyn, for the market."

"Our teyn is fleeing with a Crafty woman," said Shaldis. "If she wasn't, I'd be able to see her. They may be meeting someone between here and there." She unhooked the water bottle from her saddle, took a sparing drink. Following Rat's example, she was being stingy even though there were waterskins on both spare horses. "Will the horses be all right?"

Rat checked both remounts, then swung to his own saddle again. "Camels be better," he reported. "We give them rest in the heat of the day, they good for a day, two days. After that . . ."

"With luck we'll catch our friend within a day." Shaldis wrapped the dark gauze once again over her eyes. "Now she knows she's being pursued, this may be the last clear chance we'll have to face her down and bargain with her. This way."

THIRTY-EIGHT

B reast deep in the stinking green of the scummy pool, the young boar teyn made no sound. The guards had gagged it with a wad of leather and rags, bound it hand and foot before lowering it into the water. From where she stood behind the railing opposite it, Foxfire could see it trembling, see the terror in those huge, pale, dilated eyes.

Belial the crocodile slid through the filthy water. The bow wave of his passing sent up a reek to her, like the cesspools under hell. She closed her eyes, but she could see the pool, the reptile, the terrified, helpless victim all engraved on her mind like some inescapable dream. Through her exhaustion and her terror she repeated the patterns of the spell, formed up the lines of power in her mind.

He will go away. He will turn aside. There's nothing there.

Belial's eye was like yellow glass as he turned in the water.

And slipped past the teyn, so close that his scales scraped the huge, furry shoulder.

Foxfire's mind locked around her spells, her body sick with unbreathing terror.

He will turn aside.

Belial turned aside.

Hold the spells. Don't think about anything else.

"You've done it, girl!" Her grandmother's hand tightened like a thumbscrew around her arm. "You've done it!"

She wanted to twist her arm away and couldn't, couldn't move for fear of relaxing her concentration the tiniest bit.

"Get him out of there," she managed to whisper. "Please."

Red Silk shook her with bruising triumph. "You've done it!" Her laughter was almost a shriek. She didn't even look at the teyn.

"Úrthet," Foxfire gasped, and her brother and Soral Brûl began to gently haul on the rope that bound the teyn, drawing it to the edge of the pool.

At the same moment Red Silk snatched one of the wicker cages from Urnate Urla, the chicken within it squawking with protest, and hurled it into the water a few feet from Belial's enormous head.

With deadly speed the huge reptile whirled in the water, snapped up cage, chicken, all.

Red Silk shrugged. "He was hungry, all right." Then she cackled again, almost hugging herself with delight. "You've done it! Your father will dance! You'll be a royal princess, my girl, the daughter of a king! You'll marry whom you will, do as you please."

Marry whom I will? Foxfire fought not to cry; above all things else she couldn't let her grandmother see her cry. *Not if Father has a word to say about it.* But she glanced back to the corner of the clammy vaulted cellar, where old Eleven Grasshoppers sat wrapped in her own long arms, quietly watching her, and felt that the old jenny, if she didn't know exactly what was going on, at least sensed her sickened, desperate pain.

She held her breath, trembling, until her brother and the failed Sun Mage had pulled the bound teyn, dripping, from Belial's pool. Then she had to dig her nails into her own wrist to keep from collapsing in tears of relief. Yesterday it had been the same, and the day before, when they'd poured poison down a poor young jenny's throat and had waited an hour, two hours, three hours in sweating heat before it was clear that Foxfire's spells had worked. She'd gone to the compound to check on the jenny this morning—Six Thistles, they called her—and had found her nursing her infant as if nothing had happened. The first young boar they'd dumped into the snake pit had been ignored by the cobras until he'd tried to run. Then he'd been bitten four times, and Foxfire had clung to the rim of the pit, working and reworking the spells of the cure of poison from a distance for three hours, before

Red Silk would let one of the guards go down and bring him out.

Foxfire's spells had protected the guard as well. The boar teyn was still alive, and they'd tied up the next one they'd thrown down, to make sure he stayed still.

Afterward, when Foxfire had wept hysterically in Opal's arms in the secrecy of her own room, Eleven Grasshoppers had again tried to comfort them both.

"She said it today," whispered Foxfire when after two more teyn had been passed unhurt through the crocodile's pool Red Silk finally let her return to her room. Opal gathered her into her arms. Eleven Grasshoppers had, in imitation of the maid's habitual tasks, carefully fetched a bowl of lavender water from the wall bench, making both girls laugh. "She said, 'You'll be a royal princess.' She hasn't the slightest intention of saving the king's life."

Foxfire wiped her eyes on the bedsheet, where the two girls were now sitting—Eleven Grasshoppers, too, though Red Silk would have whipped them both for letting a teyn, however well washed, sit on a bed. "'You can marry whom you will,' she said."

"Well, that's a fairy tale, anyway," said Opal. She went to the table where a supper of couscous and lamb was being kept warm under a basket. Evening light slanted harsh and golden through the lattices of the window. Beyond, the crests of the Dead Hills, visible above the compound wall, had a weirdly desolate beauty, abstract red shapes against a molten blue sky. "I heard Soral Brûl talking to madam this morning, when I went to get your breakfast. He was telling her that though he can't do magic himself anymore, it's in his blood. He said that your daughter by him would be Crafty born for certain."

Foxfire was so exhausted that the flash of anger she felt wasn't enough to warm the sinking in her chest. She felt tears begin to leak from her eyes again, but her voice was steady and sharp as metal in her own ears. "That sounds exactly like the kind of thing that'll make sense to Father. And I'm sure it's never even *occurred* to that stuck-up Brûl that once I have children by him, neither Father nor Grandmother is going to let him live."

Opal's eyes widened. It had clearly never occurred to her, either.

Foxfire felt a thousand years old.

She took a deep breath as Opal came over to the bed with a bowl of food. Eleven Grasshoppers sprang neatly down and trotted to her own little bed of folded blankets in the corner; she knew if she did this the girls would give her the scraps. The jenny curled herself up neatly, wrapped in her long arms, for all the world like a little old woman in her simple tunic, watching the girls with her wise pale-blue eyes.

"How long did it take us to get here?" asked Foxfire. "We left Golden Sky not long after sunset, camped once at noon, then got here late in the afternoon. The city should be a little closer than that."

"It takes the supply trains all day and part of a second," said Opal. "I know because I asked one of the drivers to buy me the latest horoscope from Starbright—I got one for you, too." She went to the loose floor tile behind the wardrobe, under which Foxfire hid the pilfered pottery food bowl she used to talk to Shaldis, and brought out two small squares of yellow paper. They were rather dark from having been washed and reused a number of times.

"They're from two days after the half moon, and that was the day before yesterday."

She sat again on the corner of the bed, watched as Fox-fire scooped up couscous with her bread. Her brown eyes filled with concern beneath the scarred mess of lashless lids. "You aren't thinking—? We can't."

"*You're* not," said Foxfire simply. "Because I'm going to poison you—just enough to make you sleep a lot and then be really sick—so Grandmother won't think you had anything to do with my getting away." She got to her feet, carried her empty dish back to the table, and stood looking through the window at the shallow crescent of the waning moon, luminous in the burning sky.

It was nine days past full. Four days until the dark of its cycle.

"Foxfire."

"The king saved my life," said Foxfire quietly, still looking out at the moon. "I love Father, Opal, and I—I even love Grandmother, you know. But I can't go on living like this." Her throat tightened, and she forced back the tears that burned the backs of her eyes. "I can't go on waiting for the next awful thing Father or Grandmother is going to make me do. And even when Papa becomes king, you know it'll be something else. Raeshaldis . . . Raeshaldis left her grandfather. Left her family, because they would have tried to do the same thing to her, tried to make her be just a tool for getting them what they wanted, the way Grandmother and Father are doing to me."

She turned back, to look into her friend's horror-stricken eyes. "If I protect the king, he'll protect me."

"You can't betray your father!" Opal had lived in the

same house as Red Silk long enough to speak the words in a nearly inaudible whisper. "You can't go against your family!"

"The king is the head of my family," replied Foxfire shakily, though she knew Mohrvine would not see it that way at all.

He'll never speak to me again.

Just forming the words in her mind was like the earth breaking open beneath her feet, dropping her into a void that had no end.

Tears leaking down her face, she whispered, "Papa's only going to use me again and again and again, until there's nothing left of me. He doesn't mean to, but he will. I have to get out."

She fell into Opal's arms as the smaller girl leaped to her feet, rushed to her side, gathered her into a desperate embrace. For a time nothing existed for her but tears and pain and the knowledge that her own assessment of the situation was correct: that her father loved her dearly, and would use her like a spear until she broke in his hand.

He would never forgive her defection.

Raeshaldis survived this, she thought.

I can, too.

She whispered again, "I have to get out."

"Rider coming," said Rat.

Shaldis, clinging to the saddle bow of her stumbling horse, barely heard. Her eyes were half shut against the hard horizontal glare of the sinking sun and with the light trance of listening, scenting—searching for that elusive flicker of blue in all the wasteland of empty rock and wind-scoured sand.

Except for the shortest possible rest at the worst of the nooning, they had ridden through the day, blazing heat that crushed horses and riders like an invisible hammer. The teyn—and the nomad Crafty—seemed a little closer. They had stopped, too, for a time, or at least the scent and movement of the indigo speck in the distance had seemed unmoving to Shaldis's straining senses. But many miles still separated them. With the coming of night the scent of the indigo would be stronger, but sooner or later they would have to rest.

"Camels," added Rat.

Shaldis drew rein, dared withdraw her mind from the quarry, turned to blink at her companion. "What?"

"Camels. Four of 'em, heading this way." He pointed. The sinking sun, setting behind the near-invisible trace of the distant Dead Hills, drenched the dust cloud with light. Shaldis could make out black, swaying shapes amid the swooning heat shimmer that seemed to hide the horizon in an incandescent curtain. She whispered, "Jethan," half disbelieving. But when she fumbled the scrying crystal from her purse and looked within it, the young guardsman's image was clear: dust covered, veiled against heat and glare, and as stiff in his saddle as the gait of his mount would permit.

Two of the other camels carried waterskins. The third bore an empty saddle. The tassels and trappings were green and orange, the colors of her grandfather's house.

"The king needs you at the aqueduct," was the first thing Jethan said to her when he came near enough, almost half an hour later. "Two laborers there have gone mad in the past two days. Lord Soth will be going on there from Three Wells, but they'll need a true mage."

"I'm delighted to see you too, Jethan," replied Shaldis in a tone of exaggerated cheer. "And, yes, thank you, I'm in the very pink of good health. How are you?"

Jethan drew himself up in rigid indignation, like a statue wrought of dust. Then he relaxed, tapped the camel down to its knees, and sprang from the saddle to stand before her, where she stood dismounted beside the exhausted horses. "I'm well," he said quietly. "But I'm very tired and very frightened, for the king's sake and that of my lady. Though I am the better for seeing you safe."

Shaldis replied, meaning it, "And I you."

"I have water," said Jethan. "At your grandfather's house they said you took enough for two days, but in this heat . . ."

"Thank you," said Shaldis. "I appreciate that. Rat will, too, when he takes the horses back—they can't go on into the desert this way. Tell the king that I'm pursuing a nomad Raven sister into the desert, the Raven sister he and I spoke of, who can control the teyn. Maybe who can control wind as well. What tracks we've found were nearly erased by wind, but we've barely felt any—only a stream of it, sometimes, flowing near the ground. Not enough to raise dust in the distance. They're almost half a day ahead of us. I hope to overtake them tomorrow."

Without turning his head, Jethan said, "You hear that, Rat, is it? Tell the king that, when you get to the aqueduct. I'm sure your master back in town will understand the delay in your return with his horses." He didn't take his eyes off Shaldis, blue as jewels in the mask of dust. "Please reassure the king that we'll both be with him when he rides back to the city four nights hence for his jubilee."

Shaldis's head was pounding with the heat and the glare of the sun-blasted emptiness and with the need for sleep. She could have fallen on Jethan's shoulder and cried, as she'd fallen yesterday on the king's. She only said to Rat, "Rest until the sun's down. That dust cloud in the north is the workface of the aqueduct. Once it's dark you'll probably be able to see the lights of the camp."

"You're not going on now, miss?" The driver stepped between her and the saddled camel as she reached up to take its bridle to mount. "Without rest? You've rode since midnight, barring the nooning stop, and if you slept, then by the look of you you didn't get any good of it."

In fact Shaldis ached as if she'd been beaten. But she said, "In my grandfather's house last night I saw green mists, the same green mists Foxfire has said she's seen around her grandmother's house in the hills —and that Jethan and I saw near Ahure's house. I don't know whether these have anything to do with my grandfather's madness or with the glass this woman is trying to take from him or with what's happened in Three Wells or with the woman who's been crying to me in my dreams. What I do know is that the woman out there ahead of us has some answers. The only answers I've encountered so far. And as far as I know, she and her teyn are still moving. So we need to move, too."

She hooked her toe onto the kneeling camel's leg and sprang into the saddle. The camel groaned in protest, then lurched to her feet, mumbling and grousing as camels do. Jethan unhooked a pair of waterskins from one of the spare camels and laid them in the dust beside Rat and the horses. "Tell the king we will not forsake him," he said softly. "If we do not reach the aqueduct camp before he must leave, we will not fail to be in the city on the day of the new moon."

Shaldis glanced worriedly at him as he swung on his camel again, tapped it to signal it to rise. Behind his shoulder the dwindling crescent moon stood clear in the saffron sky.

She'd watched it from night to night, but its thinness struck her anew, and filled her with despair. Wasting, draining away. Like Summerchild's strength. Like the king's life.

Jethan caught her look, but didn't respond until they had started off again with long swaying strides toward that half-guessed dot of blue in the landscape, that elusive whiff of indigo.

Then Jethan said softly, "But if we come not to the city till the day of the new moon, I fear it will be to find the lady Summerchild dead and all hope at an end."

THIRTY-NINE

M ost curious." Oryn made a move to step closer to the man who sat in the stuffy brown shade of the little goat-hair tent, hands bound before him and leg-shackled to the tent pole. Ykem, foreman of the aqueduct camp, made what might have been a move preliminary to catching his sleeve, but of course a foreman didn't do that to a king.

"Watch it, sir. He's quiet enough now, but this morning he was like to kill the fellow who came in to change the latrine bucket. Lunged at him, screaming and clawing, he did, and we thought he'd snap the tent pole. We had him chained in the quartermaster's store tent, but the men wouldn't have it, sir. Said he'd put a Bad-Luck Shadow on the picks and shovels, and they'd turn in the hands of them as used 'em."

Oryn glanced back at the sunburned little man when he used that nomad term, then looked back at the shackled workman. The man looked like any of the rangeland villagers, wiry and dark, unremarkable save for the expression of mad bliss on his face as he sang.

"Been singin' like that since night before last, sir," added Ykem. " 'Cept when he sleeps, which he does every few hours. Even when he attacked Nam this morning, if you can call it singin'."

"Oh, it's singing, all right." Oryn folded his arms, watched the madman's mouth gaping, flexing, tongue quivering and curling as it gave shape to the sound that poured like a wailing river from his throat. "I've made a study of music—one can only watch dancing girls cavort day in and day out for so long—"

Ykem looked at him in startlement, then saw the joke and laughed.

"And that sounds a bit like what the deep-desert nomads do to bring on trances. Does he have nomad blood? Or nomad family?"

Ykem shook his head. "Hates 'em," he said shortly.

"He's from the City of White Walls. Said he'd never been out of sight of the White Lake, till he came here."

Oryn murmured again, "Most curious. And did he know the other man who went mad? Were they friends?"

"Probably knew him. They worked the same gang. Nobody says they was particular friends. Both of 'em, these three, four days now, the men say they'd been sickenin' for somethin'. They'd eat their food and sneak off to their barrack the minute they could, and their mates'd find 'em sound asleep in minutes." Ykem nodded toward the rough, open-sided shelter of canvas-roofed poles that stood on the edge of the camp. "Deep sleep, dead sleep, they say, but that might be hindsight, the way men do. I asked around among the foremen, and they say five or six other men are startin' to do that. Startin' to claim they're sleepy right after they come off, and sometimes not even stay for the food. But I talked to 'em and they seem all right."

"Or they wanted you to think they are, at any rate." Oryn took another look at the madman, with his lolling head and eyes fixed enraptured on nothingness, wailing words—they *had* to be words, thought Oryn, there was a regularity in them that went far beyond random sounds—in a language he had never heard before. He wondered what Soth would make of it. Though Earth Wizards were as a rule less scholarly than Sun Mages, Soth had studied ancient tongues, both the languages of dimmest prehistory and the tongues of those alien mages learned through the scrying crystals.

He ducked his head, pushed through the tent flap and out into the slanting heat, the sun-saturated dust of late afternoon.

"And none of the men have reported disturbing a tomb? Finding jewels they shouldn't have or pieces of mummies?"

"Pieces of *mummies*, my lord?" Ykem stared at him, baffled.

Oryn's head ached. Resting in the heat of yesterday's brief nooning, and riding on through the night, he felt his mind circling again and again to what Raeshaldis had told him about her grandfather and his connection with Noyad the tomb-robbing jeweler, about the howling man in Little Hyacinth Lane, and the burning of the White Djinn Tavern.

The royal cavalcade had followed the line of the aqueduct through the Dead Hills and into the desert. Last year, when the engineers had been constructing the raised waterway across the flat rangelands to the city, he had always felt a lift of hope and purpose in visiting the face camp. Every day had brought the end of the stone trough on its high stone piers closer to their goal, to the rocky, pale shoulders of the Dead Hills. Progress had been visible.

Then he had been able to tell himself, *We will reach the Oasis of Koshlar, and the deep waters of its springs will flow cleanly to the city and the fields.*

It was hard to remember that now, looking out across the waterless expanses of the desert. A hundred and sixty miles, the surveyors said. It would go faster now, of course, since they were only digging and covering. . . .

If he lived to push it through to completion.

Don't think about that, he ordered himself.

Don't think about Summerchild. About whether she'll be alive when you return, or—

Don't think about or.

Weariness settled on him like the big double baskets of earth that were yoked, before and behind, on the teyn who hauled them away from the digging crews. *Think about what you're going to say to Soth when he gets here. About what Raeshaldis will make of that poor fellow in the tent. Five or six others, who "look all right."*

He wondered how much scrub water Geb had managed to locate, and longed for a proper bath, a proper massage, sleep. He couldn't recall when last he'd slept.

He'd even accept dreams about his father being eaten by lions, or about fleeing one himself, as an alternative to sleepless fear for Summerchild's life, for Rainsong's survival.

And the madman in his tent—and the one who'd thrown himself into the teyn gang—had first shown their madness with longing for excessive sleep. Was it the same with Raeshaldis's grandfather?

There were men waiting for him outside his tent. With the sun-drenched dust that hung over the camp like lake fog in the north, he was quite close before he made out the brown and white robes of nomads.

They ran forward to him—surprising behavior for deep-desert dwellers, who mostly had little use for the king—and knelt before him, something no nomad would do save before their own tribal sheikh. Geb emerged briefly in the shadow of the tent doorway, arms folded and an expression of disapproval on his round features that would have done Jethan proud.

One of them, Oryn saw, was the tribal sheikh. So whatever was going on, it was serious. By the tattoos on their foreheads and chins they were an-Dhoki, a tribe that made its money mostly by hunting teyn in the hills and bringing them to the city for sale, though they engaged in small-time banditry when they thought they could get away with it.

"Lord King," said the sheikh, "you who have the great mages at your calling, the great wizards. We, who are your disobedient children, we beg your help. I, Urah of the rai-an-Dhoki, beg it, and we promise our service for ten generations." And though he remained standing, he folded his hands and inclined his head in the closest any nomad ever came to a gesture of supplication.

Oryn knew better than to be transported with joy at this news. They'd be back raiding the herds of the rangeland sheikhs before the moon was full. But he knew also what was expected of him, which was a grave frown and an expression of utterly uncaring haughtiness. "Geb," he called out, "send water and bread to these, my children, and make them comfortable. I will see them when I have eaten and bathed, perhaps slept a little, for I am weary." His father had never failed to impress upon him—and Oryn had found by experience that he was correct—that the longer one made a nomad wait, the greater one's power in his eyes. For the nomads, power was everything. Power, and not showing them that they had a single thing that you wanted.

The waiting game, and afterward the endless ritual of refusing to get to the point of whatever they wanted of one, exasperated Oryn to frenzy, because sometimes things *were* important. As king he was expected to make everyone wait for days, sometimes months. But the nomads on the whole accepted this with patience and generally did seem to accord more respect to him the more he turned them from his door.

Thus he was astonished when the sheikh caught the sleeve of his robe and cried, "My lord, no! They are dead, my lord, they are all dead!"

Oryn looked down into the brown dusty face within its frame of veils and saw it streaked with tears. "Who is dead?"

The sheikh whispered, "My family—my children—my brothers and their wives. All of them. They all went mad and slew one another in the night." He knelt and rested his cheek in the sand beside Oryn's foot in a gesture, not of humility, but of a despair that lifted the hair on the king's nape. "You are a king who commands wizards. You are a king who has put your life in the hands of the gods. Take this curse from off us lest these my nephews—all of us few that are left—go mad and die, too."

Hoarse with shock, Oryn said, "Show me."

※

Riding up to the construction camp that morning, Oryn had noticed the vultures, but his mind had been on the mad workman, and he'd accepted Ykem's reply to his query, that it was probably a dead cow, wandered from the hills. The nomad camp lay in a shallow wadi three miles from the vast straggle of tents and teyn pens around the end of the aqueduct ditch. As their horses flung up their heads, snorting uneasily even before the camp came into view, Oryn guessed that Urah and the rai-an-Dhoki had come this close to the Dead Hills for purposes they guessed the king would disapprove. Ordinarily, nomads traveled with their herds of goats and sheep, animals whose straying would have announced their presence (he sincerely hoped) to the construction camp's perimeter scouts.

But as the horses of the king and his squad of guards topped the rim of the stony crack in the earth, Oryn heard only the groaning and mumbling of camels and now and then the whicker of a thirsty horse. "Again, the animals survived," he murmured, drawing rein and leaning to speak to Bax. The commander nodded.

"I thought that myself, sir." The icy eyes scanned the broken ground, the clusters of dusty black birds rising and falling just where wind scour and an outcrop of harder stone offered concealment for the earth-colored goat-hair tents.

Oryn found himself thinking that vultures wouldn't have clustered that way around the hidden campsite had live warriors been lying in wait to take prisoner the king. He thought Bax's heavy shoulders relaxed a little as the commander raised his hand, signaled the guards to ride down into the wadi.

"It was thus we found them when we returned to camp this noon," Urah whispered, urging his skinny, light-built desert pony close beside Oryn's tall mount. "My nephews and I, we followed the wadi from the hills. We saw the vultures gathered, the *shar-I-zhaffa*, the servants of the gods of the dead, and we knew then what we would see. We did an evil thing, Lord King, and the curse fell upon these innocent ones."

"What was the evil that you did?" asked Oryn.

The sheikh turned his face aside and drew his veils around him in an attitude of ritual shame. "All throughout the near desert it is said that the curses that once guarded the tombs of the dead hold power no more. It is said that men can enter the sealed houses where the old kings sleep and take back from them at last the gold they stole from the people of the desert and the gold they won from the mines with the blood of slaves."

Most of the slaves who worked the gold mines in the Eanit and around the Lake of the Moon were in fact teyn, not nomads, but Oryn did not interrupt to point this out. No amount of this sort of logic had ever changed the nomads' rationale that robbing the ranchers and farmers of the realm was merely getting back their own. He didn't know if they even really believed it themselves. He said instead, "So you robbed a tomb?"

"We did, my lord." Genuine distress cracked in the older man's voice. "Had we known—had *I* known—of the doom it would bring . . ." He shook his head. "My lord, it was a few things only, for the tomb had been robbed before us, and most of the gold was already gone. Yet I see no other vultures; we have found no other camps like . . . like that of my family. I know not why the curse was visited on me and mine and not upon the thieves that came before."

As the horses rounded the bare shoulder of sun-blasted rock that sheltered the camp, Oryn's horse flung up its head again, fighting the bit, and at the same moment the stink of decay whiffed in the still, superheated air. Even in the afternoon's heat it was no more than a whiff, and looking down, Oryn saw that what he had first taken to be a twisted black hunk of wood was in fact a mummy: withered, desiccated, and curled so tightly upon itself that it appeared to have been knotted like tarred rope.

Another one lay between where his horse stood and the half-dozen silent tents that clustered in the black shade of the overhanging lip of the wadi. A man—or what had been a man—lay next to that one, covered in vultures.

Oryn swung down from his horse.

"Watch it, sir," cautioned Bax, but he dismounted, too. The other guards followed, leaving their horses with two men and advancing, swords drawn, into the hushed camp.

Beside Oryn, Urah said sadly, "I understand the caution of your men, great lord. There has been much misunderstanding between your people and mine. But I promise you, this is no trap. All here are dead."

"I believe you," said the king. "Zhenus!" he called out to the sergeant of the guards. "Please check the horse line and the camels and make sure that the sheikh here and his nephews are given all their beasts again—all of those which bear proper brands of sale." He glanced sidelong at Sheikh Urah as he said it, and the sheikh bowed again.

"We have erred, Great King, and we have been punished. Please, please, lift the curse from us, from this camp, from our tents, and all that we possess lest it fall upon us tonight as we sleep. We have done great evil and beg only your aid."

Leaving his horse with the others, Oryn waded forward through the deep sand to the tents, Bax and Urah following. Though his father had repeated over and over that one never admitted to a nomad that one was unable to do anything, he said, "You shall have my aid, my son"—the sheikh was at least a dozen years Oryn's senior, ancient by desert standards—"so far as I am able to grant it. And you shall have all the assistance that my wizard, and the Crafty woman of my people, can grant. But some matters are too great and lie in the hands of the gods."

Bax shot him a warning look, but Urah only folded his hands again and bowed.

"This I understand."

The body of a woman lay in the doorway of the tent. Her throat had been cut, and the vultures had been at her. Blood clotted in her long black hair. With the sun's descent all the tents lay under the shadow of the wadi's wall, and the interior of the first, as Oryn stepped carefully past the dead woman, was for a moment so dark that all he could see was a stray gleam caught in a vessel of iridescent glass.

Behind him he heard Urah whisper, "Ah, Nisheddeh, beloved," as he knelt beside the woman. "Forgive me, and do not pass along the evil to the one who brought it upon you." And he gathered the dead woman's hair into his hands to kiss.

Oryn turned back, blinking, to the dark of the tent. It seemed like any other nomad tent, and more sparsely furnished than most: a woman's bow and quiver hanging from one tent pole, tasseled bags holding spare clothing like some sort of exotic fruit upon another, camel saddles to sit on, and blankets unrolled on the faded rugs that kept the inhabitants' feet from the stones and sand. Sacks of dates and rice; a coffee pan of beaten copper and a bigger cooking pot; and two folding tables, one of which held a half-dozen intricately carved ivory spoons of varying sizes—Zali ware, they looked like, tomb loot almost certainly—and something that could have been a flute; as well as the round-bellied little vessel—a vase? a bottle?—of exquisitely tinted green glass. This vessel seemed to shine with glancing light for which Oryn could identify no source.

"Lord?" The sergeant Zhenus came in behind him, a burly, barrel-bellied man who retained the echoes of striking good looks. "I've had a look at the beasts. Should I . . ." His voice trailed off. Oryn barely heard him as he tried to figure out why that bottle—or vase or lamp or whatever it was—and that object alone should reflect light when the tent doorway lay in the shadow of the wadi's edge. Only when Zhenus tried to step past him, hand reaching out toward the things on the table, did he come to himself.

"Here, don't touch that."

And, when the sergeant did not appear to hear him, Oryn stepped forward quickly and laid a hand on the man's outstretched arm.

Zhenus startled, stepping back, and his eyes widened when he saw the king's hand on him: "Lord, I—I'm sorry, I didn't rightly hear you."

"It's all right," said Oryn, though in fact to "not rightly hear" an order from the king was grounds for whipping at best and possibly hanging, or it would have been if the king had been Taras Greatsword, anyway. Oryn had seen a porter condemned to have all four limbs broken for having his attention elsewhere when Greatsword had given an order. He went on, "It's just that it's best if no one touches anything in the camp, at least until Soth and Raeshaldis have had a look at it."

"But shouldn't we—" The sergeant only just stopped himself from the unheard-of crime of contradicting the king. "That is, lord, might it not be a good idea to take the things back to the camp? His lordship might not arrive till after dark; and for myself, with these teyn turning wild as they've been and escapin', I'd not like to think of anyone, even a mage or a Crafty, wanderin' about outside the camp after dark falls."

"That's a reasonable suggestion, yes," agreed Oryn. "Only there may be a curse, you see. So it's probably best that they be left as they are."

He emerged from the tent to find Bax already assigning four men to remain on guard around the camp: "Most of 'em killed each other, right enough, as you said, sheikh. Same as the village. Strangest thing I've ever seen. You and your nephews best come back with us; we'll see you put up someplace."

"At least until the mage, and the lady Crafty, arrive," added Oryn, seeing Urah's frown at the commander's suggestion. "I shall have the quartermaster set up tents for you, and your beasts will be given their own line separate from those of the camp and water and food. Bax, don't leave a guard here tonight."

"No, sir?" The commander's white eyebrows flared up at the ends, like inquiring wings.

Oryn looked uneasily at the length of the shadows that had now completely crossed the wadi, at the fading gold of the sky. "No. Whatever is going on here, I'd rather risk losing track of it through not setting a guard than lose four more men as we did at Three Wells. Soth should be here by morning, and, please the gods, Shaldis. And one or the other of them will, I hope, be able to find some answers about whatever is going on here. And elsewhere."

As he walked back toward the horses, Oryn felt his eyes drawn, as if in spite of himself, to the dark of the tent doorway. Beyond the body of Urah's wife, nearly hidden in the shadows, the glass vessel gleamed like a watching eye.

"I thought there wasn't curses anymore, sir," he heard Zhenus argue to Bax. "That's what they say is going on with the rains, isn't it? That magic don't work no more, not for good nor for ill. So that means nothing that was cursed is still cursed."

"That's what it means," replied the commander imperturbably. "But that's only the curses that work by magic. Not going along with what the king says is one of those curses that doesn't work by magic. You step out of line, and magic or no magic, you're for it. Understand?"

"Yes sir. I understand."

By the horses Elpiduyek was muttering as he readjusted the ingenious gyroscopic arrangement that changed the angle of the royal parasol's canopy, cursing the sand that fouled the mechanism. Two of Urah's nephews brought the horses and camels from the lines behind the tents, the horses stumbling and wild with thirst. Oryn stopped and turned back to look at the dark tents again, and the sheikh paused beside him, his face filled with unbearable grief.

"How can it be," the older man asked quietly, "that the curse would pass by my horses and my camels and yet take my beautiful Nisheddeh, the honey of my days, the stars of my nights? Is this what the curse is: that I who sinned should *not* die but should live on in sorrow?"

"I do not think any man, not even the great sages of old, has ever found an answer to that," replied Oryn, thinking of the still, wasted body on the linen pillows, the voices of his Raven girls raised in spells that did not seem to touch the shadow that lay on Summerchild's face. "If I ever learn the answer I shall tell you."

And the sheikh glanced sidelong at him and managed

a little smile under his grizzled mustache. "Thank you, Lord King. And I shall do the same for you, should I learn the answer first."

"I appreciate it." Oryn turned toward the horses again and paused once more, looking down at the black, writhed form of the naked mummy in the dust. "Is that common?" he asked. "I'm a scholar, and I've never encountered mention of it: of Zali mummies being deformed in that fashion. It's only recently that we've seen any that survived. But, if you will forgive my frank speech, lord sheikh, you're a tomb robber and have more experience in this matter than I. Is that something the Zali did to their dead that made them convolute that way?"

"Mummies?" Urah's eyes filled with shock and with pain as he looked down at the blackened, leathery thing at their feet. "Lord King, that is not a mummy! Look at the face—can you not see the tattoos still upon the forehead and the chin? I know those tattoos, my lord, and by them I know this man: he is my brother, Warha. It is the curse that has left him so."

FORTY

Someone was seeking her.
    Shaldis put the thought aside.
Darkness lay upon the desert. The moon had set; the evening wind was long stilled. Around here even the plants

were failing, the eerie sentinels of cactus and the clumped sleeping sagebrushes growing farther and farther apart. Very soon, Shaldis knew, they would end altogether. Underfoot the floor of the world was colorless stone and sand.

The air smelled of heat and sand, and nothing more.

And far, far off, like the ghost of smoke, the faintest trace of indigo.

Look in a mirror!

But she knew now that if she took her attention from that far-off scent, she would never find it again. Not in this world that seemed to grow wider and wider, this silence that deepened with every forward step she took.

Behind her she had the dim consciousness of Jethan riding, leading the camels. Many yards behind, but what did it matter? In this world there was no longer any concealing brush, and even the cracks and wadis that came down out of the Dead Hills had shallowed to nothing.

Anything that would come at them could be seen for miles.

Anything that came near her now would swamp that elusive scent that was more within her mind than any part of the real world around her. Like a single silk thread flying loose in a windstorm she traced it. *They have to be headed somewhere, and it has to be somewhere they can get afoot with only the water they can carry.*

I will not be outwalked.

She stumbled, numb with exhaustion, her body burning with a fever of sleeplessness, weariness, dehydration. After two days and a night, the only thing that existed was the faint scent of indigo and it was weakening, calling her soul from her flesh in order to follow, leaving the flesh to catch up as it could.

You will not escape me.
Shaldis!

I'm sorry, she answered whichever sister it was who cried to her mind. *I can't. This may be our only chance.*

A footfall in the corridor. Foxfire dumped the water from the scrying bowl back into the ewer, thrust the bowl under the mattress, slid like a cat into the high-legged bed, and whipped the sheet over herself and Opal. Both girls dropped their heads onto the pillow and shut their eyes as the latch of the door slid back: *Grandmother.*

The whisper of hinges.

No light.

Of course. Grandmother can see in the dark as well as I can.

With moonset the chamber was dark as the inside of an oven. Maybe the reason Shaldis hadn't responded to her call was because she couldn't shine light on the water in the bowl—it was something she intended to ask the older girl as soon as she was safe in the king's palace. Now she could only deepen her breathing and think dreamy thoughts about Belzinan, the gazelle-thin dancer whose performances were all the rage in the Yellow City: conjure up thoughts about what it would be like to be passionately clasped in his arms. Of course, all the gossip said that her father would be far likelier to attract Belzinan's notice than she would, even could she ever find it in herself to be interested in any man again. But never mind. The dream was pleasant enough.

She hoped Opal was doing the same. Her grandmother

was capable of sensing other people's dreams, as she herself had sensed those of the guards at Nebekht's Temple. Maybe her grandmother could even read the dreams of another Raven sister.

After a long time she heard the door close again.

Foxfire didn't know if Red Silk suspected, but she knew she wouldn't dare try to reach Raeshaldis again tonight.

Maybe not until she was out of the house completely, on her way back to the city. How close would she have to be to the city's walls before she called out for riders to meet her? How far from her grandmother to prevent Red Silk from catching her before she was met?

And how would she be able to tell that?

She was still working out the mathematics of time and distance of a single hard-riding old lady against that of a troop of the king's guards searching the broken hill territory between the Valley of the Hawk and the Yellow City when she fell asleep. At least, she reflected, she actually dreamed of Belzinian dancing, rather than of a young teyn lying bound and gagged in slimy green water, staring with frantic eyes as the crocodile swam nearer and nearer. . . .

※

A guard coughed. The one at the watch fire over by the closest of the teyn pens, Oryn thought, identifying the direction of the sound. That damned kitchen cat who'd been courting one or another of the camp toms all night started up yowling again. All the half-wild toms who prowled the desert around the kitchen tents took up the serenade, and Oryn briefly considered turning out the

entire guard to have the female captured and taken
twenty miles out into the desert and dropped. It would
take her the rest of the night to return to the camp and
resume her love life, and by that time he'd be eating
breakfast.

Chained in the quartermaster's tent, the mad digger
continued to sing in that eerie up-and-down wailing, the
same unknown words repeated over and over in an unknown tongue.

The king turned over on his gilded camp bed—carefully, since the last thing he wanted was Geb scurrying in
yet again with inquiries of had he called and did he want
a slave to fan him or someone to read to him or play the
flute or engage him in a game of fox and geese that he'd
be sure to win. *No, and no, and NO.*

What I want is for Soth to arrive.

*What I want is for Raeshaldis to come with news that
she's caught that wretched nomad Crafty her groom told
me about and her wretched indigo-soaked teyn and has
solved this entire tangled puzzle. Or even if she hasn't
solved it, I want her here to tell me if she's heard from the
ladies around Summerchild.*

*And while I'm wanting things, I want Summerchild
here beside me in this deathly not quite silence, alive and
healthy and well.*

Despairingly, Oryn shut his eyes and saw her face
again as last he had seen it, wasted, waxen, like a ghost
on the threshold of death.

People always tried to bargain with Death, but Death
was notoriously uninterested. *I shall be in Death's house
two days from tomorrow,* he thought. *What if while I'm
there, when the priest seals me into that stone grave with*

the scorpion, I see Her, and She offers to bargain after all. What would I do?

Give the land to Mohrvine and to civil war in trade for Summerchild's life?

In front of the tent, the guard stood up.

Oryn heard it very clearly: the creak of belt and boot leather, the sweet clink of sword hanger and buckle.

But no footstep had approached.

He opened his eyes, curious at the anomaly.

The outer flap of his tent was open in the vain hope of catching a breeze. Through the gauze inner curtain he saw the man clearly by the glow of the camp torches. It was Sergeant Zhenus. There was definitely no one and nothing in the darkness beyond.

Yet Zhenus looked around him, then back into the blackness of the tent. And then, to Oryn's indignant surprise, he simply walked away.

Now, see here! The king sat up, again cautiously, groped for the shirt he'd left across the foot of the bed. *Enough is enough!*

I should have had you whipped back in the nomad camp when you argued with me, my lad. My father always warned me: you let them argue with you over shining bottles with curses on them one day, and by midnight that night they'll be running off and deserting you.

Pulling a dark cloak around him to cover the pale shirt, the king stepped to the tent door, soft footed and cautious as a cat. Looking out, he saw Sergeant Zhenus very definitely walking toward the edge of the camp.

And to the marrow of his bones he knew, the man was heading back to the nomad camp, where the iridescent bottle gleamed darkly in the blackness of the nomad tent.

He knew because the image of it had returned to his own mind again and again through the sleepless hours.

Oryn pulled on boots, gathered up the dagger Bax insisted he carry with him at all times—*one of these days I really MUST take the time to learn how to use it!*—and followed his guard from the tent. Zhenus had disappeared into the darkness beyond the dim ambience of the fires and torches that dotted the camp, but Oryn had little trouble getting him in sight again. By the stars it was halfway between midnight and morning. *Dear GODS, where is Soth all this time?* They shed a wan and tricky radiance in which it was nearly impossible to make out anything clearly. But Zhenus was making no effort at concealment. Nor, apparently, did he have any idea he was being followed as he headed east over the broken and uneven ground. He neither quickened his pace nor slowed it, nor made any attempt to seek the occasional cover of rocks or cactus clumps.

Merely followed the tracks of the horses, where they'd ridden to the nomad camp that afternoon.

Even Oryn, completely unversed in the lore of tracking, had no trouble following him. Yet to cross three miles of desert mounted, in full daylight, and surrounded by one's guards is a very different matter from walking those same three miles alone in the darkness. Jethan's account of teyn lying in wait all around the wizard Ahure's house returned to him, and his own fearful vision of those hairy hordes rising up out of the sagebrush near Three Wells village. Teyn attacking, moving in formation, directed by a single command.

The fact that that single command seemed to be far to the south, being trailed by the only academically trained

Crafty woman in the known world, was a certain amount of comfort, but what if there was more than one nomad Raven sister? Shaldis had said, hadn't she, that the marks she'd found about the city had seemed inconsistent, as far as she could judge a magic that felt totally alien to her previous experience. Not to speak of the woman—another nomad, surely?—who called to her in her dreams.

Objects of accursed glass taken from Zali tombs, objects that seemed to have the effect of driving men mad.

A village and then a camp, both wiped out, their inhabitants either slaughtering one another or withering up—*Dear gods!*—into the horrible things he'd seen that afternoon. Maybe, in fact probably, none of the so-called mummies in Three Wells had come out of a tomb at all. All of them could easily have been inhabitants of the village.

But what had happened to them and to the an-Dhoki nomads of Sheikh Urah's family?

And why would nomad Crafties, with or without the services of ensorcelled teyn, want to steal objects so accursed?

Unless, of course, the nomads knew a way of using some magic that might still linger in those vessels of glass? Could that be true, with the spells of the ancient wizards turning to dust left and right? He'd heard it said that the nomads were descendants of the swarthy-skinned hunters who'd inhabited the forests west of the Great Lake and the Lake of the Sun during the time the Zali kings had reigned: had they preserved some tradition from those days that even the Sun Mages had forgotten? A tradition that let them handle such accursed objects without being sunk into a coma or driven mad?

Ahure evidently knew something, was seeking the

same thing, either in concert with the still-hypothetical nomads or, likelier, in competition.

Whichever the case, wondered Oryn, how powerful was the magic he or she or they could extract, if it existed at all?

How much trouble are we in?

And will my successor—Barún or Mohrvine or whoever decides to risk civil war by breaking with the rituals of sanctification—be able to harness that magic? Or is this going to be the final blow that will shatter the united strength of the realm and condemn everyone to death from starvation and thirst?

He stubbed his toe on a boulder, the scrunch of his feet in the sand like a drumroll to his own ears. Zhenus did not turn. Oryn debated going back, calling his guards, seeing if by some chance Soth or Raeshaldis had come into the camp. But a glance back over his shoulder at the clustered pinpoints of amber in the unearthly blueness chased the thought from his mind. He knew he didn't dare. If Zhenus took the bottle—and in his heart Oryn knew it was the bottle—and disappeared, where would they be then? Particularly if Shaldis's grandfather also vanished?

Three days. In three days this will all be beyond my ability to help or hurt, and one of those days spent just journeying back to the city—

STOP IT! You're not dead yet.

At least the all-pervasive quality of starlight illuminated the nomad camp evenly, if faintly. The tents were visible, not hidden in pockets of shadow. Oryn slithered down the side of the wadi a hundred feet from where Zhenus descended, and only the sergeant's almost somnambulistic preoccupation with his own quest kept him from seeing that he was pursued. When Zhenus stopped, Oryn halted, too. The guard unhooked something from his belt, and a moment later a spot of yellow flared into the world of cobalt and black.

He had brought a lamp with him.

Therefore, he was planning to come here from before the time he went on duty.

Was the nomad Raven sister—or *a* nomad Raven sister—waiting for him in the darkness of the tent?

Oryn shifted the dagger in his hand and edged forward as the guard ducked into the low black entrance of the tent.

No sound. No outcry. Through the coarse brown goat hair he could see the lamp moving and Zhenus's bulky shadow.

If I'm going to perform feats of physical derring-do like the heroes in all the best ballads, I really must acquire a sword and take some lessons in its use from Bax.

Oryn lifted the tent flap and looked in.

No crowd of teyn armed with sharpened bones.

No nomad Raven sister.

Only Zhenus, on his knees now and holding the iridescent bottle in both hands. He pressed it to his face, eyes closed, expression rapt. Rolled it against his cheek, his throat, his breast. His head dropped back; he began to sway, and from his throat came thin wailing, soft but growing stronger, exactly the same tune—if it was a tune—that the madman in the supply tent had been singing all day and all night.

Through half-clenched teeth, the same unknown words.

Oryn stepped into the tent, said, "Zhenus!"

The sergeant turned, and his lip lifted clear of his teeth in a snarl like a beast's.

"Put it down."

Saliva glistened as it tracked down Zhenus's chin. The singing did not stop, but the eyes that watched Oryn were watchful, ready, and quite mad.

"Can you hear me? Put it down. I order you—"

Zhenus lunged. Oryn thought the sergeant would simply try to thrust past him and flee into the darkness with his treasure, but he didn't. Clutching the bottle in one hand he drew his sword and flung himself on the king as if he were flinging himself into the line of battle, voice raised in a howling cry. Oryn ducked, tripped on the blankets on the floor, and went down. Zhenus stooped to kill him on the ground, and Oryn caught the leg of the table, slammed it into his attacker's shins. Zhenus fell, letting go of his sword as he clutched the bottle to keep it from breaking.

Oryn snatched up the weapon, and, when Zhenus sprang up and threw himself at him again, screaming, swung the little table at the man's head with all the force of his arm. Zhenus fell, dazed, and Oryn smote him again, and this time the sergeant lay still.

He's truly unconscious, thought Oryn, kneeling beside him. *He's let go of the bottle.*

He used the sword to nudge the smooth, rounded vessel clear of the sergeant's hand and into the light of the lamp, which for a wonder hadn't gone out.

Why Oryn did this he wasn't afterward sure.

Just to see it more clearly.

Because it was, he saw now, the most beautiful object he had ever laid eyes on. It was perfectly plain, round, and appeared to him to be crystal clear though he could not see through it or into it. Under the surface iridescence lay darkness, as if the bottle were filled with it.

And under the darkness, a wakeful eye of green light.

This is the answer, thought Oryn wonderingly, settling himself cross-legged on the tattered nomad carpets, letting the sword slip from his hand.

This is what will save not only me but Summerchild and the realm as well.

This power.

Relief swept him, drowning him; sank him into sweetness he had never imagined before. Like the memory of his dreams he saw himself wading into the lagoon in the House of the Twin Gods, the green water lapping around him, warm with the sunlight. Saw on the lagoon's rim not two priests but seven, and the answer seemed so clear to him, deceptively simple and beautiful with the perfect beauty of all simple things. The crocodiles merely stayed away from him, did not even turn their wicked yellow eyes in his direction. That was all there was to it.

Not two priests but seven.

And trees with lavender flowers, visible over the enclosure wall.

Relief and gladness as he waded up out of the lagoon, dripping water from his thin white garment, holding up his arms to the cheering crowds, to show himself unhurt. Then he saw her coming down the steps to him, his lady, his wife. It had to be Summerchild, from the love that filled his heart at the sight of her, but she no longer looked the same. She was dark haired and green eyed. . . .

Why was that?

The people cheered as he passed before the seven

priests, who salaamed in the style that only they used.
Crowds followed him along the dusty path back to the
city—*back* to the city? When had the House of the Twins
moved into the desert? But he recognized the House of
Death, built curiously into the city's southern wall. Death
at least had a single servant, as Death always did and always had, but after he'd gone into the stone hollow and
come out safely, with the scorpion in his hand, he saw
that the House of Wisdom—the house of the serpent
king—was also outside the city, only it wasn't called the
House of Wisdom but the House of Madness.

In either case, the pit of serpents was the same, and the
answer was the same, too. To simply walk down the steps
and lay his head upon the idol's altar. To have the snakes
ignore him. Easy, easy as a little song, and from the pit's
rim his beloved one smiled down at him from among the
nine—*nine?*—priests.

But as he approached the altar in the center of the pit,
a tiny yellow snake, the length of his hand, struck at him
from between the cracks in the altar and bit him on the
foot. He kicked it aside, stamped at it, though it eluded
him; and he heard the people who lined the pit's edge
gasp. Something went through his mind, some thought,
some terrible sense of déjà vu, gone as soon as it touched
him.

He turned back to the altar knowing the pain would
start as he turned, and it did. It hit him first in his chest,
like the blow of a spear or a knife, searing so that he
gasped like a landed fish. Then the next instant knives of
pain slashed every joint in his body, so that sweat poured
from him, tears flowed from his eyes. His knees gave way
and he fell, catching at the altar, crying out. Above him,

Shibathnes of the Serpents, the lord of the darkness in the mind, stared down at him with eyes like the darkness behind the stars. Pain, and worse pain, and still worse, and he was screaming, and the nine priests of Wisdom (or Madness) stepped closer to the edge.

At the same instant men came rushing down the steps into the pit, men with drawn swords. His brother's men— not Barún's but some other brother's, the same way his dark-haired beloved whom he knew so well wasn't Summerchild but someone he'd never seen before. The pain made it impossible to think. Madness seized him, madness born of the pain that set his brain on fire, and he snatched up the sword that he'd let slip from his hands and flung himself at them, screaming in pain, knowing he was going to die and not caring.

Anything, anything to end the pain.

And to take them with him, traitors who had bribed the priests to let him die, when the answer had been in his grasp.

Then his eyes cleared, the dream shifting to waking for one moment, or what would have been waking but for the glowing iridescence of the bottle still burning in his mind. His attackers were but shadows in the darkness around him, but where the starlight touched their eyes he saw they were pale, with slitted pupils like cats.

They seized him, held him down, and the knives all slashed at once. The snake's venom rushed out with the blood as darkness poured in.

FORTY-ONE

They're out there somewhere.
They can't simply have vanished.

Raeshaldis stopped, letting her slitted eyelids drift that last fraction of an inch into complete closure, sank her mind into the emptiness that now smelled of nothing but air and rock. The desert floor was bare here, even of sand. Only rock stained dark by the slow leaching of the sun. The air was like a diamond, shriveling the tissues of her nose and lips even through her veils.

They have to stop somewhere. She may be a Crafty but she's no more than human. She has to rest.

As her eyes slipped closed that final fraction of an inch, her mind slipped back down into trance, her senses reaching out over the desert like the farthest extension of a single drop of blood spreading in a still pool that taints all the water with its presence. Through weariness like the pounding of a hammer she was aware of Jethan and the camels, some half mile behind her, waiting in the dove-gray twilight of the coming morning. Was aware of her own fatigue and thirst—she couldn't even remember when she'd let her mind be distracted long enough to go back to them for water.

Was aware that this was the hour called the Bird Sun, when back in the lands where there was water all the birds would be waking to cry their territories, to hunt insects, to coo and twitter at one another: in her grandfather's little garden and the king's great ones, under the eaves of every house in the Yellow City and in the palmeries and fields and pastures all along the shores of the lake.

Here there was no sound but the sob of the wind across the bare black rocks and now and then the creak of saddle leather far behind her and the jingle of a camel bell.

It would be full light soon. Full sun.

The night before last she'd followed the teyn's scent far into the bare desert, as she'd followed it through the Dead Hills with Rat on the night preceding that. And the one before that she'd ridden with Jethan to the house of Ahure. She knew she'd dozed and eaten at some point in the past three days but couldn't remember exactly when. Despite her training in long fasts and nights without sleep, she knew she was coming to the end of her physical endurance.

Just what was that other woman made of?

Was she like the teyn, who could go for seven days, it was said, without rest or food?

Was she getting her tame teyn to carry her while she slept?

Were her spells over them that strong?

Shaldis realized she was nodding on her feet, and jerked her mind to wakefulness. Like a wolf she scented the air, turning her head again, sifting and sorting the dry, hard air of dawn.

And finding nothing.

Still she started forward, eyes half shut, trusting that in time she would pick up the trail again.

"Lord King?"

The voice came from a thousand miles away in the darkness.

"Oryn?"

The image of the nine priests on the edge of the crocodile pool dissolved and Oryn opened his eyes. "Where in the gods' names were you?"

It was Soth kneeling beside him.

Morning sun glared in Oryn's eyes, and the next second a vulture's shadow passed across it. The world smelled of the birds and of blood. His skin was on fire with pain.

"And what happened? There were nine priests, though Death still had only one." He brought up his hand to touch a burning line of pain on his forehead and saw that someone had drawn a circle on the back of his wrist in blood to which stuck sand grains and dust. The movement brought back the knives of all his enemies. The henchmen of the brother who wasn't really his brother, or something.

Soth's face looked ghostly white in the pale wrappings of his veils. "Can you sit up?" Behind him a whole squad of guards crowded close, as if they expected their monarch to utter prophecies or give birth.

"Of course I can sit up! I only . . ." He tried it and sank back with a gasp. "On second thought, please have the palace baths transported out here." He managed to get up on one elbow and looked around.

He lay on the ground in mid-desert. Far off a column of dust proclaimed the aqueduct camp, but it had to be a good five miles away. Vultures circled overhead.

At least with such helpful fowl in the neighborhood,

once they knew he was missing he couldn't have been difficult to find.

"My lord, what happened? Who did this?" Soth reached back for the dripping waterskin Commander Bax passed forward, propped Oryn's shoulders, and helped him drink. Oryn's hands were shaking so badly he found he couldn't support the skin's weight himself. "The relief guard found Sergeant Zhenus missing. He fetched Geb to go in and check on you, and you were gone, too. Bax tells me they were searching for you for the rest of the night. I saw the vultures myself as I rode into camp at dawn. I thought it odd that they didn't land."

Oryn turned his hands over. His shirt was ripped in a hundred places; shallow cuts marked his arms, chest, thighs. Between the cuts, circles and zigzags had been drawn in blood on his reddening, sunburned skin. Stammering a little, he said, "I don't really know. I followed Zhenus to the nomad camp. He was . . ." Oryn turned his head, saw another column of vultures two or three miles off, where the camp must lie in the wadi that was invisible from here, concealed by the rise of the ground. A pale crescent moon hung in the daylight sky.

He looked back at Soth, suddenly frightened. "No one's at the nomad camp, are they?"

The librarian shook his head. "We came searching for you first. Who—?"

"Post guards around it. No one is to go into it, no one, for any reason. There was a bottle. A bottle of iridescent glass. Zali ware, I think."

Soth held up a fragment of it, a shard about three inches long. It was tipped with dried blood.

Looking past him, Oryn saw that where he had lain on

the ground was surrounded by a minute hedge of broken glass, pieces buried so that their bloodstained points protruded from the earth like uneven teeth, glittering in the hot morning sunlight.

He shook his head, trying to clear away the burning fantasies of dream, to separate them from memories scarcely less unreal.

He'd been a king, he thought. Or someone had.

His enemies had seized him, dragged him to his death; and looking down he saw that between the gashes and the blood circles, his arms were bruised. As Soth and Bax helped him to his feet he lay his own hand gingerly over the darkening finger weals. His hands and feet were small for his height, but at six foot three he was still a big man, and the span of these marks exceeded his own by over an inch.

"What do you remember?" asked Bax gently. "Did you see who attacked you? Or what happened to Zhenus?"

"Zhenus attacked me," said Oryn hesitantly. "Circle the nomad camp, find his tracks if he left it, but whatever you do don't go into it looking for him. It wasn't he who did this," he added, seeing both his friends open their mouths with the same question. "Send a message, at once, now, immediately, to Lady Moth at the palace. A squadron is to go to the house of Chirak Shaldeth in Sleeping Worms Street and arrest every person in it. Slaves, camel drivers, teyn, and every member of the family from lowest to highest, excepting solely the Lady Raeshaldis, if she's there. They're to be taken to the palace prison and given new clothing down to the skin, decently and with respect, mind you. But no single member of the household, and I mean *none*, is to keep by them so much as a toothpick that was in that house. When the house is empty it's to be cordoned off and no one is to touch anything within it. Lady Moth is to go with the squadron and stay with the guards on the empty house. Lady Pebble is to remain with the household members until they're put in their cells, and then she's to remain in the guardroom until I personally speak to her.

"It wasn't a curse that destroyed the nomad camp, Soth." Oryn turned back to his tutor, tightened his grip on the sinewy, black-robed arm. "It wasn't a plague that killed everyone in Three Wells and then later took those poor guardsmen. No one brought mummies or hex-ridden gold into the village. Maybe not even a piece of glass such as the one that—that trapped me."

He turned his hands over again, staring at the ragged cuts, the daubed lines and rings that reminded him of the sigils and runes that the mages had drawn for centuries, to focus their power.

"I think it's the Dream Eater we spoke about," he said softly. "It was supposed to haunt tombs, to eat the dreams of the dead. And I think it was a dead man's dreams, a dead king's dreams, that I saw and felt. A Zali king, by the way everyone was dressed. The ancient wizards warded against the Eater of Dreams just as they warded against the lake monsters so long ago and so effectively that everyone forgot that it was real."

Behind him, he heard one of the guards whisper, "Bad-Luck Shadow."

"What?" Oryn swung around.

The guard gulped and looked as if he'd been caught sucking his thumb at a review. "Nothing, sir. Just my granny used to stick broken glass in the ground just like that, on certain nights of the year, around the house, to keep the Bad-Luck Shadow away. My dad complained as how we kids were always cuttin' ourselves on it, and she just said, 'All the better.' "

"Did she, indeed?" murmured Oryn, and turned to look back toward the circling vultures that marked the nomad camp. Rising wind lifted and whirled them like smoke and threw a bitter scatter of sand in his eyes.

"Broken glass is a very common element in old protective spells," began Soth, and Oryn frowned.

"Exactly what *is* the Bad-Luck Shadow?" he asked.

The men all looked at one another, baffled to put a description to the bogeyman that all their parents had shaken before their eyes. The first guard shrugged and said, "Something that'll get five-year-old boys if they don't do what their granny says, sir?"

"Someone knows." Oryn's eyes passed from the faces of his guards, his tutor, back toward the distant wadi where, he strongly suspected, Zhenus lay among the withered black corpses of the an-Dhoki, perhaps withering and blackening himself by this time, his mind lost in the dreams of ancient kings. "Someone who commands the teyn, who's been using them as cat's-paws to keep us away from the places where the Eater of Dreams has risen from the ground. What are these marks, Soth?" he asked, extending his arms. "Do they look like anything you know of? The dreams that took me—maybe the Eater itself—were lodged in glass; I think there's another such glass talisman in the house of Chirak Shaldeth. Does glass draw the Eater of Dreams or repel it? Was I being protected by this"—he looked back at the ragged ring of glittering points, half obscured now by the blowing sand—"or being sacrificed? Or used as bait?"

Soth only shook his head.

"We have to find out," said Oryn. Wind lashed him again, strong enough this time to make him stagger. All tracks would be gone, he thought; whatever the earth could have told Bax. "We have to find this person, this woman. She holds the key to Summerchild's life, and she seems to be able to command the teyn.

"Bax, we'll start back for the city the moment we're saddled up, but send your messenger now to the house of Chirak Shaldeth. Sooner or later our friend's going to go back there."

"Do you think Pebble can cope with it?" asked the librarian. "Or Moth? Or even Raeshaldis?"

"I don't know. They'll have to, or we're—"

Another gust of wind thrust them all, like a giant hand, and the morning sunlight shifted to a yellow cast. The wind burned Oryn's lungs as he drew breath, wind saturated with—

"Dust, my lord!" A guard pointed toward the south, where a deadly line of billowing yellow was beginning to rise above the horizon.

Oryn said, "Dear gods!" and Bax said something considerably less refined. "Can your man get through?" Oryn added. "It looks like a bad storm."

"I'll get through." Bax transferred Oryn's arm to the nearest guard, strode away toward the horses.

"You? But—"

"With luck I'll reach the hills before it hits," the commander yelled back over his shoulder, then quickened his pace to a run. Before Oryn could call out, the older man sprang up onto the strongest of the horses—Oryn's own, he noticed—and spurred away at a gallop toward the line of the distant hills.

"Come on!" Soth dragged Oryn toward the horses, who were tossing their heads and fighting the guards who held their reins, frightened by the dust-laden wind. "We can make it to the camp and take shelter! Can you ride?"

"I'm jolly well not going to sit here and wait to be buried."

If anyone could make it back to the city through the storm, Oryn reflected, *Bax could.* He should probably have tried to stop his commander—a man old enough to be his father—from risking a ride through the killer storm, but his half-guessed fear of what was being drawn to Chirak Shaldeth's house was too strong now to put aside. Had no one else been available he knew he would have at least tried to make the ride himself.

Whatever the Eater of Dreams was that seeped from the walls of tombs and transmuted the dreams of the dead into madness, the ancients had feared it, and it did not seem to have lost strength in its years of enforced quiescence. He'd seen what it could do in Three Wells. What it could do if it was drawn to a city of a hundred thousand people, he tried not to imagine.

But he did imagine it, and it turned him cold with fright.

The dust storm came out of nowhere.

Shaldis realized she must have fallen asleep on her feet, because it seemed to her one moment that she walked half blindly, numbly, following the hope or illusion that maybe the scent of indigo might lie before her and the next that she was on her knees, with the hot wind ripping at her veils and her clothing, the sunlight yellowing away toward darkness. Dust burned her eyes and filled her nose, and the wind's howl filled her ears. A gust of wind threw her to the ground, and when she fumbled for the spells she'd learned, to part the winds around her and turn aside the dust, she barely had the strength to lessen them.

Jethan, she thought wildly, *where's Jethan?* She had to get to him, to protect him, too, with whatever she had strength for.

A darker shape blotted the growing darkness of the howling world. She yelled, "Here! Jethan!" and he stumbled out of the dust to her, face wrapped in his veils but still moving like a man blind and deaf.

In one hand he held the end of a rope; he dragged her to her feet without a word, half carried her along. Staggering, Shaldis formed the spell again in her aching mind, splitting the wind behind them so that it rushed by on either side. Gusts whirled onto them nevertheless, and the dust that hung in the air choked and smothered her. The dark around them grew, illuminated by flashes of dry lightning; the wind rose to a scream.

"I got the tent up," Jethan yelled over the din, and the wind snatched his words away. ". . . camels . . ." she heard him say, and ". . . should be safe . . ."

He made a place of shelter, thought Shaldis, as they reeled into the low-pitched triangular tent, *before he came for me.*

What a blessing to have a friend who thought things out.

Most of the room in the tent was taken up by the camels, grumbling and moaning and stinking as only camels can. Shaldis tried to anchor her spells to the goat hair and the poles, to the small patch of earth that was the only place safe amid the shrieking wildness of the storm. The darkness of the dust blotted out the sickly remainder of the morning light. Mind aching, body aching, she thought she could see the spells themselves, like floating balls of marsh fire, clinging to the tent.

Then her mind darkened, and she slipped unconscious to the ground.

FORTY-TWO

Through the stillness of concentration, the deep weariness of power raised and power expended, Pomegranate heard the voices in the lower chamber of the Summer Pavilion and shivered.

Lotus was saying, "I'm sorry, they're working great magic. It's a matter of life and death."

And a voice that Pomegranate recognized as belonging to Shaldis's aunt Yellow Hen—who'd always given her food and sometimes clothing in her begging days—retorted, "You think I'd have walked all the way here from the Bazaar District and put up with that snippy porter at the gate if *this* wasn't life and death? Tell her I need to see her, and I need to see her at once."

Since she'd come back to the Yellow City four days ago, Pomegranate had been plagued by the nagging sense there was something wrong somewhere. She had spoken of it only once, to Shaldis, but the uneasiness, the feeling of listening, had never left her.

Pontifer sensed it, too. All day yesterday the white pig had trotted back and forth from where Pomegranate sat at Summerchild's side out into the terrace garden, then back again, restless, the way he'd done back when he'd been a real pig when a storm was brewing. When, during their watches at Summerchild's side, Shaldis had spoken to her in passing of her grandfather's obsession with an object that came out of a tomb, Pomegranate had wondered if that was the reason for the prickling sensation in her palms and scalp, for her sense of something always lurking around the next corner, watching.

Since last night she had felt as she frequently felt when her dreams were bad, when she'd wake in the middle of the night and gather up blankets and clothing and quietly flit through the silent alleys to another of her hidey-holes in the Slaughterhouse District. Moving on, so that it wouldn't get her.

Whatever It was, in her dreams.

This was the first time she'd felt like this in waking life and she couldn't explain it, but she knew it wasn't good.

"I'll see if she's even able to hear me," whispered Lotus's voice downstairs. "But they're working to save my lady's life now, and she's been unconscious so long."

Silently, Pomegranate withdrew her mind from the Circle of Sisterhood that held together the magic of the others. Pebble looked haggard with weariness, her plump cheeks marked with lines of concentration grimly at odds with her usual placidity. The paint on Moth's face had a doll-like appearance against the pallor underneath. Neither opened her eyes. Pomegranate padded from the chamber on bare feet and met Lotus as the maid was coming up the stair.

"My lady . . ." the girl began, and Pomegranate lifted her hand in acknowledgment and nodded.

"How is the lady?" asked Yellow Hen when Pomegranate emerged from around the stairway screen. "My niece has been in a fair stew over her, with my father and that brother of hers both tearing at her like a couple of dogs."

"What's happening?" Pomegranate met the other woman's eyes: like herself, no longer young, and like herself unwanted in the world that had too many husbandless women already. For as long as she could remember, Pomegranate had seen Yellow Hen come and go from the house on Sleeping Worms Street. Knowing, as she did, everyone in the city, she'd heard all about Chirak Shaldeth's attempts to sell his crooked-backed, stubborn daughter to whomever would take her long before she heard that Shaldeth's granddaughter had power in her veins and hands.

More than the old skinflint deserved, for a fact.

"One of the maids disappeared last night," said Yellow Hen briefly. "And my brother Tjagan the night before that. I've been up and down the house searching. I found Six Flower's hairpins on the attic stairs but no sign of the girl herself. My sister-in-law won't come out of her chamber and neither will my father, but they're both singing—singing music such as I've never heard, the one of them answering the other from court to court. Some of the camel drivers are gone, too, and their mates swear they went into the kitchen court, not out into the street."

"And you found nothing in the attic where you say you saw this one girl's hairpins?"

"I found nothing." Yellow Hen hesitated, regarding Pomegranate as if wondering how much of what she'd seen or thought she'd seen she could speak of without sounding demented.

And evidently remembering the woman she was talking to was widely regarded as mad herself. "The attic was . . . was changed. Or there was something there that made it appear different. I can't explain, but it seemed when I went in there, there were more rooms than there had been, more doors where doors hadn't been before. And something moved up there, something green that glowed."

"Yes," whispered Pomegranate, "yes. I've smelled it, felt it . . . heard it singing far-off in my sleep. What about Shaldis's father? Your brother?"

"He won't come from his study. He isn't singing yet, but I didn't like his voice, when he told me to go away. His wife tells me he won't let anyone in."

"And his son? That snotty-nosed brat who Shaldis tells me is now running the house?"

Yellow Hen's face twisted. "He keeps swearing there's not a thing wrong. I left him cursing Shaldis for not doing something to keep the teyn from running off, and cursing Strath Gamert or Noyad or whoever he thinks is doing all this just to ruin the family."

"Sounds like him." Pomegranate remembered Tulik as young as the age of eight, ordering the servants to drive her away from the kitchen court. She glanced through the doorway into the gardens, where the light was sickening to yellowish brown and gardeners were scurrying to put cages of wicker and gauze over the rosebushes. Up until a few years ago, when dust storms howled in from the desert, the Sun Mages in their Citadel could be counted on to send them elsewhere. She could hear the old gardener cursing, as if his inconvenience were the worst calamity to be faced as a result of the change in the structure of the universe.

It was an attitude Pomegranate had met with all up and down the shores of the seven lakes.

There probably were men, she reflected, who thought that poor Oryn's death and replacement would solve that problem, too.

"Wait here for me," she said, and sprang up the stairs again with the lightness of a far younger woman.

Pebble and Moth had emerged from their healing trance and were consuming tea and honeyed fig balls with the ravenousness of athletes after a race. Lotus and another maid were going around the room, fastening up the gauze-backed lattices that would allegedly keep most of the dust out of the beautiful blue-and-gold chamber, though Pomegranate knew that, like every other dwelling in the city, the palace was in for a massive sweeping out by tomorrow.

The two young women listened to Pomegranate's tale with expressions of deep uneasiness; she saw their glances meet. "I have to go," she finished, prodding more hairpins into the random coils of her hair. "I know Yellow Hen and I know she wouldn't come here for help unless there's something really scary going on in that house—and I think there is. But this isn't a rangeland village. It's a city—and we have no idea how far or how fast it will spread."

She started to wrap one of her many ragged scarves around her hair and face, to protect against the rising winds and dust. Even broken by the Dead Hills, the storm's violence was a force to be reckoned with; lightning was beginning to flash in the darkening sky. Wordlessly, Lotus went to one of the wall cupboards and brought out airy lengths of pink and white gauze. "I know it would be all right with her," the maid whispered, glancing at the still face of the woman on the bed.

Pomegranate smiled. "Thank you, dear." She turned for the door.

Pebble asked, "Isn't Pontifer going with you?"

Pomegranate stopped, looked gravely back at the younger woman's shy smile. She knew perfectly well that none of her colleagues could see her pet and that most of them—Pebble included—didn't believe him to be any more than a madwoman's delusion. It touched her that the girl would ask after him anyway. "Pontifer's gone," she said. "He left an hour, maybe two hours ago, I don't know where. If he comes back, tell him I need him. Maybe we all need him."

✳

Raeshaldis opened her eyes, knowing that she dreamed. She lay in Jethan's arms, in sleep far deeper than she ever recalled in her life, her body depleted, her mind drained. Jethan, holding her, looked just as bad, she thought. Under the film of dust his face was like a dead man's, save for the sweat that tracked through the gray-brown crust. The hour was that of the Sun of Justice, the Hammer Sun, the crushing nadir of afternoon, the heat brutal, the darkness almost complete. The howl of the winds all around them drowned every other sound, as if they were lost, adrift in some alien world of ashen midnight, unable to return to their own.

She was glad that Jethan was beside her. That she wasn't alone.

In his dream, she wondered, was he scandalized that the tiny confines of their tent had broken all possibility of a woman's space being separated from a man's?

Probably.

And she smiled.

Dust hung thick in the air. As she had before she'd fainted, she could see her protective spells like fluttering rags of light, clinging to the tent poles. The goat-hair cloth above them sagged with the weight of dust. She rose to her knees, leaving her body behind her, still in the crook of Jethan's arm—shocked a little at how gaunt she was, sunburned and haggard—and crawled to the entry flap. Untying it, she looked out, saw how the winds rose up on either side of the little tent in walls of blowing dust. These met overhead as if the tent were enclosed in a fragment of glass. Even in her dream, she was simply too weary to reach out her mind to feel for the storm's edge, to judge how long it would last.

The howling of the storm's voice filled the earth.

She had lost the marked teyn and the woman who controlled it.

After all this long pursuit, to the very edge of the world it seemed, she had after all failed. And in failing, had almost certainly condemned Summerchild and the king to death.

Nothing remained except to go back, to take up the threads of things as she found them, and help the situation as best she could.

Through the whirling brownness beyond the limits of her wind ward, she saw something moving, something white and low. It was quite close to her before she realized it was a pig, and for an instant her cracked lips smiled. "Hey, Pontifer," she said. Then fear flashed through her, fear that Pomegranate was somewhere in the storm, lost. Pomegranate wouldn't have come looking for her, would she? Not all the way out here.

Tentatively she reached out her mind for the animal's—for though she'd never made mental touch with Pontifer she guessed he was perfectly capable of it—but received nothing. The pig only turned and trotted off into the storm again. He stopped, looked back at her over his shoulder. Shaldis pulled her veils around her face, then turned her head to look back into the tent.

She saw herself sleeping, curled into a ball at Jethan's side. Did he dream, she wondered, of the granny who wouldn't let him pick on his brother? Of that low brown hut and parched fields, where he should have stayed to look after his family?

Did he dream of his friends, of Riis and his men who now lay beneath the rangeland's hard yellow earth?

Far off, Shaldis heard—or thought she heard—the rhythmic crashing from her earlier dreams, nearly inaudible beneath the screaming of the wind.

She stepped from the tent and followed Pontifer into the darkness.

In time the crashing grew louder, the wind less. Through the darkness she heard what could only be drumming and saw light—fire?—and the thin gleam of the waning moon. She felt—and she could never afterward explain it—as if the sun turned over, and instead of its being the grilling Hammer Sun of afternoon it was the hour of the Sun's Dreams, the deepest hour of the night.

And still. The air on her face was moist and sweet, as if she had walked into the time of the winter rains along the jungled shores of the Great Lake. The scents of vegetation and flowers nearly intoxicated her.

Woven reeds crunched under her foot. She put out her hand and touched a wall of bunched grass tied to a framework of poles. A fire built just outside the low door opening showed her the sharp slant of an enormously high roof and, along the grassy walls, children sleeping.

They dozed fitfully on woven mats. Brown skinned, dark haired, thin with sickness. Around them, bunches and bundles of plants had been laid, and the whole surrounded with the familiar runes of healing that she'd been meditating on for so many nights, crudely but carefully scratched in the earth.

Drumming outside, and the soft rhythmic crashing that had led her here. Shaldis put off her veils, dust sliding from their creases in pale streams, knelt at the nearest child's side. It was a girl the same age as Twinkle, her skin dry and her lips cracked. A gourd beside the child's mats held water and by it a wet handful of pulpy felted cloth. Looking more closely at the bunches of plants, Shaldis recognized the bark and leaves of the fever tree, the dried flowers of the hand of Darutha.

She heard, thought Shaldis, knowing where she had to be. *She gathered the plants, but didn't know what to do with them.*

Like us, with our spells against crocodiles and snakes.

She passed her hand gently over the girl's face, drew signs of courage and life with her finger in the dark. Then she took the gourd of water and the branch of the fever tree and went to the door, to see if there was a way to heat the water for the necessary tisane.

Outside, the waning crescent of the moon was almost bright enough to cast a shadow. The grass house stood on a little rise of ground among dense trees, but before it the ground fell away to sand.

And beyond the sand . . .

Shaldis thought, *It's the sea.*

Tears flooded her eyes, of shock, of delight, of emotions for which she had no name.

The water—infinite water, endless water—rose up in a wall, curled, and fell foaming, roaring, onto itself a dozen yards from the white sand. It was a little like the waves of the lakes when the wind was high. *So a child,* she thought, *might mistake a bowl of leaves for a forest.*

What I heard was the noise of the sea—which neither I, nor anyone I know, has ever seen.

On the edge of the sea women danced in a ring by moonlight, young women and old, an outer circle of fifty or more and an inner group of five. Men played the drums for them, a heavy haunting rhythm. The dance was like nothing Shaldis had ever seen, yet it drew her, as if she could have walked down the sand to them and joined in.

They're raising magic with the dance. The power hung palpable in the flower-drenched air, the way the power of the Sun Mages haloed the Circle at the top of the Citadel, when the adepts and the singers and the masters had all assembled, to sing the Summoning the Rain.

This was the first time, she realized, that she'd been sleeping at the time they raised power: sleeping deeply

enough in the daytime, her mind exhausted past the point
of all its defenses.

Their day is our night. She didn't know what this
meant or why it was true, but in her bones she knew it
was. Long training homed her mind to the distant sun.

But these people have never needed to summon rain.
Clouds sailed free as elephantine birds above the sea.
*They live with the sound of that crashing water every day
of their lives.*

The tallest of the women stopped dancing, stood still
in the center of the circle gazing up the hill at Shaldis in
the door of the grass house, transfixed. Then she stepped
out of the ring, walking slowly first, signaling the others
to stay back, then running. Shaldis stood waiting for her,
a pale shape in the firelight, the water gourd and the
healing branch in her hands.

"You came." Because it was a dream—or maybe because Pontifer Pig lurked in the dark of the house behind
her—Shaldis again heard in her mind the thought behind
that musical language.

She said, "Puahale?" knowing it—the way things are
known in dreams—for the other woman's name.

Puahale smiled, white teeth in a round face like dusky
honey. "Rae-shaldis?" She pronounced the name hesitantly. "Old One?"

"Father calls me that."

The other woman laughed, still uncertain, as if not believing that they stood face-to-face. "My father calls me
Little One."

Shaldis looked up at her—she stood considerably
more than six feet, several inches taller than Shaldis, who
was as tall as many men. "I hope that's a joke."

Puahale laughed again, then put out one big hand to touch Shaldis's face wonderingly, as if expecting her fingers to pass through the flesh. Shaldis half expected them to as well. But they didn't. Puahale's hand was warm, and sweat glittered on her face from dancing. Her hair was black, straight, and hung almost to her knees. Her body and limbs were patterned with tattoos. She was, Shaldis thought, a few years younger than Summerchild, and, like Summerchild's, her smile radiated both power and peace.

"You came," she said again, and Shaldis took her hand.

"I came to show you how to get healing from plants and leaves," she said. "And I came to beg your help."

FORTY-THREE

Was that you I spoke to by the lake of fire?" Shaldis asked as the two women sorted through the bunches of leaves and roots. In the fire before the house door, chunks of rough-textured black rock heated, to be dropped when red-hot into the huge water gourd, an ancient method that Shaldis had heard Rachnis the shadowmaster speak of. Some of the deep-desert tribes still used it, the ones who seldom came in touch with the traders from the Realm of the Seven Lakes and might not see a metal pot from one year's end to the next.

"That's the Dreamshadow." Puahale's round face grew somber. "It lives under the ground, *in* the ground. It's a thing, a spirit, but not like the djinni that used to dwell in the sea and the air." The word she used was different, but because they spoke in the language of dreams, Raeshaldis knew at once that it was indeed those glittering entities of magic of whom she spoke.

"We don't even know if the Dreamshadow is one creature, or many, or just a kind of poison that the earth exudes in some places. The voices it speaks with seem to be just the voices of those whose dreams it scavenged. Its music is the music that lingered in the hearts of the dead after their souls had been taken back into God. Back before we came here, Wika tells me—Wika is my teacher, the teacher of all us priestesses—our people used to put the dead in holes in the ground or in tombs cut into the rocks. But the Dreamshadow lived in those rocks, and in the earth of the Old Islands, and it grew so strong eating the dreams of the dead that it started oozing out of the tombs and out of the ground near the tombs, to attack the living. It would burrow into their minds until they thought they were in the dreams of all those long dead. Sometimes—not always—it would eat their bodies as well, making them wither up and turn black. Other times they would just go mad and die singing or be killed by those they attacked."

Gime. Shaldis saw again the flash of Jethan's sword, the crimson fountain of blood in the morning sun.

Saw the blackened mummies in the streets of Three Wells.

Saw the drift of green mist in the garden courtyard below her grandfather's rooms and Summerchild, in a vision like a dream, surrounded by the glowing mists, protected by the power of the sigils drawn around her but unable to break free.

"How do you get rid of it?" she whispered, panic closing over her throat like a strangling hand. "How do you save someone who's been taken by it?"

And for an instant she felt sick with terror that Puahale would shake her head and say sadly, *There is no way*.

But the woman said at once, as matter-of-factly as Shaldis would have prescribed willow bark for fever, "You cut them, where the lines of the body's energy run near the surface. It breaks the Dreamshadow's hold. There are spells to say—"

"Tell me," said Shaldis. "Teach me. A friend of mine was taken. And my grandfather has a—a glass ball, an ancient thing that came out of a tomb, that I think is drawing the Dreamshadow to it."

Puahale's eyes widened. "Wika told me about that! On the Old Islands the wizards would trap it in something called glass. Do you know glass? Wika says it was made out of melted sand—"

"My people have it, yes." And a little wryly, despite her fear, she added, "Sand is something we have plenty of." She held up the amulet Twinkle had given her, with its huge central bead of pink glass.

Puahale touched it wonderingly, brushed its smoothness against her lower lip. "Our people who came here didn't know how to make it," she said. "And our wizards found that obsidian works better, the black glass from within the volcano's crater." The last words she used, Shaldis could form no mental image for. But Puahale went on, "That's where the Dreamshadow dwelled, here, where the molten heart of the island seeps forth. What you called the lake of fire. It was weaker here, because it hadn't been devouring the dreams of the dead for all those lifetimes as it had on the Old Islands; from the first the wizards put boundaries against it, of obsidian rocks, and gave the dead to the birds of the air. But it's still deadly dangerous."

Puahale stopped her grinding to touch one of the several disks of highly polished obsidian that she wore, strung on braided strands of fish sinew around her neck. "It will go into obsidian before it goes into a living person." She held up one, not a disk, but a small, flaked blade. "In the Old Islands, some of the wizards used to make glass traps for it that men would put under their pillows, so they could dream the dreams of the dead. When I went up to the crater and saw you there, I was seeking the learning of the dead, hoping there might be a way to hear it without being trapped. But Wika my teacher stopped me, as I stopped you. Wika said the men who used such dream-traps were ensnared by the dreams within them, until they'd rather dream than do anything else and so went mad. And because of the dreams concentrated in the glass, the Dream-shadow was drawn to them also, drawn out of the ground, out of the tombs, and took those men and whoever else was nearby."

"*Damn* him!" Shaldis's hands shook so badly she dropped the fever bark. Rage burned up in her at her grandfather, at Noyad the jeweler. At the ancient king or land-chief, whoever he had been, who'd had the glass trap made, the repository of poisoned dreams, for his own pleasure.

The Dreamshadow was being drawn to it, glutted and strong with the energies of deaths it had been feeding on for ten years, since the old spells had failed, that had for centuries kept it at bay.

It was drawn to her house. To her father, her mother, Twinkle, Foursie.

"I have to get back," she whispered, fighting to steady her breath. Feeling as she had felt, when the masters had blindfolded her and whirled her around, had shouted at her and shoved her and she had to form spells neatly and accurately through and against all the distractions and panic. "Before I go, show me how to cut and what to say, what spells to use. But now—" She steadied herself with an effort. "This is what you do with this bark, to bring down fever. You'll soak it in hot water, the hotter the better, for a count of two or three hundred. But while the water's heating, make a diagram, like this, in the earth. Call on the power of—"

She stopped herself from saying *the sun* and asked instead, "Where does your power come from? What is its source?"

"The moon," said Puahale, and sounded a little surprised. "Like all women's power. The moon, and for some women, for the strong women, the sea."

"You're not going *out* in it?" Opal turned from the open door of the bedroom, through which she'd been staring, hypnotized, out at the weird, still gloom of the court. Though dinner was just over and it was the hour of siesta, the dust storm had swallowed the sun in impenetrable brown haze. Torches burned dully in the murk within the arcade around the house's central court, the flame struggling against the dust that hung, despite Red Silk's ward spells, heavy in the motionless air. Beyond the compound walls—and the edges of Red Silk's spells—the wind could be heard shrieking like the damned in torment. On her bed of folded blankets, Eleven Grasshoppers rocked back and forth with her arms wrapped around herself, gazing at the girls with wide, apprehensive eyes.

"Hssh. It'll be over an hour before daybreak tomorrow." Foxfire rolled her veils into a tight ball—and some spares, if she could induce Eleven Grasshoppers to keep them on—and tied them around the strap that bound two of the waterskins together. "I've been listening—I can sense the far edge. The winds will be worse in the early part of the night, but we'll be following the road then. They'll be less by the time we need to leave it. You know the city, Grasshoppers?" She turned and bent to lay a comforting hand on the old teyn's shoulder. "City?"

"City," agreed Eleven Grasshoppers.

"Foxfire, you can't trust her as a guide! Not through a dust storm!"

"City," asserted the old jenny more positively.

"See? She knows where I want to get."

"Oh, *please*! Grasshoppers, Hell?" She mimicked precisely Foxfire's nod and optimistic inflection.

Eleven Grasshoppers replied in the same tone, "Hell."

"She doesn't know what you're saying."

"She does, too. Grasshoppers." Foxfire walked the fingers of her right hand along the bed's edge, bound for her spread-out left one. She patted the left hand. "City. I want to go to the *city*."

"City," agreed Eleven Grasshoppers again, the pupils of her pale-blue eyes widened to black pits by the dimness.

Foxfire turned back to the carved chest at the bed's

foot, dug out the earth-colored peasant robes she'd worn for the expedition to Nebekht's Temple and the satchel containing the food she'd been stashing away, bit by bit, from every meal. "The sand will cover our tracks," she said. "With luck I'll be able to reach one of the others and tell them to get horses and riders to meet me at the edge of the hills, to get me into the city. Don't stop me, Opal."

She turned back to her friend, caught the girl's small, burn-scarred hands. "The stuff I'll give you should keep you so sick it'll be the day after tomorrow before Grandmother can even talk to you," she promised. When Opal gulped and nodded bravely, Foxfire added, "It won't be so bad. You'll be mostly dopey and half asleep. Just don't tell her *anything*. Not that she'll ask," she added. "I mean, out here, there's only one place I *could* be going."

"And one reason to go there tomorrow," whispered Opal. "Can't I go with you?"

"Sweetheart, I wish you could. But we have to travel really fast. And I think the tracks of two people and a teyn would be hard to hide. Besides," added Foxfire half jestingly, "I checked our horoscopes and tomorrow's a badluck day for Air Butterflies—you're Air, aren't you?"

"I'm Air," agreed Opal glumly. "And if your grandmother decides I let you go, it *will* be a bad-luck day for me."

"What could you have done?" argued Foxfire, and poured a little water from the skin into a gourd bowl stolen from the guards. From a twist of cloth hidden in the folds of her sash—she knew far better than to leave it anywhere in the room—she took several pinches of the powder she'd made up from the stems and roots harvested in the scraggly courtyard garden, dropped them in the water and laid her hands over the bowl. "My horoscope says—for Fire Butterflies"—she and Opal were almost exactly one year apart in age, but had completely different stellar aspects according to the complicated patterns of women's horoscopes—"that the sixth day of the moon's last quarter is well aspected for travel as long as I wear yellow. Can I borrow your yellow hair ribbons?"

"Is there anything you need?" Geb wrung out the sponge into the cloisonné bowl of herbed water, drew the sheet up over Oryn's chest. Useless gestures, and rather silly, thought Oryn. He could feel the ambient dust that fuzzed the air within the royal tent already sticking to his damp face, could see where it scummed the water in the bowl. "Anything I can do?"

Somewhere beyond the wall of wind and dust and flying sand is the moon, thought Oryn. *The dwindling crescent that no amount of magic, no amount of strength, no amount of money or intelligence or prayers to the gods will prevent from wasting away.*

Somewhere beyond the wall of wind and dust and flying sand Summerchild is dying.

Command of time and distance is what I need.

And there is nothing anyone can do, including myself.

But he smiled at his chamberlain, who in the sicklied lamplight looked as exhausted and grief-twisted as he guessed he appeared himself, and said gently, "No, Geb, thank you. I'm fine."

Geb blew out three of the lamp's four flames, and retreated

to his own little annex of the big royal tent. *To do what?* Oryn wondered as the tent flaps dropped behind the servant. To read the treatises on astrology and perfume distilling to which Oryn knew he was addicted, trapped as they all were in the suffocating oven heat? To plan what he would do when Barún, or Mohrvine, took over residence in the palace?

To lie awake in the choking gloom, ensnared by all the things that could not be done until the winds died down?

Soth was right, he knew. Neither Moth nor Pebble, nor probably Raeshaldis, could trap the Raven sister whose strength was such that she could command the teyn, could force her into an alliance.

Would his successor even recognize the degree of danger until it was too late?

Oryn folded his hands on his chest, stared at the sagging tent cloth above him, propped by a forest of extra poles and leaking sand at every seam.

The lion can be drugged, he thought—Soth had discreetly let him know that the matter had already been arranged—*and the path through the fire secretly soaked with water rather than with oil.* The scorpion traditionally sealed into the king's mock tomb beneath the House of Khon, the House of Death, was usually one of the enormous black kind whose sting was barely more uncomfortable than an ant bite.

But it wasn't the perils of the world, or the perils hidden within the circle of the fire's realm of home and pleasure, or even Death that he had to fear.

It was the baffling two-faced seesaw of yearning and powerlessness that drove even the wisest to folly. It was the madness that rises from the abysses of the mind, masquerading as inspiration. It was the silent endlessness of time.

And like the king entrapped with the fearsome-looking, harmless scorpion of Death, Oryn could only lie in the breathless heat, thinking of Summerchild, thinking of Bax riding through the storm. The commander wouldn't even reach the city much before nightfall, and the gods only knew what could happen between now and then. If Bax did not reach it while some vestige of light lingered in the flying dust he would almost certainly be doomed. As poor Zhenus had been doomed, dead now in the storm if he hadn't been before.

And when he himself returned to the Yellow City, Oryn wondered, would it be to find what he'd found in Three Wells?

He supposed he would even have to say that he'd welcome—or at least acquiesce to—being eaten by crocodiles if his people were still alive and safe to see it.

And maybe that's what it was to truly be a king.

FORTY-FOUR

Our people never had call to make these—these *tisanes* and *poultices* and *medicines* from plants." Tentatively following Shaldis's lead, Puahale spread the paste of aromatic *sima* leaves across the face of the oldest girl. The child stirred a little in her sleep and cried out, but the tall priestess laid a hand on her chest, and the girl did not wake. "The wizards, the wise men, would just lay hands on the sick, and the sickness passed away. This fever came on the people perhaps fifteen, perhaps twenty years ago, and none died because the magic of the wise men was strong. But their magic did not pass to us in the same fashion. Many have died from wounds that turned dirty, despite all our repeating of the spells the wise men taught us. We even tried to summon the Little People of the forests to our aid; they did not come."

She shook her head and looked across the sleeping girl at Shaldis. "Thank you that you came at last. And thank you that you stayed to show me this, though I know you're afraid for your family with the Dreamshadow glass in the house. Every night we have been dancing, to draw power from the moon, but it has been on the wane. Spells in the waning moon work differently."

She returned to the doorway, where the plants lay sorted in the power circles the two women had drawn. Sourcing power from the moon, following the marks Puahale had shown her, Shaldis could feel the strength of healing within the leaves, the bark, the roots, far stronger than she had ever felt it, when sourced from the sun or the earth. Fearful as she was, apprehensive as she was and fretting to return, she felt a wild surge of triumph at this new and steady power.

God of mages, she whispered within her mind, *don't let me forget all this when I wake. Don't let me forget the spells to source from the moon and the sea.*

"When I started dreaming about the plants," Puahale went on as she checked the stones in the fire to see if they were hot enough to boil the water, "I had everyone search for anything that looked or smelled like the things I saw in my dreams. There's a huge pile behind the healing house of things people brought that didn't look or smell like what I saw in my dreams. As you see, we were able to find only a few, though canoes went out even to the Far Island, which is a journey of a week without sight of land."

"A *week*?" Shaldis couldn't imagine water great enough that one could sail over it for a week.

Puahale nodded gravely. "Those who came here from the Old Islands brought many plants and flowers, as well as animals—chickens and pigs and dogs. But for them, the power in the hands of the wise men was all they needed for the healing of the sick.

"Those who came here first sailed for months. The Old Islands were that far away and there is nothing in between but the ocean. The canoes had to be very large, to carry enough water and food. Our families here did not make the journey back very often—once every few years, for twenty generations, and they would be gone for a third of a year.

"Then one night something happened to that land." She turned her face away and made a business of turning the rocks with wooden tongs, to hide the tears in her eyes.

"Did the Dreamshadow destroy the people there?" Shaldis remembered again the carnage in Three Wells, the howling man running through the crowded streets of the Yellow City with a knife.

Puahale shook her head so that her long straight hair rippled in the firelight. "No, nothing like that. The land itself was destroyed. My mother's great-great-grandfather was a wise man, when on the dreadful night the wise men here and on the other islands all woke in shock and terror, all at the same moment. They spoke first to one another, mind to mind across the distances between our islands— it is a day's sailing from here, from the Island of Rainbows, down to the Big Island, and two days to the Little Island and the Island of the Gods—and when they saw nothing amiss here, they all turned their minds together to the Old Islands. But there was nothing there. Only visions of the black sea steaming and covered with debris. They sent out a fleet to the place where the Old Islands were, and found nothing, only coconuts floating on the water, waterlogged almost to sinking, and some pieces of carved wood that had come from the temples and palaces. I think the gods must have gotten very angry with them, or else some terrible demon came out of the sea. My mother's great-great-grandfather said that the air stank of doom and terror and that his dreams were fearful in that place."

"Did they come back?" asked Shaldis softly when Puahale's silence had gone on for some time. "You said they needed extra-big boats even to get there."

"They tried to. They even made special boats, hoping they could thus carry enough. The wise ones here watched them in their dreams and their trances, night by night, and knew that even with all they took they were starving. I think when the great storm struck them, there were simply too few men strong enough to keep the big canoes into the wind. They swamped, and the mariners all died, my mother's great-great-grandfather with them. And since that time, there has only been the islands here."

"Like us," said Shaldis softly, "in our desert, with nowhere to go but the coast of the ocean that is all rock and barrenness."

Puahale lifted the stones from the fire, dropped them into the gourd. Steam hissed, and Shaldis showed her how much *sima* to crush to make the healing paste and how much fever bark to use. For a time they spoke only of healing and of spells to keep life in the failing flesh until medicines could take hold. Shaldis thought again of the sisters of her circle, pouring their power into Summerchild's frail body.

Of the scars on a little gray cat.

She could understand a nomad sister burning the ruins of Three Wells, lest the Dreamshadow still haunt them, brooding over the corpses as Puahale had told her it did. Could understand a nomad Raven sister summoning teyn to hold the king's forces at bay until all the glass in the town could be smashed, to make spells of aversion and traps to absorb the Dreamshadow and channel it back into the earth, traps that would have protected poor Riis and his men, she thought despairingly, had they camped in the ruins themselves and not at a careful distance away.

Strong with the strength it had drunk from the tombs, the Dreamshadow had come upon them in their sleep, as it had come upon Three Wells. Like poison rising from the ground. Like poison soaking into the adobe of the walls—adobe that was in truth only the earth that was the Dreamshadow's home.

She could almost understand a nomad Raven sister trying repeatedly to get her grandfather's glass dream trap away from him and burning the White Djinn Tavern lest traces of the Dreamshadow linger there and summon more of itself, in greater strength, though it wasn't really like the nomads to put themselves into danger for the sake of the town dwellers, who treated them with frequent scorn.

Would a nomad Raven sister linger in the town long enough to heal a dying cat?

She reached down and felt the face of the little boy nearest her. He seemed to be sleeping easier, and his skin was cooler. While they'd been working, she'd heard rain begin outside, from those floating masses of cloud. Heard it sweep through the jungle, then rush over the healing house's thick grass walls in effortless waves, filling all the universe with its sweetness before it trailed away over the ocean again.

Now birds were beginning to sing, a thousand voices waking and lifting to the coming dawn.

"I have to go," said Shaldis again, and looked back into the darkness of the healing house, where she thought she could glimpse the white shape of Pontifer Pig. "Puahale, listen. I thank you—I cannot thank you enough—for the help you've given me, the spells you've taught me. In my own land, it's not just the Dreamshadow that's a danger. The king—the man who can keep my people together long enough to ride out this change that the world has gone through—is in peril."

And in Puahale's mind she saw the image of a canoe captain who keeps his crew together with his own courage and wit and laughter, and keeps the vessel's nose turned into the oncoming deep-ocean waves. "Men seek to put him to a test, men who blame him for all the evil that has befallen since magic began to change."

"People fear change," agreed Puahale. "We had some trouble here, too, a few years ago, when some of the men wanted to kill the Little People after they realized they too had magic. What a king is I know not."

"He is my friend," said Shaldis, and Puahale nodded, as if there were no more to be explained. "The tests he faces are against poisonous insects and serpents, against poison that he must drink—we know not what kind it will be—and against"—*did they have crocodiles here?*—

"giant water lizards. We have no spells to defend against these."

"I'll tell you the words that will turn aside stinging insects. You have to change your spells, depending on where you yourself are in relation to the course of the moon. The spells work at a distance, as do the ones for snakes. There are snakes in the jungles of all the islands, and some very bad ones on the Big Island. The elders say they were there before the first of us came. Water lizards I know not."

She frowned, trying to picture them—maybe trying to pluck the image of them from Shaldis's mind, but by her expression, not succeeding.

"The Little People may know," she said at last. "Do you know the Little People? They live in the jungles and on the slopes of the mountains. We have often wondered how they came here, for they do not live in houses or build canoes or use tools of any sort, yet they were here before us. They don't even speak. Where they call their power from we don't know either, though they did not used to have power at all, before ten years ago. They have it now, though, and make ward marks and other magic signs on the trees and rocks. So it is as well that we always let them alone, even when they sneak down to steal our pigs and poi pots. Even before they had power, their skill was very great."

Shaldis stared at her, openmouthed at the image that came to her from the other woman's mind.

"You do not have Little People?" asked Puahale again. "They are covered with hair and have long arms that they use like legs sometimes and pale eyes with pupils like slits."

"We do," said Shaldis softly. Dawn light was trickling

into the sky, dyeing the ocean heliotrope and pink. The steady heartbeat of the surf boomed into the silence, and Shaldis felt almost dizzy as cascades of inferences dropped into place.

The teyn have magic.

The teyn knew about the Dream Eater. It was they who were trying to destroy it, to get it away from Grandfather. They tried to stop Ahure from his tomb robbing. Not a child Crafty, not a nomad—a teyn.

And very clearly and distantly, she recalled the mad wizard Aktis, who had murdered Raven sisters in an effort to absorb their power. When he'd kidnapped Foxfire and hidden her in the tombs of the Dead Hills, he'd also kidnapped and killed a jenny teyn. She, too, must have had power.

Then suddenly, like a desperate, far-off clamoring, she felt the tug and drain of magic, magic drawn from her through the Sigil of Sisterhood that bound her to Pomegranate, Moth, Pebble. They were calling on all the power they could muster, calling in frantic need, in danger of their lives.

Calling for help.

FORTY-FIVE

Pomegranate halted in her tracks, repelled and terrified, whispered, "Dear gods!"

"You feel it, too?"

And the next second, peering through the slashing dust at the high red wall, the shut gate, the old woman could not for the life of her lay a finger on what was so different, so frightening, about the house of Chirak Shaldeth. Windows shuttered behind their lattices, ward signs against mice and insects and Bad-Luck Shadow—just to be on the safe side—painted neatly around all doors. A house like other houses in the street.

Was it the emptiness of the street that gave her the impression of having wandered into a nightmare? The sickly brown darkness and the gusts that whirled her veils and her straggly hair into tangles around her?

She didn't think so, and glanced over at her companion. "What *is* it?" she asked. "Why does it feel like this?"

Yellow Hen shook her head, her dark eyes narrowed. "I don't know. But it's worse now than it was when I left for the palace."

It wasn't surprising, of course, that the house was closed up tight, and neither woman had ever entered the front door of a dwelling in their lives. The main gates were only closed, not latched; the wind was less in the main courtyard owing to the height of the walls. Nevertheless the stables and storerooms were closed up as well—with the drivers undoubtedly inside—and the court empty.

The gate through to the kitchen court was latched, but it had been years since latches had troubled Pomegranate. As the two women advanced down the narrow tiled passageway, the deadly stillness seemed to press more purposefully around them, the shrieking of the wind only emphasizing the silence that lay between its moans. It would help, she thought, if Pontifer were with her—she couldn't imagine where her pet had gone.

They stepped into the kitchen court.

Into clear sunlight and the sound of splashing water in a central fountain. Pomegranate froze, her hand shutting hard around Yellow Hen's wrist. The court seemed oddly angled, and there were gateways leading into courtyards beyond where she knew only the surrounding streets and houses lay. Three children she'd never seen before knelt on the fountain's tiled rim, dabbling their hands in the water.

In the next instant a woman burst from the shuttered doorway of the kitchen, fled across the court, her clothing in flames and her hair streaming. Something followed her, something that could have been a cloud of dense smoke or a billowing swarm of stinging insects, something that reached tendrils for her as she plunged past the pool, through the tiled archway that led into the front part of the house. Pomegranate and Yellow Hen raced after her, Pomegranate grimly trying to collect whatever spells of protection she knew, wondering if they'd work in this place.

"What the hell are you doing here?" Tulik stepped out of the archway, blocking them. Grabbed Yellow Hen's arm. "And who's that and what's she doing in this house?" The chilly brown gaze that Pomegranate had found so unpleasant in the child had not improved in the young man.

"What's *she* doing?" repeated Yellow Hen incredulously. "What are *you* doing? Didn't you see Six Flower just now? And can't you see—"

She turned wildly back toward the kitchen court, but

Pomegranate, looking back as well, knew what she'd see: the yellow mists of dust, the basinless stone wellhead boxed with makeshift boards, the kitchen archways closed with lattices hastily erected against the dust.

And no sign of the burning woman or her pursuer in the tiled passageway beyond Tulik.

But something moved in the shadows—maybe only an eddy of dust.

And Pomegranate wasn't sure, but she still thought there was one extra archway leading out of the kitchen court, one that hadn't been there the last time she was here—admittedly several years ago—and, if she remembered the layout of the neighborhood aright, *couldn't* be there.

Above the howling of the wind she could hear someone singing somewhere in the house.

"Are you part of the plot, too?" Tulik shook his aunt roughly by the arm. "That old faker Ahure was here this morning already. *He's* the one we have to thank for the teyn all running off, him or whoever's paying him to ruin us! He bribed Nettleflower—oh, yes, I know all about that! I should have known he wouldn't stop at just one!"

He bared his teeth, just the way his grandfather did, Pomegranate thought. He really was turning into the old man.

He looked like an old man, too, in the ghastly twilight of the storm. Hair dirty, face haggard. Had he been old enough to have it, his cheeks would have been stubbled: they were certainly days unwashed. He wore only a sheet wrapped around his waist and his eyes were the eyes of a man who has not slept in so long that sleep and waking merge.

"But I *will not* be pushed from command of this house," Tulik whispered. "Grandfather is well—he is only tired. I do exactly as he bids me and no one—*no one*—is taking over our affairs. Hamar! Dzek!" He raised his voice to a shout, and two of the camel drivers came running down the passageway behind him. Pomegranate saw their faces, slightly dazed or slightly drunk, beyond clear thought in any case. "Take Yellow Hen to the cellar and see that she stays there out of trouble. This one you can throw into the street."

The men moved to grab Yellow Hen's arms, but Pomegranate caught the skinny woman's elbow, wrenched her from Tulik's grip at the same moment Yellow Hen herself whipped and slashed her arm around to break her nephew's hold. The drivers lunged at them, but Pomegranate struck at them with her stick, called a spell of explosive light to burst in the air between them, but absolutely nothing happened.

Hand in hand, she and Yellow Hen turned and ran.

Tulik yelled, "Stop them! Make sure they're in no condition to make trouble for me again!"

They darted across the kitchen court and through the gate, but it wasn't until they reached the street that Pomegranate was able to call a howling blast of the dust-laden wind to surround their pursuers, to cloak her and Yellow Hen in curtains of dust so thick as to hide them from sight. They flattened, panting, into an alley some distance away, still holding hands to keep from losing each other in the dust and the wind.

"What do we do?" gasped Yellow Hen. "Where's that fat fool of a king when you need him? I have nieces and nephews in that house that I care about. Even that fool prig Tulik, for that matter. Where's Raeshaldis? She went off two nights ago after a teyn that Father claimed was trying to murder him, and hasn't been seen since—that blockheaded sweetheart of hers came the next day and took four camels and went after her."

"We've heard nothing," replied Pomegranate grimly, for she had tried twice in the past two days to contact Raeshaldis, but she had not looked into mirror or crystal to answer her call. "As for us, I think the first thing we'd better do is walk the alleys around the house and see if it's the only place that's affected, or if this—this evil, this sickness—goes beyond its walls."

She tucked her face veil in more firmly into the random knots of her head veil and hair. After many hours of working spells of healing, spells of life, to try to keep Summerchild from slipping away from the precarious borderlands where she now wandered, Pomegranate was deeply weary. Maybe only that lay behind her inability to make spells work within the walls of Chirak Shaldeth's house, she reflected. Neither Moth nor Pebble would be in better shape, she knew. And her instincts told her that whatever was in the house—whatever had drawn parts of it into the halfway world of dream, where the waking world's magic was altered—was strong.

She took a deep breath. "But whatever we find, I think someone needs to stand watch over the place until we can figure out what to do. And I think I'm going to need help."

※

"Of course my brother will be back." Barún's soldierly spine stiffened in indignation at the merest notion that his uncle might think otherwise. "He has great faith in the gods—as have I. There has been a great deal of foolish talk lately, but the simple fact is that they will not desert him."

For a time Mohrvine regarded his nephew across the rim of his wine cup, marveling for the thousandth time that his older brother's two sons should so absolutely divide the qualities of their father. Barún was nearly the double of Taras Greatsword, as Mohrvine recalled him in his fiery prime: arrogant, handsome, able to spear a gazelle at a distance of a dozen yards with a single throw and to fight all day, untiring. But he was stupid as a wooden peg. Greatsword's canny intelligence had all gone to his older child, that plump, curly-haired, self-indulgent painted harp strummer.

Oryn had inherited Greatsword's stubbornness, too, reflected Mohrvine irritably. Stubbornness that saw only a single answer to the perplexing questions facing the realm.

Not entirely of his conscious volition, Mohrvine's hand stole to the velvet purse at his belt, where his mother's folded message lay. *All things continue well here. The roses have bloomed, as I know you hoped they would.*

The roses have bloomed. He shut his eyes with a shiver of anticipation, relief, ecstasy.

They had found spells that would take him through the tests that ringed the kingship in a hedge of peril.

The tests that would slice Oryn to pieces.

"And if the gods choose otherwise?" asked Mohrvine softly. "Do you think that they will desert *him* and stand by *you*?"

Barún's eyes shifted toward the latticework wall that divided this lower chamber of his private pavilion into two. The lattice, as was common for such divisions, was curtained on the other side; Mohrvine could smell the drift of incense and perfume, and guessed that the Emerald Concubine—the woman he had given Barún a few months ago—was there.

Listening.

And silently, by her delicate scent, reminding the king's heir of her presence. Reminding him of the privileges of being king, if he lived to enjoy them.

Barún said, "That is a matter that I leave in the hands of the gods." He almost sounded as if he believed it.

"And if your brother dies the day after tomorrow," Mohrvine pressed, for he did not seriously believe Oryn would renege on the jubilee, "will you put yourself in the hands of the gods?"

Barún's big, sword-callused hand toyed with the delicate coconut candy on the inlaid platter between them. Beyond the tight-fitting screens of lattice and gauze, the late afternoon sky was dark with blowing dust, and lamps had been kindled in all the niches of the chamber. Intermittent flashes of lightning illuminated the gloom, and between them, the air prickled as if perpetually charged for the next explosion. Before leaving his house Mohrvine had ordered all the teyn put under guard. They often tried to run away during storms or wind.

"Surely," said Barún, "these ceremonies . . . these superstitions . . . surely the gods would not demand adherence to them in all circumstances. And I'm not certain that a precedent exists for two rites to be held so close together. . . ."

"You're right!" exclaimed Mohrvine, raising his eyebrows like a man suddenly enlightened. "I shall have my secretary inquire into it—Soral Brûl, who used to be a Sun Mage, is well acquainted with ancient lore. But surely a precedent can be found for a crowned king to delay the tests of consecration, if the need of the realm is desperate . . . as all must agree that it surely is. Even Lord Akarian cannot argue that."

Barún nodded, visibly relieved. He clearly hadn't the smallest suspicion, Mohrvine reflected contemptuously, that Lord Akarian most certainly *would* argue that, and would probably step in demanding to take the tests of kingship himself, when Barún backed out. Or would step in did not Mohrvine step neatly before him.

And if Akarian really wanted to make himself a meal for crocodiles, he was perfectly welcome to do so. It would be neater than having him assassinated, which Mohrvine knew he would be obliged to do at the earliest possible moment, despite the fact that he would then have to deal with an uprising in the Akarian heartlands around the Lake of the Moon.

With luck it wouldn't be a bad one.

Watching his nephew's face, Mohrvine could see that none of these contingencies troubled him. Barún had been presented with what looked like a solution. Faced with the spectacle of Oryn's death and his own ensuing peril, Barún, Mohrvine guessed, would accept any position—commander of the guards, for instance—that permitted him to go on fighting nomads upon occasion and bulling lovely women and willing youths.

What neither son of Greatsword seemed to have inherited was their father's ambition. And the gods be thanked for that. If only Oryn . . .

"My lord Barún?" A red-clothed guardsman bowed from the doorway. "A page has arrived from the Summer Pavilion. They beg that you come there as soon as may be." It was unheard-of, of course, even in these unveiled times, for women to directly initiate a visit with a man, though Mohrvine supposed that would be next.

Barún looked discontented. Mohrvine didn't doubt he'd planned to go straight into the Emerald Concubine's chamber next door. "Thank you, Cosk," Barún said. "Send the boy with my message that . I will come presently."

Which meant, Mohrvine knew, he'd go tomorrow if he didn't forget.

"Might I accompany you there, nephew?" he inquired, rising and gesturing toward the door. "I long to know how the lady fares."

Barún frowned, put out, but didn't object to being maneuvered.

Probably didn't notice he *was* being maneuvered, reflected Mohrvine, following the guardsman out to the anteroom of the green-tiled chamber and plucking the colorless military scarves from the arm of a waiting servant.

The roses have bloomed. His mother's code phrase sang like music in his mind. *The roses have bloomed.*

If he was to be king, he reflected, he would have to win as many of Oryn's Crafty ones over to his side as he could—after allowing the Summer Concubine to die, of course, which she clearly would soon. And that was not going to be easy, especially when it became obvious to the survivors that he'd hidden for himself the spells that would get a king through the consecration and had let Oryn perish.

FORTY-SIX

With heavy screens over the windows to block out wind and dust, the lower chamber of the Summer Pavilion had the appearance of a cave beneath the earth. The flames of a few lamps glimmered back from the designs worked in gold among the cobalt tiles; the gauze curtains billowed with strange restless animation, like ghosts in the darkness. The girl just rising from a Flower in the Wind salaam—the standard for the wives and daughters of shopkeepers when encountering customers—must be the one Foxfire (and Mohrvine's half-dozen palace spies) called Pebble: a contractor's daughter, Mohrvine recalled. Big-framed and fair—as far as he could tell from blue eyes and the slip of pale skin visible between her veils—with a sweet matter-of-factness in the way she stepped forward.

He was interested to observe that Moth, whom his daughter spoke of as being a spitfire, hung shyly in the background, overawed.

"Lord Prince," Pebble said. "Please forgive us for asking you to come, and I thank you, more than I can say, for coming so quickly. We've heard that there's danger in the city, an evil thing growing in a house in Sleeping Worms Street, a curse. Our partner Pomegranate is there, and she says she thinks there'll be trouble."

"What kind of trouble?" Barún's eyes narrowed with suspicion. He clearly, thought Mohrvine, didn't care to have policy dictated to him by a woman who dressed like a servant and salaamed like a shopkeeper's daughter.

"She doesn't know," said Pebble. "Nor even if it's something that can be dealt with materially."

"And what house? Who in the city is dealing in curses?"

"It's the house of Chirak Shaldeth," said Pebble. "His granddaughter told us that—"

"The girl Raeshaldis?" asked Barún sharply. "The one Shaldeth put out of his house? I shouldn't wonder she put a curse on him, but if she—or you—think I'm going to go against one of the most respectable merchants in the city on the say-so of a rebellious granddaughter—"

"It ain't her who put the curse," snapped Moth, stepping forward, her shyness in the presence of the king's family forgotten in her impatience. "Pomegranate is out there now—"

"That frightful old beggar woman?"

Moth made a clear effort to keep hold of her temper—causing Mohrvine a moment's amused speculation on the true purpose of veils in the hiding of women's exasperated expressions when dealing with men. "My lord," she said, "we don't know what's coming down—going on." She corrected her market slang to the vocabulary and accents she'd clearly been taught in some recent deportment class. "But there's evil growing, and we think we're going to need your help in dealing with it."

"My dear young lady, before I make any promises

about 'help' against the head of the largest merchant house in the city, I'm going to need more than speculations about 'something evil.' Now, I suggest you and your girlfriends find out what's actually going on, and then come to me. My time is not to be wasted in this way."

"Lady Moth." Mohrvine bowed to the two Raven sisters as Barún strode out into the windy gloom. Moth glanced sharply at him again, warned by Summerchild for six months past to expect treachery, no doubt. "Lady Pebble. What do you need? How may I help?"

To her credit—his informant in her master's household had been right when she'd said Moth was the most intelligent person there—the girl didn't react with the suspicion she was clearly feeling. She said, "Pomegranate needs help. One of us—maybe both of us, Pebble and me—needs to go out there, to watch over the place. But Summerchild . . ." Her dark eyes moved toward the screen that concealed the stair.

"No change?" he asked, and she shook her head.

"And no word from Lady Raeshaldis?"

"No. And we tried, just now we tried. We ain't heard nothing from her for three days now. I don't think she's dead—I think we'd know if she snuffed it. But if we can't go to Sleeping Worms Street ourselves, we need at least for there to be guards or something with Pomegranate. There's gonna be trouble, she says, and soon. When it gets dark, she thinks. You know the king would send out men on her say-so."

"I know he would," replied Mohrvine.

Moth hesitated, as if considering the man who stood before her, and how far he could be trusted. Then she asked, "What about your girl Foxfire? If you could send her here it would help, to at least go with me to Sleeping Worms Street or to stay here with Summerchild."

"Unfortunately that isn't possible," said Mohrvine smoothly. *The roses have bloomed,* whispered in triumph through his mind. But the next moment compassion touched him, the wary compassion of a sentimentalist who learned long ago never to give way: a kind of pity for Oryn, who had the love of a remarkable woman, as Mohrvine once had had.

And not too long ago Oryn and Summerchild had saved Foxfire's life. That, at least, was a debt he could repay. "What I will do is send for Cattail to come here and pay her for her time, whatever she asks. Will that do? There is nothing that I can do to save my nephew's life," he added, not quite truthfully. "But for good or for ill, he can at least go to the consecration without that added grief in his heart."

Moth said, "Thank you, yes. That will do. That's way good of you."

"If I pay Cattail enough," added Mohrvine, with a slight curl to his lip, "she'll even do exactly as she's told."

The concubine's eyes glinted. "She damn better."

"I'll make sure of it."

Shaldis wasn't much surprised to see Pontifer lying in the warm sand of the beach, a few feet above the tide line, watching her as she emerged from the healing house. The dawn air was moist and heavy, tepid rather than hot. Puahale gathered a cloak of bright-colored feathers elaborately knotted together about her shoulders; Shaldis was glad for her rough trousers and for the sleeves of her shirt. She hesitated in the doorway, then turned back to her new friend. "Do you see him?"

"The white pig?" Puahale seemed surprised at the question. "He is yours, is he not? He is beautiful. If I did not think he was precious to you, I would ask that you leave him here awhile, to father piglets that would be a marvel to all."

"It is he who brought me here," said Shaldis. "And I hope, he who shall take me back." She walked down the beach to where the pig lay and, kneeling in the sand, took from her belt the pouch containing her scrying crystal. How many times, through headache and exhaustion, had she felt the others calling her during her three days' pursuit of the teyn in the desert and last night as she'd worked healing magic over the herbs that had saved the children. She was asleep and dreaming, she knew, back in Jethan's arms in her little shelter in the desert, and she was not actually here.

Nevertheless, she cradled the crystal in her hands. "Pomegranate?" she whispered, calling to her mind her friend's wrinkled face. "Pomegranate, are you there?"

"Dear gods, girl, are you all right?" The beggar woman's image in the central facet was tiny, but beyond her Shaldis could see nothing but a whirling darkness. The dust storm must have enveloped the Yellow City. Pomegranate's face was veiled, but her voice was hoarse with strain. "Where are you?"

"I'm all right." Shaldis didn't want to go into where she was. "Pontifer's with me."

"Oh, thank the gods! Is he all right? The thing—the thing you said was in your grandfather's house—it's stronger. It's starting to devour people, I think. We can't get in, that brother of yours won't let us. Magic won't work the same way inside the walls, because it seems like the thing's making its own world the way the djinni used to. And it's starting not to work out in a couple of the alleyways behind the house as well. We're trying to hold it, Moth and Pebble and I—"

"Who's with Summerchild?" Panic twisted at Shaldis's heart. *Not this choice,* she prayed. *Not the choice of whether to let Summerchild die in the hope of having enough strength to defeat the Dreamshadow.*

"Cattail. Mohrvine's paying her. We're using all the spells of ward we can, but we can see it. It's a green mist that's coming over the walls and under the gates of the court."

"It's a thing called the Dreamshadow," said Shaldis swiftly. "It comes out of the earth; it lives on the dreams of the dead. If it takes hold of you it can be driven out by bleeding, by cutting the victim with an obsidian knife. There has to have been some kind of ward or spell against it, written on tombs as part of the funeral rite, because we've never had trouble with it before, like the lake monsters. Get someone to look it up, fast, but it can be trapped with spells into obsidian or glass if necessary. And listen, Pomegranate! The teyn—"

"Dear gods!" Pomegranate whirled, as if at some sound in the blackness all around her, and the image in the crystal died.

"Pomegranate!" She shook the crystal, as if that would somehow bring Pomegranate back. "Damn it! Pontifer, take me back."

"What is it?" Puahale came running down the beach as the pig got to his feet.

"My friends are in danger from the Dreamshadow. It's big there and it's strong."

"Then take these." The priestess took from around her neck the biggest of her obsidian amulets, and from her belt an obsidian knife. "Source your power from the moon and the sea. Trap the Dreamshadow with these words: *Lolo ano ti, ti, lolo walana.*" As she spoke the spells in her own tongue, Shaldis felt their meaning in her heart, in the marrow of her soul, where magic had its birth. *Black doors into black, black earth where you come from.*

"The words are from the Old Islands that are no more," Puahale said. "My sister, come back if you can. . . ."

Puahale had never heard of scrying, and there was no time to teach her. In the course of the night Shaldis had joined them together in the rite of the Sigil of Sisterhood—that they might call upon each other's magic, that they might know each other's hearts—but there was no guarantee it would work across who knew what kind of distance. This might, Shaldis thought frantically, be the last time she might speak to this tall heavy woman with the beautiful hair.

Would she even be able to carry things from dream to waking? she wondered desperately as she thrust the knife into her belt, strung the amulet around her neck. Would she remember the words?

From around her own throat she pulled the silver amulet Twinkle had given her, pressed it into Puahale's hand.

"I will. I promise."

They caught each other in a hard embrace, where the sea beat with a great crashing on the shore. Pontifer Pig was already trotting away down the shoreline toward the trees. Shaldis turned and ran after him, her mind racing ahead of her in despair. She would wake, and she would still be a day and a night from the Yellow City, and who knew what would happen in those hours?

"Jethan," she called as she ran. "Jethan, are you there?"

And awoke, in Jethan's arms, with her skin and lips cracked dry, her hair full of dust, and a strange amulet and a dagger of obsidian clutched in her left hand.

FORTY-SEVEN

The dark brought madness to the alleyways around Sleeping Worms Street.

Crafty ones might see in the dark, but blowing dust reduced visibility to a foot or less, and the wind masked the sounds of screams and cries. Pomegranate, bent over her broken fragment of looking glass in the shelter of the alley behind Chirak Shaldeth's house, didn't hear the men coming until they were upon her, shrieking shapes emerging from the storm's wildness armed with clubs, swords, chains. She rolled, dodged, scrambled behind the mountain of broken baskets at the back of the alley; and they hacked and waded through the matted straw after her, heedless of the cloaking spells she flung around herself. Either the influence of the Dreamshadow reached out this far, she guessed, or they saw something or some-one else in her place.

She slashed and struck with her staff, as she'd learned to on those rare occasions when a beggar more desperate than she had tried to rob or rape her. She jabbed with the pole's end and saw it do damage she knew a sane man could never have sustained, but these men were not sane.

Their eyes stared with madness, and the words they screamed were in no language she knew. When Pebble came rushing down the alley with a broken-off length of cartpole and rammed it like a dagger into one man's back, the man turned and fell, not upon Pebble, but upon his two companions. Pebble grabbed Pomegranate's wrist and dragged the old woman past the ensuing brawl to-ward the empty windy street.

Dreams, Shaldis had said.

The dreams that lingered in corpses' brains after their death.

Dreams of dying, of being killed.

Two of the men—they'd looked like respectable mer-chants and householders of the neighborhood—sank down, both eviscerated and still clawing at each other with their nails as Pomegranate looked back. The third man had collapsed into the pile of baskets, his body curl-ing in on itself and darkening as if burning up in some in-visible oven. When he opened his mouth, a little green mist flowed out.

It had started.

Above the storm's howling Pomegranate dimly heard shouting coming from somewhere close by and else-where, dimly, a snatch of singing, instantly lost in the wind. Even before the tug of Shaldis's mind on hers, she and the others had begun walking the perimeter of the area that felt wrong—evil and frightful for no reason they could ascertain—marking the walls with chalk. Now they pounded on the door nearest them, and a boy answered, ashen faced with confused terror. He whispered, "My mama . . ." and Pomegranate heard from the steep black stairway behind him a sustained and eerie wail.

"We're here to help your mama," said Pomegranate. "You run now to the Citadel of the Sun"—he looked to be eleven or twelve, old enough to find it with ease even in the tail end of the storm—"and take them a message." She held out her hand; Pebble slapped a note tablet into it and a hairpin for a stylus.

Pomegranate scrawled, *Dreamshadow eats dreams, burial wards, obsidian, glass, Sleeping Worms Street, spreading, need help NOW,* and shoved the tablet into the boy's hand. "Go. Now. Quickly." The boy pelted off into the darkness. Green light glowed at the top of the stairs, threads of mist moving downward. Pomegranate listened for other sounds within the house and heard nothing. The wailing had stopped. Dead already? Sleeping unaware? In need of rescue or past it?

Was anyone really there at all?

She stepped back into the street, slammed the door.

"If it takes one of us, cutting will let it out," she said.

"Is that with a spell or just cutting?" asked Moth at once, since none of the three knew how much time they might have to share this information. " 'Cause those guys back there was cutting each other plenty and didn't look like they was gettin' no saner."

"I don't know."

"Then it's probably better none of us gets took."

They backed from the door, their hair and veils tangling in the screaming wind. "Was that Shaldis?" whispered Pebble after a few moments, when nothing further happened.

Pomegranate recapitulated in as few sentences as possible her conversation: "She said Pontifer was with her, which I'm glad of. I worry about him. If anything should happen to me, who would be his friend then? I'm glad he's making new friends."

Pebble and Moth exchanged a look.

"She said the Dream Eater can be spelled into obsidian or glass," added Pomegranate, "but she didn't say how. Could we put a barrier of glass around the bad area, the way my granny used to put broken glass under the doorsill to keep the Bad-Luck Shadow away?"

"You think maybe this green stuff *is* the Bad-Luck Shadow?" Moth speculated doubtfully.

"If it is, we're in trouble," said Pebble, " 'cause I've heard about sixteen thousand spells to keep the Bad-Luck Shadow away and not one of them was anything like any of the others. And as far as I could see, none of them worked."

Moth patted Pebble's arm. "We figured out already we're in trouble."

A trickle of green mist began to creep through the lattice of the shut door. Pomegranate edged closer, scribbled with her fingertip on the wall nearby the strongest ward she knew, mingling with it the name of Dream Eater and the signs of earth. It flowed past this without the smallest check, the women backing away before it. "Where can we get glass?" whispered Pebble. "Even if that boy runs it'll be an hour or more before anyone comes."

"Grand Bazaar," said Moth. "It's two streets away,

way closer than the Glassmakers' Quarter. I think I can get through the locks. Pebble, you stay here—"

"No, both of you go," said Pomegranate. "Two of you can carry more, and one of us not being able to do anything here is just as good as two of us not being able to do anything."

The two young women disappeared into the whirling gloom; Pomegranate retreated down another alleyway, her heart pounding. Someone or something rushed down the street at the alley's far end. When the wind lulled, she heard the incoherent clamor of voices and a woman's scream.

And the night, she knew, was only beginning.

※

Raeshaldis. Raeshaldis, please . . .

Pomegranate? Shaldis slipped her crystal into her palm, angled its central facet to the thready light of the stars.

It was close to midnight. Dusty winds still breathed across the sand in a steady river, but visibility was up to several miles now and overhead the sky was clear. She didn't dare tell Jethan to stop the camels, wondered if she even possessed the strength to scry without sliding into sleep. Despite the profundity of her sleep, when she'd woken at Jethan's side, lying in the crook of his arm, she'd felt crushed by exhaustion, as if all her hours on the Island of Rainbows had been hours of waking.

She had moved away from him, as silently as she could, so that when he woke they would be at opposite sides of the crowded little tent. She told herself that it was out of kindliness, since she knew Jethan would be disturbed enough that he'd gone to sleep under the same undivided roof as a woman not of his family. He would be so horrified that he'd fallen asleep with her in his arms, he wouldn't know what to do or say.

But the truth was that she feared he would turn away from her, if he remembered that in his exhaustion he had held her so.

And that, she realized, she could not bear.

Her mind aching, she reached into the half trance of scrying, and the scratched, dirty face that appeared in the crystal was that of Foxfire.

"Oh, thank the gods," the girl gasped, and her words poured out like a spring mountain torrent after the rains. "I was afraid. . . . I tried to reach you last night. I didn't think I could ask for help any sooner because Grandmother has her spies in the king's palace. Shaldis, I've left, I've run away. I'm on my way into the city, but I need someone to come and meet me. They're after me, I know they're after me even though I can't see them. Grandmother's with them—she can track like a hunter and I can't use spells to hide from her."

"Where are you?"

"The Dead Hills. Father has a house in the Valley of the Hawk. That's where we've been, Grandmother and I. Shaldis, I can do it! I can work the spells to send the crocodiles away and the serpents, and to undo poison, any kind of poison, at a distance. We did it with teyn and yesterday morning we did it with some of the guards." Foxfire's voice caught on a sob, even as Shaldis's heart jolted, as if she'd swilled raw wine.

The king would be safe.

"Shaldis, I can't let her catch me! I don't know what she'd do if she caught me. The king's got to protect me."

"He'll protect you," promised Shaldis, almost light-headed with shock, relief, wild fear that even yet something could go wrong. "Are you alone?"

"I have a teyn with me, to carry water and food. She's really smart; she helped cover our tracks when she saw me trying to do it."

In other words, she was alone. Shaldis wondered if she'd left that poor maid of hers back at her father's house and what awful thing Red Silk would do to the girl in retaliation, but it meant that Foxfire would be that much more difficult for her grandmother to find.

They needed to get word to the king.

Fear flashed through her, and an instant later, despair. Pomegranate had cried, *Dear gods,* and her image had vanished. *We're trying to hold it,* she'd said, *Moth and Pebble and I.* Shaldis had waited an hour, then tried to reach each of the three in quick succession.

None had been able to reply.

And she had only to think about what Cattail would do with the information about Foxfire's defection to discard the idea with a shudder.

Which left who?

During the preceding weeks of weaving over and over again the spells of healing—and the preceding months of contemplating the upcoming Summoning of Rain—she had frequently been in despair at how few they were. Now their fewness became, not an inconvenience or a worrisome peril, but a crisis, like an injury in the deep desert, not fatal in itself but guaranteeing inevitable death.

Shaldis took a deep breath. For all she knew the other

three Raven sisters might be lost in the kind of coma that had engulfed Summerchild, and the deadly madness of the Dreamshadow might be spreading out from her grandfather's house to turn the whole district—the whole city—into the horror she'd seen at Three Wells. Even if they were still conscious, they would be fighting for their lives.

And whipping, twisting at those fears was the wild triumphal chorus. Foxfire had stumbled on the spells—or found within herself the necessary power to fuel her spells—to get the king through the ordeals of the jubilee. And she was willing to give her allegiance to the king.

No mention of Red Silk being able to do them. Presumably that grim old lady couldn't, if she was hunting her granddaughter like a gazelle through the hills. Unless she was simply so infuriated at the girl's defection from the family that she'd rather have a rebellious prisoner than an ally not completely under her control.

And Shaldis shivered, remembering the formidable old lady's anger. *Foxfire better run, and run fast.*

"Foxfire, listen," she said, trying to think through the buzzing exhaustion of days without sleep. "There's no one—none of us—at the palace. I don't think I can reach the other three—I've been trying for hours. I'm going to send Jethan to meet you; he's the only one with me." She glanced ahead of her at the strong square shoulders, the turbaned head bowed before the wind, outlined in the faint glimmer of starlight.

Did he know where the Valley of the Hawk was?

She certainly didn't.

"Can you get yourself close to where the road runs out of the hills onto the rangeland? Don't show yourself on the road but hole up where you can watch it. Jethan will show himself there—"

"I'll what?" He drew rein, let his camel fall back to keep pace beside hers. "Who are you talking to? What are you saying I'll do?"

He must know that for Shaldis to reply—especially as exhausted as she was—would cause her to lose the image in the crystal, possibly past recovery; or at least he should have known. Even her flash of anger at him was dangerous, like taking her eyes off a single goose in a flock if she hoped to find it again.

"Can you come?" Foxfire sounded desperately forlorn. Terrified, too, thought Shaldis, and well she should be.

We're trying to hold it, Pomegranate had said.

And the images of the bird-chewed bodies in the lanes of Three Wells, the tiny picture of far-off carnage in her crystal when she'd looked at the camp of the guards who'd been left there. Dear gods, had anyone gotten Foursie and Twinkle out of her grandfather's house? Had anyone gotten her mother away or Tjagan's children?

Her voice shook with the effort to keep it steady and cheerful. "I'll come if I can," she said. "I'll send others if I can, the moment I can—I probably won't reach the city till sunset tomorrow, and at sunrise after that, the king goes to his consecration."

If the city is still standing, she thought. *If anyone remains there alive to care.*

"And if the king fails," whispered Foxfire, "my father will be king. And then there will be no escape for me. Ever."

FORTY-EIGHT

"Don't be stupid," said Jethan when Shaldis told him what she wanted him to do.

"Don't *you* be stupid," retorted Shaldis, wondering why she'd ever cared enough about this stubborn man's feelings to take such pains about where he thought she'd slept. "The king's life depends on you getting Foxfire safe to the city."

"The king's life also depends on you getting safe to the city—"

"And you think I won't, without you standing guard over me?" If they'd both been standing on the ground she'd have turned and stalked away in a huff, but since they rode side by side on swaying camels her movements were limited.

He made no reply to that, but his upper lip seemed to lengthen as his mouth pressed into a line of disapproval. He saw his duty, she thought furiously, and he was going to do it come death and destruction.

"She's better than I am," said Shaldis softly, the admission like a fishhook in her flesh. Not that Foxfire was better, but that a girl younger than she had had that greater power given her.

Jethan said, "I don't believe that."

"Whether she has as much power as I do or not," said Shaldis, "she's the one who knows the spells that will save the king. I don't. You have to go to her, to keep her from falling into her grandmother's hands again. To keep her from falling into Mohrvine's hands. You have to."

He looked aside for a few moments, his face like stone in the ragged frame of his veils.

He knows I'm right, she thought, *and won't admit it. Doesn't think I can look after myself. How dare he, after I turned aside the winds, after I tracked the Crafty woman and her teyn for three days out into the desert? How dare he think I can't take care of myself?*

"Take care of yourself, then," he said, as if he'd heard her thoughts, and turned back to meet her indignant eyes. "I don't mean fight off wolves and bandits and lake monsters and tribes of ravening teyn. I know you can do all that, or could, if you weren't so tired you're falling out of the saddle. I mean rest when you need it. Sleep if you can. You push yourself too hard. Why do you think I—?"

He stopped himself mid-sentence, lips closing on whatever he was going to say. His face in dust and starlight had a remote harshness to it, as if, in weariness, he had passed somewhere beyond human emotion.

"If things are as bad as they seem to be in the city, you'll need your strength when you get there. I'll join you as soon as I can."

Without waiting for a reply he tapped his camel's shoulder with the stick and moved away from her, the beast and the remount lengthening their strides, like long-legged wading birds through the streaming dust along the ground.

Shaldis watched those dark, swaying shapes for a long while as they retreated through the starlight toward the distant hills.

She pushed on through the night, and on into the deathly silent stillness of the following day alone. Toward morning, with the last of the storm dying to whispers, she dropped into uncontrollable sleep, and only the camel saddle kept her from falling long enough for the jerk of sliding sideways to wake her. She stopped after that and slept for nearly two hours in a little camp ringed with whatever ward spells she still had energy to write. Waking, she summoned the image of her grandfather's house in Sleeping Worms Street and saw only a confusion of images: one of a house burning—but not her grandfather's house—and another of her grandfather's house with blood running from the windows and the door transformed into a mouth that grinned and spoke unknown words.

Attempts to view the familiar streets of the Bazaar District yielded tangled images of alleyways she had never seen in all her years, fading into the sight of familiar streets with men and women racing about in the duned dust of yesterday's storm or fighting one another bloodily in the doorways. The king's red-clothed soldiers were there, and the constables of the city guards: she thought she glimpsed Commander Bax striding among them in the square before the Grand Bazaar, shouting orders.

Neither Moth nor Pebble nor Pomegranate responded to her pleas to look into their scrying tools, not much to her surprise.

Though she knew it was idiotic to suppose that Jethan was more than a quarter of the way to the northern road leading into the Dead Hills, she summoned his image anyway and saw him riding fast and steadily through the broken brown emptiness under the glare of morning sun. Why this sight comforted her she didn't know, but it did. Over the six months she'd known him, she'd come to value that big, quiet man whom nothing could disconcert.

Maybe it was because, as he had said about animals, he acted rather than spoke.

She ate a little, drank some water, and rode on. When she stopped at noon, unwillingly recalling Jethan's instructions—only they'd sounded more like orders—the images she was able to summon were no less frightening and no less ambiguous. If what she saw in her crystal was true— and she reminded herself desperately that it might not be— fires and riot were spreading through the Bazaar District, with the brain-infected mad roving the streets, attacking whomever they met, and looters from the Slaughterhouse slums moving in to steal what they could. She saw the city guards fighting with men who, like the howling man who'd attacked her in Little Hyacinth Lane, seemed unaware of their hurts. Saw, too, city guards emerging from houses as mad as those who'd slept there in the previous haunted night.

I have to get back, she thought desperately. *I have to get back.*

She was only once able to look inside her own house, and the carnage she saw there she hoped was only the Dream Eater's illusion. Where her three Raven sisters were she did not know, but sometimes she saw ward signs new marked on house walls, signs that incorporated formulae that she recognized from her studies of ancient tombs (*they must have contacted Rachnis!*)—and in many places she saw where broken fragments of mirrors and glass had been wedged into window frames or doorsills.

Through the whole of the night and the morning, she had felt the draw of their energies on her, calling her magic through the Sigil of Sisterhood, to assist their own waning strength.

She did not think she would be able to sleep, but to her surprise she did, and dreamed of Foxfire, asleep in a shallow cave in some rocks, with a white-furred old jenny teyn sitting beside her, rocking in silence.

Riding through the Dead Hills in the stifling late afternoon, she saw smoke rising in the west, where the Yellow City lay. Coming out of the hills' shadow into the final fading of evening light she saw the red-gold flames licking up above the city wall. Shaldis cursed and whacked her camel with a quirt—encouragement that got her only a grumbling moan and an infinitesimal quickening of its stride.

Her hand closed around the obsidian amulet. *Puahale. Puahale, my sister, if you can raise even as much power as would fill an orchid's heart like dew, send it to me, send it to us. Send it to this amulet.*

Above the city walls, above the shrunken azure waters of the Lake of the Sun, the moon's thin crescent hung. As she rode toward the city Shaldis fixed her eyes on that great shape in the sky, conscious of its wasting as she'd been conscious of it for three days in the desert.

Power was more difficult to call from the waning moon, Puahale had said. But Puahale had taught her the words, the meditation to do so, and she called upon them now, as the Sun Mages had once called upon the sun's. She had no idea if she was doing it right, but a sense of comfort and strength filled her heart. She drank from the depleted waterskin, settled into the swaying of the camel, and remembered the pounding, steady pulse of the sea.

From that eternal pulse, too, she called power, as she'd once called power from the sun below the horizon, and felt strength flow into her veins.

Her scrying that afternoon had told her to avoid the Slaughterhouse District, so she swung lakeward and came to the city's southern gate beside the basin of the Fish-market canal. Only a short length of street separated the gate square from the greater square before the Grand Bazaar, and through the open gate she could see the flames, the running shapes of the red-clothed city guards. The shouting carried to her with the reek of smoke, of burning wood and flesh. She left the camels tied among the dusty poplars on the bank of the canal—Tulik would skin her if they got stolen but she was past caring—and ran through the gate, stumbling with weariness and cramp.

The Grand Bazaar was in flames. Its doors, usually locked at sunset, stood open; men and women—children, too—in the grubby rags of the Slaughterhouse District's disreputable denizens ran in and out, carrying away bolts of silk and handfuls of gold and silver chains. At least a dozen lay sprawled on the flagstones of the square, the arrows of the city guards in their backs and not a fragment of loot still in their lifeless hands. Their friends and neighbors had relieved them of it the minute the coast was clear, probably before they'd stopped twitching. Others ran in and out, too, screaming, wild-eyed—Shaldis's heart twisted in her chest as she recognized her own friends and neighbors, people she'd known in her childhood on Sleeping Worms Street or in the alleyways around it. Once she thought she saw Cook from her grandfather's house, but her face was so distorted—as if the bones were beginning to fall in—and so covered with soot, filth, and blood that it was hard to tell.

"Oh, no, you don't, boy!" A guard caught her arm as she tried to run into the smoke-clogged canyon of Sleeping Worms Street. "You get the hell— Miss?" It was Cosk, Jethan's friend from the palace barrack.

Shaldis realized she was still in boy's garb, filthy and sand covered from the desert. He'd probably taken her for a looter.

"I have to get in there. My family's in there."

"Nobody can get in there. They get lost, two feet in, even the ones who're from this district. They're looking for you, miss. Bax!" he yelled over his shoulder. "Commander!"

A guard came toward them, red clothing torn and face and hair black with filth. Only when he got close did Shaldis recognize the pale-blue eyes, the glints of white beneath the soot and grime of his hair, as belonging to the commander of the guards.

Knowing Bax, she expected his first words to be *Where the hell have you been?* But the commander only gripped her shoulder hard enough to break it. "Thank the gods. It's coming from your grandfather's house—nobody can get near there. This morning it seemed the other ladies had it in check—they had a perimeter up, spells and broken glass."

"I know." She looked around her for Pomegranate and the others. Since Bax's command post seemed to still be in the Bazaar Square, they had to be close by.

"Damndest thing I ever saw." Bax wiped some of the grime from his face, the soot reduced to mud by blood and sweat. "I thought the rioting would spread to the rest of the city, but it's only the thieves from the Slaughter-house District and those who're mad from this—this thing. Half the city's already flocking to the Sealed Temples. Just standing there, waiting. As if they expect the gods to come down and deal with *this* situation when they've finished with the king."

"Has Jethan come in?" demanded Shaldis, hoping against hope though she knew they couldn't reasonably reach the city before her. "Jethan and Foxfire?" The last time she'd scried for them had been hours ago and in her weariness it was taking her longer and longer to get an image. Even that little energy, she was increasingly aware, would be taken away from what she knew was a battle ahead.

"Foxfire?" The blue eyes slitted. "Mohrvine's girl? No."

They might have been pursued. They might have been forced to abandon the camels, to hide.

"Get as many men as you can spare out looking for them where the northern road comes in from the Dead Hills. They may be pursued—they'll be hiding."

"As many men as I can spare?" Bax flung out his arm in wild rage. "That'd be the one who's still back at the barracks with an infected toenail, and I've been thinking of sending for *him*. At sunset tonight the madmen started coming past the ladies' barricade, and that mist—that green light—started flowing in streets where it hadn't been before. What'll happen in this city before daylight—"

"Please!" Shaldis caught his sleeve as he started to

turn away. "Commander, please!" And lowering her voice, she whispered, "She can save the king."

He turned back. His voice was a murmur under the shouting as creatures burst out of the bazaar, blackened things that had once been human, crawling, shambling, even as they died scratching at the guards. "Mohrvine's daughter?"

Shaldis nodded.

"The witch?"

"The lady of power," said Shaldis. "Yes."

"*Cosk!*" Bax's voice rose to a bellow. "Get twenty men and get out to the north road!"

"Twenty?"

"Twenty, same as your fingers and toes. If I wanted to argue I'd have stayed with my wife. Camels and horses. You're looking for Jethan and a girl and you'd better be ready for trouble. Now go!"

Hands seized Shaldis from behind as Bax ran to join his men; it was Pomegranate. "You were right about the glass, child! But it got stronger, as it's been taking the living. It slipped out again. . . ."

"We found obsidian in the Citadel storerooms," panted Kylin, filthy and bloodied like everyone else, standing between Pomegranate, Hiero the Citadel cook, and old Yanrid the crystalmaster, the only one of the master mages young and spry enough to go running through the night carrying a couple of sackfuls of black volcanic glass. "It's expensive! It comes all the way from Tewash Oasis. Most of it's virgin—there aren't many spells that use it."

"I hope you separated out the stuff that had been used?" Though she was virtually certain that the residues of old spells on glass had failed along with everything else, the Dreamshadow might still have some unknown ability to use it. Better not to take chances. And when they nodded—and Pebble and Moth came running up, tattered and exhausted—she went on, "Glass will hold it—glass will absorb it, but not as strongly as obsidian. It can't escape from obsidian." She took the hands of Pomegranate and Moth, and Pebble closed the circle of four. The men who had been Sun Mages stood back, looking on, and for one instant in Yanrid's eyes Shaldis saw the bitter grief of regret.

"These are the spells that will drive the Dreamshadow into obsidian," she said softly. Closing her eyes, she whispered the words and formed up the rites of focus with her thoughts, recalling what Puahale had told her. "Source your power from the moon, from the moon's last night. And from this." She took the obsidian amulet from her neck and hung it around Pomegranate's.

The old woman's eyes met hers, startled and shocked. "Who is she?" she asked, and Shaldis knew Pomegranate felt the power that the priestess of the moon and the sea was sending to the enchanted fragment of black glass.

"Puahale is her name. She's one of us, one of our circle. Start at the perimeter, in a triangle around the infected area, and trap it as you work inward, into those pieces Kylin has. After this is all done we can use the old spells to bring the remains of the Dreamshadow out of the walls, bury all this in the desert surrounded by the old spells, worked with new magic, to seal it up forever."

"Triangle?" said Pomegranate. "And where are you going?"

Shaldis said, "Home."

FORTY-NINE

Cosk had been right when he'd said that even guards raised in Sleeping Worms Street were getting lost a yard from its mouth. Two of those who'd tried to get to the house of Shaldeth before her had carried balls of twine that they played out behind them, to guide them back should they become confused in the tangled illusions of dream alleys and dream courts that manifested themselves along the way. Bax gave her twine as well, taken from a looted shop. Shaldis found both previous balls of twine around the first turning of the street, one still clutched in the hands of the guard, hacked to death in a pool of blood.

She took the dead guard's knife and sword, to add to the short sword and the spear Bax had given her. The silence in Sleeping Worms Street was more frightening than the din in the square behind her. Smoke hung thick between the high stuccoed walls and poured from the latticed windows on the upper floors of the houses on either side. Dust curtained the air, hanging like salt in water, as if the Dreamshadow were able to draw it up from the dunes the storm had left against every wall. It mixed with the smoke and completely negated her ability to see in darkness.

Men and women—children, too—lay sprawled in those waist-high drifts of dust and sand, killed by those whose minds the Dreamshadow had filled with its ancient illusions of terror, violence, pain. She saw one dead man lying facedown, wearing a tunic she recognized as her uncle Tjagan's. Once a man in the red tunic of the city guard threw himself screaming out of an open house door at Shaldis, hacking at her with his sword. Shaldis held him off on the end of her spear, but he drove himself halfway up its shaft trying to get to her before he finally died. Sickened, trembling, she took several minutes to work the body off the spear shaft, and as she did she could see the flesh and bones blackening and shrinking as the mindless, elemental spirit that had infected it devoured the meat within the skin.

Yet others she'd seen had seemed completely whole, as Puahale had said. Looking down at the mummifying corpse, she wondered what made the difference.

When she looked up she found herself in completely unfamiliar streets, narrow alleyways branching in all directions, choked now not with dust but with vines and lush weeds whose smell came to her thick and green.

Whose dream had that been? she wondered. *Whose memory, sucked out of a decaying brain within some ancient tomb?* She shut her eyes and closed her hand around the obsidian knife Puahale had given her, pressing the sharp edge into her flesh, and summoned in her heart the beating of the sea.

She opened her eyes to darkness again, to dust and smoke and the familiar twists of Sleeping Worms Street. Green light glimmered in the windows of every house along the way. She paused to bury fragments of glass in the heaped sand along the walls, with the whispered incantation Puahale had taught her. At least, she hoped, she could keep the street behind her clear and safe for a retreat and with luck make sure the Dreamshadow wouldn't seep after her and take her from behind.

The door of her own house stood open, and stairs ascended to blackness. She could hear her father's voice singing in the dark.

Shaldis took a deep breath, touched the obsidian knife again, and took a firmer grip on the blood-sticky haft of the spear. The stair curved right as if ascending a tower; she could see nothing of its true course, the one she knew existed in real life. She closed her eyes, summoned up all the power she could call into her heart, to slowly return her perception to reality. The body of a woman in a servant's dress lay at the top, so withered and deformed that she couldn't make out who it was—Six Flower, maybe. Again she placed fragments of glass to guard the path behind her, hating to take the time—and even the small outlay of energy they cost—but knowing she must.

She called out, "Mama? Papa? Aunt Apricot?"

She listened. Listened deep into the house she knew so well.

The crackle of fire, the smell of smoke. The kitchen was burning, she thought, but the fire was old and most of the damage already done. Eerie sounds, sounds she knew were as illusory as the extra doors that kept appearing in the walls as she edged along the gallery over the first court; moans and cries and the sweet jingling of alien music. Green mist flowed suddenly from beneath one of the doors before her, her father's room.

Heartsick with dread, she backed a half-dozen paces, knelt, and laid a tiny flake of obsidian on the tiled gallery floor, traced around it the signs Puahale had shown her, signs Shaldis had learned with the quick trained memory from two long years of drilling with the Sun Mages. The mist curled away like a live thing, started to flow along the gallery away from her.

No you don't, you glowy bastard. I want to know where you are.

She repeated the spell, calling on the strength of the sea and the strength of the moon in the hours of its death. Strength went out of her like blood from a wound, and she put forth her will again. More green smoke flowed along the gallery floor, the luminescence of it bright enough now that she could have read by it.

As it glowed brighter she felt it pull against her, and she repeated the words of the spell: *"Lolo ano ti, ti, lolo walana."* Black doors into black, black earth where you come from.

She put her strength into the old formulae that she had written around the glistening little chunk of shiny black glass, the formulae that had been marked on the walls of every tomb, automatically, along with pious wishes for the safe passage of the dead: the Sigil of Earth, the Sigil of Binding, the nearly forgotten Sigil of the Eaters of Dreams.

Weakness filled her, as her power went into the obsidian, as if she were trying to lift a lead chest bolted to the floor. Then in its wake, like a whispered counterspell, despair. The grief of those who had lost everything, the grief of those who understood that all life ended, that all light would fail.

Lolo ano ti, *you filthy green nothingness. I don't care if I'm going to die one day.* Lolo walana, *and the sea will beat on the shores though none here has ever heard its sound. The power is there.*

Slowly, slowly, with a sensation as if coiled wire were being pulled out of the muscle of her heart, she saw the green mist flow into the obsidian, into the annealed essence of the heart of the earth. Flow in and be trapped.

It wasn't like fighting another wizard, not even like struggling against the power of a djinn. She felt the heaped-up dreams of good and evil people, the confused rages and sorrows of their dying hearts, and the petty malice and greed they might have all their lives suppressed; felt, behind those chaotic shrieks of pain and despair, the raw magic that wizards of the suppressed Black Cult had once distilled from the decaying brains of the dead. Glimmeringly, she felt the knowledge of those Black Cult wizards themselves, trapped and absorbed by the Dreamshadow, the Eater of Dreams, and turned against her. But if the Dreamshadow itself had any thought, any self, any awareness behind the glamour of those dreams, she could not feel it. Only the mindless malice of a carnivorous worm, like water polluted by a thousand poisons. She clung to the wall, feeling as if some enormous river of lightning were being sucked from the distant sea through her body and poured out at the dead green that glowed before her, forcing it into the volcanic glass: as if she were no more than a focus, a window through which flowed the power of the moon and the sea.

When the last of the green mist disappeared Shaldis barely had the strength to stagger forward and make the final signs to close the circle around the obsidian flake. Her hands were shaking and her face and hair soaked with sweat. Ordinary magic, she knew, the magic she had used before, sourced from the sun or the earth, would never have worked against the Dreamshadow's deepfounded power. So tired was she that she wondered how long this newer strength would last. She felt faint and knew that if she passed out she'd never wake up—and even if she did, Jethan would give her That Look and put on airs about what women weren't strong enough to do.

The mist within the house was caught within the obsidian, but she felt already that more were nearby. The same creature? An identical one? Did it make a difference? She didn't know, but knew she'd have to be quick.

She didn't have the strength to go through that again.

Her voice was a bare croak. "Papa?"

He had ceased singing. She pushed open the door of his room and saw him sitting on the edge of his bed in the dark. His eyes were open, but he gave no sign that he saw her. "Papa?"

When he still made neither move nor sound she drew the obsidian knife from her belt, pulled his shirt open and made slits in his chest and arms, and used her finger to draw the patterns in the blood. He hadn't begun to deform, to be consumed from within, at least. He gasped as the blood ran down, blinked and tried to focus his eyes on her in the threads of yellow firelight that leaked through the windows. "Old One?"

"Old One!" The cry from the door made her turn. Foursie and Twinkle came running in, stumbling over each other, their long hair hanging over the ragged shirts that were their only garments; faces, filthy and streaked with tears, turned up toward her.

They clutched her, sobbing, clinging. "Oldflower hid

us—Mama's gone crazy—Cook ran away scream-
ing. . . ." And more incoherent stammerings of a day and
a night of terror.

Their father turned his head, brows pulling down in
dazed pain. "Foursie?" He spoke as if his mouth were numb.

Shaldis took her sister's hands, wrapped them around
the twine that still trailed from her belt. "Foursie, Twinkle, this will lead you out of the house and away to safety.
Take Papa with you. Don't let go of his hands, and whatever you do, don't let go of the string. Everything around
you will try to make you but don't let go. All right? Can
you do that?"

Foursie caught back her sob and wiped her eyes. "Uh-
huh. If you can get in here, we can get back."

"Old One," whispered Twinkle desperately, "we're
hungry."

"They'll give you food and water when they get you
out of the square, sweetheart. That green mist, the green
light . . ."

"Oldflower said it was the Bad-Luck Shadow. It's all
over the house. She said don't let it touch us."

"Don't," said Shaldis. "It is the Bad-Luck Shadow.
Don't let it get near you. Where's Tulik? And Mama?
And Oldflower and the others?"

"Up in your attic," whispered Foursie. "Where you
used to hide from Grandpapa."

Shaldis got their father to his feet, pressed his cold,
thin hands into those of his younger daughters. "Go," she
said. "And hurry." There was no knowing how long the
wards she'd put on the glass down in the street would
hold, and she could already feel the presence of more
Dreamshadow elsewhere in the house.

In her grandfather's bedroom, she thought.

Flowing out of the iridescent glass dream-trap that had been in an ancient, unprotected tomb. Glass that had been spelled to hold dead men's dreams.

If she waited and sought the rest of her family in this madhouse, it would grow stronger yet.

She picked up her spear, walked through the dormitory of the maids and down the stairs to cross the kitchen court, for the gallery was burned and the court itself filled with smoldering debris. Beyond lay the silent, sand-filled ruin of her grandfather's garden.

A woman was singing. Her mother? Aunt Apricot? Shaldis hesitated, almost turning aside to look for her, but from the windows of her grandfather's room she saw the faint glow of green light beginning to strengthen.

She tried to call up the memory of the sea, the power of the moon. But the moon had long ago set, on the last day of its brief life, and Shaldis had not the training to locate it as she could the sun. Her body felt empty and cold, as if the very marrow of her bones had been scraped out. She leaned on the spear shaft for support. In the heart of her home, it seemed to her that this was as it had always been in her childhood: filled with smoke and sand, with dark and terror, and she stood there alone.

Gathering strength to confront her grandfather and the nameless thing that filled his mind.

Jethan, she thought, *you're right. I can do this alone— but I'd rather you were here at my back. Or by my side.*

Feeling a strange and enormous calm at the thought of his friendship, Shaldis climbed the stair and walked down the gallery to the old man's room.

Idiot, she thought as she walked. *Selfish, self-satisfied*

- idiot. The teyn knew it was deadly and tried to get it away from you. And you called me in, claiming your life needed protecting, when what you really wanted to protect was this thing that gave you the sweetest dreams, the sweetest illusions, that your mind had ever known.

Other people's dreams, the dreams of those who'd actually led lives that gave them joy. Who hadn't spent their precious days wresting money from others and then trying to keep everyone in their proper places so the money wouldn't wander away. Your life was so joyless you had nothing from which to build sweet dreams of your own.

Were the dreams so all consuming when Grandfather first got the glass ball from Noyad? Probably not. Their strength grew as he let them into his living brain, she thought, *night after night. And those dreams called the Dreamshadow from the tombs where it hid, drawing it into the city at last and bringing him dreams a thousand times sweeter still.*

She wondered if it was his realization of what he'd done to protect it—of strangling Nettleflower when he caught her conspiring to steal it—that had broken his last link with the pain of the waking world. *The men who had such dream-traps were ensnared by the dreams within them,* Puahale had said, *until they'd rather dream than do anything else.* Had that final shock of seeing what he was becoming driven him back to the solitude of his room and the comfort of other people's dreams?

And Tulik covered the whole thing up rather than have the other merchants take away from him the power that was so close to his hands.

She wanted to take them both and knock their heads together.

But she had to save their lives first.

If she could.

In the darkness there were a hundred doors along the gallery where her grandfather's room was, all the doors alike. Looking down over the rail into the garden, Shaldis could see, not the sand-drifted trees and the fountain in its covering of boards and straw mats, but a patterned marble floor lit by a thousand lamps, where couples made love on beds of silk and the scattered petals of roses. She could smell the drifts of sweetness and sandalwood and salt, could hear the jingling of the bells the women wore in their oiled hair.

Kneeling, she placed and spelled a few more pieces of glass, to protect her back.

There were still a hundred doors, but now only one of them looked like that of her grandfather's room.

She opened it.

She went in spearpoint first, which was fortunate. Something—a table? a small bookshelf?—crashed down onto the spear, wrenching it out of her hand, and sinewy hands groped for her throat.

Shaldis wrenched at them, kicking, as she was borne back onto the floor. Her knife was in her belt, but she could not draw steel on her grandfather. He had burned her books, beaten her, torn her mind daily with his invective and his blows, but she could never, ever hurt him. . . .

And he was trying to kill her. He pinned her down, seized her hair, trying with all the force of his arms to beat her head on the floor, screaming, "Thief! Whore! You won't get it! You won't get it!" She could only twist to get away, could only grab his arms as he bit her hands, drawing blood, and jabbed her with his knees. "It's mine! Mine!" The stink of him filled her nostrils, and somewhere she saw the glimmer of misty green light. "Thief!"

Shaldis's hand went for her knife hilt, but she knew wounding wouldn't stop him. He slammed her into the floor, his greater weight—a man's weight—bearing her down. "Thief!" His hands closed on her throat.

Then his grip broke; a black tangled form fell through the door beside them and struck her grandfather aside. Chirak Shaldeth went rolling, sprang to his feet, and fell on the newcomer with a shriek like the demons of ancient legend. Shaldis, wrenching away from the tangle of kicking feet and clawing hands, saw that the newcomer was Ahure. "Thief! Cheat! Liar!" the Blood Mage howled as he grabbed Chirak's hair, then tried to beat his brains out on the floor as moments before Chirak had tried to beat out those of his granddaughter. Blood streamed from a dozen cuts on Ahure's arms, breast, and scalp. *No wonder he's been able to resist its takeover for so long.*

Shaldis staggered to her feet, saw in an instant where the green light was glowing, flickering over the bed, over something lying in the pillows.

With the obsidian knife she drew cuts into both her arms and into the skin just below her collarbone; as the blood flowed down she dove for the bed. Both Chirak and Ahure flung themselves, shrieking, after her, but neither would let the other reach it, so they locked again, ripping and hammering at each other. Shaldis sprawled over the bed, caught up the ball of brownish glass that glowed with green light deep within, and dashed it with all her strength to the tile of the floor.

It shattered into a thousand pieces. Misty light flickered over it, swirling, as some formless creature sought to lick up the trapped dreams as the shattering of spell-wrought glass released them, and she slapped the obsidian knife blade down into the midst of it, screaming out the words, "*Lolo ano ti, ti, lolo walana.*"

Someone screamed in the darkness like a gutted horse. Hands seized her, sticky with gore, dragged her away from the shattered fragments of glass. But the mist had gone.

"What have you done?" Ahure shrieked at her, shaking her so that her head rolled on her shoulders and she thought her neck would snap. "What have you done, hag? Bitch! Whore! You've broken it! Broken it!"

And he collapsed suddenly, face buried in his mutilated hands, rocking on his knees and howling with grief.

Shaldis stumbled past him to her grandfather. One look told her he was dead. His neck was broken. Even as she watched, his body blackened with the mummifying infection of the Dreamshadow, desiccated like sun-dried leather. It crossed her mind that he might have been dead when he attacked her.

FIFTY

Shaldis found her mother in the attic, in the same sort of trance that had held her father. Tulik and their other brother, twelve-year-old Zelph, were both deeply asleep in Oldflower's little back room off the kitchen, with Tjagan's two children and Oldflower and Five Flower keeping watch.

Five Flower, good nomad girl that she was, had arranged broken glass and a dozen other chasers of Bad-Luck Shadow across the door.

Her mother and the two sleepers responded dimly to the bloodletting that had awakened her father. She led them back along the track of the twine, glimpsing down alleyways she'd never seen before courtyards that opened into scenes of carnage, of beauty, of strangeness. She felt the presence of the Dreamshadow still in the neighborhood, saw the green corpse glow at windows and the mist flowing out doors. But she felt, too, the power of the Raven sisters, the power of the Circle of the Moon, slowly driving the rotted semiconsciousness of it into the black glass traps.

The fires were out in the Grand Bazaar when she and what remained of her family reached the square. As they emerged from the mouth of Sleeping Worms Street, Soth ran up to her, still clothed for a desert journey and covered with dust. "Yanrid took your sisters and father to the Citadel, along with others who were removed from the infected area," the king's tutor said. "You only just missed the king. He came straight here the moment we came into the city, but Bax sent him on to the palace."

Shaldis realized with surprise that the night was far spent. The last thread of the moon was gone, and the air, outside the infected alleyways, was clear. It was only a few hours till dawn.

"The way your father was cut." The former Earth Wizard looked past her at the dazed Tulik and Zelph, then back to Shaldis's own gashes. "Who told you about that?

Pomegranate said the bloodletting breaks the hold of the Eater of Dreams. The night before last the king was taken by this thing, and someone knew to cut him and to trace spell marks on him with his own blood. I've made a copy of the marks, but we didn't know what they meant until your father came out with them. Are you well enough to come to the palace with me and try them on Summer-child? Cattail's done her best keeping her alive, but it's clear her last strength is failing."

"Get me a horse," said Shaldis, and checked her belt-pouch for a flake of obsidian large enough and sharp enough to use in place of Puahale's knife. "You put me in a chair and I'm going to fall asleep on the way, and you may not be able to wake me. Has Jethan come in yet? He went to help Foxfire. Cosk and about twenty riders went after them just after sunset."

"Bax told me." Soth took her hand as Kylin led up a cav-alry horse. "If they'd had to hide somewhere in the hills— Jethan and Foxfire, I mean—Cosk might not even have found them yet."

"Is there any way of stopping the jubilee ordeals until they get here?" Shaldis swung into the saddle, and to his great credit Soth didn't attempt to help her. Only mounted his own horse and rode beside her through streets still duned deep in dust. No one seemed to have made any at-tempt to sweep, though tracks crisscrossed the soft sand. Hundreds, thousands of foot trails, all flowing like a river toward the northern gate of the city, beyond which lay the Place of Kush, the Place of the Lion.

The place where the king would meet the first of the six ordeals.

"That isn't possible," said Soth quietly, and followed

Shaldis's gaze. "They're waiting all around the walls of the pit," he went on. "They've been waiting since sunset, in spite of the riot in the Bazaar District. Even when the flames there rose above the roofs of the city, more people went to gather around the lion pit. Waiting to see the king."

Cosk, thought Shaldis, *you'd better bring Jethan and Foxfire back fast.*

There was no time to scry. And she feared, moreover, for the loss of the energy the attempt to do so would cost her. She knew she would need everything she had left.

In the Golden Court before the palace gates, the sand had been swept up and disposed of. Passing through the gate into the gardens was almost like stepping into one of those illusions that she'd glimpsed around the dark turnings and flame-lit doorways while trying to get up Sleeping Worms Street: small lamps shed flakes of golden light on rosebushes still in bloom, and the air was heavy with the scent of jasmine and the waters of the lake, like the Island of Rainbows.

Walking along the paths to the Summer Pavilion, Shaldis missed the pounding of the surf.

No one stirred in the gardens save the king's cats, stalking crickets in the dark. Shaldis wondered if Pontifer Pig had returned to Pomegranate's side and if he was somehow helping her and the other sisters draw the Dreamshadow into their obsidian traps.

Her grandfather was dead. Her scalp still hurt, where he'd dragged her by the hair trying to kill her. The stab of her breath with every step she took told her pretty clearly that he'd cracked one of her ribs—not for the first time in her life.

She was too tired to feel anything about any of this.

Only that Summerchild was dying.

Puahale, she thought, and brought to mind the silver amulet that Twinkle had given her, the silver amulet she'd left with her new sister, *if you have any power left to lend me, lend it now.*

A few candles still burned in the lamp niches of Summerchild's pavilion. The chamber downstairs had been cleared of its screens and of the dust that had filtered through them; Lotus was waiting with dates, coffee, and balls of sweetened bean paste that Shaldis walked straight past to climb the stairs. In the upper chamber, the lake breezes drifted through the open archways, bringing the scent of the gardens. Only now and then, when they veered, the air was gritty with smoke.

Cattail rose from beside the bed, a startlingly different Cattail from the one Shaldis had visited a dozen nights ago in her vulgar new mansion in the Fishmarket. She was dressed in the plain clean linen frock of an ordinary Fishmarket housewife, and her gray-black hair was knotted into a businesslike bun. She held a sponge with which she'd been washing Summerchild's still face. The steamy scent of lavender water filled the blue-and-gold chamber.

Candlelight wavered over the maze of power lines chalked on the tiles around the bed. The scent of coffee lingered in the air, and of herbs.

"I'm glad you've come," said Cattail, all her boldness momentarily gone. "I've done everything I can, but she does not stir—she barely breathes. The king was here earlier"—his harp still stood near the garden door—"and I hoped . . ."

"We all hope." Shaldis came to the tall woman and embraced her. "Thank you. Thank you so much." She knelt at once beside the bed, drew out the sharp obsidian flake and the little papyrus roll of diagram that Soth had pressed into her hand.

They were obviously spell marks, though from what system Shaldis could not guess, nor what words were said with them, if any. Still, she set a ring of broken glass around the bed, drawing between the shards the signs Puahale had shown her and the formulae from the tombs. When that was done she drew back the sheets and made the cuts in Summerchild's fragile silky skin exactly as they appeared on the diagram—most of them corresponded precisely to what Puahale had showed her—and used the blood to draw the circles, the lines, the zigzags on the unconscious woman's hands and face and throat, as she had done on her father's.

Since she did not know the formulae of those spells, she used Puahale's, calling on the strength of the sea, the slow hammer of the surf on the faraway shore—and beyond that shore, the dimmer, stronger knowledge of the water that stretched away out of sight of land.

The waves that ran forever, as the desert around the valley ran, under the ever-altering eternity of the moon.

She sat back, holding Summerchild's hand, and let the power flow through her. She was far too exhausted for it to be more than a slow drift, and she knew that, too, would be gone soon. She didn't even know if the power was real or was merely the sweetness of her memories.

She heard Cattail come back into the room and smelled fresh coffee, though the big woman did not speak. For once, it appeared, Mohrvine had offered genuine help in paying for the former laundress's services. Later she heard Pomegranate's voice below, and those of

Moth and Pebble. From some great distance she saw, as if in a dream, a double circle of women dancing on the beach of the Island of Rainbows, the outer ring moving one way, the inner—with Puahale's tall head standing above the rest—moving in the other. The sun westering over a pink-dyed sea made a sharp golden square of the silver amulet on Puahale's neck.

In the garden she heard the first birds begin to waken and sing.

Summerchild's fingers tightened around hers.

"Shaldis?"

"I'm here." She opened her eyes. The whole eastern sky above the palace gardens was a wash of blazing gold. The shadows of a new day stretched lakeward. Every bird and bee in the world seemed to be awake.

Summerchild was looking up at her with the incurious eyes of the last extremities of weakness. "What happened?" she asked.

"What didn't?" Shaldis almost laughed, and held out her hand, into which Cattail instantly pressed a cup of milk, which smelled of the sweetness of honey, and a silver spoon. "Can you drink?"

She propped her friend a little—Summerchild couldn't have weighed more than an eleven-year-old girl—and put the spoon to her lips. Pebble was already vanishing through the door in quest of something stronger. Beside the stairway screen, Pomegranate and Moth hugged each other in a silent ecstasy of joy.

"The thing that drove mad the people in Three Wells seized you. You've been unconscious for twelve days. I'll tell you all about it later, but we thought we'd lost you."

"I dreamed about you. I dreamed such strange things.

Do we really have a new sister?" The milk and honey—
and the spells of strength Cattail had written on the cup
and spoon, which Shaldis felt through her hand—had
their effect. Summerchild's eyes focused a little more and
her fine-drawn brows pulled together in concern. "Darling, what happened?" She brought up a feeble hand to
touch Shaldis's face: grimy with soot, cracked with the
sun, fresh cuts clotted with blood, and her tangled hair
full of sand. She realized her bloodstained clothing
smelled like camel. "Are you all right?"

"Just tired. There was . . . much evil from the thing
that was in the village. But it's gone now. And I've
learned new things, many new things about our power."

Pebble approached with a cup of chicken broth. Summerchild murmured, "Thank you," as she took it, and
then, "Oh, you poor child!" to the big lank-haired girl.
Pebble, too, was filthy and soot grimed, her eyelids
smudged with dark exhaustion. Looking past her at
Pomegranate and Moth, Shaldis saw they were the same.
If their lives had depended on lighting a single candle by
means of magic, she guessed, between the four of them
they would all perish.

But by their calm faces—by their mere presence here—
she knew that the eater of dead men's dreams had been imprisoned.

And Summerchild was alive, and awake, and would live.

"Thank you," whispered Summerchild again, as
Shaldis laid her back into the pillows. "I feel so weak.
Twelve days, you said? My poor Oryn. Where is he?"

In the shocked, deathly silence that followed this,
Shaldis turned her eyes to the others. They, too, in their
exhaustion and their joy, had for the moment forgotten.

The sun stood high above the Citadel bluff, flooding the Yellow City with light. The king would have set out for the Sealed Temples with the first stains of the dawn light on this day of the new moon.

Stoutly, Moth said, "He be back before night, Summer. You rest now." And she grabbed the maid Lotus by the arm as Lotus came in with another honey posset and gave her a glare whose urgent demand for silence could not be mistaken.

The four Raven sisters and Cattail clustered together at the head of the stairs that descended from the upper room. "They've fixed the lion and the fire," breathed Cattail as they descended. "And Lord Mohrvine told me they got one of those big ugly harmless scorpions. The king'll be coming to the Temple of the Twins just about now."

"I been listening," said Moth. "It's all been silent, I haven't heard no crowd howling, like they would if—if something went wrong."

"Can you help us?" Shaldis looked straight into Cattail's eyes.

The older woman hesitated, then shook her head. "I've been trying for two weeks to come up with spells," she said, not adding—she didn't have to—any speculation about who might pay her for such efforts and how much.

"We may not need much extra power," said Shaldis, leading the way down the stairs into the soft gloom of the Summer Pavilion's lower chamber. "If Jethan . . ."

She stopped in her tracks.

Jethan stood in the center of the room. He had washed his face, but still wore the sand-worn tattered clothing he'd had on in the desert, torn now and stained with blood. He'd worked his veils into makeshift bandages, around his head and on his upper left arm, where an enemy's sword would be likeliest to nick. Bruises blackened his cheekbones and jaw.

His face was expressionless, his eyes desolate with grief, self-blame, defeat.

"I'm sorry, Shaldis."

She said the first thing that came to her. "Are you all right?"

A flash of anger passed across his eyes, and his gesture seemed to be an attempt to push his own pain aside. "They took her. Red Silk and her riders. I tried to follow but I was afoot, and they turned back to hunt me. Cosk and his riders got me away from them, but they—we— were outnumbered; to try to fight our way past would have been death, and to no purpose."

Looking into his eyes, Shaldis understood that had his friends not arrived—had his friends not been in danger— he would have gone on fighting, and died, rather than retreat.

"I'm sorry," he said again, his voice like the scrape of stone. "I did what I could."

He's lucky he wasn't killed, thought Shaldis, sick in her heart that she'd sent him to do a task that he couldn't hope to succeed at. "No, I'm sorry," she whispered, stepping up close to him under the glum gaze of two of Summerchild's eunuchs, who had all this time watched from a corner. "You did well even to get out of there alive, and better, to know when to come back here. We'll need you."

He glanced at the stair.

"Summerchild's alive," said Shaldis softly. "She's awake, she'll live. Will you come with us now to the Temple of the Twins?"

"And do what?" demanded Jethan, almost spitting the words. His eyes, cold with self-reproach, raked her, then passed to the others: haggard, shaky with fatigue, clearly far beyond even the smallest of magics, even had they known the spells to save the king.

"And stand by him," said Shaldis, "as his friends. Even if there is no hope."

Jethan was silent, the bitterness of his blue gaze terrifying. Then he sighed and took her hand. "Let's go, then," he said.

FIFTY-ONE

They got as close on horseback to the Temple of the Twins as they could—Shaldis, Jethan, Pomegranate, and Pebble, Moth having volunteered to remain behind with Summerchild. The crowd filled every street, alleyway, and square of the Flowermarket District, in whose boundary wall the small black Temple of the Twins was set like a bead in a ring. More people crowded the lower temple fence that extended beyond the city wall, as the wall of the Temple of Death extended beyond the southern wall on the opposite side of the city. Men stood on ladders and on one another's shoulders to look over into the enclosed and rather scummy lagoon from which a wide channel led out to the lake itself.

Under other circumstances any of the three Raven

sisters would have simply extended the minor spells of illusion to open a path for themselves through the crowd. None was capable of doing so now. Jethan pushed and thrust, Shaldis clinging to his belt with one hand and to Pomegranate's wrist with the other. They were halfway to the small, guarded door when a noise, like a sigh or a gasp or a stirring, ran through the crowd, a buzz of anticipation.

Damn it, Shaldis thought frantically, *damn it.*

What any of them could have done when they reached the inner enclosure, if they reached it, she hadn't the faintest idea. Only that they had to be there, they had to at least try, even though not a trace of power remained to them now.

The temple's small door was closed, but as Jethan and the three women came near, it opened. The black-veiled figure who regarded them enigmatically from the threshold was alone, but not another soul of the crowding multitude even attempted to push forward. People took liberties with the gods all the time, pilfered from their temples and falsified their tithes and took their names in vain, but they treated differently those who dwelled in the Sealed Temples.

The single, small, high-roofed chamber was empty and clean swept. As she and the others walked through, Shaldis glimpsed a niche curtained in black. The northern side of the chamber was open, pillared, and looked out onto the lagoon, down to which led shallow steps. The stink of dirty water and crocodiles was overwhelming. It was as if, Shaldis thought, the temple had been built only as an adjunct to the lagoon, existing solely for the consecration of kings and in disuse for centuries. Crocodiles must creep up the channel from the lake and bask on its steps and in its cool shelter all the time.

There was a space of about twenty-five feet between the lagoon's stone brim and the enclosure wall. It was jammed solid with watchers, but they stayed away from the steps.

Two priests stood on the steps, alone. Shaldis came to a halt still within the temple's shadows. She could see the king wading steadily, breast deep in the green water, across the pool to touch the far edge, which she knew he must do and come back.

The pool was full of crocodiles. It was a hot morning; they basked on the lower steps, floated in the murky verges of papyrus and reed that had rooted over the years all around the lagoon's sides. They swam, gliding in the green water with the heavy deadly sinuousness of water snakes. One of them came close enough to the king that the bow wave of its passing slopped over his shoulders; he had to step back a pace so that its scaled side wouldn't brush his face.

Shaldis's eyes scanned the crowd, frantically searching for a face she knew. She saw Yanrid, Rachnis, Hathmar clustered together with Hiero and Kylin. By the way the Sun Mages clung to one another's hands it was clear they were in terror and were not even attempting magic. Nearby them Geb, the king's fat little chamberlain, held his hands pressed over his mouth, weeping.

There was no sign of Foxfire. *Was it only chance?* Shaldis's mind screamed at her. *It can't be chance!*

It crossed her mind to wonder dizzily if in fact the Veiled Gods *did* express their preferences by a miracle.

She felt as if her heart ceased beating, for as long as it

took the king to touch the worn spot at the pool's far edge and to wade slowly back.

Two more crocodiles swam near him, as if investigating, then glided indifferently away.

He came up the steps, dripping filthy water from the thin white shirt he wore, then collapsed to his knees on the stone. Shaldis could see him shaking with shock; she thought he was going to be sick. Then Soth came forward out of the crowd, and from the other side the two black-veiled priests, to help him to his feet.

After a long moment he turned and held up his arms, showing himself unhurt, though his face was ashen as a dying man's and he looked about to faint.

They could probably hear the shouts and cries, thought Shaldis, on the Island of Rainbows.

Soth offered his arm again and the king shook it off. He walked by himself up the steps, through the bare little sanctuary—where he knelt for a moment before the curtained niche—and then to the simple door. He passed the Raven sisters without turning, too numb and shaken to see. Jethan whispered, "What happened?" And Shaldis could only shake her head. The cheering went through her skull like the stroke of an ax, and it was ten times worse when the king came out the little door and walked barefoot, dripping, as if in a trance down the narrow streets that led to the Temple of Shibathnes, the Serpent King, the lord of the dark within the mind.

The Temple of Shibathnes, in its obscure square near the great holy place of Rohar, was in the form of a black tower, sunk into the earth so that only its circular top protruded like a wellhead, and a stairway spiraled down into the rock. A gallery had been built around the top, so that spectators could watch the king descend; and again Shaldis reflected that the place seemed to have been constructed for this one occasion only, for the consecration of a king. The gallery was wood, and had been many times renewed over the centuries, but as Shaldis and Jethan—and hundreds of other people—crowded onto it, it swayed and creaked.

"I think the last time this thing was repaired was before the rains quit, six hundred years ago," muttered Jethan, clinging hard to Shaldis's arm. Nevertheless, Shaldis pushed forward toward the rail, and people continued to stream through the round temple's narrow door and onto the gallery behind her, until she thought the rickety platform must collapse.

If it did, it would be death for everyone. Below her, and visible through the gaping, crazy boards, was a sheer drop of a hundred feet to a stone floor. The stair spiraled down the sides, stone treads worn to a shallow runnel. At noon the sun must shine straight down the roofless well to the bottom, where a statue of some kind stood, presumably Shibathnes, though it was too foreshortened by height to tell. At this hour of the morning the stone deeps were cool.

From the cracks and hollows in every wall, snakes had crept out to bask. Magic of some kind must linger around the place, thought Shaldis, for she could see that most of them were adders or cobras: big spectacle-backed olive-colored king cobras and the vile little brown-black swamp snakes that would pursue men for miles through the mud pits. Her mind groped for the spells Puahale had taught her, to turn snakes aside, but she knew there was no power left within her, after the fight with the Dreamshadow and the saving of Summerchild's life.

Yet the crocodiles had been turned aside. As the king descended, clinging to the rock cracks of the wall to keep his balance on the crumbling stairs, Shaldis closed her eyes, sank her mind toward trance, listening.

Feeling for the taste, the touch of magic.

It was there. She felt it immediately, the same magic that had marked her grandfather's house and Ahure's.

The strange little spells that she'd thought must belong to a nomad Crafty or to a child.

It's a teyn.

She knew it, with a kind of dazed wonderment and a relief so intense her head ached. The magic was the same, that familiar sweet lightness that she'd felt on the walls of her grandfather's house, on the scars of Murder the cat. She opened her eyes to scan the crowd on the gallery again. Nearly a dozen teyn had slipped in with the crowd, scattered among them fairly evenly. All domestics, of the tamest sort that owners would send down to the wells for water or the marketplaces for corn, with notes of credit to the dealers.

All back against the wall, of course. No human was going to let a teyn take the rail-side place where the view was best.

There. A white-furred jenny in the usual ragged tunic given to house teyn. Why did she know her, or feel she knew her?

She'd dreamed of her. Dreamed of Foxfire sleeping in the desert.

She's really smart; she helped cover our tracks when she saw what I was trying to do.

Why in the name of all the gods would a teyn remain in captivity—especially in captivity with Red Silk!—when she had the power to escape?

The king reached the bottom of the stair. He'd nearly stepped on three cobras and an asp, sleeping on the steps; the stone floor of the pit was carpeted with them. He walked forward gingerly, placing his bare feet as delicately as a dancer. There was scarcely room for him to kneel before the image, but he did, his knee inches from a knot of coiled scaly rings—he put his arms around the statue's black base, rested his head against the Snake King's foot, the way teyn were taught to, at the feet of their masters.

He remained there a long time. Trying to gather up enough strength, Shaldis realized, to climb back out.

Praying Shibathnes only knew what.

The stairs were steep. He had to climb on his hands and knees. When he got past the last snake coiled on them the cheering started, and the deep hollow picked up the echoes like a mammoth didgeridoo, racketing the noise upward to the sky.

"I've heard that the priests of old used to let the candidate get through the first five ordeals, only to let him die on the sixth, if he displeased them," whispered Hathmar, coming up beside Shaldis as the crowds—swollen to every man, woman, and child in the city, it seemed—followed the king through the streets to the Fishmarket Gate and then out and across an old path through the fields, to where the black Temple of Time stood alone. The priests of the other gods of the city—BoSaa and Darutha and Rohar and the other daylight gods of everyday life—formed a ring around the king, with a ring of his guards outside of that. In any case it was considered the worst kind of ill luck to touch a king on his way to his consecration; and after what they'd seen that morning, evidently nobody in the city was willing to risk anything at this point. The feet of the crowd threshed through the deep dust still lying in the streets and between the field rows beyond the gates, and the whole city lay under a thick golden cloud of it as the sun climbed toward noon.

Looking back, Shaldis saw Mohrvine riding his black horse among the crowd, dressed with his usual careful simplicity, his face blank as a stone wall.

Ready to step forward and volunteer to take the tests of kingship, the moment a crocodile devoured his nephew or a cobra fastened its fangs into his ankle?

Walking along with her arm through Jethan's, Shaldis prayed Foxfire was all right. She wouldn't be killed or even physically harmed, Shaldis knew—she was far too valuable—and probably her maid Opal would survive as well. Red Silk was far too canny to commit an act that unpardonable. But she guessed that both girls were in for some hard times, and her heart ached for them.

Softly she said to Hathmar, "No. He'll survive." She could see more teyn attaching themselves to the crowd. She sensed more than a single source of that odd, unfamiliar power, but surely there couldn't be *that* many teyn Crafties? They shambled inconspicuously in its wake and wandered out to circle the black stone of the enclosure wall.

Like the Temple of Shibathnes, the Temple of Time was also a pit, but wide as the grounds of a great house. There was, in fact, no temple at all: simply the maze, whose twisting walls stood higher than the head of the tallest man and whose convoluted corridors opened into six small, identical chambers, open alike to the sky.

Each chamber held a stone altar, some eight feet long by two broad. On each altar stood a cup.

The king entered the maze at noon, with the sun standing straight overhead. The people around the edge looked down, but such was the height of the walls that Shaldis, pressed against the railing that surrounded the pit above, could tell there was no way for a man within to orient himself.

In times past, had five of those cups been charged with poison, the sixth with harmless wine? Or had all six held different poisons, so that no one could know what antidote to carry, nor could a mage keeping watch know exactly what spells of healing to place upon the king? The king had walked the maze before, twelve years ago, and had presumably been coached fairly recently by Hathmar in its windings. He made his way without faltering to the central chamber.

For a long time he knelt before the altar, as he had in the Temple of Shibathnes, his arms stretched across it and his head pressed to the stone.

"He's going to make it," Jethan whispered, and where her arm pressed his in the crowd Shaldis could feel him trembling. She herself could see the pattern of scabbed cuts on the king's arms and chest and thighs, exactly as Soth had reproduced them. *It was the teyn themselves,* she thought, *who came to him in the desert, when he'd been taken by the Dreamshadow.*

Not anyone controlling them. No nomad Raven sister at all.

They had saved him then, as they were saving him now.

After a long time he rose, drank the contents of the cup, and laid himself on the altar, his hands folded over his breast, the noon sun beating down on his face.

Waiting for the will of the gods.

Here kings had died. Shaldis could feel the echoes of those deaths whispering in the stone. She looked along the railing, all around that enormous sunken labyrinth, and glimpsed again, far back in the crowd, the white fur of Foxfire's jenny teyn. It occurred to her to wonder if Foxfire had *ever* had the power to turn aside the crocodiles or the snakes, had *ever* actually been able to make spells work that would evaporate a deadly poison out of a man's system.

Or had it *all* been Eleven Grasshoppers, who followed her so inconspicuously about her grandmother's house?

If nothing else, she reflected, she'd better communicate this theory to Mohrvine as soon as she could, before he got it into his head that he could pass through the ordeals and decided to assassinate the king and make the attempt.

A dark shape moved through the maze, the veiled Servant of Time. The black form stood beside the king's stone bed, stretched forth a thin hand to touch the king's head, throat, wrists. Shaldis saw the king move and take the shadow's hand to sit up, then to stand.

Shouting spread outward from the railing, across the fields to the Fishmarket Gate and from there into the city. Jethan swept Shaldis into his arms and kissed her. Hathmar flung his arms around Pomegranate, Geb embraced Pebble, and everyone was hugging everyone, shouting, whooping as the king was led from the maze. Lightheaded with relief, Shaldis thought, *Summerchild will hear it from her garden.*

Mohrvine, his face a rictus of congratulation, stepped forward at the maze's entrance to embrace his nephew.

Shaldis noticed that Bax stayed very close during that demonstration of affection, and kept between the two men thereafter.

Flowers pelted the king, garments were spread over the drifted sand. He saw the Sun Mages and the Raven sisters in the crowd, embraced them before he was torn away to the embraces, it seemed, of everyone in the city, before the priests and the guards closed in to conduct him back to the city gates, the city streets. A huge tiredness washed over Shaldis, and she stumbled, clinging to the unvarying strength of Jethan's arm as he led her among the crowd back toward the palace. Everyone was singing, voices blending into a black buzzing wave of noise; and Shaldis found herself thinking, *I'll have to see to Father when I get back, and Tulik and the others.* She staggered again, and Jethan lifted her in his arms.

He set her down in the Golden Court, before the palace gates. Beneath the crimson and gold archways of the Marvelous Tower a curtained chair had been set up. As the king approached the archway the curtains parted and Moth and Cattail helped Summerchild to stand, Summerchild frail as a single dried flower stalk and beautiful in her veils of pink silk, her soft escaping tendrils of mistfair hair.

Oryn stopped as if transfixed by a spear, staring at her, as if not believing what he saw. Then he ran forward and in the sight of all the people of the city caught her in his arms, a huge fat man in a dirty white shift holding the most perfect Pearl Woman in the city; the cheers would have deafened the gods. Then Oryn turned, and held Summerchild's hand up, wordlessly proclaiming to all the city that this was his woman, his wife, and his queen, though the loudest herald crying this news would have been drowned by the din. Turning, he cupped her face in his hands and kissed her, before seating her again in her chair and following it, on foot, through the gates.

FIFTY-TWO

Raeshaldis left word at the palace that she'd return in the morning to relay vital information to the king. More than anyone, he deserved rest. Everything else could wait.

"Are you all right?" she asked Jethan as the two of them stood pressed against the crimson-tiled tower gate by the crowd still milling in the Golden Court. She reached up, touched the bandage on his head, the bruises that blackened his left cheekbone and eye.

Gently he took her hand. "*You* ask *me* that?"

She'd forgotten what she must look like, covered with soot, blood, dust. *Father,* she thought. *Grandfather.*

And she had to push the thoughts away. Thoughts of her responsibilities now—her family would be up at the Citadel. She really ought to go to them.

The thought of doing one single thing more made her weep with sheer exhaustion, and Jethan put his grimy hand against her cheek. "Come," he said. "Let's get you to bed."

The crowd in the Golden Square seemed to be ready to make a day of it, despite the heat. Vendors were setting up

carts of sherbets and fruit, impromptu bands were forming, and a cheer went up as palace servants rolled three
huge wooden hogsheads of wine to the fountain in the
center of the square. More cheers went up: "To the king!"
"To the king and his lady!" And, amazingly, words that
hadn't been heard in the Yellow City for centuries: "To
the queen!"

Shaldis hoped Mohrvine was choking.

"He'll want to see you sooner than the morning,"
warned Hathmar, edging out of the mob with the other
Sun Mages around him. "The Red Pavilion is ready for
you as usual. Ladies . . ."

The fragile old Archmage turned to Pomegranate, Moth,
Pebble, and Cattail; all of them shook their heads. "Papa's
been so sweet about letting me stay in the palace all these
days and nights," said Pebble, "but the poor dear's been living on my sister's cooking. I really must go back and rescue him. It will be heaven," she added with a sigh, "to sleep
in my own bed."

"It'll be heaven to *sleep*," declared Moth. "And I don't
care in whose bed as long as nobody wakes me up. Just
get somebody to fetch me a litter and take me home."

"I'll give you a ride, honey," promised Cattail. "Mine's
a double, and it's on its way."

"I'll be back in the morning," said Pomegranate, stepping forward to give Shaldis a quick hug. "I had enough
people for now, and enough palaces, too. It was Foxfire,
wasn't it?" she added. "That saved the king? You thank
her for me. Thank her for us all. Let's go, Pontifer."

As she walked away, Shaldis almost thought she
caught a quick glimpse of a white pig, following the old
lady away through the crowd.

But when the others dispersed, Shaldis looked back up into Jethan's face and saw his blue eyes grave. "It wasn't Foxfire, was it?" he asked, and Shaldis shook her head.

"No."

He seemed to read in her short reply that no alternative candidate was forthcoming. One eyebrow rose. "Whoever it is," he said, "the king owes her his life."

Shaldis said softly, "Oh, yes. And that's what I need to talk to him about."

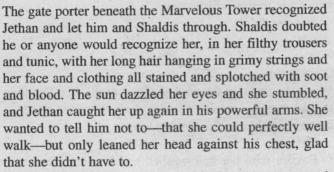

The gate porter beneath the Marvelous Tower recognized Jethan and let him and Shaldis through. Shaldis doubted he or anyone would recognize her, in her filthy trousers and tunic, with her long hair hanging in grimy strings and her face and clothing all stained and splotched with soot and blood. The sun dazzled her eyes and she stumbled, and Jethan caught her up again in his powerful arms. She wanted to tell him not to—that she could perfectly well walk—but only leaned her head against his chest, glad that she didn't have to.

The Red Pavilion, in its jungles of jasmine, was cool even in the heat of noon, the door a haven of shadow and solitude as Jethan set her down. "Will you be all right?"

She nodded, and he turned to go.

"Jethan . . ."

Blue eyes enigmatic in a face as sunburned and blistered as her own. Black hair escaping from the pushed-back snaggle of turban and veils. Waiting.

"Thank you. Thank you so much." She stepped out of the shadow to where he stood in the dappled green shade. "For going to fetch Foxfire—for coming after me in the desert. You always look like you're thinking I'm such a hoyden and not what your family would approve of; and every time I turn around, you're there like an oak tree to lean on. Not like Papa. Not like Grandfather . . ."

I must be tired, she thought confusedly, *to be saying all this. . . .*

He said, "Raeshaldis, don't you understand?"

She could only look up at him, shaking her head.

He stepped forward, pulled her into his arms, and kissed her with a hungry and tender violence so utterly at odds with everything she'd known of him that her first instinct was to thrust him away.

But she didn't.

When she woke in the cool shadows of the Red Pavilion the sky outside was just growing dark. Someone was trying to reach her on the scrying stone.

Foxfire.

Foxfire with her hair washed and her face clean and prettily painted, but not so prettily as to cover savage claw rakes on one cheekbone and a bruise on her chin. "What happened?" the girl asked at once. "Father was here, just *furious.* The king is all right? Shaldis, I've lost the power! I've lost the power to make the spells work, the spells against crocodiles and serpents, though my other magic seems all right. The guard barely got away from the crocodiles and the other one's in the infirmary now with snakebite. And Father's blaming Grandmother! They had a shouting match you could have heard clear back in the Valley of the Hawk."

Shaldis rolled up onto her elbows among the cushions of the bed. She could already see behind the younger girl that she was in some more luxurious chamber, probably down at Mohrvine's lakeside compound at Golden Sky.

"What happened? Did you— Did one of the others—?"

"The king got through the tests all right," said Shaldis. She tried to unclaw some of the tangles of her hair and gave it up, and ran a hand over her aching head. "I can't tell you yet—it may be something that's kept secret for some time, but I think your father will tell you."

If, she reflected, Oryn chose to pass the secret along to Mohrvine. She couldn't imagine, with Red Silk investigating, that it could be kept long. "Are you all right?"

Foxfire nodded. "Thank you, thank you for sending Jethan. That's why Grandmother beat me, for keeping her and the guards from killing him when he tried to get me away. And I didn't dare do more, because of Opal. Grandmother said she'd kill Opal, but we're both here all right, because Father was so angry at Grandmother for hitting me, they aren't even speaking. Thank you so much for trying to help."

"Do you still want to be helped?"

Foxfire closed her eyes, as if turning in her mind the love she bore her father and her position as the second princess of the realm. The security of knowing that she had her father's heart, now that the crisis was past. Then a tear crept down her cheek, and she whispered, "Everything's fine now, but there will be a next time. I don't know what it will be about, but I know Papa. There'll be something. Yes. I want to get out of here."

"Then we'll work on that." Shaldis sat up, drew the sheet around her. "In the meantime, what happened to the old jenny who was carrying your things when you ran away? Did she escape?"

Foxfire nodded. "The minute Soral Brûl and his riders showed up. We ran in different directions. I hope she'll be all right. Grasshoppers is a household teyn; she's never been in the wild. I've tried looking for her in my mirror already and I can't see her. Is that because she's with you? Or because I don't know her real name? Do teyn have real names among themselves? That they call each other, I mean?"

"I think they do," said Shaldis. "I'll find her and make sure she's all right."

She folded her hands around the crystal, and let the image die. *Some of the men wanted to kill the Little People,* Puahale had said, *when they realized they too had magic.*

Would they here?

Faced with creatures who were everywhere, who were not human, whose thoughts could be neither predicted nor manipulated? Some men, certainly, would try to get control of them, as they did women.

Was that why they'd kept silent about their power all these years?

For a very long time she sat, gazing out at the last daylight fading above the gold-stained waters of the lake.

The light was gone from the sky and she was sitting in the dark when Jethan scratched softly at the archway that led to the stairs. "Are you awake?" he asked. "The king wants to see you." He was clean and smelled of soap, and was dressed in the crimson tunic, the golden armor of the palace guard. Under one arm he carried his plumed helmet; over the other, the clean white robe of a citadel novice, which he crossed the room to lay on the low table beside the bed. He looked as collected and businesslike as ever.

Only, when he passed her, and she put out her hand to touch his arm, he bent and very gently brushed her lips with his.

She thought then, *It wasn't a dream.*

And a long shiver went through her, as she saw the new road that opened before her feet. Change she had not expected, something else—within herself, this time—that could be neither predicted nor manipulated. Her feelings terrified her, made her want to flee. To go back to a time when, no matter how harsh her life had been, her heart had been undisturbed.

No wonder people wanted to kill that which they did not understand. Shaldis had a quick scrub with water that silent-footed servants brought to the red-tiled bath chamber, changed into the white robe, and braided up her hair. Jethan walked with her to the Peacock Pavilion—the king's official favorite residence—where all the lamps were kindled, blazing like a giant lamp itself in the twilight. As they approached it, Jethan's stride checked. He looked around sharply and in the same instant Shaldis smelled it, too: the musky pong of teyn and, almost worn away by sand and the passage of days, the wry echo of indigo.

For a moment she saw them, crouched in a great tangle of sand-choked jasmine that the wind had torn down from its arbor—three jenny teyn. Two were domestics, one of them white with age and the other big with child. To her astonishment she recognized Five Cakes from her grandfather's household, the faded rags of her tunic still stained with indigo dye. The third was a wilding, small and black and very young. The younger two were watching the Peacock Pavilion and the paths leading to it, but the blue eyes of the old one—it had to be Eleven Grasshoppers—met Shaldis's.

Those are my sisters, thought Shaldis. *Members of the circle like myself.* But before she could speak, the three watchers faded away into the shadows of the tangled vines.

Shaldis had half expected to see the other Raven sisters at the king's pavilion, and the Sun Mages as well. But the only ones in its latticed lower chamber were the king, Summerchild, and Soth the librarian. Shaldis paused a yard from the threshold, glanced up at Jethan, aware that he had no place in the conference but torn by the unaccustomed sensation of not wanting to send him away.

He didn't smile, but his hand was warm, for an instant, on her back, and he said, "I'll be near."

The king got to his feet as she came through the door. He'd clearly spent part of the afternoon in the baths and looked much more himself. To Shaldis's utter shock, he knelt before her and took her hands to kiss.

She drew them back, as confused by this as she had been by her sudden fear of hurting Jethan's feelings. "Wrong hands, Your Majesty," she said.

The king looked up at her: hair newly curled, earrings and necklaces that matched his rings, like a giant blossom of color and perfume, with the eyes of a man who's waded into a pool of crocodiles without the hope that any magic was there to protect him.

The eyes of a man who's put himself completely in the hands of the gods.

"Oh, please don't tell me that, my dear child," he said,

rising rather stiffly and bending to kiss her hand anyway. "In spite of everything you'd told me, when I came up out of the pool and saw you I dared to hope that somehow you'd put together some kind of spell. It was the only thing that got me through the serpents and the maze. Don't tell me the gods really care that much who's king?"

"They care," said Shaldis softly. "But they send messengers dressed in clothing we don't expect. You're not going to like this, Your Majesty—you're not going to like what it's going to mean for the realm. You were saved by the teyn."

King Oryn looked at her blankly, for a moment literally not understanding. "But the teyn don't . . ." he began. And then, his eyes changing, "Are you sure?"

Shaldis nodded.

He drew in his breath, let it out, and said, "Oh, dear."

And in his silence Shaldis saw every slave compound and field gang that kept the mines, the farms, the economy of the realm running. Saw the digging gangs of the aqueduct and the sweepers of every courtyard in the city. "Dear gods," sighed the king at last, "and I thought we'd had trouble with women coming to power."

From the divan where she lay, Summerchild said, "Tell us about it, darling. How did you learn this? And when did this power come to them? When it came to us? To the women? Is it only the jennies or the males as well?"

"I think only the jennies, and I don't know how many of them. I should have suspected last spring, when the mad wizard Aktis was killing Raven sisters to raise power. He killed a jenny teyn, you remember. But—"

Summerchild's head turned. At the same instant Shaldis smelled the unmistakable animal scent of teyn and, turning herself, saw framed in the archway the three jennies she'd glimpsed in the garden: Eleven Grasshoppers, Five Cakes, and the little black wilding. They waited, silently, between the darkness and the lamplight, their slit-pupiled blue eyes reflecting the glow like beasts'.

Then the king crossed the room to them and knelt, as he had knelt to Raeshaldis, and kissed Eleven Grasshoppers's hands.

The little jenny looked down at him solemnly, put her knotted hands around his face, and brushed his forehead with her nose and lips.

The wilding jenny made a clicking sound with her lips. From the scented garden bed a snake crawled, a little brown fruit asp, one of the deadliest. The king got hastily to his feet and stepped back, and Shaldis could have sworn Eleven Grasshoppers almost smiled. But the old teyn only made a small movement with her finger, and the asp coiled itself into a neat circle and hid its head.

Then Eleven Grasshoppers met the king's eyes again, as if saying, *You see?*

He replied, "Yes. I see. And I thank you, more than words can ever say. And I apologize, for my people, from the bottom of my heart."

There was silence, in which Shaldis heard the scrunch of boot leather on gravel and then Jethan's voice. "You can't—"

"Oh, get away from me, boy. I have every right to learn who saved my nephew's skin and what he plans to do with the power it's brought him."

Steel hissed as Jethan drew his sword. The king's eyes went to those of Eleven Grasshoppers. The old teyn nodded, obviously without the slightest qualm about meeting her master, and as Oryn called out, "Let him pass, Jethan," she plucked a lamp from the nearest niche and blew out its flame. *So much for the old tale that teyn are afraid of fire,* thought Shaldis. As Mohrvine stepped through the door, Eleven Grasshoppers set the lamp on the floor close to the asp. She looked at the king, then looked at the lamp.

Flame rekindled on the wick.

Summerchild said, "You will have to free them. All of them."

The king said, "I know."

Transfixed, Mohrvine whispered, "Dear gods."

The teyn regarded him in silence. Shaldis found herself wondering what kind of information they passed among themselves—and by what means—about the lords who for over a thousand years had enslaved them in the Valley of the Lakes. They had quite clearly known who to save and when.

The king made no reply.

Mohrvine's voice was hoarse. "You *dare* not!"

The king held out his hand in silence. Eleven Grasshoppers picked up the asp and placed it in his palm. The little snake, whose bite killed in minutes, wrapped its brown tail around the plump bejeweled wrist and laid its head, tongue flicking contentedly, on the king's hand.

"I dare not not dare," replied Oryn softly. He moved to hand the snake to his uncle—Mohrvine backed quickly away.

"I came to ask you, Nephew—now that you are favored by the gods—what you plan to do about the increasing escapes of the teyn. And I must say I was ready for almost anything—except this." And he gestured at the teyn in shocked disgust. "And I can promise you that magic or not—and they do seem to have power of a sort—if you attempt to free them, if you so much as *touch* the property of myself or any of your landchiefs, no matter what opinions about you the gods expressed this morning, the carnage that swept through the Bazaar District last night will be *nothing* to the rioting that will break out."

Mohrvine turned in a great swirl of white cloak, as if to make an exit, but the king's voice stopped him. "That is why I need your help, Uncle. Your help, your example, and your wisdom."

Mohrvine looked back at him, no expression in his turquoise eyes.

"I have seen and fought the teyn in the desert, Uncle, and they fought like a trained army. We have no idea how they communicate or what they know. And if, after today, you think we can keep the teyn enslaved in spite of the debt that I personally owe them—and in spite of what they now must all know about their own power—all I have to say is that the attempt had better work the first time and keep on working infallibly. For if we now attempt to keep them as they have been, we will not have a second chance to win their trust or their aid."

Still Mohrvine said nothing, but faced his nephew— faced the beautiful Summerchild and the watching teyn enigmatic as animals—in the angry silence of a man who has no reply.

"We thought last spring that the world had changed," the king went on. "We did not know how right we were. The power that protected us is gone. Threats that it had kept at bay for so long we've forgotten their existence are now free to rove the earth, of which the lake monsters, bless their simple hearts, and the Eater of Dreams may have been only the first. We cannot now afford to think that anything is constituted the way it once was."

"I perish with anticipation," said Mohrvine through gritted teeth, "to learn what other changes have taken place that we do not yet know about."

"Don't fight me, Uncle," said Oryn softly. "I'm begging you. I need your help."

Mohrvine said nothing, but swept back his cloak and executed a profound bow to the three teyn standing silent in the garden arch. Then he turned and stalked from the room.

FIFTY-THREE

I t has all changed." Raeshaldis perched on the top of the knee-high wall of black stone that circled the little group of healing houses and looked out over the beach to the sea. It had rained just before sunset, and in the final fading of the twilight, the jungle gave back the perfume of water and wet plants. Though the night was warm, clouds moved like a silent army across the sky.

The moon was waxing toward full.

She would wake soon, in her chamber off the Citadel's Court of Novices where she had fallen asleep, but lingered within the green enchanted circle of her dream.

"Things that used to keep us safe don't protect us anymore. Even with the jennies—the females of the Little People—to help, we still don't know if we'll be able to bring the rains in the spring. And without the teyn to help, farming's at a standstill, and the situation's only going to get worse. Everyone wants things to go back to the way they were, and nobody wants to hear that that's impossible."

She sighed and made a helpless gesture with her hands. Oryn's story, one Mohrvine was backing up, was that the gods had decreed the teyn be liberated: a source of endless trouble but not nearly as dangerous, to the teyn themselves, as the truth would be. "The thing I want to know—the thing all the mages want to know—is what caused it? Why is this happening? Why did the world change? Do you know?"

She turned to look down at Puahale, who sat at the foot of the little wall, with the spell diagrams they had worked on that afternoon still spread around her in the tree-sheltered sand. She had taught Puahale to scry, and they had spent some time memorizing words of each other's languages. The thought that the nature of magic, the nature of the universe, might further shift to make it impossible for her to return in dream to this place filled Raeshaldis with grief, but at least, she thought, they could be prepared to establish other means to communicate.

And the Sigil of Sisterhood, the circle of those who called down their power from the moon, would bind their souls and their magic forever. That much she knew in her bones.

"Why did magic change?" she asked softly. "Why did it go into women and leave men? Why can the females of the Little People now do it, as well as women of our race?

One of the lords of my country says that magic changed because the gods are angry with us, even though the king passed through the tests that are supposed to say the gods approve of what he does. Another lord says that there's some massively evil superwizard somewhere, who's placed a curse on every mage in the world."

That was Lord Sarn. And presumably, thought Shaldis, when his lordship managed to find that superwizard he'd try to hire him.

"Do your wizards, your teachers, know? Or know anything about it?"

"We asked the djinni that," replied Puahale, after some moments spent in thought.

"Are they still around?" Shaldis spoke in surprise, though she had her suspicions about where other djinni had gone to, besides the mad spirit hiding in the idol in the deserted Temple of Nebekht.

Pontifer Pig, she was almost certain, was a djinn, who had taken his shape from the form within Pomegranate's genial hallucinations.

And sometimes she thought she glimpsed a shimmering intelligence looking out at her from the eyes of some of the palace cats.

"Well," said Puahale, "they had to become something else, too. The way we used to be little girls before we became women, and the way my father turned from an angry warrior into a gentle old man.

"My teacher Wika had a dream, ten years ago, when the djinni disappeared and our wise men could no longer bring the big schools of fish into the lagoons. She and I took a canoe far out into the ocean, where the whales swim. Do you know whales?"

Shaldis shook her head, the image coming to her mind of hugeness and water. Perhaps like the lake monsters Soth had described?

"The djinni live inside them now," said Puahale. "The whales themselves don't mind, they said. But the djinni can no longer live as once they lived. Some of them are angry about it, and some of them went mad. But the one we called Red-Haired Woman, one of the djinni most friendly to us, told my teacher why this happened. And it didn't make any sense."

She shrugged, dismissing the matter, as if it were of little moment.

Shaldis sprang down from the wall, suddenly angry with this big, easygoing woman who had never had to worry about the rains, who had never had to struggle to learn spells that men grudged to teach her, nor to twist with pain inside wondering if a day would come when she must choose between her power and Jethan's arms.

"How can you say that?" she demanded. "How can you just let it go with that? Didn't you ask what the djinn meant? Or seek in other legends, other tales, for the meaning of what it said?"

Puahale raised her eyebrows, surprised by this outburst. "What good would it have done?"

"We might be able to find a way to . . ." Shaldis hesitated.

To what? Give magic back to men, if it meant that women would lose it again, and go back to what they had been?

Send the teyn back into the bondage of people who killed them as casually as they slaughtered stray dogs?

Would that bring back the rains?

Helpless, she was silent for a time. Then, "What did she say? Red-Haired Woman, I mean."

Her friend looked relieved, that the quick, frustrated rage had vanished from her voice and her eyes. She frowned for a moment, looking out to sea, as if to call back the djinn's exact words to her mind. Except, of course, Shaldis realized, the djinni did not speak in human words, but rather in this precise dream language that she used with Puahale, of thoughts and images transferred mind to mind. And like the crashing of the sea before she had seen its waves break on the shore, that which could not be recognized was meaningless.

"Red-Haired Woman said," recited Puahale, closing her eyes and holding up one finger, "that the world, the sun, and all the stars had fallen through a giant hole into another part of Everything, so that all the little pieces of—of sand—of something, that make up Everything, have all started to vibrate at a different speed than they used to. This changed the way the sun shines and the way this—this magic water that is in people's bodies—works, and so our brains work differently."

Shaldis said, *"What?"*

Puahale opened her eyes. "I told you it didn't make any sense."

Shaldis tried to imagine offering that explanation to Lord Sarn, with the added remark that it came from something a giant fish had told a woman she'd met in her dreams.

A malign superwizard casting a spell on the world was a far more believable tale. And keeping Lord Sarn looking for him would distract that powerful landchief from making trouble over the emancipation of the teyn.

The information that the djinni had taken refuge in giant water creatures, she thought, she would also keep to herself, at least until she could pay a call on Hokiros.

But even an explanation that made sense, reflected Shaldis as she walked with her friend down to the sea, might well have been useless, if there was nothing that could be done to change matters.

After a time she asked, "Is that how magic really works?"

And Puahale shrugged again. "Maybe the djinni don't know any more than we do."

It was a disconcerting thought. The waves crashed on the beach, sent their warm sheets of water rushing up to curl around the two women's ankles, the touch of it a whisper of power. The great wise ones, Puahale had said, could source power from the strength and movement of the sea, and Raeshaldis felt that power like a glow in her heart.

"No one really knew how magic worked before it changed, did they?" Shaldis asked. "Much less afterward."

Puahale shook her head. "Any more than we know—or ever knew—what life is, or why we love and need to be loved. All we can do is live as well as we can, use our magic for the highest good of the world, and love, ourselves as well as others, with the whole of our hearts."

"Is that possible?" asked Shaldis softly. "To love someone, and still keep your heart strong to do magic?" She still ached inside with the confusion and grief at her grandfather's death, with the way Tulik was stepping in already to command the family, as if their father was simply another child. He'd pushed and maneuvered their father into the proctorship within a few days of Chirak

Shaldeth's death, and neither he, nor any of the other family members whom Shaldis had rescued, recalled much about the incident, though in all other respects they were well.

The previous week, Tulik had hired Ahure as an adviser. Some things, at least, didn't change.

And she still felt a tangled confusion of emotions about Jethan, worrying when he was silent, aching with passion when he took her in his arms, her mind returning to him again and again when they were apart. Wondering what he was doing and thinking, praying that no act of hers would somehow destroy the delight of his love. *How can I be a Crafty woman, a Raven sister, when the mere touch of a man's hand makes me melt like this inside?*

It can't last, and then what will I do?

"Of course it's possible." Puahale put her arm around Shaldis's shoulders, hugged her like a sister, like her own family back on Sleeping Worms Street. "You'll find how it works best for you, the same way you found how your power works best. Look!" She turned and pointed out to sea. "There they are. The whales."

Shaldis stood in the froth of the surf, gazing across the moonlit ocean at the far-off shapes of monstrous flukes, of black curving backs glittering as they dived. *The djinni,* she thought. Adjusting to their new lives, in exile from the magic that had been theirs.

Could they, like she, source magic from the sea?

Would they, like Pontifer Pig, gradually strengthen in their new shapes and one day become something more than a shadow in someone else's mind?

It was time to go home. The surge of the wave washed around her knees, dragged on her white robe where she'd kilted it high. The sun was rising above the Yellow City, as the last of its light flickered and slipped from the sky above the endless sea to the west. The crashing of the waves seemed to gather her up, to bear her back through the darkness. Having touched the strength of the limitless waters, having heard the sea, she felt that she could do anything, learn anything, conquer anything.

Anything except the yearnings of her own heart.

And maybe, she thought, waking and turning her head to see Jethan still sleeping beside her in the sun-streaked quiet of the Citadel of the Sun, *maybe even those as well.*

She reached across, wanting to touch his hair, like rough dark silk pillowed on her arm, but not wanting to wake him. And as she moved her head, she saw on the other side of the room her white novice's robe, lying where she'd discarded it last night across the little table beside the door.

Its hem, she saw, was soaked with seawater, just beginning to drip down onto the tiles of the floor.

ABOUT THE AUTHOR

Barbara Hambly was born in San Diego on August 28, 1951, and grew up in Southern California amid daydreams, Beatlemania, and Flower Power. She attended the University of California, Riverside, where she obtained a master's degree in medieval history and a black belt in Shotokan Karate. She later taught a year of high school, waited tables, taught karate, shelved books in the local library, and was "downsized" out of the aerospace industry two days after signing her first book contract in 1981. For many years she was best known for writing sword-and-sorcery fantasy, with occasional excursions into vampire tales, Star Trek and Star Wars novels, but has recently branched out into a series of well-reviewed historical whodunits as well. A world traveler, she has served as President of the Science Fiction Writers of America, is the holder of a Lifetime Achievement Award from *Romantic Times BOOKclub Magazine*, and at one point in her life wrote scripts for cartoon shows. She currently lives in Los Angeles.

CAPTIVATING FANTASY FROM
BARBARA HAMBLY
SISTERS OF THE RAVEN

The Yellow City is in crisis. Men have always possessed the magic that sustains civilization, from healing the sick to calling the rains to keeping mice from the granaries. Now the rains are weeks late, the wells are drying up, and the Sun Mages cannot summon the powers that the empire needs to survive. When magic appears—inexplicably—in the hands of a few women, the men react swiftly and furiously. Raeshaldis, the only girl ever accepted to the College of the Sun Mages, finds the mages won't teach her the spells. Corn-Tassle Woman's budding powers can't protect her from an abusive husband. And the Summer Concubine must play the dutiful consort even as danger looms for her Raven sisters. For while famine threatens and fanatics riot, someone is killing the most gifted female magic-workers . . .

PRAISE FOR
SISTERS OF THE RAVEN

"Smart, thoughtful . . . keenly imagined . . . vividly convincing."
— **SUZY MCKEE CHARNAS,**
author of *The Slave and the Free*

"This is Barbara Hambly at the very top of her form . . . Read this one!"
— **HARRY TURTLEDOVE,**
author of the American Empire series

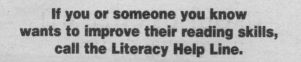